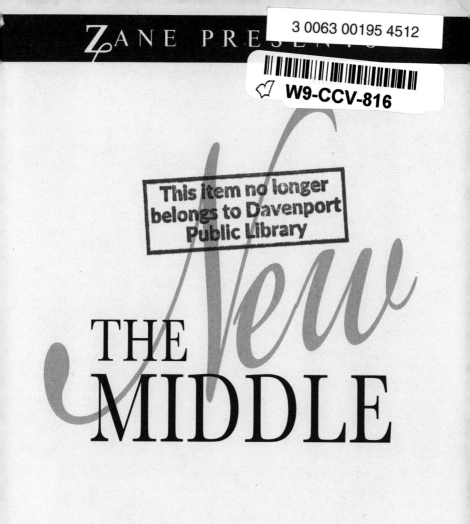

ZANE PRESENTS

THE *New* MIDDLE

Dear Reader:

In the literary world, we sometimes discover titles that are focused on those considered "middle aged." Now we have *The New Middle*, Bonita Thompson's debut novel with a cast of characters surely to please readers of *all* ages.

From the single parent, Joseph, a widower who has taken a hiatus from the dating world and whose son keeps him on his toes to Phoebe, who is reinventing herself after reaching midlife and childless to Dianne and Torrick, a couple who are playing out their marriage roles to Jacqueline, a single woman who makes the ultimate decision that changes her life, this journey reveals the lifestyles of those in between the aging spectrum.

This fascinating tale explores multiple topics including matrimony, relationships, loneliness and middle life crisis, complete with the ups and downs. She pokes humor at the old school technology such as Walkmans and answering machines and deals with aging realities of reading glasses and graying hair. There's even a middle-aged booty call.

As always, thanks for supporting myself and the Strebor Books family. We strive to bring you the most cutting-edge, out-of-the-box material on the market. You can find me on Facebook @AuthorZane or you can email me at zane@eroticanoir.com

Blessings,

Zane

Publisher
Strebor Books
www.simonandschuster.com

ZANE PRESENTS

THE *New* MIDDLE

BONITA THOMPSON

STREBOR BOOKS
NEW YORK LONDON TORONTO SYDNEY

Strebor Books
P.O. Box 6505
Largo, MD 20792
http://www.streborbooks.com

This book is a work of fiction. Names, characters, places and incidents are products of the author's imagination or are used fictitiously. Any resemblance to actual events or locales or persons, living or dead, is entirely coincidental.

ISBN 978-1-59309-622-9
ISBN 978-1-4767-8322-2 (ebook)
LCCN 2015934634

First Strebor Books trade paperback edition September 2015

Cover design: www.mariondesigns.com
Cover photograph: © Keith Saunders/Keith Saunders Photos

10 9 8 7 6 5 4 3 2 1

Manufactured in the United States of America

For information regarding special discounts for bulk purchases, please contact Simon & Schuster Special Sales at 1-866-506-1949

The Simon & Schuster Speakers Bureau can bring authors to your live event. For more information or to book an event, contact the Simon & Schuster Speakers Bureau at 1-866-248-3049 or visit our website at www.simonspeakers.com.

For BYT

Acknowledgments

Having heroines and a hero is a blessing to a novelist, and the publishing of *The New Middle* was potentially doomed without them. When I penned *Middle* in 2012, it never, ever entered my mind that one year later the manuscript would reach Zane's inbox. I am indebted to Charmaine Parker and Zane for their choosing to greenlight a story about five baby boomers. Before pitching *Middle* to Strebor, it landed on the desks of skeptics, and most of whom were over the age of forty. I was struck by a repetitive theme—that a fictional narrative strictly about "middle-aged characters" was not "sexy" or "marketable." I am notorious for inventing new words, but have been unable to come up with one for Maurier. So let's just say serious gratitude goes to this selfless human being for taking on the assignment as first reader, and offering brutally honest feedback.

CHAPTER 1

It took a lot of soul-searching for Venetia to finally choose to make the call. She'd done enough internal inventory over the years to know when she wasn't in the right place to go this completely alone. While praying was at the top of her must-do when she was off balance, her go-to-God moments generally required patience in order to receive divine guidance. Venetia had none at the moment. And that still, small voice she was supposed to rely on hadn't kicked in. She ran two miles along the lake thinking that would do the trick. All she got out of that was a good workout. Was it possible to still have the same feelings, the same thinking, after running two miles? She understood from her work as a life coach that feelings weren't static, but adjusted to incessant changing circumstances. So why didn't she feel differently? Why was her mind still on the same thought? After all, subsequent to running, she'd stopped to chat with a neighbor walking her dog. They'd disgusted the hostile tone of the presidential election, the prolonged dry spell, and a *Housewives* franchise. Afterward, Venetia had showered, paid a few bills online, and made several business calls.

She never felt this stuck.

What she needed was some one-on-one. Something touchy-feely; not an elusive message swirling around the ether. Okay, so she preferred secular instead of spiritual communication. There was go-to-God and there was go-to-Phoebe. Her godmother, as the pathetic, overused cliché went, had been there *and* done that. Venetia's thoughts stopped in midair when she heard the buzzing coming from the direction of her mobile device. She reached for the smartphone set beside her cup of barely touched tea and glanced fleetingly at the familiar number. She replaced the cell on the table.

Venetia spotted Phoebe entering the bright and open space of the downtown mall. The stores weren't open for business yet and Venetia loved it when it was quiet. Save for a few people who probably worked in the mall, sitting at tables and benches, here, there—the place was empty. Those sitting in the mall were alone, their eyes fixed to an electronic device they held in their hand. Occasionally, they reached blindly for a ubiquitous cup containing something caffeinated.

Venetia, half standing, waved to Phoebe. Clad in a sporty suit that had the Loft brand look, Phoebe hurried toward her godchild. With a judgmental eye, but without looking too long, Venetia admired the heather-gray pinstripe suit; it was acceptably stylish. But it gave her a bit more insight as to how rough her godmother was having it. Venetia felt a startling sorrow in her throat at the very thought Phoebe had lost so much, and it appeared from no-where. Nothing about life ever happened suddenly, though.

Phoebe greeted Venetia, "I just have a few to kill."

"Oh, that temp gig, huh?"

"Yeah."

"Not enough time for a tea?"

"Sorry." She sat in the accompanying stool. "So why did you want me to meet you here?" Casually, Phoebe looked up to the skylight. Effervescent sunbeams escaped from the glass ceiling, circulating generously inside the opulent mall.

"Barry's cheating on me."

Her eyes wide, Phoebe swallowed hard and suppressed the words at the tip of her tongue. She said instead, "I thought he was in Libya. How did you find out?"

"Well," Venetia began in an insecure voice. "I didn't find out that he was cheating...exactly. I know something's off. Something's not right. He's...different." She reached for her tea and sipped through the small hole, leaving a lipstick stain on the plastic lid.

Phoebe sighed. Of course she remembered what it was like to be a newbie in the third decade of her life. In the thirties—oh, yes, we were smarter than the twenties, with a sliver of self-assuredness that was impossible to have before our twenty-first birthday. Moreover, we were insightful, while not necessarily psychologically mature to take full advantage of the awareness the years leading up to forties produced. Women in their forties had *some* distance; enough to be conscious of the wisdom and know how to use it to their benefit. A lot of seemingly unfair experiences in the thirties began to make sense in the fourth decade. Yet the fifties? We found a way, oftentimes unconsciously, to prioritize and minimize. But even with all the knowledge and wisdom leading into the fifth decade, we managed to cling deeply to embedded wounds and private pain. Phoebe reached across the small table and squeezed Venetia's hand.

"I have to go. I'll be late."

"I'm in the middle of a crisis."

Phoebe came to her feet. She wrapped an elegant warm-weather scarf loosely around her neck. "Do you really need *me* to tell you what you should do? Come on, Venetia. If he's cheating..."

"B-b-b-but..."

"Your mother couldn't possibly give birth to a fool!" Phoebe pressed her cheek against Venetia's. "If you still have doubts when I get home, let's talk. Thoughts generally change during the course of a day. We can open one of those expensive bottles of wine you have in your…that's one hell of a wine collection you have…and we can talk all night. But I have to go."

Phoebe had turned to leave when Venetia called out, "Good luck! And, Phoebe?"

Phoebe looked over her shoulder.

"You're right about my wine collection." Venetia grinned. Oddly, she even felt—not so much better; she felt lighter.

"Love you!"

With wide aqua-blue eyes, the concierge looked up at Phoebe. She stood on the other side of the all-glass desk and the concierge knew she looked familiar, but she wasn't exactly sure why she recognized Phoebe's face. A courteous smile touched her lips in the way she had become accustomed to by being the first impression of Media Capital. With a trendy bob haircut, colored in a quiet blonde so not to overstate her pseudo-blondeness, she was Madison Avenue attractive. Cute blouse. The style typically found on racks at Forever 21 and H&M—the youthful clothing stores of her generation with affordable short-lived trends. Delicate eye shadow, a popular shade at the moment, added a quiet maturity to her youthful face. Her glossy-sparkly lipstick was subtle and made her lips look fuller. Phoebe wasn't keen on shiny lipstick. She didn't want to look as though she'd forgotten to wipe her mouth after finishing off a few Buffalo wings, or lobster.

"Good morning," the concierge greeted Phoebe. She lifted her forefinger, the short, manicured nail polished indigo blue. "Excuse me." She pressed a button and adjusted her earpiece. "Good morning, Media Capital. How may I direct your call? He's not in the office yet." Smoothly, familiarly, the concierge touched the screen of an electronic tablet with her forefinger. Concentrating with an acute attentiveness unusual for someone her age, her eyes scanned the details. It took a matter of seconds for her to resume: "He's expected in about nine." She listened professionally. "I'll put you through to his voicemail. Have a good day, Ms. Kendricks. Thank you." The concierge pressed a button on the multiple-lined phone that Phoebe could scarcely make out through the thick-plated glass. "Sorry. Can I help you?" The concierge talked very fast—no pauses, not even to take a breath.

"Phoebe Pleas. I'm from the Next Generation. My contact is Gloria…"

"Oh right. Yes, correct." She pushed a few buttons and said into her mouthpiece, "A temp associate from Next Generation is in reception." She listened briefly. "Take a seat. Gloria will be right with you. Coffee?"

"No, thank you," said Phoebe.

Sitting in one of the plush chairs, Phoebe stole glances at the concierge. Had Phoebe been so poised, so mature, and exuding pseudo confidence in her early twenties? Would this young woman be wiser and smarter and savvier than she'd been in her youth? Had all of Phoebe's choices been so careless that each one led her to a seat and waiting for someone named *Gloria* about a temp job—at fifty-two? Was the twenty-something born at the right time, in the right atmosphere—when women really did excel in ways her generation hadn't been able to do? Women were not yet where they should be, even in the concierge's time. After all, Americans were more accepting of a black *man* as president than they were a *white* woman. Helen Gurley Brown, God rest her soul, would gasp at Phoebe's thoughts. Well, Phoebe was never the feminist type. Before *Sex and the City*, there was Helen Gurley Brown's *Sex and the Single Girl*. Could the concierge honor a pioneer whom she might or might not have heard of who contributed to American culture to a degree it paved the way for the concierge's independence, her myriad of options? Moreover, the very style this young woman was wearing, Ms. Brown wore the same trends in the previous century. Brown, a '60s diva, had a fingerprint on the purported sexual revolution—contraception, premarital sex, abortion, homosexuality, feminism—which transformed a generation.

A lean, attractive woman stood in front of Phoebe, interrupting her mental chatter.

Phoebe stood. "Good morning!"

"Gloria. And I'm so glad you could make it on such short notice. Come, let's go to my office."

Gloria's office was small, but there was a snapshot view of the downtown skyline; personal touches—fresh flowers in a tasteful vase, and framed photographs of family and/or friends. Two business-styled, heather-brown chairs overcrowded the space, and a flat-screen TV, muted, was tuned to the Bloomberg channel.

"So, Phoebe, did you have trouble finding parking?"

"No."

"Public transportation?"

"Right."

"So you won't need a keycard for parking?"

"I think I'll be using the Rail."

"So!" Gloria exhaled. "Let's see…" She sought out specifics on Phoebe's résumé. "Well," she said with an elevated brow. "You've lived in Paris, Toronto, and wow, Sydney?" *She's temping; I don't want to know the whats and whys.* "It's great you've worked for a restaurant. And Rules? That should impress Chef. Are you sure you want to do *this*? Next Generation informed you it would be a minimum of four weeks?"

"I understand."

"A hospitality assistant didn't work out. Chef's particular so we'll need to really find the right fit. Are you okay with the potential of perhaps six weeks?"

"I *am* starting today?" *Please, God, tell me I didn't just sound desperate?*

The talent acquisitions director took a closer look at Phoebe. If Gloria had to guess from her résumé, she was about five, six years her senior and Gloria was forty-one. Although her suit was dated, she had a timeless look about her, and men noticed her. Conceivably, not in the same way they did when she was fifteen years younger. Gloria assumed, like a few of her friends from grad school, Phoebe needed to take whatever she could get in this Great Recession aftershock. *I'll do whatever deemed necessary not to be* this woman *in six, seven years! She looks so familiar. Hmmm.*

"Of course. Let's get you settled in." *She's way overqualified for this position, but apparently Phoebe needs the work so she will stick around. I'd be remiss not to help a sister in this economic climate.*

Phoebe followed the TA director down a corridor, and Gloria, despite wearing five-inch, gladiator open-toe heels, acted as though she was rushing to put out a fire. Phoebe was wearing a pair of shoes she could hardly wear all day and be comfortable. Who was she kidding? She wore platforms to her high-school prom. Now here she was, decades later—what, pretending she could still hang?

"Coffee, tea?" Gloria asked over her shoulder.

"I'm good."

"Here we go. This will be your office. I know it's no bigger than a bread box. No window," Gloria said, being facetious. "You can put your belongings here. Chef's PA will come and direct you on everything. IT will assign you a laptop."

"Thank you, Gloria."

"Any questions, my door's always open."

"Cornell! Cornell! Damn, that boy!"

Joseph attempted to resume reading the *Times*. That unnecessarily loud music made it a challenge to concentrate on the words printed on the paper—Obama's camp accused Romney's camp of reinventing the truth. And Romney's camp accused the Obama administration of ruining everything once sacred about America! Politics was always a blood sport. Back in the day, people focused on character development. In this century it was *look at me*! Politics wasn't so vicious two decades ago, and the money spent on campaigns these days? Billions used entirely to bash one another with mendacious television ads. With that level of cash flow, they could get the country out of hock! Joseph took a deep breath; the loud music rattled his nerves. "Cornell!" he yelled. His restraint had reached a breaking point. He dropped the newspaper to the granite countertop and placed the coffee mug next to it with force—so much so, some of his black coffee splattered onto the surface. Joseph shouted over his shoulder, *"Cornell!"*

Annoyed, he stood, and with long strides headed for the front of the house. That hip-hop noise was so loud the house vibrated. The landline rang, and before he headed up the stairs to confront his son, he stopped and looked at the phone in its carriage across the room. As if to decide which had precedence, Joseph looked from the telephone to the stairway. The ringing telephone abated.

"Cornell!" he yelled, much louder this time.

Within moments, Cornell popped his head around the corner of the spiral stairway. Tall and lean, he had the looks of a male model. "Yeah, Dad? You call me?" He held the iPad that Joseph, regrettably, purchased for his son on his birthday; primarily since a few weeks later, he dropped out of university, and in his senior year. Then his son announced ever so casually that his girlfriend—with a name like Sin—was four months' pregnant. Cornell wasn't raised to drop out of school and get a girl pregnant out of wedlock. His behavior was completely irresponsible. He had no job, no income. What could Joseph do? He had to let him come home. *I didn't raise my son like this! I worked hard—his mamma worked hard—so he could have the best of everything. I gave my children more than enough. If his mamma was alive, I know her heart would be crushed.*

"Can you turn it down a notch?"

"What?"

"If you take those things out of your ears, you might be able to *hear* me." He yelled, "Why you need the music so loud anyway? What are the earphones for?"

"These are ear*buds*." He held one with the tips of his fingers. "I'll turn it down, as you say, a notch. Anyway, didn't you do the same thing at my age, with—what was it called in your day—the Walkman?"

"I didn't listen to my Walkman and a stereo at the same time. It makes no sense!"

"Whatever, Dad." Cornell slipped his earbud back in his ear.

"Turn off the stereo. If you're listening to the iPod, you don't need the stereo blasting, too!"

"Man, it's music."

"Did you just refer to me as *man?*"

Cornell frowned, giving his father a *Dad, please* look.

"You asked me to buy you that tablet because you needed it for school. You drop out! The laptop can do the exact same thing as that fancy iPad! Don't try to finesse me, Cornell. Stop messing around on that thing and look for a job!"

"Like I'm not looking."

"Go out and buy a newspaper, knock on some doors. But *look* for work!"

"A *newspaper? Seriously!* They don't list jobs in the newspaper; everything's online. And *knock* on a door?"

"It might not be a lot of good jobs out there, but surely something's out there. I can make a call, get you something—and it might not be full time—working at the post office."

"What, and get laid off? The post office is barely surviving. They raise the cost of stamps every six months. Who uses stamps anymore anyway? Postal jobs—that's old-school." He shrugged with a natural smugness. "You were a blue-collar man, but that's so last century. Outsourcing, green jobs, tech, stuff like that. Those are jobs of the future. There's no potential at the *post office.*" There was a subtle arrogance in Cornell's tone.

"And without a degree? How far will that get you?"

"Steve Jobs didn't have a degree and look where that got him. It's a semester. I'm going back."

"Steve Jobs, huh? Look, get a job! If it means flipping burgers, get a *job!*"

"You are like so antiquated. You think I'm not looking. And flip a burger? Heck, that isn't even minimum wage work."

"You'd better find something. Something that'll help you take care of your unborn child. I'm not taking care of Sin and you and a baby, too!"

"*Zyn*, Dad!"

"What normal person names their child Zyn anyway?"

When Joseph returned to his cup of coffee and took a sip, it was no longer warm. That's how he preferred his first cup—*warm*. He barely touched his coffee before the music started blasting, waking up the dead. A waste! Joseph wiped up the spill he'd made earlier. With a sigh, his eyes wandered out at the sunny morning. The dry spell made his once perfectly green-colored lawn look like straw. He'd cancelled the services of the gardener when Cornell moved in. That boy hadn't picked up so much as a broom, let alone pulled out the lawnmower. Now that the leaves were starting to fall, did he really expect his son to reach for a rake?

"I might as well go tend to the lawn. Nothing but bad news in the paper anyway," he mumbled to himself. "That illegal shooting a police officer in cold blood. So brazen, with witnesses looking on. Endless wars…inequality." Dismayed, Joseph shook his head. "Well, let me go on out here." He headed for the back door.

"Good morning."

"Good morning. Do you have an appointment?"

"With Dr. Wang."

"Please sign in. And your name?"

"Dianne Lewis James." Dianne scribbled hurriedly on the sign-in sheet. Casually, she glanced at her watch.

"Fill this out, and we'll need your insurance."

Dianne reached for the clipboard. "Thank you."

The small waiting room was half-busy. While several women focused intently on their devices, a child sat on the floor and drew in a coloring book. Dianne couldn't guess who the child might have belonged to. Not one woman was paying her any attention. She felt lighthearted observing the child so engaged. Both of her girls were excited when she bought their first box of crayons, but they started coloring a little older as Dianne recalled. When the little girl with soft gray eyes looked her way, Dianne winked. The child blushed, returned to her coloring book but occasionally looked to Dianne with a slobbery giggle.

She heard her cell vibrating. Since both of the girls were in school, she doubted either one of them was calling her. Henna always texted anyway. Daniela reminded Dianne that if she wanted to keep tabs on her to check Twitter. Dianne's mother called every morning and they'd had their twenty-minute daily catch-up. Torrick was in a meeting. She took a quick look at his schedule prior to his leaving the house; that way she'd have a sense of his day. The vibration ceased. Dianne pressed her eyes shut. *I know these symptoms aren't because of a yeast infection. God, please don't let this…"*

Dianne's eyes shot toward the sound of a door opening. A young woman with long, thick, chestnut-colored hair spoke cordially, "Dianne Lewis James?"

Very few added the Lewis to her name. She was *Mrs.* James. Her big sister, to this day, teased her about turning into *Mrs. Somebody.* Dianne was, among the circle of her youth, the type *not* to get lost inside a marriage, or become one of those women who gave up a career and supported her husband while she raised children. Life never did turn out as *planned.* If there was a *Cinderella* sequel, who knew what her story would look like. She'd probably regret her foot even fit that slipper. Dianne stood, rested her designer handbag on her wrist, and walked toward the young, chestnut-haired woman.

"Dianne Lewis James?"

"Yes."

"Good morning!"

An hour later, Dianne sat in a large boardroom in one of the newer buildings downtown. One of several committees she chaired was meeting to discuss how the elimination of the Ride Free Zone would affect the working poor, homeless, and the physically and mentally challenged. The view from the boardroom was stunningly breathtaking—mountains and clouds were vivid ivory. The Sound was congested with sailboats and the sun was citrus-bright, streaking diagonally against the intense sapphire sky. The recently opened Ferris wheel modernized the city's skyline. Henna pleaded with Dianne to let her take a ride on it before school resumed, but so much was going on at the time, she failed to get it on her calendar.

"Dianne, good morning. Glad you could coordinate on such short notice." The woman claimed the seat next to Dianne. "Can we do coffee soon? There's so much to catch up on."

"We must!" Dianne exaggerated. Her cell vibrated against the desk. She reached for it and said, "Excuse me." A photo of her sister illuminated. "I need to take this." She rushed to her feet. "Before the end of the meeting, let's coordinate our calendars." Dianne left the boardroom and entered the bustling hallway. Nearby, a news crew was setting up for an interview. She said, "Thank you for calling me back. Look, I was wondering...Are you open for a much-needed martini diet and black-and-whites weekend? Yes, I can get away. Torrick's in town. He needs quality time with the girls anyway. Yeah, sure. I'll text my details."

Dianne returned to the boardroom and took her seat. She turned off her cell and dropped it in her purse on the floor. With a casual flip of her glossy, shoulder-length hair, she took a deep breath and grabbed the bottle of water set before her.

Following the meeting, she was standing at the elevator checking messages when she heard someone call out, "Dianne?" Instinctively, Dianne turned. It took only a split-second to recognize her. An involuntary gasp slipped out. "Phoebe?"

"Oh, my God! Girl, how *are* you?"

They met each other with their back-in-the-day greet: air kisses. Laughing, they each studied—assessed—the other. A decade had come and gone since they *talked*. The last time they actually saw each other was at their dear friend Cordia's funeral, but they politely acknowledged each other's presence solemnly.

"Do you live here?"

"Just moved up."

"San Francisco was the last address I had for you. Girl, it's been so—awhile."

"Are you and Torrick still…?"

"And the girls are fifteen and twelve."

"We have to catch up."

"What are you doing here?"

"It's a long story. Look, I'm coming off a lunch break. Can we exchange numbers?"

"Sure, of course. We have to do lunch. Where are you staying?"

"Do you know SoJo's?"

"Best Cajun shrimp ever! We're almost neighbors. I'm on Cascadia."

They swapped numbers and promised to catch up, embracing and laughing as if the affection purified the three-decade-old animosity.

In the elevator, Dianne ransacked her brain trying to determine whatever happened to Phoebe. She disappeared. Their old circle had no clue what Phoebe had been up to, or where she was, and she wasn't on Facebook. Dianne would hear—by several degrees of separation—a tidbit here, a rumor there, but it was all so sketchy and downlow. No one had any concrete details. Why was she in the office building where Dianne's committee met biweekly, and working? Doing what? Dianne couldn't imagine Phoebe sitting in an office all day. *SoJo's? Oh, she must be staying with Venetia.* What the hell was going on with her? Last Dianne heard Phoebe was involved with an architect or graphic designer. Word had it, he was married. Before that, there was the retired ballplayer who owned that popular restaurant. The once very controversial athlete wooed one of those reality TV chefs from somewhere and his name created a buzz; even slipping the maître d' a Benjamin didn't guarantee a table. Phoebe ditched him because he got physical. At least that's what Dianne heard. Her girlfriend from days gone by didn't look her usually well-dressed self. That suit had to be from—2006? She'd seen photographs of her online, arriving at some affair with the controversial ballplayer. She looked really good *then*. Dianne always, always envied her old friend—her style, her natural beauty, her worldly, wanderlust nature. At least she managed to maintain her figure.

Dianne stepped into the elevator. She searched for a number in her contacts. She pressed the name with her forefinger, and when the person answered, Dianne said, "You'll never guess who I just ran into…"

"Good afternoon Jacqueline. How may I help?" Claire listened politely. "Sure, but I would need it to be on my break. Is that all right?" Respectfully, she listened. "Sure, three. Right, 'bye!" Claire disconnected the call and noted the time on her tablet. Taking a deep breath, she pumped hand-sanitizer inside one hand and massaged it into both hands until the germ-killer dissolved into her palms. Her mind was distracted, elsewhere. She tried to conjure up why she'd need to go to Jacqueline's office. When Jacqueline rushed in—always hurried, in one hand her cell glued to her ear, the *Times*, *Wall Street* and *Business Journal*, and an electronic tablet tucked under her armpit; each day dressed to the nines—she passed Claire a fleeting acknowledgment. If she was in the mood. Occasionally a subtle nod. Claire was convinced it was only when she'd gotten laid that Jacqueline even hinted at a smile.

Claire answered the ringing console, polite, professional. Once she'd forwarded the call she studied the time again. She received a message. An assistant requested that she hire a car for someone in Strategy, Claire's dream department. She replied with "On it!" and made arrangements for a car via e-mail. She answered several calls, and once the hire was confirmed, Claire forwarded it to the assistant in Strategy. Drumming her squarely shaped nails on the glass table, she waited. Two calls came in; she forwarded them accordingly.

Back to Jacqueline. Since she'd started at Media Capital, Claire had seen Jacqueline through two temps, followed by a temp-to-hire who left for lunch and never returned. There had been a lot of talk surrounding the whole matter, presumably because the temp-to-hire was black. Since then, several other assistants were sharing the role of supporting Jacqueline. She was difficult, to put it ever so gently. Because Claire had her eye on her own clients someday in the very foreseeable future, she'd fallen into the team-player role splendidly. She'd done her share of butt-kissing. Without hesitation, she took on "other duties as assigned" by offering to support several of the overworked assistants.

Earlier that morning, the lines were ringing off the hook; a local station was taping an interview with a client; some outside committee, which used one of the conference rooms every other week, needed assistance; *and* Claire needed to pee. Badly. Chef was preparing a private lunch for a meeting that had everyone walking on eggshells; therefore, two other meetings had to be catered, which Claire helped place orders for, all the while the lines were buzzing like mad! And because yet another hospitality assistant was "let go" or walked out—who knew? And for reasons Claire wasn't privy to, they brought in a temp. *She* wasn't even trained yet, and Claire took notice that she was on top of it, particularly under the circumstances. So there Claire was—helping with orders for two separate lunch meetings, answering calls, signing visitors in, *and* printing out visitor badges. All of it—the phones, assisting in a pinch, greeting visitors, not to mention managing twelve con-ference room calendars—was her job. It wasn't that she was making excuses for the mistake, but it did justify *why* it happened.

The *issue* took place in the midst of the morning rush, and Claire was convinced it would tarnish her résumé for eternity. *The* call. Not just any call. *The* call. And Claire, of all the people at Media Capital, had forwarded the call straight into Jacqueline's voicemail. A client—a reality TV personality—was arrested in Los Angeles the evening before, and she could hear snippets here and there about what to do to get ahead of the social media chatter. It slipped Claire's mind that Jacqueline wanted to get the call NO MATTER WHAT! *Bad Judgment 101.* There was no doubt in her mind she was being requested to Jacqueline's office because she'd transferred *the* call into voicemail, *mistakenly*. Jacqueline wanted to chew her out, remind Claire she was inept, the worst concierge the company had ever hired. Claire believed in her heart of hearts because Jacqueline wasn't only friends with one of the founders, but she was also a major asset to Media Capital, that she could have Claire fired—*like that!*

A series of calls came in and Claire handled them efficiently, resourcefully. Still, she felt stupid. There was no way Jacqueline would summon her into her office for anything else. Claire was confident the woman loathed her. Once, shortly after one of her temps quit, Jacqueline called reception and said something like, "Will you *please* find Jan and tell him I want a café au lait?" When Claire reminded Jacqueline that Jan was no longer with Media Capital, she snapped: "Well, whoever took his place. I *want* a café au lait. Is that too difficult for you to handle? Or are you too simple?"

The constant interruptions exasperated Claire. She couldn't find a second in her day—but for her breaks!—to think! The phones? Never-ending. And if it wasn't the phones, it was constant deliveries and one person asking for this and another asking her to do that! *Sigh.* The pay was good; at last she was able to move out of the small two-bedroom apartment she shared with a casual friend from college whose lifestyle clashed with Claire's. Being hired as the concierge at Media Capital, she was able to find an affordable Capitol Hill studio. Claire was unaware how much she liked working at the top media consultant firm until she felt the threat of no longer having a job where she could capitalize off the connections that could stair-step her career.

Could she lose her job? Media Capital was high-profile. Their client list consisted of top music names, models, athletes, media personalities, and even politicians and physicians with high-profile visibility. These were media magnets that could easily take their public cachet to New York and Los Angeles media consultant firms. She spent four years in college expecting to be a media strategist. When she'd graduated, unemployment topped 11 percent. She couldn't find a *real* job, and with benefits. Instead, she worked part-time, and cleaning dog parks to being a coffee/tea/espresso runner for a startup to delivering packages to even being of all things, a barista. Finally, she fell into the perfect spot at one of the most prestigious media organizations in the country, with offices in Milan, London and Paris. Claire wanted to be here. Now? She might well be kicked to the curb by end of business, and by the end of next week, applying for unemployment benefits. And all because of one call out of 100-plus she handled in a given day. Of all the clients, it had to be one of Jacqueline's.

"Claire, hey! I'm here for your break."

Claire, so deep inside her head, hadn't realized her relief had arrived. "Just so you'll know, Jacqueline's summoned me to her office, I might need a few extra minutes. Do you mind?"

"What, about that call?"

With a chuckle, Claire said, "I have a feeling that's what it's about, so if you hear her…"

"Good luck!" her relief said. "That's a woman you don't want to cross."

Her heart pulsating, Claire walked toward Jacqueline's office feigning confidence. Coincidentally she was wearing a new biz-casual suit she'd purchased last payday. It wasn't a power suit per se, but wearing it made Claire feel not so powerless. Still, her mind was preparing itself for a beat down. She knew the slip-up made her come across, at the very least, inexperienced. She was upset the moment it had happened, and apologetic. And in her six months with Media Capital, she had never done anything remotely irresponsible. Surely Jacqueline had made some mistakes along the way to a corner office. Surely she could relate. Well, Miss Perfect, Miss All That and Butter Doesn't Melt In *Her* Mouth? Perhaps not.

Claire stood in the doorframe. Jacqueline was on a call, using her earpiece. Her back to Claire, she stood near the window. The view from Jacqueline's office was breathtaking this time of year. The bright sun, the vivid sky, the Olympics. *When I make it, will I have an office like this?* Jacqueline was talking in another language. Claire wasn't sure—it didn't sound like a language she was familiar with. Tall, slender, very style-conscious, Jacqueline was, without question, so stunning. And smart. With degrees from top universities, time spent working abroad; she was savvy, and a light-skinned black. PC: *African-American.*

Claire cleared her throat. Not wanting to be presumptuous, she remained in the doorway.

Jacqueline looked over her shoulder. She lifted a long finger. *Wait*, the raised finger implied. Claire waited. A few moments went by and Jacqueline walked to her desk, instructing Claire with her hand to come into her office. She motioned for Claire to close the door. *Merde*. Claire closed the door, her heart starting to pump faster, as it did when she ran up and down Harbor Steps five times each morning. She stood at the closed door. An assistant, one of the young women temporarily doing Jacqueline's travel logistics, passed. She eyed Claire standing in the office with a picture-perfect view. Scarcely, but Claire noticed her gentle green eyes widen as if to suggest *uh-oh*!

Jacqueline, while on a call, listened. She pantomimed, *Have a seat*.

Merde! Claire sat at one of the chairs facing Jacqueline's desk.

"No," Jacqueline said very softly. "Sit over there," she added, pointing to a sage loveseat, matching chair and two chocolate-hued, cube-shaped ottomans.

Claire stood, and feeling even more awkward, walked over to the loveseat. Sitting ramrod straight, she hoped her body language gave the impression she was a warrior—it was her favorite yoga asana. She gazed out at the day, staying focused. Claire chose not to awfulize beyond that moment. She needed this company on her résumé so she'd dare not be confrontational. But she wasn't going to be bullied either. She'd stand toe-to-toe with Jacqueline Daye and let the pieces fall where they must.

"So," Jacqueline said, sitting in the loveseat. "Conference calls. Sometimes…" She took a deep breath, tossing her flat-ironed, silky straight hair off her shoulders. Jacqueline crossed her bare, shapely legs. "Sorry to call you in on your break. You must get bored up there all day."

"Bored, Well, I'm busy, though."

"My day has been completely turned upside down because of that fiasco you pulled this morning. That said, without an assistant…I have to do everything around here. Moira…It's hard to believe she went to NYU. Totally ineffectual. I recognize she's my colleague's assistant, but she's an educated young woman—really! She can't walk *and* chew gum simultaneously?" Jacqueline leaned forward, pressing her elbows to her knees while she massaged her temples with her fingertips. "I need someone. Someone *competent*. I like your style. You're quick on your feet. I cannot afford to lose another assistant. Three inside of five months…"

Three months, thought Claire.

"You're smart, Claire. Yes, that mishap you pulled was inexcusable. But I've watched you since you've been the concierge. You're professional and adaptable. You never lose your cool. The way you handled—you made no excuses for what happened this morning. That took…it showed a sense of reflection. I want you on my team. I've talked to Gloria in talent acquisitions. She was fine with my inviting you in for a chat. Are you interested?"

"Interested. You mean…"

"Look, I'm really not the B-word that I've become highly regarded as." Jacqueline uncrossed her legs. "And I know I have the reputation of a prima donna." The tone of her voice suggested that she couldn't care less what people thought of her.

"I…" Claire was stunned. Being offered a position as Jacqueline's assistant was so far off her radar.

"Well…" Jacqueline said, spreading her hands. An expensive, classy set of bangles jingled.

"Yes!" Claire said, much too quickly—as if she were desperate. Even if she asked Jacqueline to let her sleep on it, she'd still have no idea what was waiting for her when all was said and done. Jacqueline's assistants were known for working long hours.

"I'm going to ask you a question, which I hope doesn't offend you."

"Okay."

"Will you have a problem working for a black woman?"

Huh? Claire said too quickly, "No no," shaking her head, the angular cut of her bob swinging side to side.

"Do you have a problem going to get coffee or tea or water? Do you have a problem with running errands for me?"

Pause. Dry mouth. Swallow. "No."

She just lied to my face.

"The pay is competitive. It's hard work. You must know how to anticipate my every need. You'll need to be a social media maven. You have to learn to write press releases, and good ones. I under-stand you're a wordsmith, which is attractive. I need someone who can edit my speeches. You have to know how to be prepared for the unexpected. I do not like 'I'm sorry' assistants. It's imperative that you be discreet, hoard personal and extremely private data as if it was life or death. Since you're the concierge, you had to pass a back-ground check…You'll have access to my credit card accounts so we'll need to vet you. A more in-depth…at least seven professional refer-ences that will sing praises. Is that going to be a problem?"

"Not a problem."

Jacqueline studied Claire critically.

"I want to learn and from the best." By the subtle lift of one side of Jacqueline's mouth, Claire trusted that was exactly what Jacque-line wanted to hear.

Jacqueline gave Claire a swift appraisal. "Good. Okay. So I'll call Gloria and we'll take it from there."

Each woman stood. Claire could feel the stillness in her heart. Jacqueline *was* a prima donna; there was no doubt about it. Still, for the first time, Claire saw something new, something she hadn't seen in Jacqueline in her six months with Media Capital. There was no female consultant at the company she'd rather learn from more than Jacqueline. *This is business, not personal.*

When she walked back toward reception, Claire never felt more relieved.

"Torrick?"

He looked up from his once-upon-a-time hot lunch. His face suggested to his trustworthy personal assistant that he really needed some down time.

"The timing's not perfect, I understand."

All he needed was ten uninterrupted minutes; that's all. The owner of the take-away place on the ground floor of the office building knew how to prepare the chicken fettuccini he liked. It never tasted the same if he heated it up in the microwave. His expression told his PA, *don't bring me no bad news.*

"Dianne's holding."

"Thank you," he said, monitoring his tone. "Torrick speaking."

Dianne was waiting to have her weekly mani-pedi. *Jacqueline recommended this place. She saw it on Angie's List. Hell, I should one-star them on Yelp.* "It's me."

"Hey, what's going on?" Torrick said.

"I'm at an appointment. Look, I wanted to give you a heads-up that I've arranged to go to New York. I'll be gone through the weekend, so please don't make plans. I need you to be in town for the girls."

"You always pull these last-minute trips on me, Dianne." Torrick reached for a plastic fork—and how he loathed eating with plastic utensils—and attempted to grab a bite or two while Dianne went into complaining mode; more like a soliloquy.

"My sister's going through something. I thought I'd take a quick trip to New York. We could use some time together."

Torrick managed to catch words here and there, and nearly finished his lunch listening to Dianne. Today was one of those days where he couldn't bring himself to debate with his wife. She'd picked a good time to drop a bomb on him. Two back-to-back meetings; and he left his cell somewhere but couldn't recall where. For over an hour, Torrick went without his mobile device. It was such a strange thing: he felt so out of touch. Disconnected. Finally, someone brought the cell to reception and his PA returned it to him. When he reached for it, Torrick sighed with utter relief.

"Torrick?"

"Yeah, okay. Do what you have to do. But Saturday I have the BPOA…" Torrick released a harsh sigh when his wife let out a disapproving grunt. "The Black Professionals of America summit, Dianne! So, Daniela and Henna will have to fend, understand?

"Torrick!"

"I attend the BPOA every year, and it's on my calendar. You decided last minute to go to New York. Daniela is old enough to watch after her sister." When his wife took a deep breath, Torrick's brow arched. It was Dianne's way of suppressing what was really on her mind. "Look, I still haven't had a chance to finish my lunch. We'll talk when I get home."

"I leave tomorrow, Torrick! We need to discuss how you'll utilize your weekend *with* the girls. Daniela was eleven, twelve the last time you had them all to yourself. Finally, it's time for my appointment. I've been here waiting for nearly twenty minutes."

"Later, baby." He pushed the intercom button and said into it, "Can you do some digging? Find out what might be going on around town this weekend. Something I can take the girls to." *Henna is crazy about the Cheesecake Factory.* "Find something fun. The girls haven't taken a ride on the Ferris wheel since it opened. Dianne would've mentioned it otherwise. Oh, but I have that thing at the convention center on Saturday. Yeah, but I'm not sure how long that'll be.

What's playing at the movies? Find something, okay? Thanks."

With his mind elsewhere, Torrick finished his lunch. His cell hummed nearby. He reached for it, and a brow shot up when he saw the name illumine on the screen. "Torrick James," he answered. "Jacqueline *Daye!* What's going on with you?"

"Are you attending the BPOA this year?"

"Well, now, you know I wouldn't miss that. You obviously haven't had a chance to see the itinerary; I'm keynote speaker."

"I've been traveling for the past couple of weeks, and it's been a busy time. This all-about-me culture is stressing me out! I haven't had a chance to even glance at the itinerary. Truth be told, my memory is starting to go."

"So you'll be there?"

"Well, of course."

"Look forward to seeing you."

"How's my girl?"

"I just hung up from talking to Dianne. She's off to New York."

"To hang with her sister, Vanessa?"

Torrick wiped his hands with a napkin. He attempted to balance the phone with his shoulder. While he listened to Jacqueline, he laughed with a lot of heart. "Wow," he chimed in, and "Woman, you're something else," he added. He needed to wrap it up, so Torrick said, "Listen, let's make an effort to talk Saturday. Sounds good. You, too…"

Torrick began going through a slew of e-mails. He hadn't even started working on his speech. He thought he might be able to do it on the fly, but that was careless, even a bit risky. Once he answered a few e-mails and jotted down some ideas for the speech, he leaned in his chair tossing a football back and forth, from hand to hand. The CEO of his own private security firm, Torrick took great risks to get where he was. He liked what he did to earn a good living, but he'd lost a lot of time with the girls which he couldn't make up for. While he didn't travel as much as he did in the past, travel was still a necessity. Each time he came home, he saw something new about one daughter or the other. Daniela was even wearing makeup now. Henna was tall—she'd shot up out of nowhere. He was still young. Forty-eight. Too young to retire. Besides, he wanted his family to be secure before he retired. The economic climate was iffy. While he was interrupted by a few lengthy calls, he managed to pump out a strong first draft of his speech. He knew it wasn't exactly the best speech he'd ever written, but he'd waited too long to approach it with thought and now he was forced to extemporize. He'd have his PA do a touch-up.

He stood, stretched, and decided to call it a day. Before heading home, he'd put in an hour at the gym. For the first time, since he couldn't recall when, he was going to have a sit-down meal with his beautiful wife and the girls.

"This is Venetia." A frown sketched her face. "I'm sorry, who's calling?"

Venetia heard Phoebe walking downstairs. She planned to surprise her with a delivery from SoJo's, a place Venetia practically grew up eating at, a few blocks away. She knew the owner, and his son would make a home delivery if the place wasn't busy. She'd spent upward of two hours with clients; each typically in need and often had consultations by phone. Along the way, Venetia had lost track of time.

Phoebe called out, "Venetia!"

She could hear Phoebe's heels against the hardwood staircase. "I actually have some time next week. I'll be in L.A.…Sorry, say that again." Unconsciously, Venetia stood. "Oh!…"

Phoebe entered the doorway, visibly tired. Venetia put her finger to her mouth to give Phoebe a heads-up: *Shhhh!* Phoebe, compliant, went to a chair and flopped in it as if she was dead tired. And she was. She hadn't been on her feet like she had today, not in years. Her body felt as though it had traveled through several time zones. Phoebe had no idea the work was going to be so physical. Or had challenging work and long days become too demanding for her body?

Venetia reached for a nearby pen and scrawled in rushed handwriting. "I can do that. Yes. Sure. And thank you for the referral." When she disconnected the call, she flopped in the chair.

"What?" Phoebe knew that look. Venetia was her godchild. They had been close, especially in Venetia's early twenties, which had been a complicated time for Venetia. Phoebe had become somewhat of a surrogate mother to Venetia, and maternal instincts she never thought she had kicked in when Venetia's mother passed away.

"I just got a really good referral. You'll not guess who wants to hire me. *Girl!*"

"Who?" Phoebe slipped off her shoes.

"Gwen Jackson."

"Gwen Jackson?"

"Gwenology?"

"You're referring to the reality TV show?"

"That was Jacqueline Daye. She's Gwen's media consultant…"

"Jacqueline Daye. I heard that name. Today, in fact. Wait, she works at the place where I'm temping."

"Get real. Seriously? You're temping at Media Capital?"

"That woman had me on my toes at least three times today. A café au lait, and not just any café au lait. A chef salad, a veggie smoothie…"

"Is she black?"

"Actually, she is."

"Mon Dieu. I have to tell you, I thought I could always detect a sister…This lady, though—she didn't give me the slightest hint that she occasionally went to the hood. But for no other reason than to get her hair done."

"Oh, now her hair. It's hers."

Venetia laughed out loud!

"Why's Gwen Jackson needing a life coach?"

"Last night she got her third DUI. Her reality show—the execs are threatening to release her from her contract. Apparently, there's a clause and she's more than abused it. She has to *demonstrate* that she's making an effort to get her life back on track. For real this time."

"I thought the reality TV playbook was to be as obnoxious as possible. If she gets sober, that'll change the whole dynamic. She risks losing her following."

"After all, it's why the show's so popular. *Her* drama. If someone followed me around with a camera all day, they'd be yawning and definitely changing the channel." Venetia perused a few sheets of paper. "Jacqueline's having her contract with the studio PDF'd to me, along with some press clips. She wants me to meet with Gwen tomorrow. In L.A."

"Well, I must say. This isn't the same Venetia I met up with this morning. I was worried about you."

"I could still use that drink and some mature advice. I was going to have something delivered. You want to go out? My treat."

"You know, I think I'd like to go out. I feel better now that I've been off my feet. I forgot how hilly this place is. What made me wear platforms!"

Venetia laughed; she was always uninhibited in her godmother's company. "The place I thought we could go to is informal, and it's walking distance. I can drive if you want. If you're too pooped to walk."

"I'll slip on my ballets. It's good to see you smiling. Your energy was off this morning. Have you talked with Barry?"

"I ignored two texts. We agreed to Skype when he could, but at least one text per day was the deal. No exception. That way I'd know he was safe.

"He's…I don't know…acting different. I think he's unfaithful."

"Unfaithful comes in many forms. Let me change. Say ten, fifteen?"

"Fifteen. I want to go online and check out Jacqueline Daye's client list."

"Venetia?" With a stapler in her hand, she looked up at Phoebe. "Thank you for letting me crash at the guesthouse."

"Love comes in many forms, too."

CHAPTER 2

Dianne's sister instructed her to take Metro-North from Grand Central. It was a quiet train ride from Midtown. Only a handful of people shared the car with her. The last time she was in New York, Dianne and Torrick made the decision to move back to the West Coast. Her marriage was different then. *She* was different back then. Running into Phoebe had reminded Dianne of her life prior to meeting Torrick. Before she'd had the girls and immersed herself into the roles of wife and mother and everything that entailed, she'd lived a life of independence. Back then she had no idea how her life would unfold. She loved her girls and had no regrets where they were concerned; still, something was missing—in her life; in her heart. A sense of guilt began to touch her in a way she hadn't experienced before. To want more meant that she didn't have enough. God only knew that wasn't true. Her life was a perfect imperfection. So why—especially since she'd run into Phoebe—did she feel an odd sense of regret?

The conductor announced her sister's stop. Vanessa lived in New Rochelle, roughly a thirty-minute train ride from Manhattan. Dianne grabbed her bag, a designer tote she carried whenever she took short trips, stuffed with weekend attire. She dashed through the doors just before they began to close. The sultry evening air that greeted her felt refreshing. Fall was a heartbeat away, and Dianne had a soft spot for East Coast autumn.

"Dianne!"

She twirled at the sound of the familiar voice. She vaguely made out her sister in the early evening hue. Two years ago, Vanessa had relocated to New York where she was able to land a job earning what her talent was worth. Four years ago, she'd been laid off by the company she'd worked for for nearly twelve years in Los Angeles. It had been a good job, which helped pay her daughter's tuition at San Jose State.

Vanessa greeted her baby sister with a loving embrace. They held each other for quite some time until Dianne took the initiative and released Vanessa. Finally, they were in the same time zone.

"How are you?" Vanessa asked.

"I'm okay."

"You don't call me for a martini diet and black-and-whites weekend if you're okay. Come on, let's go."

Once inside the car, Dianne, anxious, buckled her seat belt. What was she going to say to Vanessa? There was no one who saw through her exaggerations and little white lies like Vanessa. Torrick, at one time, was demonstrative when it came to his love for Dianne; these days, though, he was too preoccupied. *Is he still attracted to me?*

"So…" Pulling out of a parking space, Vanessa broke the ice. "I went and got a lot of DVDs. Do you know how hard it is to find black-and-whites these days? I stopped at the library earlier and found—you won't believe it…"

"Imitation of Life."

"You and Mama are crazy for *Imitation of Life*. It was there, but I decided not to grab it. It was in color!"

"They colorized that? That's crazy!"

"People under thirty-five don't appreciate the black-and-white era. Whatever it is they want, we have to grin and bear it. Go to a mall! Instagram and Pinterest...Lord!" Vanessa sighed. "My daughter, she makes me feel *dated*."

"So what did you get?"

"Back Street."

"I haven't seen that...It was probably the last time you, Mama and me saw it. I think I was carrying Henna. Please, don't tell me they colorized that, too."

"The one I got is in black-and-white."

"Thank you, Vanessa. I could do with some Susan Hayward. You know, she was born to be in that era."

"Mr. John Gavin. I think George Clooney is the John Gavin of our day."

"No, Clooney's Cary Grant." Vanessa stopped at a signal. Slyly, she stole a glance her sister's way. *Something's up.*

"Well, true. Cary was a charmer." She sat quietly until Vanessa turned into a quaint street crammed with high-rise apartment buildings with fire escapes. "So what else did you get?"

"How could we have a martini and black-and-whites weekend without Bette?"

Dianne grinned, and she sensed herself starting to let go. For now. "There's no such thing as a martini and black-and-whites weekend without Bette."

"So, who's the new Bette Davis? Meryl Streep?"

"No, no way! Meryl is fabulous, but Bette is an original and can't be duplicated."

"True." Vanessa pulled into a parking space. "Do you mind a pizza delivery? I didn't get a chance to drop by Stop & Shop. "

"I'm going to have to put in extra gym time when I go back."

They walked toward Vanessa's apartment building, and she asked Dianne, "How are my favorite nieces doing?"

"Your two and only nieces are doing splendid." Vanessa unlocked the door. They walked through the vestibule when Dianne said, "They are so independent. I don't know what it is, but they are *grown*. They don't need me anymore."

Vanessa called for the elevator. She looked into her little sister's baby browns. "You're their mother; they'll always *need* you. I guess we have some talking to do."

"Why did I need to meet you *here?*" Gwen asked, annoyed. Her eyes shielded by fashionable large-framed shades, she wore skinny jeans. A trendy scarf hung loosely around her neck; her linen fedora tilted slightly to one side and beautifully dyed strawberry-blonde hair cascaded in ringlets past her waist—the Gwen *de rigueur*—along with a penciled-in birthmark near her upper lip. She looked around the room, jittery and high-strung.

"Why don't you take a seat," Venetia said.

Gwen looked Venetia over as if to decide if she even liked her. "I really don't want to be here."

"But since you're here, why not take a seat."

Gwen walked to the window and examined the late Southern California morning. The sun colorized the day like an image on a postcard. Her driver was leaning against the Navigator he chauffeured her around in, smoking a cigarette. He was her day driver. *He's a fine white boy.*

"Gwen?"

Her cell rang and she reached for it in the back pocket of her black skinny jeans. Gwen assessed the information on her touchscreen cell. Seconds later, she placed the device back into her pocket in the same familiar way a man slipped his wallet in the back pocket of his trousers. Intently, she looked out the window.

"Gwen?" Venetia kept her voice controlled, but she added

emphasis. She thought a hyper-casual approach was a better idea, but would it get her the desired result?

Gwen looked at her. "What?" She shrugged.

"Have a seat. We can talk for a few minutes, and if after that you want to leave, you can leave. This benefits you."

Gwen remained at the window, studying the outside. "I know the paparazzi are within blocks of here. I can't be seen with you. You get that?"

"You have my word: there'll be no paparazzi here."

Gwen familiarized Venetia's face well enough that should she run into her again, she'd dimly recall they met. She wanted nothing to do with this—whatever she does, or this meeting; her people set this thing up.

"Gwen…"

"You're one persistent chick, aren't you?" She walked over to a plump aubergine chair and flopped in it, exaggerating an audible exhalation. "I need a cigarette."

"There's no smoking in here."

"Then we got to make this quick."

Venetia sat across from Gwen, who was now pushing back her cuticles. "*Your* people hired me, Gwen. To work with you on…"

"I'm aware of that."

"I'm sure we can work together."

"There's no way for me to go to some clinic or whatever without the media finding out. I'll stop drinking on my own."

"You'll stop drinking?" Venetia snapped her fingers. "Just like that?"

"I like to have fun. Drinking's the thing I do with it. That doesn't make me an alcoholic."

"You realize you can't even drive right now. Three DUIs in… And what's going to happen when you have to show up in court?"

Gwen put up her hand in that *stop in the name of love* way, and with a voice that sounded final, said, "I'm not going to some clinic or whatever. And I damn-sure won't be a Lohan. No damn way, Auntie Em!"

"Okay, look." Venetia suppressed the sigh at the back of her throat. "Let's not discuss the drinking issue. Let's start with some of your personal…"

"What are you, a shrink? Huh-uh, Jacqueline D. didn't tell me I was meeting some shrink."

"I'm not a *shrink.*"

"So what exactly are you?" Gwen's body language spoke volumes.

"Jacqueline should have run my credentials by you."

"Credentials?"

"I work with certain types of people whose lives are…frenzied."

"Frenzied?"

"I'm a life coach."

"*Life* coach?" Gwen laughed.

"I'm sorry, what's funny?"

With arms locked over her chest, Gwen asked, "Why do I need someone to coach me on my *life?* Valerie, this is about my *career,* you read me. Whatever I gotta do to get the paparazzi off my back because of some so-called DUI…"

"Venetia."

"What?"

"My name is Venetia. And if you're here merely to get the paparazzi off your back about a *so-called* DUI, I cannot help you."

"Jacqueline D. said we were hooking up to make this shit work."

"I…"

"What's a—what you call it—life coach do exactly?"

"Gwen, no one can ever be prepared for a sudden abyss of fame." She frowned. "I really don't need someone that doesn't even *know* me telling me whether or not I can handle *fame*. I am not a parasite, okay!"

Venetia understood she was getting nowhere and she was tired from a very early morning flight; and she wasn't exactly in the mood to go up against a twenty-two-year-old who believed she had her life all figured out. At Gwen's age, life put Venetia in her place. She had her fair share of bumps and painful bruises, and it took a minute to get what life experiences were attempting to teach her. So Venetia's decision to meet with Gwen wasn't just business; she genuinely wanted to help someone she assessed was clearly in pain.

"Let me ask you something." Gwen looked up from her finger-nails painted in two different shades of polish. "If you were not on a reality TV program, what would you be doing?"

Gwen was visibly becoming uncomfortable. Her reality show was all about attitude. While Venetia had never seen the show, she'd caught an episode On Demand prior to leaving for L.A. The tone of the program rested entirely—at least from Venetia's perspective—on Gwen's lifestyle: club-hopping in L.A., high-priced spas with friends in chic cities like San Francisco, shopping at trendy boutiques on Robertson, getting a new tattoo, a spur-of-the-moment trip to Miami where she changed clothes in her stretch limo—all taped for the viewers to see. Venetia shook her head, trying to ascertain the entertainment value.

"What do you mean what would I be doing?"

Venetia asked every client this question; by the time they reached the place of needing her, they were at a crossroad. Not so much professionally as they were personally. It was the personal that interfered with the professional; and in some cases, vice versa. With regard to Gwen, it interfered with the public persona she'd manufactured.

"What would be, say, your raison d'être?"

"Raison *whah?*"

"What would you be doing to earn a living if you weren't on a reality TV show? Would you have gone to college and gotten a degree? Would you have become an actress or…?"

With a smirk and a hunch of her shoulders, Gwen said in a quite cavalier way, "I don't know," then her eyes immediately went back to her cuticles. It was a gesture that clearly demonstrated that she was in a situation she wasn't accustomed to. The meeting was a dead-giveaway and proved one thing: Gwen was out of her depth. She was far more comfortable in front of the camera changing her clothes in a limo and drinking champagne from a pair of never-worn platforms.

"Okay, let's try asking this in a different way. If you knew without a shadow of a doubt that you wouldn't fail, what would you choose to do with your life?"

"This is bullshit."

"Gwen…"

"What kinda training do you have to come at me like this, huh?"

"I…"

"You say you aren't no shrink, so…" She shrugged sarcastically.

"I don't have a degree in psychology, no."

"So…"

"My educational background is in sociology. And I have been trained to be a life coach."

"There's training for this kind of gig?"

"I think if you'd read my CV…"

"CV? What, is that some kind of…"

"Résumé."

"Oh, so you can't just say résumé. You gotta get all Brit."

"Gwen, why are you angry?"

"Are we through here? I'll tell Jacqueline D. you were cool."

"First I'd like you to at least answer my question."

"Which is?" she asked, leaning into the chair. She crossed her legs, one foot shaking.

"If you knew without a doubt that you wouldn't or even couldn't fail, what would you like to do? And I mean do with your *life?*"

With a judgmental gaze, Gwen chuckled sarcastically. In all honesty, and deep down, she never even thought she'd be on TV; let alone doing anything that got her the attention she now received—fame and whatnot. Tweets mentioning her dozens of times each day, popular on TV, Sunset Boulevard and Times Square billboards, late-night TV hosts saying what she did, going somewhere as simple as Target and creating a scene, and a lot of attention from men! Even women came on to her in bathrooms—in clubs, restaurants, at parties. They would hold up their cell phones, snapping photographs and published them on their various social media walls. She'd caught a few videos taped by camera phones and posted on YouTube. The attention—she loved it, and it brought her a sense of pleasure. Secretly, it validated her in some strange way; and the jealousy she had to deal with? She'd lost some of her friends from Baldwin Hills, her old hood, who couldn't handle the attention, her fame, her new money. She had to drop her old friends because they couldn't relate to her new friends, or her (new) world. There was always a downside to an upside. For Gwen the downside was the lack of control.

She removed an imaginary piece of lint from her jeans. Her eyes darted to a scrape on the side of her ankle boot. *Damn!* "I don't know. Maybe I'd like to be like Oprah."

"Do you admire Oprah?"

"She's a positive role model."

"Why not Condoleezza Rice, or…?"

"Who? Oh, her. Why would I admire *her?*"

"You realize the distinction between Oprah and Condoleezza Rice, right?"

"Uh, *yea-uh!*"

"Do you think Oprah would admire you?"

Gwen's eyes shot straight up at Venetia. *I wonder who does her brows.* "Well, if she even knows who I am, I doubt it."

"And why would you think she wouldn't admire you?"

"I get your point, ah-ight? I *get* it. You trying to manipulate me. It. Ain't. Working!"

"I'm trying to get you to examine your life. Not just your image. You can't like how you're portrayed by the media. Are you comfortable with how you're selling a fake you to the world? I'd like to work with you, Gwen. But not so it can help your career. It's to help you with your life—the way you choose to use it and live it. If you stay on this path, you'll burn out. Listen, your fate won't arrive in a Navigator to pick you up. Do you want to be a burnt-out, ex-reality TV personality at twenty-five?"

"I'm twenty-two!"

"But by twenty-five, if you aren't careful, you'll burn out. You should care about, not just ratings and whether the paparazzi are following you around L.A. You should care about your health and your mind."

"Look, let me think it over. Ah-ight?"

"Your life needs a new trajectory. The third DUI is a game-changer. You're intelligent enough to understand that."

Gwen stood, and reached for her cell in her pocket. She studied it for a few moments. Venetia took notice that she was responding to something. She was typing speedily with her thumbs. Venetia came to her feet.

Gwen looked over to Venetia. "I gotta split." She headed for the door.

"Gwen…"

"Jacqueline D.'ll be in touch."

Before Venetia could stop her, in an energetic pace, Gwen walked out and toward the Navigator that dropped her at Venetia's doorstep. Gwen slid on her shades and cased the immediate area—a narrow street, and palm-tree lined. So paranoid that a paparazzo was lurking around, Gwen began to trot. The driver was leaning against the SUV but stood and opened the door. Gwen disappeared inside and was safeguarded by tinted windows.

Venetia had no expectations of ever talking to Gwen Jackson again.

"Okay, tell me this. If you hadn't gotten pregnant, would you have married Torrick?"

Dianne was at one end of the sofa bed and Vanessa at the other. The Saturday morning offered soft sunlight. Both took their time getting up. They'd stayed up all night watching DVDs. Not to mention the seven martinis between them—they had hangovers. Besides, Dianne had flown from the West to the East Coast. Vanessa was forced to get up because of the persistent ringing landline. It had been her daughter in San Jose. Afterward, Vanessa made coffee and toasted frozen waffles. Dianne frowned at the idea, but once she took her first bite, she said, "These aren't bad, Vanessa."

"I've asked myself that question several times."

"I always believed you never quite got over Gregory."

"I did, eventually."

"But do you really *love* Torrick, Dianne?"

"I wouldn't have married a man I didn't love. Really!"

"Let me ask this: Are you *in* love with your husband?"

"I *love* Torrick."

The tender sun trickled in through partially opened mini-blinds. Dianne was wrapped in a vivid-colored throw. Vanessa, wearing leggings and a stretch zip up-styled jacket, held a cup of tea.

Vanessa rubbed Dianne's leg affectionately. "I'm not questioning whether you care for Torrick. He's the father of your children. You've been with him for sixteen years. That's some history. Do you *like* him? Do you still *want* him? You can like someone and not love them and love someone and not like them necessarily."

"It sounds to me like you're talking about your second—and might I point out—failed marriage?"

"I wasn't good at marriage." Vanessa yawned. "Anyway…You come three thousand miles to tell me you had a one-night-stand with a personal trainer and two days ago went to see your internist and learned that you had chlamydia. That's an expensive excuse to come to New York."

"I also wanted to see you."

"And of course you're trying to buy time. Expecting that prescription to kick in and cure your STD before you fly back home."

"Nothing gets by you, does it?"

"You're confident it wasn't Torrick and not the personal trainer?"

"We haven't had sex in a month. No, it's the personal trainer."

"Condoms? I know it's been a while so they aren't something you'd carry on your person as a possible precaution. But if you're *married*—duh! Use protection when you cheat."

"It happened so fast…"

"You made a vow; that should mean something. And who gets chlamydia in their fifties? That's something I worry my daughter will get. Really, Dianne! Look…" she sighed. "Marriage is a partnership, which is why you should marry someone who's like a good girlfriend. When that in *loveness* thing goes away, you have something to fall back on. It's inevitable: sex will be a routine, like brushing your teeth—very *un*Zen. You won't even *think* about it; you just do it. I stopped *enjoying* sex with both of my husbands well into…Mmmm, year three. I miss male connection, but I don't miss being married."

"Marriage ain't easy. By the way, I want that pomegranate recipe." Dianne looked out the window; her thoughts wandered to and fro.

"You know Mama's repeating herself, and forgetting names now. She called me Dianne twice yesterday. I had to stop myself from correcting her." They sat wordless for a short while. Vanessa broke the silence and asked, "How do you decide to sleep with someone on the fly while you're married? I don't think I could ever do something like that. Unless I was contemplating leaving the marriage. Sleeping with someone else, especially when you don't use a form of protection, is insanely disrespectful. Why did you do it, Dianne?"

She began to feel a mounting sense of unease. Coming to New York made her start to feel guilty. But Dianne knew her sister was only saying what she needed to hear. She was the tough-love type to the core.

"Okay, so what about Phoebe, your erstwhile friend? How did it really feel seeing her after all these years?"

Dianne reached for her ringing cellular. She acknowledged the name and, meeting her sister's gaze, answered, "Hi, Torrick."

Jacqueline was savoring a delicious white coffee while reading through her e-mails. Every few words, she'd stop and take a quick peek at the various hues of black professionals that paid good cash to attend the yearly black professionals' summit. It was the only time she was a spectator to so many thriving blacks in one space. Jacqueline wasn't the type to jump to conclusions without hard facts, so she trusted that the extra security had more to do with the huge crowd, not because the people walking the four floors of the convention center were black. Besides, they looked more like Torrick's security detail. Jacqueline placed her white coffee on a nearby table and reread a text from Venetia Street. Perchance she needed to pull out her reading glasses. Jacqueline couldn't believe what her eyes were telling her. She read the text again, raising the cell closer to her face. *Unbelievable!* Gwen walked out of the appointment! "Oy!" she said.

"Are you that beautiful woman I saw step out of a black Crossfire? Parking level two-A?"

"Excuse me." Jacqueline tried to concentrate on the text, but the man standing in front of her—handsome, well-preserved forties, extremely polished—was a distraction.

"Wasn't it you I saw this morning? Those long legs"—his eyes lowered to take a fleeting look at Jacqueline's shapely legs—"stepping out of a Crossfire."

"Have we met…before?" Her right brow elevated.

"If only," he said. "Daniel Terry." The charismatic man slipped her a business card.

Reluctant, and keeping her eyes on his, Jacqueline reached for the card. She barely noticed the printed words. Her usual on-top-of-it self was off guard. Had she not gotten the text from Venetia, perhaps she would have been on her game. "I thought one-hundred and forty characters was the new business card."

"So I heard. Let me guess…" Daniel placed his fingers beneath his chin.

"Media Capital."

"Media Capital?" The tender line between his eyes creased deeper.

He was too smooth; Jacqueline couldn't detect how impressed he really was. "And you…" Jacqueline eyed his business card with her genuine panache. "Ventures Anonymous?" *Why anonymous?* Jacqueline's cell vibrated and she eyed the number, which didn't look familiar. She hesitated for a split-second. In a short span of time, she needed to decide whether to answer it or to continue talking to Daniel, who was a seriously attractive diversion from Venetia's unexpected text. "Excuse me," she said to Daniel, "for a moment, please." She turned away from Daniel, but sensed his presence lingering nearby, waiting. *That suit fits like he was born in it. Those slim slacks accentuate his lean, taut thighs. No wedding band. Appearance-wise, he's too good to be true.* "Jacqueline Daye. Who's calling?" Jacqueline listened briefly. "Can I get back with you on this? Yes, of course. Thank you." She adjusted her charm. Daniel stood in close proximity, his arms crossed, glancing nonchalantly at a crowd of businessmen nearby, laughing with animation over drinks from the open bar. He turned and immediately his face shifted as if it was a compliment to be back in her company. "So, Mr. Terry, what do you think of the summit thus far?"

"Captivating. It's my first. And you?"

"My third. Every year it gets larger, and that's a good thing. The power in this space. It's exciting to witness."

"Torrick James gave one hell of a speech."

"Do you know Torrick James?"

"Casually. We work out at the same gym. Went to his Super Bowl party last year. He's a great guy. Beautiful wife, children. He made all the right moves."

"Are you married?"

"Divorced. Three years."

"Children?"

"With a woman I was involved with prior to my marriage. My daughter is a freshman at UCLA." Daniel slipped his hands into his trouser pockets. "Let me guess. Never married, no children?"

Jacqueline was ill at ease by his all-too accurate assessment of her, but she was now a pro at revealing secrets. "Perceptive."

"Well…Unmarried women, and especially unmarried and childless women, carry themselves in a certain way. They're more conscious of themselves. Do you? Have children?"

"I don't."

"You're okay with your status?"

"What exactly does that imp—mean?"

"I think I hit a nerve."

Jacqueline's cell buzzed and she sought out the caller. "Jacqueline Daye." Her eyes rested on Daniel studying her, perhaps closer than she felt comfortable with. "Of course. When? And where again? Sounds good. Okay…" She released the call.

"That was a man," Daniel presumed, confident.

"I have your business card, Daniel." She produced her hand. "It was fun getting acquainted."

"Lunch soon?" He released her hand and closed his suit jacket by buttoning one button with natural finesse.

"Let's check our calendars, shall we?"

"I take it you're listed on Media Capital's website."

Joseph preferred early morning walks. There was a consistent rain the evening before, and it continued well past dawn. Damp weather did nothing for his arthritis—what his son called kneemonia. He decided not to walk along the lake, even while the walks were something to look forward to. Nature—something about it. The wind in the trees, the sound of birds he couldn't see; the simplicity of these things made life less chaotic, rushed. Here, in this time and place, life moved in God's pace. People were too preoccupied these days. It felt like a lifetime ago, but Joseph remembered "sir" and "ma'am." He recalled "thank you" and "please." Nods and thoughtful hellos by strangers. Nowadays, people didn't have time to be polite; not that polite required time.

Now that there was a sliver of sun, he thought he could do at least a quarter of a mile without his knees aching later on. A runner occasional acknowledged him when-they passed, and with those things in their ears, like his son. *Earbuds.* He'd been living near the lake since they 'd bought the house back in '88. It was a vibrant neighborhood. The houses nearly touched one another in an enchanting tableau, with well-cared-for lawns and clean, curvilinear streets. At the time they purchased the home, it had the potential to double in value. If he wanted to, Joseph could put it up for sale and get a decent price. But the value, despite the ZIP code, wasn't worth nearly what it was prior to the downturn in '07. Or was it '08? Every other economist had a different theory, a different timeline when the recession hit, and the housing market took a nosedive. Jobs being shipped away to places like China; half of the possessions Americans purchased were imported from elsewhere. Whenever he needed to talk to customer service by phone, they always had accents that weren't American. He couldn't recall when last he spoke to someone with English-as-a-first-language accent.

"Good morning!" Joseph said to a passing jogger.

"Morning, Joe!" He kept his pace, not missing a beat.

He was fit, a tax attorney who drove a Porsche convertible. Roughly three, four years older than Joseph, he looked years younger. Joseph was envious that his neighbor felt comfortable at his age wearing an earring like he was a twenty-year-old rock star. *That happened after the divorce.* They used to play racquetball together back in the day. Admittedly, Joseph had developed a beer belly or a couch potato pouch around the same time his daughter graduated from high school and went off to college. When his wife became ill, he no longer tended to his own needs, and in all honesty, he stopped paying attention. His interest in living changed, although Joseph was still attracted to life. As the path bent, and he was getting to the point where he would head back to the house, he noticed a woman he hadn't seen before. It wasn't unusual for strangers to be on the path. The woman caught his eye primarily because she wasn't running like everyone else. Joseph stopped running some years back; when his RA made it impossible for him to run. He had to be in his mid-forties then. It felt like yesterday.

It was impulsive on his part; Joseph stopped in his tracks and spoke to the unfamiliar woman. "Beautiful late morning, isn't it?"

Phoebe barely paid him any attention, despite his standing in her way. "Yes," she replied politely.

Joseph was immediately drawn to this mysterious woman. Although he knew, from past experience, he was out of her league. She was classy, and Hollywood attractive. She took such care of herself, he couldn't quite guess her age. The way she spoke to him and the way her eyes met his, he wouldn't stand a chance with her. There was no feeling in her eyes that suggested she even cared what his name was. She only stopped because Joseph blocked her way.

"The trees," Joseph said. He observed the leaves flittering in the gentle breeze. "And the sky. The rain cleans the air."

He wanted a sign that he had a chance.

"I'm from Southern California. We really need rain. We're going through a drought."

"Oh, so you live in the Golden State?"

"I'm here temporarily."

"Are you…staying nearby?"

Phoebe replied with a nod.

"Well! I'm just around the curve," he said, turning toward the arc in the road.

With a smile that leaned more toward sociable than solicitous, Phoebe said, "Oh." She started walking, having to step on to the fading green-hued lawn in order to get around him. Casually, she said, "Enjoy your walk."

"Thank you. Oh," he called out. "Whereabouts are you staying?"

"Up there." Phoebe was vague.

"Love those homes. Priceless views."

Phoebe repeated, "Enjoy your walk."

Joseph read between the lines. Women were so difficult to meet these days.

"There you are. Look at *you*," Torrick said, coming to his feet.

Jacqueline laughed a break-the-ice laugh as they pressed their cheeks against each other's. "Here I am." *Why am I nervous?*

"Have a seat."

Torrick had ordered a cognac and was sitting by a burning fire and the opened French doors that allowed the noise from the street to compete with Adele's powerful voice singing "Rumor Has It." The adjacent restaurant was energetic and eventful. When he'd arrived, Torrick asked the maître d' if he could be seated in the Purple Room since he wasn't planning on dining. His business provided security whenever high-profilers stayed at the adjacent hotel. Torrick received VIP treatment as a result.

Jacqueline sat, crossed her long, bare legs exposed from a split skirt, open to the left. Casually, she flipped strands of her coal-colored hair away. Her long legs and *good* hair were undeniable assets.

"You should insure those legs of yours," Torrick teased.

"How long has it been since we last saw each other?"

With a shrug, he guessed: "What, three months? Daniela had just upgraded to a smartphone, so…"

"Sweet Daniela. Her age, the kids are always in FOMO mode." Loosening up, Jacqueline laughed. "I suppose at that age we, too, had to be on top of everything. It was simply a different time."

Jacqueline always, always liked Torrick's company. While he was easy to look at, she enjoyed being around him because he had energy, spirit. He loved to talk and nothing he ever discussed was trivial. If he wasn't married to one of her dear friends, she'd have been on top of him years ago.

A waiter approached them sitting in velour, overstuffed chairs.

"What are you having, Jacqueline?"

"Whatever he's having, I'll have the same."

Torrick lifted his glass as if to let the waiter know his drink. Swift and smooth, the waiter nodded with a thin-lipped smile. Torrick leaned into the chair, relaxed and contended. "So, tell me…"

"You were brilliant!"

"Oh, you mean the speech?" Laughing, Torrick said, "Well, thank you. But I was actually going to ask how's the media business doing?"

"It's a hustle is what it is. Ten years ago I worked less hours and had time to *live*. This social media…it's a time-snatcher. What it would be like to be in my thirties again. Before all this oversharing of the effluvia, of the mundane…"

"Trust me; you don't want to go back to the thirties."

"Why not?" she asked, sincerely curious.

"Look, men have these fantasies from time to time, too. But women obsess over it. I believe Dianne feels as though she's lost some of her worth as a woman. Remember her fiftieth?"

"That was one fabulous party. And you went all out, too."

"I won't divulge what that cost me. Besides, it's not the point. When the guests and the caterers were all gone…We were getting undressed and Dianne sat in the middle of the bed and cried like a baby." Torrick hunched his broad shoulders, still baffled by it several years later. "Seriously…"

Jacqueline, with downcast eyes, said, "Her first hot flash; she was depressed for a few days. And then her first colonoscopy…it was a defining moment." Their waiter interrupted and placed Jacqueline's drink on the table. Before she resumed, she let the cognac wet her tongue. She held the glass, gazing into it. Their eyes met. "Earlier, when I was at the summit, someone approached me."

"Some*one*? Only some*one*?" he mocked. "Who?" Torrick was rather curious to know. He was familiar with some of the women, but many of the men who attended the summit he knew socially or had done business with, on both the East and West Coast.

"That doesn't matter, really." In a somber voice, Jacqueline continued. "He said something to me I might have been in denial about for years, I'm not sure."

Torrick held his drink in one hand while his other arm rested on the arm of the chair. By her expression, Torrick decided it stayed with Jacqueline long enough for her to bring it up. He'd always seen her as beautiful, smart, fascinating, and remarkably sure of herself. A friend of Dianne's since they'd relocated from Los Angeles, Jacqueline was intensely self-contained. A few years back, he'd tried to set her up with someone he golfed with on occasion. He was a heart specialist used to being the center of attention and was intimidated by a woman who couldn't care less about his status. Torrick had no intentions of ever putting someone else, or himself, in that situation again.

"What did he say?"

Jacqueline breathed heavily, swirling the liquor in the glass. "I was satisfied with being unmarried and childless." She took two good sips and the liquor burned her throat.

"Are you?"

She looked over at Torrick. The fire burning nearby glowed against the side of his dark and handsome face. *Dianne has no idea how lucky she is.* "I never second-guess my life choices, Torrick."

"Hmmm, I like that answer."

"Do you?"

"I'll put it this way: I sleep good at night."

She laughed, adoring his company more than she should.

Torrick leaned forward and held out his drink. "Let's toast."

She bent forward. "To?"

He winked. "Good friends."

"What do you plan to do, Dianne?"

Martini and black-and-white weekends always did the trick, but coming to see her sister did nothing but open up old wounds. Even her sister didn't know about the sorrows that had haunted her all these years: the might-have-beens, and the wishes and hopes that were like dust in the wind. Meeting Torrick was her saving grace. At least she felt that way, and even believed it, for years. She admitted to her sister seeing Phoebe brought back memories— painful, sad, but also some of the happiest moments of her life were when Phoebe and she were friends. She was a reminder of who Dianne thought she *would* be.

"Some part of me wants to tell him the truth. I don't feel like carrying around all this excess baggage. It's a burden."

"When did you start feeling like this? Before or after you went to the doctor?"

Dianne couldn't be sure. "Why?"

"Because the same day you went to your doctor is the same day you ran into Phoebe."

"Are you suggesting there's a connection?"

"I'm not suggesting; there *is* a connection. But let's stick with Torrick. Phoebe's not your pressing issue."

"Phoebe…I forgot how angry I was at her."

"Listen, you had a one-day-stand with a personal trainer. And he's thirty-one? That screams confusion. Oh, I know right now it's all chic to be a cougar. Hell, I want to be a cougar. But, Dianne…"

"It's not always easy to consider someone else when you have intense needs. I would never do anything to bring harm to my daughters. I have devoted my life to them, and without ever complaining about it."

"You think I don't know that. I was lucky because Mama did a lot of my heavy-lifting. I wish I had been as attentive and selfless with Carmel as you've been with Daniela and Henna."

"You think you've been a bad mother?"

"I've been good compared to a lot of mothers I've come across. But I wasn't as available as you've been. Hindsight has excellent vision, so I can now see all the mistakes clearly."

A tear slipped leisurely off Dianne's cheek. She swiped away the tearstain. "You asked me if I loved Torrick and I told you that I did. I've thought about it over the past few days. And I've been thinking a lot about my first real love, Gregory. Maybe I did hook up with Torrick for the wrong reason. Anyway, he's a good man. He has excellent qualities. But I think what you're asking me is if what I feel is love or comfort?"

With a somber face, Vanessa said, "It's okay. You don't have to go into a lot of detail." She came to her feet. "I'm going to shower and dress. Let's go to the city and spend some of Torrick's hard-earned money before you head to LaGuardia. Dianne?"

Solemnly, she looked up at her sister.

"You'll get past this."

She offered her sister a weak smile. "And in the meantime?"

Hours later, sitting on the flight back home, Dianne tried to concentrate on a trilogy she'd been attempting to finish. She borrowed her daughter's e-reader, but on the flight to New York her mind kept wandering and she never quite got through a chapter. Dianne pressed her eyes shut and tried to get some much-needed sleep.

CHAPTER 3

"This damn traffic!"

Jacqueline's cell buzzed. She said into her Bluetooth, "Jacqueline Daye. Who's calling?" Jacqueline was determined to beat unanticipated morning traffic. She turned off the main street and decided she had a better chance of not being late for the Weekly Huddle if she took side streets. She never, *never* overslept. "Richard?" She grinned. "It's been awhile, my friend. How's the legal profession?" She switched gears and turned sharply into a street where garbage was being picked up. *Damn!* "Yes, that sounds lovely. Who's the client? Of course I heard about it. I'm listening. I'm on my way into the office and it's one of those horrible Mondays. Everyone seems to be going in the same direction." With laughter, and feeling a tad tingly hearing Richard's voice, she said, "Brilliant! Absolutely. Cheers!" The garbage truck was moving at a snail's pace along the narrow street. Jacqueline called into the office and greeted the concierge, "Claire, Jacqueline. I'm on my way in. Traffic's absolutely crazy this morning! Let Michael and Stefan know I'm running late. Have Stefan's assistant get everything—social media—all of it, on the police shooting a few nights ago. Correct." Jacqueline shifted gears and sped past the garbage truck parked in the middle of the cluttered street, and nearly ran down one of the workers hauling a compost bin. She put her gear in second when she reached the roundabout. "And Claire?" she resumed. "I want this to be a topic in the Huddle."

Within a mile, between home and the office, Jacqueline's phone rang six times. She decided, entering the garage elevator, she would insist—no, demand!—TA start the process of getting Claire to transition as her assistant. Jacqueline spent her entire weekend going through mail and e-mails, and making one too many calls her assistant would otherwise handle.

"Good morning!" Claire said to Jacqueline when she entered reception.

"Good morning." She didn't stop, but slowed her pace to add, "What do I need to know?"

Claire rushed to her feet. "The meeting's pushed back. Stefan didn't want to start without you." Claire walked around the desk and tailed behind Jacqueline who didn't miss a beat. She maintained a brisk pace and power-browsed a document on her iPad. "You have two Fleetfoot packages on your desk," Claire continued. "They just arrived. And the information you wanted on the police shooting is on your desk, too. And I'll let Stefan's assistant know you've arrived and they'll be ready to start—"

"I need to speak with Gloria in TA," Jacqueline interrupted, walking hurriedly down the hallway.

No sooner than she entered her office, Jacqueline received a text from Venetia Street, the life coach. She debated whether she should even bother reading it. Gwen, with her *Gwenology* self, was more trouble than her being a client with Media Capital was worth. If she hadn't spent a "minute" with her father eight years ago, Jacqueline would drop her like she should a depraved habit. She plopped her purse on the desk and reached for a pile of clipped papers marked *Anthony Perez.* If she and Stefan weren't such good friends, she'd woo his assistant in a heartbeat—she was good. Jacqueline tossed the profile back on her desk and thought better of ignoring Venetia. Not only did she come highly recommended, her website showcased the I-know-where-you-live-I-know-where-you-work-I-know-where-you-shop clientele—hardcore social-networkers, and high-profile bloggers. Not to mention she was the daughter of the late and deeply beloved Cordia Street. Jacqueline didn't want to alienate someone with her reputation and connections. She read the text. It was to the point: *Gwen is going to crash and burn. I recommend intervention immediately.*

When Jacqueline received the text from Venetia while at the BPOA summit stating that Gwen wasn't interested in working with a life coach, she'd gotten sidetracked by that too-sexy guy at the summit—Daniel. Out of curiosity, she did an online drive-by, and before she wrapped up her weekend, they'd indulged in a handful of flirtatious texts. Her entire weekend was inundated with nonsense—one crisis after another. Gwen, and Daniel too, became an afterthought.

"Hey, we're ready." Stefan was tall with fading good looks. He verged on anorexic; his features were gaunt and he looked years older than his age. Jacqueline looked up to him standing in the doorway. He continued, "Before we head into the Huddle, can you tell me why Anthony Perez is a topic?"

"Good morning, Stefan." She reached for her electronic tablet and held it like a schoolbook. "I think he's a potential client."

"Why would we handle an alleged drug dealer?"

"Do you know who he is?"

"It's been all over the news."

"And it's also national."

"Does this have anything to do with who's representing him?"

"You know me better than that. Have you looked it over?"

"Flip through thirty-eight pages and try to *participate* in a conference call. One's going to get less attention."

"At least you're honest about your declining attention span.

When we started in this business, there was no online social-net-working. We had to dig deep to get someone's four-one-one. People need to be careful what we say on those social-networking sites. It's insanity—hashtag drug mule." Jacqueline placed the dossier beneath her e-tablet. She walked toward Stefan. "How are you feeling?"

He touched her familiarly on the arm, and with a wink, said, "It's a good day."

"Sweet. And, Stefan, can you do something about getting Claire on board sooner than next week? I'm swamped."

"Excuse me!"

Phoebe was placing dishes in the dishwasher. She'd borrowed Venetia's iPod and was humming to John Legend's "Ordinary People"; she didn't hear Jacqueline.

"Phyllis!" Jacqueline snapped her fingers, intolerant. "Phyllis!"

Phoebe yanked a bud from her ear. "Are you talking to me?"

In a sarcastic gesture, Jacqueline looked around. "Aren't you Phyllis?"

"No." She shook her head.

"What's your name? Look, forget that. I need a café au lait. And as an FYI: the coffee in the conference room is *warm*."

"I'll let Chef know."

"Thank you for the café au lait, dear." Jacqueline rushed into the hallway calling out, "Michael!…"

Dear. Rolling her eyes, Phoebe stopped what she was doing to prepare a café au lait. Chef walked in, whistling. "What are you doing?" he snapped.

"Making a café au lait."

"For?"

"Jacqueline, I think that's her name. Tall, light-skinned black woman. *And* she says the coffee in the Cascades conference room is *warm*."

"Please don't ruin her café au lait. She's very particular. Not too hot, not too warm. Make sure it's right, will you? I don't want to have to hear about it…" He rinsed his hands in the sink and started reaching for vegetables with a habitual rhythm. "I'll handle the coffee. You know we have two meetings this afternoon. Can you manage?"

"I can manage," Phoebe said.

Three minutes later, Phoebe entered the large conference room facing the striking Cascades. Everyone in the room was either talking to someone on a mobile device, or looking down at one. Several assistants, seated on charcoal-colored exercise balls along the wall, were tapping away on laptops or electronic tablets. No one was talking to each other. Phoebe sought Jacqueline. *Why did she have to be on the opposite side of the room?* She made her way toward her, but was stopped by a man she had not seen before, and who looked borderline sallow. "Could you bring me a glass of soy?"

"Sure."

Jacqueline reached for the café au lait. "Thank you."

When Phoebe returned to the kitchen, Chef's PA was scribbling on a notepad. "A man in the conference room—I didn't get his name—wants a glass of soy."

"He's the sixty percent of Media Cap. He has cancer."

Phoebe poured a glass of soy. "Yes, he looks…"

"Phoebe, put it in the microwave. No more than fifteen seconds. He prefers it warm. Also, I'd sprinkle a touch of vanilla to give it flavor."

"By the time I learn everyone's idiosyncrasies, they will have hired someone permanently."

"No one's going to say it, so I will: you're doing a fabulous job." The PA began to leave the kitchen, but added, "You can always come to me; I have your back."

Phoebe pressed the start button on the microwave. "I appreciate that."

On her break, Phoebe slipped into one of the hospitality suites primarily used for visitors or clients. She checked the calendar; no one was scheduled to use it. She needed the break. She had to get away from the toxic nature of Media Capital. The company was the personification of manufactured needs and wants. No wonder Chef bit her head off—the placating he had to do. Phoebe was no more than a glorified waitress, but the pay made up for the cons of the assignment. Gloria, in TA, had stopped in to say hello to her at the end of her first week. She had that I-didn't-expect-you-to-last-this-long look.

A ringtone interrupted the rant inside her head. The number was local; Phoebe hadn't given out her number since she'd arrived. "Hello? Dianne, hi. Drinks? Yes, it would be fun to catch up." She stood and walked to the window. The view from her vantage point wasn't that good, but there was a spectacular vista—a faint sun sheathed the waning summer day. "Okay. I can find it. See you then. *Ciao*."

For a few seconds, she stared at the mobile in her hand. On the one hand, she wanted to meet Dianne for drinks so they could fill in the blanks in their lives. The last time she'd heard from Dianne was by way of a Christmas card, which was a photograph of her family—the girls, Torrick, and Dianne seated strategically in an enchanting room with a burning fireplace and poinsettias in the backdrop. The only thing missing was a beautifully coiffed dog. Daniela and Henna were probably no more than eight and five. On the other hand, she wasn't particularly sure enough time had come and gone for Dianne to still not hold bitterness toward her. Their history—their life in the public eye—was impaired because of misinterpretations and a trivial row that led them to go their separate ways. Phoebe had been young and selfish; she'd be the first to admit that. But the details of that time, when they were young and had so much life ahead of them, were blurred by the labyrinth she'd traveled that led her where she now stood. Dianne had married, started a family; she got lucky.

"Oh, excuse me," said a man with a British accent. "I was told this room was booked for me."

"And it is."

Phoebe was walking toward the kitchen when her cell rang. The number was private. She had a hint as to who it might be, and she hesitated before she said, "Hello?"

Dianne spent far too much time in the neighborhood supermarket. She decided against making dinner and thought Torrick could whip something together. Thinking better of it, he would run into traffic; his calendar indicated that he would be escorting a client to the airport. In traffic that time of day, he wouldn't make it home before seven. Her instincts kicked in and Dianne bought a rotisserie chicken and romaine for a salad. Her oldest, Daniela, made very tasty salads, adding mixed veggies, nuts and dried fruit.

While she drove the main street toward home, she decided on what to wear to her meet-up with Phoebe. Were it not for her sister, Vanessa, Dianne might have let it go and not bothered to call Phoebe. When they ran into each other, admittedly she was curious what had happened to Phoebe. It would seem something went wrong. Of course, even at her worst, Phoebe could pull herself together without much fuss. Regrettably, to look naturally good at their age took more time.

She pulled into the drive and her next-door neighbor's dog started barking. *Please don't let her come out and talk. I'll never get away.* She managed to sneak into the house unseen. Dianne rushed into the kitchen. She put away the items swiftly. Her cell buzzed and Dianne reached for it. It was a text from her oldest asking if she could stay at her best friend's for dinner. Dianne texted Daniela back, telling her that it wasn't a good day; that her sister couldn't stay home alone once it was dark. *Get home on time,* Dianne's response stated firmly. For a few years now, Dianne had let her oldest get away with more than enough. She was lenient as she, too, gave her mother a hard time at her age. She recognized the hypocrisy if she were too stringent. Dianne, as well as her sister, turned out fine. Every now and then, to let her know who was boss, Dianne threw her daughter a curveball: *No, and don't even debate with me.* When she heard the beep that she'd received a text, she knew it was Daniela pleading urgently. *Home by six-thirty, no exceptions!* she texted back.

"She'll get over it." Surprisingly, she heard a beep. "I know she's not going to argue with me about this." Dianne picked up her cell and within a single heartbeat gasped, oblivious as to her action. "Oh, my goodness." The text was from the personal trainer she'd had a—as her sister framed it—one-day-stand with. Dianne replaced the cell and tried to recall whether she had even given him her number. It was possible he'd gotten it from the gym where she worked out. The pace of her heartbeat accelerated, and Dianne was starting to freak out about the very fact that she would have to fess up to Torrick about the chlamydia. She couldn't bring herself to read the text. It was understood—he in a relationship and she married—their indiscretion was a one-time incident. They wouldn't reach out to each other again. When her internist had informed her she'd contracted a sexually transmitted disease, Dianne's first thought was how she would work through it with Torrick; she never once thought of contacting the personal trainer. *Shoot!* She looked over her shoulder at the microwave. She would be late meeting up with Phoebe if she didn't leave soon.

She pressed Vanessa's name in her phone. Dianne was immediately greeted by her voicemail. She pressed disconnect. Her heart was pounding. She broke down and opened the text. It was short and sweet: *We need to talk.* Her instinct was to delete it and move on. Then she thought better of it. She needed to prepare the asparagus and she needed to freshen up. *Shoot.*

Like her mother had warned her when she'd first learned she was pregnant with Daniela, and Dianne was afraid to tell Torrick— "nothing ever goes away; we block it out as if it's not there." Dianne focused on making the asparagus; afterward, she carved the chicken. The landline rang, but Dianne chose to disregard it. She needed to stay in the moment. Hastily, she wrote out instructions to her daughters. She would call Torrick in the car.

For twenty minutes, Dianne debated on what to wear. It wasn't as though she was having a clandestine meeting with a lover. It was drinks and catching up with an old friend. Finally, she decided on jeans, a silk tee and a fall-weather leather jacket Dianne had been debating whether to donate to the church's yearly wardrobe giveaway.

In the car she sucked in a deep breath. She buckled her seat belt. Dianne tried Vanessa again, but received voicemail. She pressed Jacqueline, but disconnected the call before the third ring. She couldn't talk about the personal trainer with her. She wasn't even sure why. Their friendship was solid and Dianne liked hanging out with Jacqueline. She was single and fun; a guilty pleasure.

They shopped, shared books, went to hot yoga, and ate out whenever their schedules permitted them both to do so. They attended the same church. But in reflection, Dianne rarely talked about her marriage to Jacqueline. She probably assumed, like everyone else at church, that Dianne and Torrick were happy and had a good marriage. She gave Jacqueline no reason to assume otherwise.

"Vanessa, call me when you get a chance. I know you're three hours ahead, but I need to talk to you." By the time she managed to find a parking space a few blocks from the Blue Bar, her anxiety subsided. When she entered Blue, it was crammed—mostly professionals unwinding after a stressful day at the office. Dianne had no idea what that life was really like. On occasion, she'd find herself envying Jacqueline because of her glamorous, time-consuming career. No sooner than she started working as a buyer, Dianne met Torrick and got pregnant with Daniela. She never really had a chance to balance a corporate career and personal life simultaneously.

Dianne spotted Phoebe standing with a man holding a drink. Back in the day, he would definitely have been Phoebe's type. Upon approaching them, the man's face rang a bell.

"Dianne," Phoebe said.

They received each other's cheek warmly.

"You're Torrick James's wife, right?"

"We have friends in common?"

"I came to your Super Bowl party last year. Daniel Terry."

"Yes. Right!"

"That's what I like about L.A. You don't coincidentally run into anyone you know."

Dianne agreed with Phoebe, feeling her nerves finally settle. Still, she could definitely go for a drink.

"Are you joining us?"

"I'm meeting someone. A potential client, but he's late. Not a good sign."

Agreeably, Dianne and Phoebe laughed.

Dianne sought for an available table, and from the corner of her eye, she could see Daniel put his hand up to his ear as if to suggest he would give Phoebe a call. Obviously, they had exchanged numbers prior to her arrival.

"I think that couple's leaving. Phoebe, let's grab the table. Hurry!"

"Henna! Come on down. Dinner's ready!" Torrick called out to his daughter.

"Where's Mama anyway?" Daniela asked.

"She's meeting up with an old friend."

"What old friend?"

"You might not remember Phoebe. They were best friends. You know your mother was in a famous singing group. Phoebe was also in Venice."

"She's the one who wrote that mega song, huh? 'Plan B'?"

Torrick placed tossed salad in ceramic salad bowls while Daniela put asparagus on the plates.

"What happened between them? Mama acts weird every time she talks about her. She talks differently about Cordia."

Daniela took after her mother, Henna her father. Both were strikingly pretty with espresso-colored hair and high cheekbones, like Dianne's. Torrick was very proud of his daughters. They had been good children and he never had any real trouble with them. He and Dianne built a good life; they were in no position to whine.

"Hey, Daddy!" Henna said. She stood on her tiptoes to kiss his cheek perfunctorily. "Chicken, again?"

"What did you have a taste for?"

"Pizza!" Daniela chimed in.

"Your mother already prepared dinner before she left. Pizza another time, all right?"

The girls started gossiping about a reality TV program, *Gwenology*. Torrick had finally caved in and let Henna watch it because there were so many reality TV programs on the air he didn't have time to monitor them all. His cell rang and he reached for it. "Torrick James." He listened momentarily. "Additional security for the first lady? Absolutely. I'll arrange it right away. Sure thing. You'll receive my confirmation. Enjoy your evening." He noticed an unread text from Jacqueline. She was inquiring about possible security for a potential client. He decided to deal with it after dinner. He called his head of security for high-profile clients and arranged additional protection for the first lady's visit. He answered on the first ring. They talked less than a minute.

"Okay, girls. Everything's ready." They sat at the kitchen table. Henna reached for Daniela's hand and her father's. "I take it you want to say grace?" She nodded. "Then by all means."

"Girl, you have lived some roller coaster of a life since Venice broke up." Dianne had already drowned two glasses of white wine. She felt mellow, not high.

"And you. This love story of yours…"

Dianne would never consider her life with Torrick a *love story*. "Torrick and I have been so blessed. We really have."

"Now that you can look from your current bird's-eye view and see how blessed your life has been, aren't you happy that your life took the direction that it took?"

"Well…" Dianne had no idea such a question would come at her. She wasn't clever at being dishonest. Oh, she lied like everyone else. But it was never to be deceitful necessarily; more so to protect some part of herself she felt needed to be guarded. And if she needed to protect someone else. When she decided to call Phoebe and meet for drinks, she told herself that she was over their past. "Let's put it this way," she'd continued. "I like my life. I love my children. I really can't complain."

They'd sat and reminisced over the good old days. Phoebe no longer knew Dianne. It had been some years since they were close. Dianne was different yet essentially the same. Phoebe sensed it; she, not for a minute, expected Dianne to confess whatever was going on with her to her, but something felt off. A line had been drawn in the sand some time ago. Even if she came to the Blue Bar armed with love, the forgiveness was still, still too hard to do. Phoebe felt it in every chosen word. She would catch it whenever Dianne's eyes dodged hers. But Phoebe was at peace with it. Some experiences were so radical that they shifted the entire trajectory of a life. Phoebe believed—and not because it in some way absolved her of her actions—she did Dianne a favor.

"None of us should complain."

"You have every right," Dianne said, reaching for her nearly-empty wineglass.

"What do you mean?"

"Between the three of us, you, Phoebe, did it all. And now, you lost your home…That charming Santa Monica bungalow? I liked your Coldwater Canyon home, but it…Who did the landscaping for the bungalow, by the way?"

"I forgot…no, Miguel Sanchez, I think."

"You were an events director for that swanky oceanfront boutique hotel. You managed Rules…I mean the hardest place to get a table in California. Their Mexican prawns are serious. Torrick finessed us a table when we were in San Francisco two years ago. You weren't running it by then. You don't think losing everything isn't unfair?"

"I didn't lose everything."

She finished her wine. "Oh, girl. You are better than me. I'd be pissed!"

"I was *pissed*, as you put it. But it didn't last long."

"Do you believe in karma?"

"To a degree."

"Do you think this—what you're going through right now—is karma?"

Phoebe dared not hesitate. She swallowed thickly, for she knew what Dianne was hinting at. "It could be," she managed to say in a convincing, tempered voice.

"I have to apologize."

Phoebe was turning her wineglass around in circles by its stem while staring into what was left of the burgundy-colored wine. Her eyes met Dianne's. She leaned into the table. "Why?" Phoebe tilted her head to one side.

"I never once asked about Venetia."

"Yes you did."

"Yeah, but it was like saying hello to a familiar face in passing. I didn't ask for details."

"Well, let's just say Cordia would be very proud of Venetia."

"I haven't seen her in years. How does that happen? We live less than a mile from each other. Actually, it was because of Cordia's house and neighborhood I talked Torrick into buying our house when he started his business here. Cordia's views…"

"Venetia has changed nothing. You know, she spends a lot of her time in L.A."

"She never thought of selling the house after her grandmother moved into that nursing home?"

"She sees it as home. She had no connection to the Benedict Canyon house."

"Oh, I loooooved that house."

"Venetia's a life coach."

"Life coach? Girl, I could use a life coach right about now."

Phoebe picked up her wineglass and held it with both hands. "Why?" She finished off the smooth-tasting wine.

"I need a new focus. The girls don't need me like they used to. When I was Daniela's age, I was hardly as independent and resourceful. I envy her sometimes."

There it was. Phoebe caught it a few times since they sat, ordered drinks, shared a plate of calamari, and started, albeit gently, talking in the way two people talked who hadn't seen each other in quite some time. Phoebe couldn't even guess what it was, but something wasn't quite right with Dianne. And that *I'm so blessed* thing was phony.

"I'd like to see your girls. Do they know who I am?"

"Of course they do. You know that portrait done of us?"

Phoebe nodded.

"It takes up an entire wall. Oh, it was so funny. Remember how we all squeezed in Cordia's Corvette and drove to Sunset when we heard it was up? We were still so naïve."

In a quiet voice, Phoebe said, "I remember." She glanced at her watch. "Are you okay to drive?"

With a chuckle, Dianne said, "Now you know me."

"You were always good at holding your liquor."

Dianne pulled out her wallet with a devious grin on her face. "Remember that night in Chicago?"

"Oh, you mean the backgammon and Long Island Iced Tea night?"

"You were smashed!" Dianne giggled. She pulled out her debit card and searched for their waiter.

"What about that time at the Playboy Club? You acted a complete fool."

"Oh, my goodness." Dianne rolled her eyes. "I forgot about that night…

"What about you and Cordia? You two were…Oh, do you remember that night at the Speakeasy? You guys sang really loud to Prince's 'Head.'" Dianne laughed so hard, she snorted. "Every time…" She pressed her hands against her high cheekbones. "Prince sang *head*, you guys bobbed your head to one side and sang with him so loud, *head!* You guys were loud."

"Remember that night at Jackie O's? You were kind of dating that player with…was it the L.A. Rams or the Oakland Raiders? You ordered all those drinks—what, about twenty-five?—and charged them on his Diners card because…"

"Yeah. He was hitting on other women right in my face. Yes! He was such an ass!"

"That was evil." Dianne slid her glass to the side. "We had a lot of fun at Jackie O's. Cordia knew how to have fun, with her leather pants-wearing self."

"She knew how to wear leather pants. Remember me and leg warmers?"

Somber, Phoebe said, "We really lived out loud. It was…Life was good to us."

Dianne reached for Phoebe's hand. She squeezed it with affection. Their eyes met and Dianne, in a solemn voice, said, "We're blessed to share the tale. Cordia…" But her voice trailed off.

"You don't regret those days, Dianne?"

She fingered for the waiter. "No. Absolutely not. Frankly—let's say I had the time of my life."

The waiter arrived at their table. "Check?"

Dianne said, "Please."

The house was deathly silent. Even though half the time his son got on his nerves, when Cornell wasn't home, Joseph was overcome with loneliness. On some level, he failed to acknowledge that his son's presence added substance to his days. Stillness didn't greet him at the front door since his son had come back home. His companionship made Joseph feel less alone in the world. Cornell gave his life a bit of definition; he took up space that would otherwise be a void. Joseph reached for the mouse and clicked his favorites. It was about a year ago he started visiting these sites. Boredom, loneliness, disappointment. Porn had never been his thing. Oh, when he was young he had a subscription to *Playboy*, and when he was at university, he'd find the occasional abandoned *Penthouse* lying around and he'd take it back to his dorm and look through it several times. On two occasions he'd gone to a topless bar; even had a lap dance once. When he married, though, Joseph gradually stopped indulging in such things; although from time to time he gave them a cursory looking over. Guys he hung around, went to football games with, and coworkers—he appeased them; more so to be a part of the group. But he was devoted to his wife. There had been jabs by friends that it was all harmless fun. It wasn't as though he was having an affair or cheating on his wife. True, he agreed. But he thought it safe to refrain.

His tax attorney friend who jogged the entire path along the lake each morning thought having an occasional indiscretion made his life more gratifying. Eventually this led to affairs and the demise of an eighteen-year marriage. Joseph was faithful to his wife for twenty-three years, up to the day she took her last breath. Did he look at other women? No doubt. It was human nature to be attracted to other women. Was lust in his heart? Roughly six, seven years into their marriage, Joseph did find himself wandering away from his wife. But he never, ever so much as came on to another woman. If he was friendly with a woman because she was very attractive, it didn't mean he was trying to pick her up. If anything, it was no more than harmless flirtation. To be frank, he wouldn't have known how to cheat on his wife.

Joseph did nothing more than look at photographs. Even while staring at the sensual bodies and imagining having sex with them, a sense of shame always caused him discomfort. For quite some time, he was so lost in the images he hadn't heard Cornell come home.

"Dad!" he spoke up, standing in the doorway. He held a bowl and spoon in his hands.

Joseph, self-conscious, clicked the mouse to minimize the image he had been staring at. "Hey, I didn't hear you come home."

"Thank the Lord!" Cornell said, sardonic.

"What's the point of the sarcasm, Cornell?"

"I tiptoed. If I *walk* the staircase, you claim I'm stomping."

"What's that you're eating?" Joseph was trying to keep his son distracted.

"Cereal."

"I made a large pot of stew."

"You did?" Cornell leaned in the doorframe and continued to eat his cereal.

"I made more than enough."

"I'll have some. After my cereal."

It was best he keep his mouth shut. That way Cornell would eventually leave and go and do whatever he did in his room.

"Oh, by the way. Christine said Thanksgiving doesn't look good, but she can probably come home for Christmas."

"Now that's good news. When'd you talk to her?"

"Earlier. She met someone."

"Christine's always meeting someone new. She gets bored too

easily. Maybe when she comes home, she can talk you into going back to school…" The moment the words dripped from Joseph's tongue, he knew he'd made a mistake. "But you'll do the right thing," he continued, to keep a debate at bay. He turned to the computer screen and closed out the Internet.

"What are you doing online? It's midnight. You're usually in bed by ten."

He stood. "That's a bit of an exaggeration, don't you think?"

"Whatever," Cornell said, leaving the doorway.

Joseph took in a deep breath, feeling relieved. Rubbing his hands across his half-balding head, he tried to ease his anxiety. The very idea his son would find out he looked at naked women online bothered Joseph. *That was close.*

When Dianne pulled into the circular drive, only one light was on in the entire house. Once inside, she placed her keys next to Torrick's in a tray on the table. Standing in the dim foyer, Dianne wondered how much had she changed over the years. It was apparent that Phoebe had changed; so much so, she was narrowly recognizable. She'd traveled extensively, which gave her exposure, and Phoebe had conspicuously evolved as a person. Dianne got pregnant and had, albeit small, a fairytale wedding. Before she could blink she was so deep into domestic life, she'd lost parts of herself she could vaguely bring to mind. The idea that she'd become no more than a high-end clothes-wearing mom disturbed Dianne. The mothers of her daughters' friends wore sneakers and baseball caps, and they were only vaguely interested in the latest fashions. Dianne never got caught up in play-dates, and she was by no means the "soccer mom" type. *Am I shallow?*

She slipped off her shoes and tiptoed up the stairs. When she entered their bedroom, Torrick's laptop was in his lap and the television was on but the sound was off. Last year his optometrist had prescribed reading glasses. Unlike Dianne, he had no problem in getting a pair. Dianne said she would get reading glasses when she could no longer read a menu. It so happened she had trouble reading the wine list at the Blue Bar.

"How was it? It looks as if you had a few."

Dianne flopped on the edge of the bed, dropping her wedges to the floor. "A few."

"And Phoebe?"

"As much as I hate to admit it, she's good. Under the circumstances. She wrote our biggest hits. 'Plan B'—that's how she purchased her Coldwater Canyon house. How does that happen—losing everything? I don't get it." The thought was fleeting, but Dianne recalled Phoebe caring little about money.

Torrick went back to reading while Dianne rested her elbows to her knees, feeling as though she drank one glass of wine too much. *It was only wine*, she thought. "Torrick?"

Mindlessly, he said, "Yeah."

With her back to him, she said, "I need to talk to you about something."

CHAPTER 4

The stones leading to the guesthouse were so slick Venetia nearly fell twice. What was she thinking, wearing flip-flops for goodness' sake! She slowed her pace and took painstaking steps on the large black stones, poising herself.

She knocked hard.

Phoebe opened the door. "What's wrong?"

"What do you mean?"'

"You were banging on the door."

"I was? Oh, I was excited, I guess."

The room felt cozy when Venetia stepped inside. Candles burned, adding a soothing ambiance to the room. The damp, chilled air came so suddenly. Two days ago, it was in the low eighties. Venetia loved this time of year, though—the hint of fall.

"So what's the excitement about?"

Venetia sat in one of the apricot-colored chairs that made the small, enchanting room look half its size. "I have something to show you. It's so awesome!"

Comfortably dressed in a pair of Lycra pants and cropped sweater, Phoebe stood at the back of the chair. "What is it?"

"Barry."

"You've finally talked to him?"

"Not yet." Venetia used her middle finger against the touch-screen to bring up a photograph.

"He's in Benghazi. Whatever doubts you have, you love him."

"I texted him with love. And before you get on me about how texting is detached and whatever, it *is* how we stay connected while he's over there." She looked over her shoulder. "Look!"

Phoebe leaned into Venetia. A stunning digitalized photograph of a little girl gazing blankly at something out of frame made her catch her breath. The girl was dark in skin tone with coal-colored hair, and tears swam inside of intense dark brown eyes. Splotches of blood were on her clothes, and face. Visible chaos encircled the child.

"It's Barry's. It made the cover of the *Times* print and online versions. It's so beautiful!"

"It's not beautiful, it's tragic."

"The circumstances, yes. But Barry's job as a photojournalist is to showcase that tragedy through his work. Remember when *Look* depicted blacks—Negroes—hanged from trees in the South? Without those photographs, the world would have been oblivious. Pictures illustrate when words fall flat."

Phoebe sat in the sofa and crossed her legs. She studied Venetia staring at the photograph, a sense of pride in her eyes. Her boyfriend—whom Phoebe believed was questionably straight if she relied on her gaydar—was doing something bigger than many. It was brave to go into places in the Middle East and be an eyewitness to the infinite bloodshed. Phoebe bent forward. "Dianne and I met for drinks a few days ago."

Venetia looked up straight away. "Really? So you two actually sat, had drinks *and* talked?"

"We did."

"So…"

"We were civil. She has everything—a good life, really. Not a life I would ever have chosen…but I can feel it; she's still resentful."

"I won't ask about this resentment thing. I don't get the whole secrecy of it all…Where does Dianne live? I'm not sure I've even been to her house before."

"She says she doesn't live far from you. Something about Cascadia."

"Nice!"

"Hey, you never have to worry."

Like her mother, Venetia exuded grace. She was reserved yet accessible. She learned how not to be treated special because her mother was Cordia Street. And despite how well Venetia lived all of her life, she was amazingly down-to-earth. Pressing her back into the chair, she said, "I work at it…making every effort not to take my life for granted. A day doesn't go by—and no matter what's going on with me—when I don't recognize that I am fortunate."

Stillness touched the air briefly.

"Maybe we can have a little get-together and invite Dianne."

"Oh, that's an idea. Hey! I have a client who's a novelist. I'll let you borrow my Kindle so you can read his book. But I've been playing with the idea of giving him a promo party. Like, have people come over. He could read a passage from the book and people can purchase a copy. Social media isn't the only word-of-mouth."

"Like a book brunch?"

"I like that idea. Yeah, that could work. I'll run it by him tomorrow. That way I can see Mother's lost best friend from the good old days. We're brilliant, aren't we?"

In good spirits, Phoebe laughed. "Devious is more like it." She came to her feet. "I have some leftovers. Have you eaten?"

"What kind of leftovers?"

Phoebe disappeared into the small kitchen. "Spaghetti!"

"Do you have bread?"

"I don't." She walked back into the living space.

"I bought a baguette this morning when I stopped at the bakery.

It's rustic—really French. And with olive oil? Bellissima! I can run and get it."

Venetia was at the door when Phoebe called out, "By the way, what happened with that girl—*Gwenology?*"

Venetia chuckled. "Let me just say she won't be a client." She reached for the doorknob but paused. "Phoebe!"

She popped her head out from behind the kitchen. "Yeah?"

"Would you be interested in meeting someone?"

"Maybe."

"I have someone in mind."

The Blue Bar was semi-busy. A handful of people took up several tables that were pushed together, laughing loud, talking even louder. A group of colleagues, thought Jacqueline, rolling her eyes. Why did Torrick suggest the Blue Bar anyway? She knew people who dropped in regularly; she wasn't in the mood to talk business. She would have preferred to talk with Torrick in his office which was adjacent to the Bell Street pier. But he had a meeting in the area and didn't think he could make it back downtown in time, so he'd requested that they meet at Blue.

Reluctantly, she'd agreed. Since she was going to be in the area, she'd tried for a last-minute hair appointment to rinse away subtle gray strands. *You can't get around aging.* Her salon was a few blocks from the Blue Bar—Jacqueline got lucky because of a cancellation.

"A penny for your thoughts," Torrick said, approaching the table.

He can be so corny at times. She feigned a smile. Jacqueline tugged at her skirt, trying to conceal her overexposed thigh. "I have to confess, I'm beginning to feel like my values are becoming superficial. I recognize the intense fluidity of our times…Still, just trying to keep pace…"

He sat across from her at the lacquered black table. "I know what you mean. It's as if you're pushed into something that on some unconscious level, you don't even agree with.

"The first lady was here yesterday…"

"I tried to make it to the hotel to catch her. A group of us from church bought a table. A lot is happening and…" She took a breath.

"We added extra security at the hotel."

"Your name has been circling around town. If little black books were still a priceless possession, I'd have to steal yours."

The waiter approached their table. Torrick said, "A beer. Imported." He looked over to Jacqueline.

"A glass of champagne, local, please."

The waiter nodded professionally.

"What's this? Champagne? I thought we were here to talk business. Did I miss something?"

"Life's a celebration. I don't need a particular reason to celebrate."

"I always did like your frame of reference. By the way, growing up, did you go by Jackie?"

"I'm a Jacqueline."

His wife's one and only single friend was never, ever dull. Torrick had several female friends, but not one held his attention in the same way Jacqueline did. With each of his female friends, his mind sometimes wandered beyond what was generally comfortable, but he always managed to pull it back. He'd turn his wedding band around and around as a cue; a habit he'd developed over the course of his marriage. Torrick loved his wife. Moreover, he loved their life together. He'd never set out to destroy what they built. Still, whenever he was in Jacqueline's presence, his imagination traveled outside of his comfort zone. She was smart, sexy, beautiful. A delicate mixture of self-confidence, intelligence, *and* easy on the eyes were dangerous traits in a woman.

The waiter brought their drinks and departed with limited words.

Jacqueline pursed her lips. "I believe we'll be needing your services."

Torrick placed his finger under his chin, engaged.

"There's a possibility that we might—*might*—take Anthony Perez on as a client."

"The Hispanic guy who shot that police officer last week?"

Jacqueline almost hesitated, but she dared not come across ambiguous. "Yes."

"I understand that your job is to maintain, maybe even to control, the public image of your clients. But this? Why, Jacqueline? He's a mule for a high-profile drug cartel, or so it's been reported."

"Hear me out."

Courteously, Torrick nodded.

"Okay, yes, this is very risky. Nine-eleven changed everything. Cameras, good grief, they're everywhere. You'd think there would be no crime these days because everyone is being videotaped. If not by the government, by each other. The shooting is clear on the surveillance video and Perez admits to shooting the officer. And bystanders—so you know the phone cameras came out. Most of the incident is caught on tape."

"Why are you even involved in this?"

"Torrick…" She placed her hands flat on the table so as to cease the intensity that suddenly swirled around them like smoke from a burning cigarette. She checked her tone and body language. "Look, I do not condone any person shooting a woman or man in uniform who puts their life on the line to protect me and you and anyone else. However, all the facts aren't out just yet; and there's such a thing as a false narrative. We—Media Capital—might assist his legal team…"

"Richard West, your ex, is his lawyer."

"That's right. There are two sides to every story. Perez pled not guilty at his bail hearing."

"West knew they wouldn't give a cop killer bail."

Jacqueline pressed her eyes shut and counted to three. "It's his job to request bail."

"Due diligence, I get it." Torrick reached for his beer.

"This reminds me of a judge I assisted once. We sat on the same board. But working with him was a bad idea."

"How so?"

"He personalized it. Richard and I have history. But he's asked us to help prepare Perez for his first two court appearances. We have a department that works strictly on reputation enhancement."

"I believe I read that the gun used in this shooting was also used in an unsolved crime in California."

"I'm limited on knowledge and that's because I don't need—want to know."

Torrick took a gulp of his beer.

"Richard has requested that his client be able to wear a bullet-proof vest. What I'm asking is that you put security in place to ensure that he gets to and from the courthouse."

"We can be no more than a shadow."

"I prefer there be someone who can protect him to and from the courthouse who doesn't have a dog in the fight. The shooting has the department all riled up. They're looking for an excuse…"

Torrick looked straight into Jacqueline's warm, brown eyes. He didn't know this side of her. Jacqueline was classy. She managed to get as far as she had based primarily on her talent. Dianne once told him Jacqueline despised women who used their looks or sexuality to make it. Everyone *used* physical attributes, so Torrick thought that was nonsense. While he had no idea of the backstory, it did pique his curiosity as to why she was willing to put her reputation on the line by taking on a client who shot—according to the videotape and a number of eyewitnesses—an on-duty police officer in cold blood.

"I can put someone on it. Would you prefer a Latino?"

"I trust your judgment."

She reached for her flute and took a sip. Torrick didn't want to look too long, but even his glance didn't deceive him: Jacqueline's hand was unsteady.

"Listen…" He wanted to put her at ease. "I know you well enough to know that you wouldn't take this on without giving it deep consideration. Besides, our judicial system says that we're innocent unless proven otherwise."

She offered Torrick a nervous smile.

"Jacqueline?"

Jacqueline finished off her champagne. "Yes?"

"If you need to talk…"

Minutes later, when she slid into the interior of her car, Jacqueline pulled out her cell. There were three text messages from Gwen, a voicemail message from a client and her nephew, and several messages from the office. Thank goodness Claire would be starting as her assistant tomorrow. She pressed a name in her contacts. When a voice came on the line, she asked, "What's Stefan's status?"

Dianne hadn't felt this nervous since she learned of her first pregnancy. That news took a minute to sink in. A beeping sound came from her cell. She reached for it in the side pocket of her purse. It was Vanessa, inquiring whether she had spoken to the trainer. The first text from the personal trainer knocked her off her feet and Dianne couldn't deal with it. But the second text? She didn't know how to process it. Too much was coming at her all at once. At the last minute, she'd cancelled her appearance at a board meeting so as to make the consultation. Now, while waiting in a small reception area of an office that played what used to be called elevator music, Dianne wasn't sure this was a good idea. And she never cancelled meetings. Torrick mentioned that morning there was a strong possibility her mother-in-law would be flying in to spend Christmas with them. Although Dianne got along with her quite well, she was a strong, opinionated and successful woman who had a clever way of making Dianne feel like a failure because she didn't have a career. "Being a buyer was ages ago, and Venice," her mother-in-law once told her, "wasn't a *career.*" Dianne had to suppress her thoughts: *Then what would you call it?* With so much pressure in her life right now, the personal trainer wasn't something she could handle. She responded to her sister's text with a quick, *Not yet—will 411 you.*

"Dianne?"

She looked up to a woman standing in a doorway. She was petite, with dark exotic looks that enhanced her aging beauty. She was Indian; Dianne realized it by her name, Shaheen. With a generous smile, she opened her door wider as if to invite Dianne inside.

"Sorry to keep you waiting," she said. Her voice was raspy, like that of a longtime smoker.

Dianne stood and walked toward the woman. "I was early."

"Join me."

The small, attractive office smelled of lavender. There were striking works of art on two walls, and enough books to fill a very small library. Dianne noted the woman's framed degrees—Cambridge, Princeton, and Yale—on a wall. A tall vase of fresh sunflowers sat on a desk by a laptop.

"Let's have a seat."

The woman sat across from Dianne and crossed her legs.

"I like the smell. What is it?"

"Scented oil."

"Lavender?"

"It really does minimize tension."

She laughed to be polite. "Does it really?"

"It's true."

Dianne took a deep breath and attempted to relax. She sensed the woman could feel her anxiety. She reached inside the pocket of her purse. "I should turn off my phone."

Once they were each comfortable in their seats, Shaheen said, "How are you, Dianne?"

"Good, thank you."

Her Mona Lisa smile suggested she didn't buy that line. But the therapist didn't verbalize her thoughts.

"Well…" Dianne spread her hands. "I mean…"

"This is only a consultation. Think of me as a trusted friend. And tell me—and let's start with one thing—what brought you to my office."

"Wow! Only one, huh?"

"Well, there can be two or three. But let's start with something simple. We won't change the world in one visit anyway."

Dianne liked Shaheen. She was genuinely kind and naturally attentive. Dianne sensed she could indeed trust her. Going to see a therapist was insane, but Vanessa told her baby sister it was a good idea. When she came home from having drinks with Phoebe, Dianne told Torrick she was having trouble concentrating, and she was going through *something* but didn't know what. He's the one that recommended Dianne see someone.

"Recently I ran into a person from my past."

"Male or female?"

"Female. We were singers. I'm not sure you heard of us, but

we were called Venice. It was four years—our friendship and the group—but it feels longer than my sixteen-year marriage."

"And this friend…"

"I was about to turn twenty-one when we met. I was taking fashion design courses in Hollywood. Are you familiar with the energy crisis back in the late seventies?"

"Yes, I recall it."

"In Los Angeles, we had these odd and even days, and it was based on your license plate. The day I met Phoebe she was in front of me in a line that was about four blocks long. When I got closer to the entrance of the gas station, I happened to notice that her plate number was odd but gas day was even numbers. I walked up to her convertible—it was an MGBGT," Dianne recalled with amusement. "I told her she was on the wrong day and that she had to get out of line.

"She jumped out of her car with her hands on her hips and told me to go to hell. That she had to be at work at the Fotomat in Santa Monica, a good fifteen miles from where we were, and we were at a gas station on Melrose and La Brea. Whatever happened to Fotomat? Digital, I guess. Anyway, she was fiesta and…*bold*. Strong-minded. She intimidated me, and I backed off. But then another girl—who eventually became my friend as well, and she was also a part of Venice—she jumped out of her car to stop these two black chicks yelling and screaming about who should and shouldn't be in the line getting gas. A friendship began that day. I'm not even sure how. But the three of us became very good friends. People used to tell us we were each other's shadow.

"Phoebe was different than anyone I'd known."

The therapist detected frustration and mild depression in Dianne's voice. "How so?"

"She wasn't trying to, but she stood out. There was something about her. Mystery, and defiance. She moved to L.A. without knowing a soul. I could never do that. She had this self-assuredness I lacked. Her ideals were grand in comparison to mine. She wanted to travel the world, learn different cultures and languages. I think I was drawn to her because of envy." Dianne could feel her eyes start to collect tears. She bit them back as best she could. She swallowed thickly and wet her lips, pressing them together to keep the swell of emotions at bay. "I really do believe," she said, talking through the pain in her throat, "Phoebe ruined my life."

The bank was crowded. Joseph rarely had to wait. All he wanted to do was make a deposit; and he had other errands to get to before the day was done. Nonchalant, he looked around and happened to catch his image on a screen. There he was, along with other customers, being videotaped. Well, if that wasn't too much! Nowadays people were so darn curious about each other. Back when Clinton was president, the word "voyeurism" became a hot topic, and highly debated. Every talk show on the air was having discussions about it. Not very long ago people wanted to maintain control over their lives, and they guarded their privacy. But with all the oversharing, twentieth-century voyeurism was old-fashioned. Furthermore, by merely typing a name in a search engine and getting details about that person's life, exposed was the new discreet.

"Good morning! Can I help you?" a teller said behind bulletproof glass.

Joseph was still looking around at the people in the bank. When he was younger, and before he had mouths to feed, male bank tellers wore suits and ties. The women wore pantyhose.

"Good morning! Can I help you?" the teller called out again.

A man standing behind Joseph said, "Sir, teller's waitin'."

Joseph casually looked at the young man behind him. Well, he wasn't necessarily young, but he did call Joseph *sir*—a sign of respect.

"Thank you," Joseph said. He stepped up to the smiling teller.

"Good morning. How can I help you today?"

Joseph produced his banking. "I'd like to make a deposit."

"Great!" said the teller. She began processing his deposit, her small lips drawn upward. "You know, you can have this direct-deposited, right?"

"What do you mean?"

"Save yourself some time. Not having to come into the bank every month. We also offer paying your bills online. Would you be interested?"

Joseph had been coming to this bank for years. No one ever tried to push all these new banking extras down his throat. He didn't trust his money going through the Internet. He posted his bills like clockwork every month. He bought stamps and *mailed* everything. No, no, he wanted nothing to do with his money hanging around somewhere in Cyberspace.

"It's at no extra cost."

"Oh, it's not about cost. But thank you, though."

"Here's your receipt. And have a great day, Mr. Morgan."

"Thank you kindly. You, too!"

Headed out the door, he bumped into a woman wearing sunglasses and not watching where she was going. *Young people. Always in such a hurry.*

"Oh, excuse…Mr. Morgan? Hi!"

Joseph took a closer look at the woman in such a rush. "Venetia?"

"It's good to see you."

"Well, how are you doing, young lady? I've come around the house a few times. Don't tell me your Hollywood clients have wooed you away from us."

"You can imagine. L.A. clients are a little more demanding," she joked. "I've been meaning to catch up with Cornell. How's he doing?"

"He dropped out, Venetia."

"Dropped out of…what, school?"

Joseph's shoulders slouched in disappointment.

"The Cornell I know would finish. What about Christine?"

"She's going to get some time off for Christmas. Can't wait. I really miss my baby girl."

"I'd love to see her when she comes. Please tell her to drop by the house."

"So, what about yourself? Any closer to getting married?"

"Married?" Venetia's head bobbed back. "I don't think I'm ready for marriage. You remember Barry?"

"He's the handsome young man who's a journalist?"

"He's a *photo*journalist."

Joseph didn't distinguish between the two.

"Actually, I'm glad I ran into you."

"Why's that?"

"My godmother is staying in the guesthouse for a little while. She just moved here from L.A. I thought you might like to meet her."

"Are you playing matchmaker, young lady?"

Venetia was quietly amused. "I thought it would be nice for her to meet someone. She's…you'd like her, Mr. Morgan."

Joseph grew curious. "Really?"

"Really."

"Well, I'd be a fool not to meet this mysterious woman." *Especially if I didn't have to approach her and make a fool of myself. Better yet, get rejected.*

"I'm in the early stages of planning a brunch for a client. He's a novelist. Can I send you an invite?"

"Well, sure."

"Sounds good."

They discussed the changing weather and the upcoming election. Polite, small talk. Eventually, Venetia had to check the time, although she tried hard not to. Over the years she'd sensed Joseph was lonely. She couldn't recall his ever not being around when she was a child. Although a bit too old-school for her blood, he was a kind man. When she'd finished at the University of Southern California and moved back home, she began to know him better. He'd drop by to make sure she and her grandmother didn't need anything. Men like Joseph Morgan were few and far between.

While walking toward his car, Joseph felt the ache in his joints yet he didn't let it impose on him on this occasion. His heartbeat felt different. Had it anything to do with having something to look forward to?

CHAPTER 5

It was impossible for Dianne to avoid the personal trainer any longer. She felt as if she was being text-harassed at this point. Silence, and ignoring him, wasn't going to do the trick. She made a conscious decision not to go to the gym in case their paths crossed. After all, they'd bumped into each at that very gym a few times before they'd ended up at a Jamba Juice having smoothies while they debated whether President Obama should be reelected. They begged to differ, holding steadfast to their opinions. They laughed with animation and flirted harmlessly. The attraction was reciprocal. Before Dianne knew it, they'd ended up at the trainer's apartment a stone's throw from the gym. One Mike's Hard Lemonade, which hardly gave them a buzz, led to having unprotected sex. It just happened.

Afterward, Dianne felt she was nothing more than a middle-aged booty call. Even back in the day when she'd slept with someone once or twice and never saw him again, they managed to have conversation afterward, and she *showered*. Once she'd had her second visit with her internist a few days ago, she felt comfortable in leaning into her husband's arms when they were in bed. Dianne felt safe making love to Torrick. But the personal trainer was wreaking havoc in her increasingly not-in-control life.

"Mama, can I have a ten?"

Daniela's voice took Dianne aback. She thought her daughter was already on her way to school.

Daniela giggled gleefully. "Did I scare you?" She looked down when she heard an alert coming from her cell.

"You think you're funny, don't you? No, you didn't scare me. I thought I was alone, that's all. Are you running late?" Dianne took a quick peek at the clock on the microwave.

"Kyndra's mom is taking us to school. Mama, do you ever keep up? Check my tweets."

"Daniela! Don't divulge every detail online. Text me that kind of information."

"Boring!"

"There's a ten in my coat pocket, I think. If not, check my wallet."

Daniela kissed her mother's cheek with familiarity and love in equal measure.

"Love you," Dianne called out.

"Love you too, Mama!"

Dianne resumed writing out her to-the-point text to the trainer. She was momentarily distracted by her daughter's fading voice. "Oh, and Aunt Vanessa called last night. She said to call her!"

Dianne called out, "Thank you!" She typed out a quick text to her sister. While she was putting the dishes in the dishwater, the trainer fired back a text and said they needed to "meet up." She agreed to meet him in the Safeway parking close to his apartment.

Her day went smoothly. She had a few more errands to run. She wasn't in the mood to cook and decided she'd grab an already-prepared something or other at Safeway since her dreaded rendez-vous with the trainer was in the market's parking lot. Dianne wasn't particularly sure she could trust herself. She didn't know why they were meeting up, and she wasn't altogether sure what, or how, she would feel. She decided it was best to arrange for an appointment with the therapist in case she needed someone to talk to. Even though Vanessa was someone she could trust her darkest secrets to, her advice often didn't align with Dianne's needs or her heart. Torrick recommending that she talk to someone was a brilliant idea. Dianne let out enough pent-up sorrow—or perhaps self-pity—at the consultation to finally feel a fragment of relief. Of course she might have to spend thousands of dollars and months of office visits to get at the root of her deepest issues. Dianne wasn't planning on investing that kind of time or money. She'd hit a rough patch and she needed to get beyond it. That's all.

She pulled into the market parking lot. The tender sun started to shrink from the cool pre-autumn day. Dianne hadn't felt jumpy until she was a block from the market. Her hands started trembling; she gripped the steering wheel tighter. She still had no idea why the personal trainer even asked to see her. Was it because he wanted to see her again? Or was he going to come clean about the chlamydia? Dianne pulled into a space where no other cars were parked in the spacious lot.

She turned off her engine and unbuckled her seat belt. Her heartbeat was rushed—she took a slow, deep breath. Dianne nearly jumped out of her skin when she heard three taps against her window. She looked up to find the personal trainer wearing a Bomber jacket and holding a helmet. He looked fine, too, which played a large part in her decision to even sleep with him in the first place. Nothing about his look suggested he wanted to rip off her thong like he did a month ago.

She opened the door and crawled out of the car. Feeling awkward, she hid her hands in the back pockets of her low-rise jeans. "Hey," she greeted him.

"I don't have time for hey! Look..." The trainer circled her. "You left something behind."

"What are you talking about?" Dianne hadn't expected him to be so cold, so distant. From a fifty-four-year-old perspective, she saw a one-nighter differently than someone the personal trainer's age. After sharing such an intimate act, could someone be so cold-hearted? So like *this?*—the way the trainer was treating her in a bloody parking lot of Safeway!

"Time is money; I don't want to waste it on you."

When those words landed on her, Dianne understood fully how unbearably irresponsible she had been sleeping with the personal trainer. He was a total stranger. Of course, she was married and other people could be affected by her selfish choice. Still, that hadn't really mattered at the time. Standing before him in an ill-lit area of the parking lot, Dianne could feel herself wanting to break down and weep. He was a completely different man from the one she actually *liked*, despite his having given her an STD. Her erect nipple in his warm mouth flashed through her mind. Dianne now felt used. Choosing to be with him had the potential to ruin her marriage. But wasn't it the risk that made it feel all the more exciting? Sure, she had learned a few things over five decades. And realistically Dianne understood sleeping with a man she hardly knew wasn't going to win his respect. Nonetheless, his attitude blew her away.

"What do you want?"

"You know why I've been texting you; it's why you've been ignoring me."

"You need to say what it is you wanted to meet me for. I have an appointment."

He closed in on Dianne and she could smell the cigarette smoke on him, mixed with a long day of sour breath. He looked down into her eyes and said straight into them without as much as a mere blink, "I got VD on account of sleeping with you. You gave me the impression this was your first time cheating on your dawg."

"*Dawg?*" She frowned. "It is the first...*was*."

"Then he's cheating on you. My lady is all over me because she wants to know how I gave it to her."

"What are you talking about?"

"You gave me chlamydia. You know what I'm talking about."

"No, *you* gave me chlamydia. How dare you!"

"How dare me?" He pointed his finger in her face. "If I really wanted to break you down, I'd put what you did to me on every social media site. I'd warn every man not to come within ten feet of *the* Dianne in that damn throwback group, Venice. You messed me up!"

"I didn't give you chlamydia!"

"Oh, so I'm lying. Huh? I'm lying?"

The personal trainer was, in a word, pissed. So much so Dianne was nervous. She was torn on what exactly to do. She knew that she hadn't given him an STD, unless—was he right? Did Torrick give her this disease? Was it Torrick and not the trainer who infected her? Had Torrick had symptoms and rushed off to his physician and gotten a prescription, as she had done? Could that be the reason he hadn't coaxed her into having sex in—it had to be nearly two months. Dianne had reached out to her husband, but his attention was elsewhere. He never once, up until a few nights ago, even attempted to have so much as a quickie. Was it a coincidence? No, Torrick wasn't cheating on her. In all honesty he could cheat, but he wasn't the type who'd cheat and not protect himself. Dianne had been careless, to be sure; Torrick, on the other hand, was far more disciplined and less spontaneous than her.

"You bitch!" he hissed. "If I was a violent man, I'd beat you *up!* To hell with your sorry ass." The personal trainer walked off and threw, "Old slut!" over his shoulder.

Reflexively, Dianne's hand covered her mouth. She stood stock-still in the parking lot. Confused, disoriented, humiliated. She watched the personal trainer leap onto his motorcycle. He powered it up and drove off, leaving tire marks behind.

Ohmagod!

It started to rain when Dianne pulled out of the now busy parking lot. She'd forgotten to go in and grab something for dinner. She must have sat in the parking lot for over thirty minutes while shame overcame her. It took a while for her to realize her cell was beeping. It wasn't until she pulled into the garage that it even occurred to her that she'd forgotten to go to her therapy appointment. For quite some time, she sat in the car. Her mind was all over the place. She had no idea how to process what she'd gone through with the personal trainer in Safeway's parking lot. It wasn't until she heard Henna, standing in the doorway of the garage, call out, "Mama?" did Dianne come out of a hazy stupor.

"Are you new?"

Phoebe turned to find a tall man, his hair a subtle salt and pepper, holding a Media Capital coffee mug. "Excuse me?"

The man reached for a packet of alternative sugar and poured it into his cup. He repeated his question: "Are you new?"

"No… Someone walked out or quit, I'm not sure which. I'm temping while they search for the perfect fit."

Amused, he held her eyes while stirring his beverage. "I see."

His lingering stare made Phoebe feel self-conscious. "Can I get you something?"

"No." He tossed the stirrer in the trash. He turned to walk out.

No sooner than she went back to arranging fruit in the enormous fruit bowl, the man returned.

"I'm Michael."

"Phoebe."

"Listen," Michael said, leaning against a counter. "What are…?"

"Good morning, Michael!" Chef's PA broke in. She held her electronic tablet in one hand and something about her look, her body language, suggested to Phoebe that she had a thing for the Media Capital co-founder.

"Good morning."

"Sorry to interrupt. Phoebe, I need you for a minute."

Michael nodded and wordlessly left the kitchen.

The PA gave Phoebe instructions to refill all the small fridges in various conference rooms and offices with bottled water and soda, and to restock both Stefan's and Michael's personal fridges with wine, which she could find in Chef's private storage. Just the day before, the PA had given Phoebe a key to the storage, which made her feel as though she was doing a good job. Unlike the first week of the assignment, Phoebe was at ease and didn't feel the need to walk on eggshells.

When Phoebe stopped to congratulate her on her new position, Claire was settling into the modish cubicle, feet from Jacqueline's office. Claire stood and said, "Oh, let me help you." She reached for a twelve-pack of bottled water.

They walked toward Jacqueline's office. "So how does it feel to work for *the* Jacqueline Daye?" Phoebe asked.

"Actually, it's only been a few days, but I like it. I have a lot to learn and I'm excited."

"You'll do fine."

They stocked Jacqueline's mini fridge with mineral and coconut water, and kale-apple-ginger drinks.

"By the way, Jacqueline also wants lemons."

Phoebe crossed her arms. "Lemons?"

"She puts lemon slices in her water."

They exchanged accommodating facial expressions.

"Ooookay!" said Phoebe. "Lemons it is." They walked out of the office together. "I'll drop some off. How many?"

Claire sat at her desk. She reached for a ringing phone and handled it in her naturally professional manner. "Okay, I don't know. Let's guess."

"Guess?"

Claire laughed. Over the past few weeks, since Phoebe had started temping as hospitality assistant, they'd quickly become chat buddies. "Okay," Claire said, putting her hands on her hips. "Let's say, how about three. You refurbish every how many days?"

"Actually, I've refilled Jacqueline's fridge twice this week."

"Oh, so let's go with three."

"Sounds good."

"See you later, Phoebe."

"*Ciao!*"

When she arrived at Michael's office, Phoebe reluctantly entered. He was on a phone call, but Michael invited her in with a waving hand.

Based on the list Chef's PA had given her, she restocked his fridge. She was leaving when Michael called out, "Phoebe!"

She stopped in her tracks. With both hands on the cart, she looked over her shoulder with a *what?* look.

"Come back in…for a minute, please."

Phoebe reentered the office, her arms crossed.

"I'll come right to the point. Would you have a drink with me? Away from the office."

Phoebe wasn't exactly sure how to respond.

"Have I made you uncomfortable?"

"This is…awkward."

"I see." Michael walked around his desk that indicated his work demanded a lot of his time. Leaning on the front end of it, he said, "It's just drinks."

So as to get back to her work she agreed with, "Where?"

"How about the Mason House bar. It's a few blocks from here. Say six-thirty?"

No sooner than Phoebe left Michael's office, she met up with Jacqueline walking toward her talking on her cell. "Hello, Phyllis," Jacqueline said, when they passed each other.

Phoebe's first instinct was to correct Jacqueline. She thought better of it and continued walking in the opposite direction.

"Get me Venetia Street, Claire," Jacqueline said, without even pausing at her new assistant's cubicle.

"Sure right." Claire had no inkling who this Venetia Street person was or even where she could get her number. No way could she afford to ask. Jacqueline would scream something about being incompetent! After training the new concierge for a week, finally, finally Claire acquired Dream Job No. 1. Without Dream Job No.1, she couldn't poise herself for Dream Job No. 2—Strategy. It was a well-guarded department to get in at Media Capital; and the likelihood of obtaining an interview—Claire had to be recommended by someone.

She reached for the laptop, pulling it closer. Claire clicked open Jacqueline's contacts. She had two different contact folders, public and private. No one had access to the private one, save for Stefan and Michael, the owners of Media Capital. She tapped the keys hurriedly, trying to find the name Venetia Street. None. *Merde.* Okay, go to the mattress she told herself. *Go to the mattress.* She searched Venetia Street online, but her website led her nowhere. White Pages offered a public listing. *Hello!*

She dialed quickly, before Jacqueline shouted, *"Where's Venetia Street?"* She'd already had that experience the day before and Claire didn't want—and couldn't afford—to hear it again.

"Hi, you've reached Venetia Street. I'm unavailable at the moment. Please leave a message…"

Merde!

"If this is a matter of importance, please call my cell…"

There is a God! Claire reached for a pen and wrote the number on her palm since there was no pad within immediate reach. She dialed her cell.

"Venetia Street," she answered.

"Hello, hi, this is Claire with Media Capital. Jacqueline Daye's calling."

"Oh, sure. Thank you, Claire."

"Hold the line, please."

Claire pressed Jacqueline's intercom and announced Venetia.

"Venetia, hello…Jacqueline Daye."

"Hello, Jacqueline. How are you?"

"Fabulous! Can we do coffee?"

"I'm in L.A. until the end of the week."

"Perfect, because I have to be in L.A. for a meeting with a client. Could we calendar each other in?"

"Sure, of course. Can you have Claire send me your available times?"

"Absolutely. Wonderful, Venetia. Thank you so much for squeezing me in."

"Look forward to meeting you in person."

"Claire!"

Claire was in her office within a heartbeat. "Yes, Jacqueline?"

"I need you to arrange a flight to L.A. for me. I'll leave from my meeting with that start-up executive in Sunnyvale. I have a meeting in downtown L.A. I need to meet with Venetia Street after that meeting. It won't be a long drawn-out thing. Find a way to work it close to my departure. Let her recommend where we should meet...And not the Ivy; it's just coffee. Casually suggest something close to LAX."

"Fine, great." She scribbled on her hand.

"Claire?"

"Yes?" She looked up at Jacqueline.

"Do you need supplies?"

"No, why?"

"So you always write notes on your arm and fingers and...?"

Laugh, Claire. "Oh. Well, no..."

"Never mind."

Leave Claire. "Anything else?"

Jacqueline reached for a pen and pad. "We've ticked the box."

"Right."

Claire wasn't back at her desk before she heard Jacqueline call out, "Claire!"

"Yes, Jacqueline," Claire said, returning to her office.

"I need a table at Purple."

"Time?"

Jacqueline glanced at her watch. "Twenty-five minutes."

"Like one o'clock?"

When Jacqueline stepped out of Purple and into the damp, crisp air, her cell vibrated. She took note of the number. Talking to her nephew was inevitable. "Hello, Simone." She rolled her eyes. "How much? Fine, a check is in the mail. Western Union?" Jacqueline couldn't believe her nephew, who was calling to borrow money she knew she wouldn't get back, would place her in a bothersome position of finding a Western Union. She had no idea where one was, let alone how to send money via Western Union. "Let me see what I can do. Simone! Listen to me. I'll see what I can do. I'll send the eight hundred as soon as I can. I'm busy, Simone!" Jacqueline's tone began to elevate. She checked herself and cased the hectic sidewalk. "I'll call you back." Jacqueline speed-dialed the office.

"Hello, Jacqueline."

"I need you to go to the nearest Western Union and send my nephew Simone—he's in my contacts—eight hundred."

"I can do that online."

"Really?"

"My father used to send me cash through Western Union."

"You have my debit card number and PIN. I can trust you to do this?"

"Absolutely. Of course."

"And Claire?"

"Yes?"

"I trust you to handle this, not only discreetly; but I'm trusting you with eight hundred dollars!"

"Yes, I know."

Jacqueline left the office without an umbrella or even a decent coat. Platforms and damp leaves. Back in the day, this would have been a walk in the park. *I need to come up out of these shoes and buy myself a nice pair of pumps. That would ruin my whole image.* She was stopped by a needy stranger, and pulled out a five and threw a *"Bless you, my friend"* over her shoulder.

At a crosswalk, she shivered, waiting for the light to change. A man, roughly in his early forties wearing a stylish all-weather coat, stood next to her. He held his umbrella over her head and said, "You never know when you'll need an umbrella."

She couldn't look too hard. Jacqueline didn't want to start something she wasn't prepared to finish. "You always need an umbrella in this town."

The light changed and Jacqueline was the first to step off the curb. The man with the umbrella halted her with, "Take my card. I'm in town until tomorrow morning. I'm here to check out talent at the Triple Door this evening. I'd hate to sit alone."

Jacqueline retrieved the business card. "If you don't hear from me in an hour, trust that I already have a commitment. But I don't think you'll have to sit alone too long." She began to trot, being very mindful to avoid as many leaves as possible, spreading like confetti along the wet sidewalks. She knew the man with the umbrella was still watching her as she made her way through the delicate raindrops.

With utter excitement, Henna jumped into her father's SUV. Finally, the boy she had a mad crush on had noticed her. It wasn't like so overt or anything. But he *noticed* that she no longer wore braces.

"He *noticed* me, Daddy."

Oh, what it was like to make eyes with a pretty girl in class. Torrick recalled that experience like—well, longer than yesterday. He himself had been a shy boy. But how could he forget what it felt like to really *like* a girl at Henna's age?

"When you met Mama, did you fall in love instantly, Daddy?"

Torrick pulled out of the school parking lot, concentrating on several things at once. Multitasking—a tautological term—challenged him to be fully present. Torrick had in fact fallen for Dianne the very moment he met her. Did he know it at the time? Probably not. Not in the way he could now look back and understand without ambiguity. Dianne had been the kind of woman he was waiting for. Although she was five years older than he, she was so vibrant. By the time they'd met, this woman had traveled to different parts of the world, and her passport was stamped in countries he hadn't traveled even as someone who once worked for the agency. She was the first woman he'd dated whom he considered "worldly." Every single male friend thought he was unbelievably lucky to snatch up one of the fine women in Venice.

"Your mother wasn't an easy woman to win over. But yes, I knew she was the one."

"How, Daddy? How do you know someone's the one?"

Henna was his youngest, and too young to even start romancing about boys. And *the one*. Daniela had already had two ostensible boyfriends this year. Would raising boys have been easier?

"Ah, it's complicated, baby. Look, I'm going to stop by Home Depot, so you don't mind, do you?"

"I don't mind." Henna started concentrating on her cell phone, texting back and forth to her best friend.

Occasionally, Torrick stole glances at Henna, so engaged in what she was doing. He loved her so much. He loved his daughters with all his heart and soul. He never wanted anything—not one thing if he could help it—to harm them. His job, for eight years, was to protect visiting heads of states and a vice president. He did both with honor, and utter integrity. He knew how to protect someone and safeguard their life. Still, Torrick understood that he couldn't protect what happened to his daughters when they were at school, or elsewhere when they weren't in his presence. He would move heaven and earth to keep them from harm.

They pulled into the Home Depot parking lot. Henna said, "What are you getting here, Daddy?"

"A new rake. Did you see those leaves when you left this morning?"

She unbuckled her seat belt. "I wanna help rake the leaves."

Torrick stopped, glanced over to his daughter with surprise. "You? The same young lady who, only a few weeks ago, poked her bottom lip out because she had to stack dishes in the dishwasher?"

She giggled. "I was going to miss some of *Gwenology!*"

Torrick's phone rang. Henna opened the passenger door.

"Torrick James." He reached for Henna's arm and pantomimed *wait*. Henna shut the door and resumed texting again. "Yes, what's going on? When?" Torrick listened for a few moments before butting in on his caller. "I'll handle it. Yeah. Give me an hour."

Henna looked over to her father. "Are we still going into Home Depot?"

"Yeah, Sweetie. Come on, let's go."

They walked toward the entrance, and Henna sensed a change in her father. He reached for her hand and while she didn't understand exactly what attentive was, Henna felt cared for. "Daddy?"

"Yeah, Sweetie?"

"Is your job stressful?"

With a chuckle, Torrick asked, "Why?"

"You're always like so stressed."

They entered Home Depot. Torrick said, "Just wait until you're an adult."

Leschi Market was semi-busy when Phoebe entered. She reached for a hand basket and roamed the aisles of the market trying to decide what to buy. Since Venetia was in L.A., she ate salads, but was burnt-out with the same-ole-same-ole. She wanted a *meal*. Wandering the aisles, Phoebe reflected on drinks with Michael, the EVP of Media Capital. The decision to meet him for drinks wasn't made lightly. The fact that she was even thinking about it perturbed Phoebe.

She'd walked two blocks to meet Michael. Mason House was a charming hotel that was easy to miss because it was small and sandwiched between a new condominium high-rise and a popular yoga and Pilates studio. When she arrived, a group of people stood around in the faintly lit, enchantingly decorated lobby. Within a minute or two, she would learn they were celebrating an engagement between two Japanese men—a gay couple. She passed through the lobby and entered the bar. It was dim, secluded-looking. She decided Michael had chosen it precisely for that reason. He wasn't inside the bar when she arrived. It worked out perfectly. She slid on to a stool and ordered Prosecco. She had no intentions of staying beyond one drink. She liked the idea that she'd bought her drink before he arrived. Phoebe hadn't followed the election, which was just under two months away. Although the sound was low, she could tell by the setup that there was a debate. She made a mental note to have her election ballot forwarded to Venetia's.

"Am I late or are you early?"

Phoebe turned to find Michael standing behind her. "I think we're both on time," she chose to say, so not to spend time on a pointless warm-up conversation that would undoubtedly be trivial.

"Let's grab a table."

Phoebe wanted to stay at the bar. She lifted her glass hoping he would grab the hint.

"Oh, you've ordered." He took the stool next to her, and Phoebe sensed from him a tried-to-conceal annoyance.

The bartender took Michael's order.

"Have you been following the election?"

"I prefer not to talk about politics with strangers—with someone I don't know. It's hard enough with someone I do know."

"I didn't ask you who you were voting for. I was merely asking whether you had kept up with the coverage. I figure that's why you sat at the bar."

"No." She looked directly into his green-gray eyes.

The bartender placed his order on the bar and Michael casually said, "Start a tab."

This is the only drink I'll be having.

"Did you know Chef's PA has a crush on you?"

"Isn't she a little old for crushes?"

"Well, she's what? Twenty-seven, twenty-eight, maybe."

"Maybe."

"Why did you invite me here?"

Michael studied her face. He reached for his drink. He nursed it so as to unwind. The day was long and complicated. He said, "I invited you here because you're a very attractive woman."

"Seriously? Is that the only reason?"

"It *was* a compliment, you know. Okay, and there's something about you."

"Like…"

"You're mysterious. You also remind me of someone."

I hate that, Phoebe thought.

"And…You were in Venice. I saw you—Venice, on YouTube. I'm impressed with the fact that you wrote three of Venice's hits."

Over the many years since her youth, from time to time someone recognized Phoebe as having once been in the late '70s and early '80s singing group, Venice. Then the recognition was "I know you (from somewhere)." After that it became, "You look familiar." Subsequently, a person would stop her in an airport or somewhere and they thought they might have known her from this thing or that. Or that she'd played in a movie or a sitcom that was no longer on the air. But they knew her face from *somewhere*. By the time she was in her early forties, a new generation was shaping the culture. Those under thirty-five had no clue who Phoebe was.

"Actually it was four—*hits*, not three. So you've heard of Venice?"

Michael said, "What, you think I'm a white guy who couldn't appreciate the Motown Sound, or R&B, or soul music? I'm a product of the seventies."

"Stefan," she said, to change the subject. "I hear has had a setback. How is he?"

"He's in the hospital."

"How serious is it? I'd heard that he was in remission."

"That's the public story. The cancer has spread."

"Well, how's the California girl?" Joseph said. "You looked to be millions of miles away."

Phoebe turned to find a man standing before her, holding a few items. He took her out of her reverie and the whole having a drink with Michael at the Mason. She needed the distraction from that experience—the fact that she even thought about it made no sense to her.

With a curious brow, Phoebe looked at the man. "We've met?"

"Yes," Joseph replied enthusiastically.

"We have?"

"By the lake?"

It occurred to Phoebe they had run into each other along the path of the lake. But they made no introductions. She wasn't in a particularly good mood so this man annoyed her. Besides, he was deeply obnoxious. She wanted to turn on her heels and leave, but she couldn't bring herself to be so rude.

"Right," she replied. "By the lake."

"What's your name?" Joseph asked.

"Phoebe."

"Phoebe? Well, I'm Joseph. It's always good to meet new people. So, you live around the area?"

Here we go again.

"Yes, nearby."

"How are you liking it here so far?"

"What do you mean?"

"Well, you said you were from Southern California. Right?"

Nonchalantly, she looked at her wristwatch. "I'm getting used to it."

"Think you might want to stay?"

"I don't think so."

"We're dignified here."

"And Californians aren't?"

"California is—exotic."

Phoebe burst into laughter.

"What's funny?" She had an infectious laugh, and Joseph liked this woman. It didn't matter what she did or where she was from and why she was living here as if she was running away from something. He didn't care about her background or any dubious details relating to her life story. He knew he liked her and wanted to get to know her. He hadn't felt that kind of interest in a woman since his wife had passed on. There had been a few women he was attracted to and wanted to get to know better. But they never made him feel the way he felt when he was in Phoebe's presence. He didn't know how to make it work in his favor. She was cordial but reserved. Perhaps she'd recently broken up with someone, or was going through a distressing divorce. No matter. He wanted to *know* her and whatever it took to make that happen, Joseph was up for it. He got stirred up inside on both occasions when they were in close proximity.

"Well, Joseph. I need to be going. It was good seeing you again."

"Can I call you sometime?"

Phoebe was heading toward the check-out lane and pivoted just enough to see a flash of his image. "We'll catch up...who knows, by the lake, right!"

Joseph's mind thought uncontrollably about Phoebe all the way home. He was blessed not to have had an accident. Was it his weight? He did need to shed a few pounds.

"Dad, is that you?" Cornell called out.

He made his way to the kitchen to put away the items he'd purchased at the market. "Who else would it be?" he said, unconsciously frustrated.

CHAPTER 6

If she didn't have time to kill before her flight was to depart, Jacqueline would have cancelled her coffee with Venetia. Because of a last-minute consultation, Venetia requested that Jacqueline meet her near her home office in the Larchmont section of Los Angeles. It was such an inconvenience. She'd made it clear to Claire that she wanted to meet as close to LAX as possible. Anyway, it was too late and Jacqueline had open space on her calendar—which was a luxury for her—before she met Venetia at Larchmont Bungalow. She hadn't asked Claire to coordinate a hired driver. The trip should have taken only half of her day. It occurred to her once she'd stepped into a taxi that she could have used Zipcar or Car2go. While she had accounts, she rarely, if ever, used the services, so naturally it didn't pop into her head to make such arrangements.

Massive mushroom-shaped trees outlined the Larchmont strip, and the taxi driver dropped Jacqueline at the foot of the bustling street. She took in the quaint, lively community. Young women—and men too—carried yoga mats as they walked to a class, and mommies still young-ish but one step closer to midlife pushed strollers. There were as many well-coifed dogs walking along the strip as were people. Jacqueline assumed it was a progressive L.A. community, with the stunningly landscaped Paramount Pictures studio only a hop, skip and jump away. Jacqueline stopped in front of Larchmont Bungalow, noting where it was located. Since she still had a little under an hour before she was to meet with Venetia, she thought she could squeeze in some shopping time. She'd hoped to browse through Stanford Shopping Center, but the meeting in Sunnyvale went over and she barely made her flight out of San Jose. Before she knew it, Jacqueline slid her debit card four times at several stores on Larchmont. It was strictly retail therapy. She didn't manage spare time in the same way she managed her time on the clock.

She dashed down the bustling street, the sun spreading over the earth like a blanket—it was a warm and clear day. "Sorry, excuse me!" Jacqueline said, pushing her way through so not to be late for her coffee with Venetia. When she arrived at the bistro, catching her breath, she was delayed by a couple with two kids and a large dog. Jacqueline didn't want to be rude, but really! "Excuse me," she said, her bags knocking against them. The couple and two children had no choice but to get out of her way, and the family dog barked ferociously at Jacqueline.

Upon entering, she looked around the semi-busy bistro for a young woman seated alone. Her hands filled, Jacqueline attempted to slow her heart rate. She went into a new section. She caught a woman, svelte and poised, seated by herself studying a menu. On the table was a cell phone set beside a glass of water. From where Jacqueline stood, it appeared her phone rang. The young woman reached for it and glanced at the screen fleetingly and replaced the phone on the table. This was the daughter of Cordia Street, Dianne's back-in-the-day BFF. Although she never said as much, Jacqueline sensed that there was bad blood between them. It wasn't worth her time to inquire for tidbits. She remembered it clearly: she was in her senior year when the word got out that Venice had broken up, and rumors spread like cockroaches. Jacqueline wasn't the type to be sensitive if she wanted her way, but Dianne always seemed touchy whenever she'd broached the subject of Cordia Street. The one with the golden voice and four number one hits—"You Think" being Jacqueline's favorite.

"Venetia?"

She looked up. "Jacqueline?"

Venetia looked so much like Cordia.

She placed her shopping bags on the floor, making apologies for interfering with her schedule.

"It's fine."

Jacqueline sat in the chair. "I love Larchmont. What a well-kept secret for someone who doesn't know L.A. intimately."

"I adore this neighborhood. I had a condo in West Hollywood. I loved my view, but it was becoming too crowded. Parking was outrageous."

A waitress interrupted and took their orders. Genially, they small-talked for a few minutes before Jacqueline introduced the purpose for the coffee.

"I want to thank you for meeting with Gwen. I was really hoping that she'd connect with you and consider it a good idea to have someone help her with all this…reality TV stardom stuff. She's not a mature girl, and it's a lot to handle: fame or celebrity, whatever; and all that comes with it. She doesn't understand the impact… the responsibility or value that comes with having a brand. I'd hoped she'd use her popularity as a means to take up a cause. Directed toward something meaningful like contaminated water in African villages. I didn't expect her to have Hindu-like compassion, but use her platform for a greater good. Reality TV has its place, but in Gwen's case…what she's doing with her life is so marginal. I have to be honest; her geographical embrace astounds me."

Venetia rested her forearms on the table and crossed her wrists.

She interjected with, "At least from what I gathered, her life *is* the reality show. How did you end up being her media consultant?"

"Frankly, I'm not sure what my role is. She doesn't listen to me. But our publicity department assists her with red carpets and public appearances. Her father and I have some history and he's asked me to guide her. Media-wise, I try. But what she really needs is life guidance."

They were interrupted by the waitress delivering their orders.

Venetia wet her tongue by taking a small sip of her iced Americano.

Jacqueline could hear her cell vibrating, but trusted it was something that could keep for twenty minutes.

"I'll tell you what I think is going to happen if she doesn't—let me say she needs someone to guide her. She has a drinking dependency, which is dangerous for someone in the position she's in. Not to mention, she's young.

"No good could come from this if she isn't monitored. She's not going to work with me; for one, she doesn't understand what a life coach does. And two, she wants to be the way she is, because something about it validates her."

"My, you got all that from talking to her for what? Ten minutes?"

"Closer to fifteen. I saw one of her episodes to prepare for our meeting. I couldn't believe it. It's lowbrow. Reality TV—those like *Gwenology*…it's such an unprincipled ambition. Sorry, I know that's cold."

"Not if it's your truth. Thank you for your candor."

"Her father has no…"

"Her father can't even get through the entourage she has surrounded herself with. They communicate via texts. When her mother up and split, they were like two peas in a pod. Now this…"

"Look, I'm glad we had this chance to meet. I was going to call you anyway. I have a client; he's an author. I know that one of your clients is a co-host for *Coffee with the Crew*, and I was wondering if he might be able to plug his book. It's a really good book, but it's not getting the national attention it needs in order to sell. Today, it's all about social media—the electronic word, right!"

"Done!"

"Just like that?"

"I'd love to hook you up." Jacqueline reached for her straw.

"I wish everything in life were so simple."

"Hey, as we used to say in the good old days: I rub your back and you rub mine. Seriously, my clients can benefit from you, and vice versa. I like to help a girl out."

"Oh, by the way." Venetia reached for a classy clutch purse in a chair. She produced a mocha-colored envelope. She placed it on the table. "Here."

"What's this?" Jacqueline picked it up. "A wedding invitation?"

"No way!"

When she pulled the attractive card from the envelope, she read it blindly, catching only the words that would mean anything. "A brunch?"

"I'm having a reading and book signing brunch for my client. The author."

"Oh, that's a great idea. Yes…" Jacqueline tried to seek out the date without having to read all the unnecessary information on the invitation. "Consider this a personal RSVP. I can bring someone?"

"Absolutely!

"I am so, so sorry I couldn't be more help with Gwen."

"If I could get Gwen to meet with you again, would you be up for that? She desperately needs a firewall."

"Absolutely. I'd like to work with Gwen."

"Now if I could just get her…" Jacqueline had ignored two calls while sitting with Venetia, and she decided she should at least check to see who was calling. The curse of her career was the twenty-four/seven accessibility. "Oh, Venetia, I'm sorry. I really do need to check with my office. Apparently…"

"Go ahead. It's fine."

Jacqueline called in on Claire's line and she answered on the first ring. "Claire?"

Venetia took notice of the swift change in Jacqueline's body language, and then her brow deeply furrowed. "What is it?" she asked when Jacqueline disconnected the call. "Jacqueline?"

"Uhhh, it's my…a friend. He has cancer and…They're flying him here. He…" Jacqueline swallowed thickly. "It's not good."

"I'm sorry." Venetia reached for Jacqueline's hand and held it tenderly. Venetia sought out their waitress; she was cleaning a nearby table. "Check, please."

Jacqueline's eyes collected tears.

Venetia said, "Let's go back to my place. It's nearby. Where are they taking him?"

"Cedars-Sinai."

The waitress placed the check on the table. Venetia pulled out her wallet and slipped a twenty on the tray. She came to her feet. "Jacqueline, come on." She took hold of several of her shopping bags. Reluctant, eventually Jacqueline came to her feet.

Venetia gingerly embraced Jacqueline, who looked quite fragile. The woman who had approached her table was self-assured, playful but never quite crossing the line into the casual nature two black businesswomen might otherwise share. She had a natural flair for balancing personable and professional. It was fascinating to watch someone with such a well-trained guise become so delicate out of nowhere.

"Let's go," Venetia said. And she ushered Jacqueline out of the animated bistro.

Everyone was gone. The house was quiet. Dianne finally had the place to herself. She couldn't quite get herself together. She made breakfast for the girls in a daze. As usual, they complained about something—the brand of cereal Dianne had already poured in bowls because she knew they would need to rush through their meal. Lately, Daniela spent too much time in the bathroom. Recently, Henna began to pout over the way she looked in jeans; she was getting in the habit of changing clothes three, four times before she finally decided on something that didn't make her look fat. Dianne and her sister weren't like that growing up: worrying over their size. But the globally embraced concept and the Madison Avenue ideology led her youngest to believe she wasn't thin enough. Realistically, both of her girls were thin enough. One other detail she'd noticed in her daughters: while close, they were equally independent of each other. Vanessa once said it was generational.

When the landline rang, she knew it would be Vanessa. Dianne wasted no time going into detail about the incident that took place in the Safeway parking lot with the personal trainer.

"He's accusing me of giving him VD. I don't know what to do." She reached for the empty bowls on the table and rinsed them out, without thinking. "No, he actually believes I'm the one who gave him VD. Yes! He called me names—like slut and bitch. He referred to Torrick as *dawg*. You know he's too young; using language like *dawg!* I couldn't believe what I was experiencing. Did I deserve this or what?"

Dianne sipped her orange juice, listening carefully to the feedback from her sister—rational, optimistic, and frustratingly reasonable. She butted in. "You know, you were right when you asked 'who gets chlamydia in their fifties?' I dodged that bullet my entire life. And now in my fifties, I get chlamydia!"

"Sorry, Mama, but I forgot to tell you to sign this," Henna said, holding out a sheet of paper.

Dianne was taken aback. "Hold on, Vanessa." She didn't even hear her daughter come back into the house. Instinctively, she reached for the paper and looked it over. "Why didn't you give this to me earlier, Henna? Did you miss the bus?"

"Catalina's mom is taking us to school today."

"She's outside?"

"Yes. Can you sign it, please?"

Dianne would never let Henna carpool without knowing ahead of time. She didn't recall even communicating with Catalina's mother, whom she occasionally shared alternate carpooling, depending on her schedule. "I really wished that you'd given this to me before. I'd like to read it over first."

"It's a permission slip. You sign them all the time."

"Well, this one's different. It's…I would prefer to talk to your father first."

"Please, Mama. I have to turn it in today."

Compassionately, Dianne studied Henna's face, which gave the look of truly, deeply wanting to go on the field trip. More so, she wondered how much of her conversation had her daughter overheard. "Vanessa, let me call you back." She disconnected the call, and walked over to a drawer and pulled out an ink pen and autographed the permission slip. "Come on. Let me go say hello to Catalina's mom."

After she showered and decided what she would make for dinner, Dianne dressed to meet a community council member for a light lunch to discuss several important topics for the next community council meeting; among them, funding to save a neighborhood library on the verge of closing. She phoned Jacqueline, whom she hadn't talked to or seen at church in several weeks. Her voicemail greeted her and Dianne left a message that they should get together: go to see a film, and have lunch—catch up. Dianne needed desperately to return to some sense of normalcy. She trusted everything would fall back into place if she went back to her routine.

When she entered the parking lot near the café where she was to have lunch, her cell rang. She reached for it tucked in her visor. To avoid missing an available parking space, Dianne didn't take the time to see who was calling. Although surprised, she was delighted to hear Phoebe's voice. "Hey, girl!" She parked in a space at the opposite end of the elevator. She turned off the engine. "Brunch? At Venetia's? Yes, that sounds great. I'd like that. You know I really would like to see Venetia. Oh, we should have exchanged addresses. But calling is so personal compared to those e-mail invites. I think that's tacky."

Dianne headed toward the elevators that led to the downtown mall, and where she was having her lunch meeting. "Oh, sure, I can remember. I look forward to it. And Phoebe? It was good to hear your voice. I am really excited. *Ciao.*" Dianne stared at her phone. She was pleased that Phoebe had reached out to her. It made Dianne feel a lot better about them being back in touch again.

Phoebe had intentionally avoided Michael since they'd met for a drink at Mason House. It struck her that she hadn't seen him around the office. He generally came into the kitchen to grab a piece of fruit, a bagel or croissant. Perhaps he was traveling. He was, after all, a busy man. Chef assigned her the task of taking inventory. Once she finished, Phoebe was to restack dishes from the dishwasher and to restock various fridges. When she made her way toward reception—the quickest path to two hospitality pantries that needed restocking—she caught sight of a tall man, and good-looking. She'd met him; she was convinced of it. Yet Phoebe didn't know where. She hadn't met many people since relocating, and—it was Daniel. The man she met while waiting for Dianne at the Blue Bar. He was giving the new concierge a large, thick cone of exotic flowers. Phoebe delayed crossing the reception area to evade him. Later she would ask herself did she do it to avoid talking to him. Or was it to preclude his knowing she worked at Media Capital, and as a hospitality assistant.

"Francesca?"

The new concierge was no Claire. She had an easygoing, quiet energy.

"Hi, Phoebe."

"Those are gorgeous flowers," she said.

"Aren't they?"

"Is the lucky girl...?"

Phoebe was interrupted by the concierge needing to answer a call. Then another.

"Sorry, Phoebe." She stood. "These are for Jacqueline."

"Jacqueline Daye?"

"A mysterious, handsome stranger dropped them off."

"I haven't seen Jacqueline. Is she traveling?"

"California. Oh, you've heard about Stefan."

"No, what?"

"It's so hush-hush. I'm to say he's out of the office, but I over-heard that a press release was to be released tomorrow."

"Press release?"

"He's been hospitalized." The new concierge pressed a button on the telephone and said to Phoebe, "Back to work..."

When Phoebe reached Michael's office, the lights were out and it looked neat—no papers scattered over the desk, and no machines humming. The flat-screen television was off, which, anytime she entered the office to restock the fridge, it was tuned to the News Mix. When she passed her, Michael's assistant was on a call and Phoebe indicated to her with hand gestures that she was refilling his fridge. The assistant nodded only half paying attention to Phoebe.

She was certainly not attracted to Michael. But while stacking his fridge with beverages, Phoebe began to feel different toward him. Unaware at that moment, but something about standing in his silent office shifted her thinking. Why had she been so hard on him? What in particular did she not like about Michael? She'd dated a Jewish man, a news producer, briefly; it wasn't that.

"Excuse me," said Michael's assistant, standing at the doorway and holding it open with her foot.

Phoebe looked up.

"Could you stock a couple of beet-apple-carrot-lemon-ginger drinks and Açaí juice?"

"Those aren't on his list."

"Stock some, okay?"

On her way back to return the empty cart, Phoebe stopped at Claire's cubicle. She was busy: between monitoring tweet traffic and watching *Coffee with the Crew*.

"I won't take up your time. I was wondering, do you have any familiarity with business plans?"

"Yes," she said. "What's up?"

"I need to write one."

"What for?" Her attention was elsewhere.

"Remember, I told you I had this idea. Tote bags."

"Oh right."

"Can you get a hold of one so I can see it?"

"You can go online, you know."

"Well, yeah…"

"I can get you one. Sure. No problem."

Phoebe turned her cart around to head back toward the kitchen, and paused long enough to look over her shoulder. Claire was intense. Phoebe wondered if she had a boyfriend or if she dated. Where would he even fit in? When she was Claire's age, Phoebe juggled several men simultaneously. Career mattered, but it wasn't the be-all. Her twenties were different in that way. From time to time, Phoebe suffered pangs of regret for not having finished college and going on to do something purposeful. Something larger—more noteworthy—than singing in a group. She consciously tried not to dwell on past choices. Still, there was something missing, deeply. A career? Not necessarily. A child? She did her best not to spend time fixating on her choice to give her child up for adoption. Without knowing anything about her—the color of her eyes, her weight, not one detail—Phoebe signed over the newborn without any sense of remorse because at the time, she was self-involved. No way would she have been ready to raise a child. Not to mention the father wasn't someone she wanted to be connected to. She couldn't bring herself to abort the child; at the time such a decision went against her values. Nonetheless, she knew in her gut that she couldn't raise it responsibly. Nor did she want to raise a child on her own.

By the time she reached the kitchen, tears were collecting in her eyes.

What brought this on?

All morning Henna couldn't stop thinking about what was wrong with her mother. Intolerably fretful, she went to the school's computer room and looked up the word "chlamydia" on the Internet. It might explain her behavior of late. Anything that came up in the search engine made no sense. Eventually, she ran out of time. While waiting impatiently for her father, her sadness deepened. She wanted to know what this word meant—"chlamydia." Was it contagious or could her mom die from it?

"You're a million miles away. Didn't you hear me calling you from the car?" Torrick greeted his daughter.

She looked up, her eyes glossy from fresh tears. "No."

Torrick sat on his heels. He took his daughter's face into his large hands. "What's wrong? What it is, Henna?"

"Is Mama sick, Daddy?"

"Sick? What are you talking about?"

"What's chlamydia?"

"Chlamydia?" Torrick reacted viscerally. "Why? What does this have to…Henna, what's this about?" Gingerly, he brushed away a tear leading down her solemn face.

"Mama was talking to somebody on the phone. She told them she had chlamydia. Is it serious, Daddy?" To Henna it sounded serious.

Torrick could barely restrain himself. But for the love of his child, and to suspend her fear, he cracked a false grin. "Ah, baby," he said. "It's…Where exactly did you hear all this, Henna?"

"When I was home."

"When was this?"

"This morning."

"Okay." He wet his lips and tried to find a way through the conversation without Henna being afraid that there was some-thing seriously wrong with her mother. Simultaneously, he was stunned and hoped his emotions didn't display how struck he was at what she'd said. Surely, she'd heard something that wasn't for her ears. Most likely she'd taken what she'd heard her mother talking about out of context. While it wouldn't come as a surprise to him that his youngest daughter could know about sexually transmitted diseases, he was relieved that at twelve years old, she wasn't as knowledgeable as he might have suspected her to be. There was still innocence in his youngest; she wasn't completely exposed to the information a twelve-year-old shouldn't be privy to and yet was easily accessible to her on the Internet. It never occurred to him that she'd spent time online attempting to find out about chlamydia but to no avail.

Torrick took her hand. "Look, Sweetie, I'm picking you up because I got a call from Catalina's mom that she had to take Catalina out of school early. But I need to get back to the office, so you'll have to come with me."

Henna tried to keep step with her father's hurried pace. He didn't completely ease her concern with his flimsy explanation. He didn't act like he even knew anything about her mother having chlamydia. She buckled her seat belt. "Daddy," she said. "So it's not serious?"

Torrick winked at his baby girl seated in the passenger's seat, and he could tell by her expression that he hadn't said enough to ease her mind. "Your mom is fine, baby," he attempted to cajole her. "She's not sick, Henna. And listen to me," he said in a tone that Henna knew all too well. "Don't mention this to your sister. Do you hear me?"

Henna nodded. Yet that made chlamydia sound all the more serious than her father dared to let on.

"And don't mention this conversation to your mother. She'll be ang—she won't like that you were eavesdropping." Torrick started the SUV.

"I wasn't eavesdropping."

He backed out of the parking space. "She won't see it that way." He barely yielded at the stop sign. He looked over to her with a stone face. "Henna, do you understand what I've just said to you?"

Henna nodded reluctantly. "Yeah, Daddy."

In his office with the door closed, and having instructed his personal assistant that he not be disturbed, Torrick went online and searched several medical sites to determine whether symptoms always accompanied the exposure to chlamydia. With the exception of an old girlfriend whom he'd slept with a week prior to marrying Dianne, Torrick had been faithful to his wife. Based on information that he read online, there was no way he could get the disease without some form of sexual contact.

Holed up in his office, when and with who were the questions that consumed him. This information gnawed at him like crazy. There was not a shadow of a doubt—Torrick trusted that he'd been a good husband. Dianne couldn't complain even if she wanted to. He had provided her with a good home, and he earned more than enough so that his family could reap the benefits of his hard work. Dianne didn't need to work, and she never gave Torrick even a hint that she wanted to go back out and earn an income. Once, she'd said to him, "Jacqueline is so lonely. All she has is her career." While Torrick disagreed with his wife, he understood her point. There was never a time when he sensed that his wife felt lack. Every marriage had its ups and downs; and a shortage of excitement and not being in synch was a part of the marriage deal. Torrick's work with the Secret Service had him traveling a lot. When he started his own business, while he didn't travel nearly as much, there were times when he would be away from home for days at a time.

For quite a while now, they'd been a solid couple. Torrick explored the corners of his mind trying to comprehend why she'd chosen—needed—to be with another man, if in fact she had. While he leaned in the back of his chair, it hit him. Dianne had been distant, even melancholy on occasion, in the past month or so. He didn't give it that much thought, even when she flew to New York to hang out with her sister on the spur-of-the-moment. But now, with the possibility that she had gone outside their marriage for any reason, Torrick didn't know what to think or even how to deal. He assumed her moodiness had something to do with her menopause. He even took into account her running into Phoebe all these years later played some part. Torrick suggested that she see someone; to get to the bottom of her emotional state.

Torrick had no idea how to handle this. He needed to confront her, but the best way to do it? Besides, he wasn't even sure his wife had chlamydia. Torrick was to confront her based on something Henna may or may not have heard accurately? Anyway, he couldn't arrive at the conclusion that it was Dianne who had chlamydia instead of someone she was merely gossiping about. Not to mention, he wasn't altogether sure how fragile Dianne was at the moment.

"Damn!" He slammed his hand on the desk. By memory, he punched numbers on the telephone. When the voice came on the line, Torrick said, "Hello, Pastor Stevens. This is Torrick James. Do you have some time to see me?"

Cornell, dressed in a hoodie beneath a weather-beaten leather jacket, entered the house from the backdoor. It led into the large kitchen that was redone for his mother only one year before she'd passed on. He walked to the fridge, holding magazines and mail in his hand, and he grabbed an almost-empty bottle of Naked. He gulped it down and put the bottle on the counter, leaning against it. He flipped through the mail. A letter from his university got his attention. He folded it and slipped it into his leather jacket pocket. Amid bills was a mocha-colored envelope addressed to his father in handwriting like that of an architect. *Whatup?* Was he being invited to something? Cornell couldn't recall the last time his father received this kind of mail. When Cornell's mother was still alive, Joseph was active, and Cornell couldn't recollect him ever being sad, or worried. His parents used to travel. Places like Hawaii and the Caribbean. These days, though, Joseph Morgan didn't go beyond the two-mile radius of his home. Occasionally he went to church, but less since he'd become a widower. Cornell watched his father age beyond his fifty-six years. Early retirement, and the death of his wife, had changed him. It was as though he had nothing to do with his time, with his life. It was another reason his sister, Christine, was spending two weeks at home over the holiday.

Cornell was curious but dared not slit the envelope open. His father would have a fit! He'd never hear the end of it. Already Cornell was feeling awkward about moving back home. While his lady—the mother of his unborn child—complained that she was tired of living with a skanky roommate and had hinted a few times about moving in with Cornell at his father's place, Cornell was actually glad he had a home to come home to. He had friends whose parents were losing, if not lost, their homes after the downturn. They were having it rough, too.

"Cornell! Do you have to park your Jeep so close to the entrance? I keep telling you…"

"Dad," Cornell interrupted—not up for the third degree. "Check this out." He held up the elaborate envelope.

Joseph put a few shopping bags on the counter. "Now you're going through my mail?"

"You know I wouldn't do that. The mail dude handed the mail

to me. Here." Cornell held the oversized envelope out to his father.

Joseph reached for it, curious.

"So?" his son asked, locking his arms together.

"So what?"

"Looks like you're invited to something. You holding back on me, Dad?"

"What could I be holding back on?" With his forefinger, he slit it open. Carefully, he read the words. "Venetia's giving a brunch. A client is having a book signing and reading."

"Venetia *Street?*" Cornell asked.

"How many Venetias have you met in your lifetime?"

Joseph moved about the kitchen, putting food away. Cornell picked up the invitation and read it.

"Why did she invite you? Venetia's crowd would be more my age."

"You're twenty-one. Venetia's got to be thirty, at least. She babysat you and your sister a few times."

"Yeah, but we're closer in age...I mean..."

"Jealous?" he joked.

It had been a while since Cornell heard his father laugh. He might have chuckled at something he saw on television, and it was funny enough for him to react to it. But Cornell had forgotten the sound of his father's laughter, which had been loud; it was as though it came from the pit of his belly.

"Jealous? What, of you?" He reached for a loaf of bread and a gallon of milk and helped his father put away the items from the bags. "So, you *are* going? You know you should go."

"I'm...Well, I might."

"Dad! Like what plan is keeping you from going?" Cornell grabbed a pluot and washed it in the sink. "You might meet some-one; who knows!"

"Meet someone?"

There went the laugh again. Something was up. Cornell knew it. His father's entire mood shifted once he read the invitation. Not to mention Joseph Morgan was one big open book. There was no mystery there.

"Something you aren't telling me, Dad. What is it?"

"Nothing." He folded the paper bags. "You know, they started charging customers for shopping bags now. No more plastic bags. I guess I'll need to go out and buy some of those tote bags everybody carries around."

"It's environmental. You changing the subject? There's got to be more to this. Why would Venetia up and invite you to a brunch? You, Mr. Recluse? Come on, Dad, give it up."

Joseph rested his hands on the kitchen counter. "I ran into her at the bank. She did mention introducing me to someone. But…"

"Get real? You serious?"

"What are you all excited about?"

"It's good to see you…a little excited. I can tell you want to go to this. You will RSVP, right?"

"I might."

"Okay, Dad. I think we should go shopping. I can help you find something kind of spiffy and…"

"All those clothes I got hanging in the closet."

"Dad, now come on. Dirt is younger than your clothes. It's not like you can't afford it. This guy I know at school…his father owns a small shop downtown. He can hook you up."

"I'm not wearing those pants that hang past my behind, now."

Cornell couldn't stop laughing. Once he pulled himself together, he said, "I hope not. I don't even wear pants past my behind. He specializes in men of a certain age."

"What are you getting at?"

"Well, Dad, you are of a certain age."

"Let's say I go to this shop. What's it gonna cost me?"

With his arms spread out as if he was about to embrace his father, he said, "Dad! Really? You're so tight. You can afford to buy new clothes."

"How do you know what I can afford?"

The sound of the landline shifted the energy, and Joseph reached for the receiver hanging in the wall carriage. "Hello. Oh, yeah. He's right here. Hold on." Joseph held the receiver out for his son. Cornell's look suggested he was curious about receiving a call on his father's landline. "It's your baby-mama," Joseph joked in a low voice. Cornell was taken aback by his father's choice of words. Amused, he reached for the receiver.

Joseph rinsed his hands, eavesdropping on his son's conversation with the young woman he didn't care for, but he hoped his son would do the right thing and marry. He hadn't been able to get a straight answer out of Cornell about what his plans were. He walked past his son and pet his back. After all, no matter what decisions he made, Cornell was his son.

CHAPTER 7

There was nothing about Los Angeles that Jacqueline genuinely liked. So many palm trees; the sun—it was always out here. There were no seeming ghettos. At least not like the ones she knew of in St. Louis, her hometown. Jacqueline never quite took to so-called Tinseltown. A hub of entertainment, it attracted a plethora of wannabes, and the people she often met here were unconsciously superficial. It was strange; Stefan fell for the City of Angels, though. Because some of his most influential clients were in entertainment, he traveled to Los Angeles so often he finally leased a house in the Westwood area. Jacqueline had a key to the place and had been staying there for several days now. She never felt so alone. When her life was out of balance and she was stressed beyond her comfort level, Stefan was the one she could go to. He was her anchor, but the armor she relied on was now cracked.

She drove along Avenue of the Stars, hoping to avoid some of the early afternoon traffic—and that was another thing: the traffic in Los Angeles unnerved her—Jacqueline's mind couldn't rest inside the knowledge that Stefan wouldn't be accessible to her. She wouldn't know how to do it. Thanksgiving, Christmas—he was the person she spent those holidays with. His family had known her for many years, and even his ex-wife and Jacqueline were causal friends.

Her idea of taking Santa Monica Boulevard to avoid traffic was absurd. Her instincts were unreliable. She made a right-hand turn off Avenue of the Stars, but it was better to have stayed on Pico. She glanced at the rental clock and sighed. Jacqueline spent hours the evening before, nearly finishing off a bottle of Stefan's expensive French wine, attempting to come up with five people who would show up for her if she lay dying in a hospital bed. She couldn't think of one soul, other than her mother and Stefan. He was her lifeline. Her line of thinking made her feel intensely lonely. She not once thought about death or dying. Not even when Stefan was hospitalized a year ago. But she understood it so clearly now: he was dying, and that left her facing her own mortality. Moreover, she obsessed over her own destiny—the when, where, and the how of her life coming to an end. What if she was alone when she met her fate? How long would it take for someone to realize they had not heard from her? Her career had been her life. Jacqueline built it, as she was now beginning to appreciate, out of some deep need to be validated. Every potential relationship ended eventually because her career took precedence, and she didn't have children like so many women, even those with a career. How did those women pull it off?

One day, when she and Dianne were having lunch, Dianne asked Jacqueline if she ever felt something missing with having a demanding career. At the time Jacqueline took that question as a sign of jealousy. She knew that Dianne, as quiet as she tried to keep it, longed for something more. She loved motherhood; Jacqueline never once doubted that. And Dianne never said as much, but Jacqueline read between the lines.

As far as she was concerned, Jacqueline had no regrets about the path she'd taken. Everyone looked back at a certain point in their life and questioned whether they could have made fill-in-the-blank choices. For the first time in quite some time, Jacqueline turned off her phone and chose to be there for a friend who championed her through more than enough distressing times over the years. While he may not have known she was present, Jacqueline needed to be there for him.

When she made it to the ward where Stefan's life was elusively slipping away, his debonair sons were just leaving.

"We thought we'd get out of here for a while. The smell, it's making me nauseous. You want to join us?" one son offered.

"Where to?"

"We thought we'd grab something quick at Chipotle. It's across from the hotel where we're staying."

"Okay, sure," she said.

They walked toward the Beverly Center. Nonchalantly, Jacqueline looked up to the cobalt blue sky; while faint smog hung like steady clouds over the city, the air was fresh. It wasn't a particularly warm day, but a jacket was enough. She wasn't sure why—in time however it would become clear—a sense of peace came over her. The intense sorrow she'd felt for the past few days, and the doubts that attempted to consume her as she drove to the hospital, had drifted away.

How long are you going to avoid me, Phoebe?

She listened to the voicemail message a half-dozen times since she'd received it two days ago. While lunching with Claire, she'd asked Phoebe why she'd left Los Angeles. There was a man— and Phoebe said to Claire a man was always in the center of the story—whom she had been with for several years and their relationship had reached an impasse. She needed space.

Claire had invited Phoebe out to lunch for two reasons: Phoebe learned that her assignment was coming to an end. Gloria in TA had informed her they'd found a permanent hospitality assistant. Also, Claire needed a break. She was overwhelmed since Jacqueline hadn't been in the office for nearly a week. Claire longed to get away from the office, if only to complete a real meal at lunchtime. All week, she was buried in work that was beyond her capability. She hardly left her desk, except to grab junk food from the nearby pantry. She drank Red Bull, spraying Rescue Remedy on her tongue, and when those failed, she downed energy shots only to stay alert. Nearly every one of Jacqueline's clients called Claire; they hadn't been able to get in touch with Jacqueline. Stefan had been admitted to Cedars-Sinai in Los Angeles and within hours, everyone in the office was talking about it. When Jacqueline advised Claire that she would be taking a few days off, Claire saw this as a window of opportunity. Yet it didn't take too long for reality to stop her cold. By the third day of Jacqueline not being reachable, she understood the pressure, the stress that her boss persistently underwent.

Over lunch in a noisy deli, Phoebe listened to Claire rant. By the time they paid their check, Phoebe saw Claire as true-to-the-bone ambitious; all she talked about was work. For perhaps the first time, Phoebe understood something she hadn't comprehended previously: she wasn't what her grandmother called a go-getter.

Even while pursuing a career in Venice, it wasn't about ambition. That wasn't the driving force. Her energy was fueled by the bonding she had with Dianne and Cordia; that was the thing that compelled her. Similarly, she was young and life looked infinite without a lot of history.

Phoebe replayed the message again. Hearing his voice brought sadness to her eyes. She missed him. She wanted him. She even felt a need for him. But that troubled her more than anything: needing and wanting him. In the past it was one or the other. But she had never felt need and want synchronously. Since Venetia had to fly to New York on business, Phoebe volunteered to call a catering friend of Venetia's to arrange her services for the book brunch; and Phoebe was to check the mail for RSVPs. Thus far, all but six had responded to the book brunch invite. She prepared a menu and faxed it over to the caterer, and made calls to those who hadn't RSVP'd as yet, leaving messages on voicemail.

The night was quiet; it rained all day. Phoebe had open space. She didn't know anyone except Venetia, Dianne, and the few people she'd become friendly with at Media Capital. It struck her, but Phoebe didn't have a reason to call Dianne, yet she felt the need to talk to someone. She decided to soak in warm bubble bath, and if she still felt lonely when she stepped out of the tub, she would connect with Dianne. She grabbed a bottle of wine and a wineglass and headed for the bath.

It might have been her own guilt, or maybe it was paranoia, but Dianne sensed Torrick being purposely distant with her. Once their marriage fell into predictability, each had a keen sense of when to give the other space. Without saying a word, he offered her just that over the past six weeks. Now, though, as she was attempting to move closer to him, to be *with* him and not in her head all the time, Torrick was backing away. The subtle nuances of married life could be challenging at times, and since Dianne had been married for quite some time, it was all she understood. To be single now—at fifty-four? She couldn't conceive of it.

Daniela and her friend went Rollerblading and Dianne had volunteered to pick them up. She invited Henna to tag along, but she didn't want to miss *Gwenology*. Dianne told her daughter she was addicted to the reality TV program, and reminded her that she could DVR it. But Henna and her friends texted each other throughout the episode and she couldn't be a part of the moment-to-moment narrative if she waited a day later to watch it. Of course Dianne remembered what that was like. She dared not miss the latest episode of *Falcon Crest*, *Knots Landing*, *Dynasty*, *Dallas*, and when *Roots*, the miniseries, played for a week, no one could peel her away from the television set. Early in their career, Venice was given a set of seats to a Lakers home game and Dianne, Phoebe and Cordia debated whether they should use the tickets or stay home to see who shot J.R. With bated breath, they waited the entire summer to see if Larry Hagman would be written off the show. The "Who Shot J.R.?" mystery was huge! Should it have been missed when originally aired, the only alternative was a rerun. Back then, program recorders were a luxury. Because they had to make an appearance at a fundraiser near the Fabulous Forum, they opted to head for the Lakers game afterward and miss the season opener of *Dallas*. Half-time was just ending when they arrived. By the time they made it to their seats, it was announced who'd shot J.R. Ewing. A sold-out game of 12,000 basketball fans reacted to the shocker, and the game was delayed by thirty-five seconds.

The road was slippery and curved sharply back and forth; Dianne was paying more attention to her erratic thoughts than she was the dark road. She reached for her ringing cell and said, "Hello. Oh, hi, Phoebe." In a snapshot flash she saw a deer, posing as if to be photographed, in the center of the deserted road. Dianne slammed on the brakes to avoid hitting the deer, but the wet street had her spinning, and she saw life slipping away before her very eyes. The car crashed inside a deep ditch and the airbag discharged into her chest. She attempted to remove the airbag, fuming beneath her breath.

Although faint, Phoebe's voice sounded urgent—yelling out, "Dianne!"

She looked around to get her bearings. The deer, which she'd managed to avoid, had disappeared into the silent night. Even though it wasn't altogether audible, she could hear Phoebe's frantic voice. Dianne couldn't identify her phone in the pitch darkness. She crawled out of the car. Rather flustered, she knew someone would be coming for her shortly. Torrick was manic when it came to security. He had technology installed in her car, Findquest, which alerted the security company when she was in distress. Torrick always knew where Dianne was.

Phoebe didn't know what to do. She heard the sound of a crash; she knew that Dianne must have hit something. She didn't know Torrick's cell phone number, or their home number. She went online to see if they were listed. She dialed the number, although Phoebe had no clue whether it was current. A young voice answered and Phoebe introduced herself. She didn't want to alarm Henna and asked if Torrick was home. When he came on the line, Phoebe exchanged pleasantries before she explained the purpose for the call. Within ten minutes of hanging up with Torrick, he called Phoebe back to inform her that Dianne was all right.

Phoebe fell asleep on the sofa waiting to hear back from Dianne. The following morning, with an intense sun spilling into the guesthouse, she was summoned from a deep sleep. At first she thought it was a dream, but finally she became aware of someone ringing the doorbell persistently, as if they knew she was home and demanded that she answer. Her neck ached; Phoebe needed a pillow when she slept. She came to her feet, tripping over a pair of Uggs at the foot of the sofa. She squinted, and rubbed her eyes. "Okay!" she spoke in an elevated voice.

She looked through the peephole. *Barry?*

When she opened the door, his back was to Phoebe. With a large travel bag slung across his chest, he turned and immediately broke open a sexy, hard-to-resist grin. With a stunning set of even teeth and a full mouth, Phoebe understood why Venetia fell for him and was drawn to his infectious charm. Barry was beautiful, with a hint of veritable masculinity.

"Phoebe," he said, and leaned in to give her a peck on the cheek. She could smell his odor—a mixture of travel and tiredness.

"Barry?"

"It's good to see you. Venetia, she told me you could give me the key to the house."

"She didn't mention you left Libya."

"I was supposed to hook up with her in New York, but Hurricane Sandy hit and I had to reroute. I thought I'd hook up with her here." After entering the cozy guesthouse, he dropped his bag and continued. "I haven't seen my girl in two months."

"Hey, make some coffee. I'll go and freshen up."

He rubbed his day-old stubble. "I could use a cup."

Phoebe checked her cell to see if she'd missed any calls. Once she washed her face and brushed her teeth, she slipped into a pair of jeans and a bulky, stylish sweater. When she returned to the front of the guesthouse, Barry was sitting on the sofa, his eyes glued to his electronic tablet. He reached for a mug and took an audible slurp. She moved toward the kitchen to grab a cup. "It's good you made it home in one piece."

He looked over his shoulder. "Tell me about it. It's intense over there."

"I saw your photo that made the *Times*. Congratulations." Phoebe poured coffee into a ceramic cup and joined Barry in the living area. "You do good work, Barry."

"Coming from you, that's a compliment. You can be hard on a brother."

She laughed. "I don't mean to be."

"Sometimes we need a strong woman to put us back in place."

Very closely, Phoebe studied Barry while he concentrated on whatever it was that had his attention. His crossed leg exposed a boot that looked as if the pair had traveled the world. She liked Barry. She wished that he was the right person for Venetia. Phoebe knew that Venetia was ready to find *the one*. A life partner; the father of her children. She was never the type of girl to go through men like she did styles. She loved, and with every inch of her heart. Barry was the first man Phoebe met that wasn't dubious in nature. Venetia's taste in men worried her. She became a bit more guarded when she got involved with a house flipper who borrowed $25,000 and Venetia never got as much as a one-dollar bill back. Finally, there was Barry. They matched well, and whenever they were together, Phoebe envied how they complemented each other. Their relationship showcased an indisputable bond, which made it all so sad.

"Barry?"

He responded with a low moan, still focused on his tablet.

"I want to ask you something."

"Okay."

"You have my word, I promise you that."

Barry, curious, looked up at Phoebe.

"Venetia is very much in love with you. Do you love her?"

"Do I love her? Yeah, of course." His forehead creased.

"Let me ask this. Is she enough for you?"

"I don't understand."

"Are you straight, Barry?"

Dianne sat awkwardly in the chair. She crossed and uncrossed her legs several times. Based upon her work over the past two decades, the therapist could sense a crisis in the making the moment it walked through the door. Dianne was one of those women caught between her self-worth and the demons that stood in the way of her feeling whole.

"We can sit in silence until you feel ready to talk. And it can be anything you feel you need to share with me. It's your call, Dianne."

A few quiet moments drifted by before Dianne spoke. "People used to ask me, 'what do you do?'"

"What do you mean?"

"I *hated* that line."

"What do you mean *do*, Dianne?"

"It was as shallow as 'what's your sign?' Oh, goodness, how I hated that line, too. So ridiculous!"

"Do you mean what do you do in terms of career…?"

Dianne nodded. "After Venice broke up and when I started working as a buyer, I'd always get the 'since Venice broke up, what do you do' question from strangers. Then one day I noticed the question didn't come up. I equated it to the fact that I was in this circle that knew who I was. But that isn't exactly true. Only recently I noticed that people stopped asking me 'what do you do' around the same time men stopped looking at me. Or at least not in the same way that they used to. It's strange—"

"Why do you suppose people stopped asking you what you did for a living?"

"One day you notice—something changed and you weren't even *aware* you were watching it change." Time—her life—seemed to have passed stealthily without a trace. "I became less interesting. We lean into people that fascinate us. We want to be compensated— we want something from people. Age changes how people deal with you. You can't prepare for getting older. Your self-esteem has to be tip-top not to *feel* the lack of interest people have in you."

"Dianne, what has happened?"

"I almost killed a deer."

"I'm sorry," the therapist said, leaning her elbows to her knees, clasping her fingers together.

"Torrick could be having an affair."

Hearing those words from Dianne didn't bring on a visceral reaction. "Why do you believe this, Dianne?"

A palpable silence played out in the room. Eventually, and with tears in her eyes, Dianne said, "Do you remember my first visit?"

"Yes."

"You asked me if I had forgiven Phoebe. At the time I wasn't sure, and frankly, I'm still not sure." Dianne pulled at a fringe from her silk scarf looped around her neck. Her eyes stayed low. "I doubt that I can ever *forgive* Phoebe. Until I ran into her recently, the only thing that remained of that time in my life was wondering what would have been. If all I get from coming to see you…" Dianne looked into the therapist's eyes "…is coming to terms with my past, then I have done something miraculous. I don't want to be stuck on what could have been."

"We finally have something we can work on—together. I know you want to put whatever you are still clinging to to bed. I assure you, this will make a difference in your life."

"Really?"

"You've spent years letting Venice shape your reality. You're contextualizing."

"I made an attempt to connect with Gregory on Facebook. I couldn't believe I did it. After what I'd done with the personal trainer, here I was spending upwards of an hour trying to connect with a man from thirty years ago. Why did I do it?"

"Why do you think you did it?"

"If I knew, would I have asked you?" Dianne's tone bordered on sharp.

"It's you that needs to answer that question."

"I really don't know the answer. That's why I'm here."

"You are impatient with complexity, Dianne."

"What does that mean?"

"Answer this: Did you find Gregory?"

"Yes."

"So where has that led?"

"Nowhere, yet."

"And if it leads somewhere?"

"I don't know."

"What do you want to get out of this?"

"I figure I'll know it when I feel it."

"And what about Phoebe?"

"Can we put her on hold?"

Discreetly, the therapist looked to the clock over Dianne's shoulder. "We have to leave it for now."

Dianne sat in her car, and she cried. She cried from someplace so deep—she couldn't make sense of this persistent and profound sadness.

CHAPTER 8

The funeral was a little bit of sadness and a little bit of jubilation. Jacqueline found herself breaking down in her room at the Four Seasons, long after wordy goodbyes, long embraces, and one last I'm-so-sorry to Stefan's family. The intense loneliness she experienced was indescribable. She wouldn't be prepared for the days to come, when it would hit her—no more laughing over wine after a long day with him, talking shop over meals Chef had prepared solely for them. One day, unguarded, she would be reminded of some quirky thing she'd do, like call Stefan to tell him about a new recipe she'd tried and failed at miserably, such as the lopsided red velvet cake that Stefan claimed was delicious! Only days before he was hospitalized at Cedars-Sinai, she reminded him that he was the one who knew her weaknesses while everyone whoever met her knew her strengths. That kind of connection was irreplaceable, and even more so harder to *lose.*

What will I do without him? She asked herself that question over a dozen times after leaving the hotel, on the ride to the airport, the flight, and once home, sitting before a burning fire with a glass of Merlot; Jacqueline clung to that question: What will I do without him?

Even though it was near midnight, she called Claire and asked that she make arrangements to go to Denver on her behalf. While she was good at doing business under some of the most extreme circumstances, Jacqueline decided to sit this one out. Claire had been working with the client, and much to Jacqueline's surprise, was amazed how well she'd handled things in her absence. Claire said she was "on it." Before she disconnected the call, her last words to Claire were, "That's why I hired you. And Claire? Impress me."

The following morning, which was a cool, damp Saturday, Jacqueline felt a touch of renewed energy and decided to be productive. For over a week, she'd put her life on hold. She spent so much time away, she hardly inhabited her condo. It was for the first time since moving into the spacious place that she became aware of that detail: that it was no more than somewhere to hang her clothes, sleep, and shower. Most of the time she ate out, or brought something home to eat while she worked. When she first purchased it, she threw spontaneous dinners, an occasional wine tasting, and when Simone, her nephew, was trying to clean himself up, she let him stay for a month. Jacqueline could vaguely recall ever having so much as a conversation with him *in* the condo.

While she washed clothes, she straightened the place up, and over a cup of tea, Jacqueline opened mail, sorted papers, went through unopened e-mail—slightly over 400—which most were forwarded to Claire to "handle." Claire had dropped off a stack of invitations for Jacqueline to respond to. She made a stack of Decline and RSVP. Since there were several errands she needed to run, she would drop the invitations at the office so Claire would handle them first thing Monday, upon her return from Denver.

It was late afternoon, and Jacqueline wasn't surprised to find no one in on her end of the floor, although it was typical of someone to be in the office on a Saturday, even on a Sunday. Before she got absorbed in work that needed her attention, she decided to stop in Stefan's office. It was untouched. His sons would arrange to collect all of his personal belongings, as well as take care of his waterfront home and other affairs. Unlike Michael's, Stefan's office was small, but stunning art on loan from a nearby gallery hung on two walls, and his good taste highlighted every corner, with artifacts and knickknacks he'd collected from places he'd traveled. Stefan was a world traveler; it then occurred to Jacqueline that she'd have no one to vacation with. She reached for a framed photograph of Stefan with his two sons on holiday on Martha's Vineyard. He looked exceptionally happy bordered with the two men he loved unconditionally. Sadness stole her breath, and with an unsteady hand, Jacqueline replaced the photograph. She left his office to break the spell.

In the garage, Jacqueline sat in her car for quite some time. She'd kept her phone off for days and needed to go through the numerous messages; her voicemail was full. At the time, clients seemed so unimportant. Besides, Claire managed to keep her abreast of what was going on. Jacqueline was confident, that in due time, she would fall back into the pattern which she'd painstakingly choreographed over the past two decades.

When she pulled out of the garage into the wet streets, it had turned dark. Impulsively, she decided to drop in on Dianne. By the time she reached the neighborhood—with handsome homes, bright orange pumpkins reminding her of the time of year, its charm and narrow, zigzag streets leading to the lake—she was on the verge of crying. There was no reason she could conjure up. Of course she was still sad about Stefan's death, but she wasn't exactly sure that was the cause. She pulled onto Dianne's street. There was a faint band of light coming from the house. Jacqueline checked the time; it wasn't late. She didn't see a car parked in the circular driveway, although Dianne typically parked in the garage. Jacqueline wasn't sure about Torrick, though.

She pulled to the curb. The street was quiet, and there was a feeling of serenity whenever she came to this privileged community. Each street was peaceful. No sooner than she made it to the front door, it began to pour down rain. She cursed beneath her breath, about her new boots and her hair. She rang the bell; Daniela answered the door. She was tall for her age, and her beauty was a fusion of her parents: Dianne's high cheekbones, her father's sensuous mouth.

"Jacqueline!" Daniela grinned and embraced her play-aunt with open and genuine affection.

"Look at you. I haven't seen you in ages. You've grown—what, an inch?"

With a cute giggle, Daniela took Jacqueline by the hand and said, "Mama's on me about not going to church every Sunday."

They walked into the living room which Dianne decorated herself. Warm and soothing colors highlighted the high-ceilinged room with a mixture of chic and traditional. "So where's the lady of the house?"

They each took a seat. Daniela folded her legs and held her bare feet with her hands and leaned forward. Jacqueline took a snowflake-colored armchair and crossed her legs.

"I love your boots. Where'd you get them? Oh, my God," Daniela said. "Those are like so-*so* awesome. Jacqueline, you have cool taste."

"Thank you."

"Mama's out…with…I'm not sure. And Daddy. Naturally, he's working."

Daniela made Jacqueline laugh. She needed to laugh. And maybe the gods had it all worked out for her: that she should choose to come to see Dianne on the spur-of-the-moment and without calling ahead, so that she could spend a spontaneous, fun-loving moment with Dianne's heartbreakingly gorgeous daughter, Daniela.

There were occasions, although not many, in which Jacqueline thought hard about having children. Stefan had asked her not one month ago if she regretted not having met someone and settled down. Jacqueline laughed heartily. "And having kids, you mean?"

Henna came downstairs to make a bag of microwave popcorn and heard Jacqueline and Daniela talking in the living room. The identical greeting she shared with Daniela, Jacqueline duplicated with Henna. The three of them talked for a good forty-five minutes: about clothes and *Gwenology*, and Jacqueline promised she'd get tickets for the group, Bomb, whenever they came to town. Daniela called Dianne twice on her cell, but it went straight to voicemail. After an hour, Jacqueline chose to leave.

She smiled for two blocks. The girls had lightened her load. She enjoyed gossiping about trivial things, and giving Henna advice about a girl whom she had been having trouble with at school. Daniela said she'd start following Jacqueline on Twitter. Jacqueline absolutely loved spending time with the James girls.

No sooner than she pulled onto the main road leading out of the Jameses' neighborhood, her car began to slow, and then the engine died. Jacqueline managed to get closer to the side of the road to avoid blocking the line of traffic. She turned the engine over twice but no luck. Ultimately, she discovered that the tank was on empty. Jacqueline turned on her phone and just the idea of seeing all the calls and texts she had to get through, she felt a sudden wave of anxiety. Before she knew it, she began to sob so violently she shook. The grief and stress and fear overtook her. Jacqueline couldn't stop the tears, even when she tried. They kept coming, and coming.

Upon exiting the freeway, Torrick pulled over and called Dianne. Her recorded voice came through the wireless which meant her phone was turned off. It had been a few days since they'd had a chance to hold a conversation. Even then, it was about the girls, or something to do with the house or their schedules. He couldn't imagine what it would be like if they were having money issues. They were walking the wire right now, so that, including other distressing factors, could be an irrevocable strain on their marriage.

Daniela texted her father and requested that he bring home her favorite Greek yogurt, so he decided to stop at the bodega near the house instead of the out-of-the-way supermarket. When he reached for the door handle, he noticed a sign posted alerting customers that the market was closed due to flooding. Aggravated, Torrick jumped back into the SUV, and the inconvenience escalated his frustration, which provoked a bad mood. Distracted, he U-turned at the roundabout. He decided since he'd have to go to another store, he might as well fill his tank; it was on the way. He turned onto the main street. Halfway down, a Crossfire with emergency blinkers blocked a portion of the road. Torrick was already on the verge of cursing someone out, and a car blocking most of the road got him riled up. "What the..." he said beneath his breath, driving around the black automobile. He glimpsed in his rearview mirror and mumbled beneath his breath about his being unreasonably worked up. He had his share of stalled cars, especially in college. Despite his frame of mind, his good nature kicked in and Torrick U-turned, feeling obliged to check out what was what.

He rushed up to the driver's window and knocked. He made out the silhouette of a female figure, but she wasn't responding. He knocked with a bit more oomph, but naught. He couldn't determine if the person was injured. Torrick brushed the sleeve of his jacket against the window to clear off the raindrops. He peeked inside. The woman sat in the driver's seat, her head buried in the palms of her hands.

"Hello! *Hello!*" Torrick called out.

The window finally rolled halfway down. "Torrick?" Jacqueline said.

"Jacqueline?" Torrick hadn't recognized her car. "Are you all right?" he yelled over the rhythm of the heavy rain.

She let the window down all the way. "I ran out of gas."

Jacqueline's makeup was smeared under her eyes, and her cheeks were streaked with dried tears. "Are you *all right?*" he asked, concerned more for her state of mind. He could see that she wasn't physically harmed in any way.

She nodded, and let out a painful cry. "Yes," she fibbed.

"Have you called anyone?"

"Yes, I mean…"

"Let me push you out of the road. Okay?"

Mechanically, Jacqueline acquiesced.

Once the car was on the side of the main road, Torrick knocked on the passenger window and he heard a sound that indicated Jacqueline had unlocked the door. He jumped inside, his designer jacket, something Dianne picked out, was soaked.

"What's wrong, Jacqueline?"

She attempted to smile away the grimace on her face. She wiped her tearstained face. Jacqueline knew she must have looked one hot mess. She peered at her mobile device in her hands.

"Jacqueline?" Torrick reached over to her. His touch was gentle. "Jacqueline…" He let out a harsh sigh and wasn't exactly sure what to do. "Listen, I'll take you home. I can arrange to have your car taken care of." He pulled his cell from his pocket and held a one-minute call.

Once they were on the road, heading to Jacqueline's on the other side of town, Torrick wanted to get to the bottom of what was going on. Jacqueline was the kind of woman most men needed to use their top skills in order to deal with her. There were some who would claim her high maintenance, although Torrick never quite understood the meaning behind that terminology. Actually, as far as he was concerned, she wasn't the *needy* type when it came to men. Jacqueline was one of those women whose appearance implied success. She had style, looks, finesse. These attributes could overawe some men. Seeing her in the state in which he found her, Torrick wasn't sure what to say to Jacqueline. Although they were friends, their relationship wasn't exactly personal. From time to time they threw each other business. She was Dianne's friend more so than his.

"Turn here," Jacqueline said. The ride had been exceptionally quiet during the entire twenty minutes it took to get to the Denny Triangle, with pricy condominiums and exclusive high-rise apartments that dominated the bay-viewed community. "It's on the left," she said. "Parking's okay on the street at this hour."

In the elevator, neither spoke. Torrick wasn't even sure why he was going up with her. He merely wanted to help her out, as Dianne's close friend. And she was uncharacteristically fragile, so he didn't want to come across anxious to get on with his own state of affairs. It could be why he'd said casually while they were still in his SUV, "Are you okay? Do you want me to come up?" After all, she'd made a reference to "parking." Torrick took that as a suggestion.

At the door, Torrick cased the place—training, really. Anytime he went somewhere new, or wasn't familiar with his surroundings, he naturally gave the place a cursory looking over. When he turned to find Jacqueline trying to slide the key into the lock, her hand unsteady as she sniffed her runny nose, he said, "Hey, let me help you out with that."

The condo was something he would expect Jacqueline to live in. Not warm and comfy, but there was a touch of a lived-in feeling. A classy setup, Jacqueline added personal touches here and there. A sequence of photographs of family; a few friends with a mass of people in the background like it was New Year's Eve in Times Square, hugging with smiles so wide they looked extraordinarily happy; and a few photos, presumably clients, bordered in stylishly frames. One gigantic work of art took up a full wall. The view was priceless.

"Have a seat," she said. "There's liquor over there." She tossed a hand out, not really indicating exactly where. "Pinot on the counter, or a Chardonnay in the fridge. I need to clean myself up." She disappeared into another part of the condo divided by walls and a lengthy hallway. Torrick studied the room nonchalantly, not really seeing exactly where the "liquor" could be. He didn't exactly feel right in opening up cabinets and whatnot. He took a seat. His cell buzzed. Torrick identified the caller and answered, "Yeah? Good. No, I'm here, upstairs. Do me a favor? Park it on the street and leave the key where you found it. Yeah, sure. Thanks, man."

A few minutes later, Jacqueline reappeared in the front of the condo, refreshed. Her hair was pulled back. Torrick had only seen Jacqueline's hair loose. She wore no makeup, and her face looked plain but natural. In a pair of fitted jeans and an oversized designer sweatshirt, she was barefooted, her exposed toenails polished in a charcoal-gray. Jacqueline traversed the room. "Did you find anything to drink?"

"I didn't look actually." Torrick crossed his legs and pressed his back deep into the sprawling sofa.

"Would you like anything? I have a bottle of white already open. Do you like wine?"

"Yeah, sure. A glass would be okay."

Jacqueline attempted to start a fire, but she couldn't get it to burn. Torrick knew she was on pins and needles, and he didn't want the slightest thing to produce another set of tears. He didn't know what to do with that. The drive to her place was awkward enough. "What am I doing wrong?" she said, feeling aberrantly insecure.

"I got it. Let me," he said. "How about that glass of wine?" He winked, hoping it would sooth her nerves a bit. He guessed she wasn't used to being out of control. He had known of several men she dated, but had not been serious with any one of them, according to Dianne, so Torrick drew the conclusion that Jacqueline was exceptionally independent.

She left the room and he could hear her moving around in the kitchen—glasses clicking, the closing of a refrigerator door, opening and closing of drawers. He managed to get the fire burning and resumed his position on the sofa. He checked his cell; his daughter was inquiring when he'd be home. He shot back a text saying he was delayed. When Jacqueline returned, she had two glasses of wine in oversized, paper-thin crystal. Wordlessly, she put his on a large table with table books stacked neatly on opposite corners, and she went to a chaise closer to the fireplace. Curled up, she looked so vulnerable without her makeup and with her long, silky black hair pulled away from her face and tied up. She held the goblet with both hands, staring into the fire.

He had lost track of time and he needed to be heading home. Torrick decided to feel his way through it. He didn't want to leave until he knew Jacqueline was all right. Much to his chagrin, he was a little more curious than he wanted to be, and attempted to exercise tender loving care, as he did with Dianne and the girls when they were upset. "So, Jacqueline," he started. "What's going on?"

She looked up from her glass and into his rum-colored eyes. She felt exposed and took a sip of her wine to avoid eye contact. She resumed staring into the glass. "My friend Stefan, one of the founders of Media Capital—he died last week."

"Yes, I read about that." He didn't finish his thoughts, and wondered if her behavior over the past hour had everything to do with that, or simply added to something she was already up against.

She looked straight at Torrick. She trusted that her running into him was a saving grace. He was a calm personality, and a standup guy. She could lean, gently, on his shoulder in the generic sense. At least at that moment. "He was a very dear friend."

The question was out before Torrick realized he'd voiced it: "Was he more than a friend?"

Jacqueline's lips curved subtly. "Once. Just once. We met at Columbia. I was a much different person back then. Shy and quiet. We had the same major and shared two classes. He liked me, but…It wasn't so much a sexual interest. He was a white guy from a family with money and he hung around white boys who also came from money. He was in a fraternity.

"We were friendly but not close. We'd go to a party or out for beers, that sort of thing. It was casual." Jacqueline took a gulp of her wine as if it would give her what she needed to hold it together. "One night, in my sophomore year, I was walking across campus from a study group. It was late; after midnight. Several white guys were walking toward me and made some derogatory remarks about me. There's a scene in *Mahogany* and Diana Ross's character is walking home in the dark and a stranger—I think he was an addict—starts to follow her. She's scared to death, but confronts the stranger with false bravado and says something like, 'What do you want?', trying to throw off a 'street cred' attitude. The addict or whatever feels intimidated and runs away. So I tried that. I said, 'What the fuck do you want?' But it didn't work." Jacqueline took a sip or two of wine. "They raped me." She said it as nonchalantly as she would hand out a business card.

Torrick wasn't sure what was coming. How could he? His entire body reacted. "What?"

"It was one guy who raped me, but his friends held me down."

"Were they…? Did they pay for what they did to you?"

"Yeah." She nodded. "I guess it's a God thing: for every bad thing that happens, God will do what is necessary to make something very good happen that outweighs that injustice. If you have what it takes to make sense of how God works. Stefan is—was a remarkable man. Without him, I'm not sure what my career would look like.

"The rape brought us—we grew quite close. I guess, in a way, I used him to find my way back to trusting men again.

"I recognized one of the guys holding me down. I'd seen him hanging out with Stefan. Stefan testified at the trial. Oh, it was in the news for weeks—the *Post*, the *Times*. These were boys who grew up spending their summers on the Cape or in the Hamptons; their fathers were on Wall Street; they had influence. Anyway, Stefan and I became very good friends after that. We were tight.

"About two years after his marriage fell apart, we grew really close, and…we realized that we were better at being friends." Jacqueline began to daydream into her glass, oblivious to the sound of her own voice. "I think we should think hard and long before we take a genuinely good friendship and turn it into something else. Sex between friends is always risky. Most friends-turned-lovers don't end up like *When Harry Met Sally*.

"I really depended on Stefan. In fact, it wasn't until he was diagnosed did I fully understand how much he meant to me. And two weeks ago, when it became clear he wasn't going to make it, I understood something I may have understood, but in a non-attached way."

Torrick leaned forward even more, holding his wineglass with both hands. He'd only taken a sip or two; he was preoccupied. "You would be alone without him."

Jacqueline shot a look at Torrick. Only an hour or so ago, she was sitting in her car holding her cell phone in her hand, not sure whom to call to help her. Now sheltered in her home, she sat comfortably before a burning fire across from a contentedly married, quite attractive man. The last man to sit at the corner of that sofa was Daniel.

They'd gone to see a film; afterward, she invited him in. They'd shared leftover peach cobbler and talked. Both of them had entertained his staying overnight but not once verbalized the idea. Daniel didn't stay. How could Jacqueline pull her dear friend's husband into her mess? It was selfish. It wasn't fair.

"You know me better than I'd like you to know me, Torrick. That's right. It hit me hard that I had taken Stefan for granted."

He butted in. "We all do that. It's never intentional. It happens the way a lot of things happen."

"I get that. But some part of me is beginning to look into my life in a new way.

"Do you remember when we last saw each other? At the Blue Bar?"

"Sure."

"Thank you by the way for the good job your people did for Anthony Perez." Torrick nodded. "You asked me if I had any regrets. Do you remember that?"

"Vaguely—"

"I was honest with you that day. Where I stood *that day*, I was completely honest with you."

"And now?"

"Some part of me is not the same. Whether it's because of Stefan, or he attributes to that sudden realization that's based on a culmination of things, I don't know.

"Oh, and when you rescued me? I had just left your home. I

spent almost an hour with your beautiful girls. They are so sweet, Torrick. You and Dianne should be proud."

With slight hesitation, he said, "And we are. Very much so." He crossed his leg and asked, "Was Dianne not home?"

"No," Jacqueline said, shaking her head. "In fact, Daniela called her twice trying to reach her to find out when she would be coming home."

"And…Did she ever call home?"

With a shrug, Jacqueline said, "Not while I was there."

A few subdued moments shifted the energy in the room. Jacqueline didn't feel better necessarily, but she felt something else; something she didn't feel an hour ago. It was because Torrick was there. He respected her enough not to probe, and yet inquired enough to show heartfelt concern for her state of mind.

"Is everything okay? I've tried to reach out to Dianne a few times over the past few weeks, but with no luck. It's not unusual, but…"

"She's…" Torrick couldn't find a way to be subtle, and he didn't want to disclose details of their marriage.

Jacqueline tilted forward. "Torrick? Torrick, is something going on with Dianne?… You don't have to give me details, but is she okay?"

"She's just bumped into a wall. You know how that goes."

"Of course I do. But what are you saying exactly?"

Jacqueline was so caught up in the crap dumped on her life in the past few weeks it never once occurred to her that Dianne might have needed a lifeline. But now that she was put in a position to think it through, she realized that the girls were naturally polite, but something did feel off. Then, when Jacqueline's car ran out of gas, her mind, her feelings, took a different direction and she had forgotten she was at Dianne's and why she was even on that side of town.

"Torrick?"

He finished off his wine and came to his feet. "I should be getting home." He pretended to care about the time, glancing fleetingly at his wristwatch. "I told Daniela I'd stop to get her some Greek yogurt. She's probably caught up in her social media world, she might have forgotten all about the yogurt. It's when they *need* you that they call."

Jacqueline picked up on his levity; it was as fake as a three-dollar bill. She rushed to her feet and hugged herself. "Thank you for bringing me home."

"By the way. My guy brought your car home. It's parked outside, near the entrance. The key is under the seat."

With crossed arms, Jacqueline said, "How much do I owe...?"

"He filled the tank and it's all good."

She walked him to the door.

He stood outside the door and made an off-handed comment about Jacqueline paying more attention to her gas gauge. Facetiously, she made a cross against her chest with a finger and promised that she would.

He headed for the elevator but going in the wrong direction. Jacqueline said, "Elevator's that way."

Standing in front of her, Torrick took notice that Jacqueline was calmer, more relaxed. Something changed; Jacqueline was right about that. She might not be the Jacqueline he once knew, but she wasn't the same Jacqueline he rescued ninety minutes ago.

"It's good to see you smiling again," he said.

She laughed warily. "Promise not to tell anyone how you found me. My reputation as a cold bitch could be ruined. I don't think I could handle some tweet about my diva-ness being feigned."

He reached for her hand and squeezed it. "It's our little secret." Torrick grinned.

She held his hand longer than she should have, and when she released it, Torrick reached down and caressed her lips with his, gingerly. Jacqueline slipped her tongue in his warm, saline-tasting mouth, and they stood in her doorway and kissed long and hard and with an intense, concentrated hunger.

The early bright sky poured into the guesthouse, and the faint sun that caressed Phoebe's face alerted her to the morning hour. While she lay in bed, mentally forcing herself to get up, she felt lazy and wasn't particularly in the mood for a house filled with mostly female energy. She didn't do well at mingling with women. Probably because she wasn't the type to sit around with women and talk about shallow things that women routinely discussed. So often when she was encircled with women, she engaged in conversations about clothes, other women in judgmental tones, celebrities, and male-bashing. Phoebe often felt left out in conversations. She learned that women were careless with details and shared your personal business, consciously or involuntarily.

While dating a former ballplayer, they'd had a heated argument which became physical. He'd left bruises that took weeks to heal, and in sharing it with a friend, the information made its way in an online gossip magazine. Phoebe had only shared the altercation with one person. Those details were shared in confidence and should never have been made public. From her own personal experience, she'd learned that women could talk too much.

Her cell rang, and she reached for it blindly. "Hello," she said, still attempting to wake up. "Gregory?" Phoebe raised her torso, resting weight on one elbow. "How did you get this number?" She pushed her hair away from her face and picked at sleep in the corners of her eyes. "Gregory…Look, I don't under—" Her eyes darted to the pocketwatch-styled clock on the bedside table. She listened for two minutes. "Can we talk about this later? No, no… I'm not putting you off. It's…I don't understand why you'd be calling me with this." She listened for quite a while. "Can I call you back, Gregory? I'll see Dianne today. I'm living here. It's a long story…" She sighed, and after a few moments of listening to Gregory, she laughed. "You haven't changed a bit, have you? I can call you at this number?" When she disconnected the call, she stared at the phone mindlessly until it rang. Venetia's name appeared on the screen. "Hey! I was just about to crawl out of bed before I got a call. Give me about fifteen."

After she freshened up, Phoebe trotted to the house. When she entered, the kitchen smelled of fresh-brewed coffee. Phoebe poured herself a cup and leaned against the counter.

Venetia entered the kitchen. "Everyone RSVP'd. You did fabulous, Phoebe. The invites, the arrangements for the menu, even the flowers—great choice! Everything is going to be fabulous. My client will be pleased."

Phoebe watched Venetia moving about the kitchen. She hummed while she occasionally glanced at her electronic tablet so as to stay abreast of the online life. Observing Venetia, Phoebe couldn't help but be reminded of her conversation with Barry.

Just by the look on his face, Phoebe understood that Barry never saw such a question about his sexuality coming. Especially not from her.

"Why do you ask such a question?" was how he'd responded.

Phoebe said, "I've had a sexual encounter with a man who was— is—bisexual. A straight woman—an emotionally healthy straight woman—doesn't want to share her man with another man. After that experience—I can't explain it. But you question whether he's on the downlow, is he bi."

"Well…" Barry laughed it off. "Reasonable people don't ask stuff like that."

"Reasonable people?"

"I know you've never approved of me, Phoebe."

"Why would you not just say no?"

"What's it to you?"

"Venetia loves you."

"And I love her, too."

"Okay," said Phoebe. The conversation would get her nowhere, and she only wished she'd not brought it up. "This is all I'll say about this and I'm done. If you love her, you'll find a way to end this. If you cannot be *monogamous*—walk away. Find a way to end it, but walk away."

"Hey!" Venetia snapped her fingers in Phoebe's face. "Where did you go? You haven't heard a word I was saying."

Feeling awkward, Phoebe said, "Sorry. What *were* you saying?"

"What did you not hear so I won't repeat myself?" Venetia was in a good mood. "Okay, did you hear me when I said Dianne called me?"

Aghast, Phoebe said, "When?"

"Yesterday."

"She didn't cancel?"

Venetia was cleaning plates with a dishcloth. "The opposite. She's excited to see me. I mean, really? We're technically neighbors and I haven't seen her since we had the tree planting for Mother in the backyard. That was, let me see, six, seven years ago. But I don't hold a grudge. I was graceful, and I am looking forward to seeing her."

"Did I ever tell you what really happened between your mother, Dianne and me?"

Venetia looked over her shoulder. "Well, as I understand it, what *really* happened was a to-the-grave secret."

"Gregory—"

"Oh, that name rings a bell. He was in Mother's diary." She bent over to reach for a plate in the dishwasher.

"He was a guy that Dianne fell very hard for."

"Oh, yes. Right! Gregory. It's coming back."

"He called me this morning."

With a strange look on her face, Venetia stopped wiping a plate and placed her hand on her hipbone. "You two stayed in touch?"

"No," Phoebe said, almost too adamantly. "I was as shocked as you appear to be."

"Hold up. What's the story? I'm missing some details."

"Venice opened at the Roxy and afterward, we all jumped in this limo and headed for Pink's. Dianne and Cordia had the munchies. You know Pink's; there's always a long line. We were standing on line and Gregory started hitting on Dianne. A week later, she was so in love she was missing rehearsals and…She loved—it was fevered obsession she had for this man." Phoebe's mind, momentarily, left the room, but Venetia cleared her throat which snapped her back into the present. "I doubt Cordia would have written it in her diary, but there was this big fight. Cordia had the voice, I had the talent to write decent lyrics to songs we were singing because I dabbled in poetry back then; and Dianne, with those cheekbones of hers, was very attractive and could dance her butt off. We all could dance, but Dianne could *dance*. Plus she designed all of our outfits. She—Dianne and me—could carry a tune, but unlike today, back then…a solo career without a *real* voice…The big fight led to her quitting Venice…"

"It was always a touchy subject, but something bad happened, didn't it? Was Gregory in the center of it?"

The doorbell rang and Venetia looked at the kitchen clock.

"The caterer. I asked that she come an hour early. Do you mind? I'll hurry and finish up the dishes so we can start putting them out. Oh, and Phoebe? Dianne volunteered to let Daniela come and help out. Is it possible you go and get her instead of having Dianne bring her over here? It's not even ten minutes there and back."

"I'd be delighted."

When Daniela opened the door, it was as if Phoebe was looking at the teenaged version of Dianne. Daniela's skin tone—a gentle sepia—was a tinge darker than Dianne's, her hair thicker, and she was tall with an androgynous quality. It was striking to see how Dianne's oldest was morphing into a spitting image of herself.

"Good morning," Phoebe greeted Daniela.

"Hi." Her mouth exposed healthy teeth, and within seconds, she fell into a bashfulness Phoebe didn't perceive as authentic. She glided her hands in the back pockets of her in-fashion jeans. "I'll grab my jacket. Come on in."

When Phoebe stepped into the house, some part of her felt relieved, even vindicated. The warm home was large, full, and rich with the scent of love. It was discernible, as if it were burning incense caressing the air. The photographs that lined the walls exhibited a family that vacationed together, enjoyed being around each other, and displayed their love openly. Phoebe saw it at once—taking up a full wall was a painting of Venice. Nearby on a table she spotted five statues: three Grammys, two American Music Awards. Like Dianne, Venetia had the same memorabilia in her home, and Phoebe's was locked securely in her L.A. storage. Torrick had provided Dianne with everything she needed and then some.

"Mama's on the phone with Grandma. She'll be down in a minute. Can I get you something to drink?"

"I'm good. Thank you, Daniela."

Although her face was friendly, Daniela's eyes stayed on Phoebe longer than was comfortable, and with that feigned bashfulness, she left to go grab her jacket. Phoebe took a seat in an oversized chair and leaned forward, embracing the warmth of a burning fire. She looked at her cell to note the time. She stared into the fading fire. Phoebe decided the Jameses had a good life. She had been blessed herself—excitement and complexity added meaning to her life's journey. But as she sat in Dianne's home, with love and comfort and the blessedness of having more than enough, a hint of envy brushed against her heart. She wasn't disappointed with not having raised children; and although she had been proposed to, Phoebe never once looked back with regret because she chose not to marry. Dianne lived inside a kind of sanctuary, and married a man who clearly loved her, and children she should feel comfortable in bragging about. One needn't spend a lot of time with Daniela to observe how well-raised she was. It wasn't something even the cleverest fifteen-year-old could fake.

"Phoebe!" Dianne called out. "Oh, there you are." Phoebe came to her feet and Dianne greeted her in that back-in-the-day way she had greeted her when they first ran into each other—air kisses. So much had come between them and their individual lives had been confronted with the depth and richness of experiences; yet and still, Dianne treated Phoebe as if they had picked up where they'd left off. "Daniela—I heard her talking; she must be talking to…" Dianne whispered, "this boy." She sat in the matching chair and crossed her legs. "He lives in L.A. She has been begging me to let her go there for Christmas break. I'm not sure. Torrick's mom plans to come and…Wait, but this is the kicker: she's trying to talk me into talking Torrick into letting her get a tattoo."

"Girls her age—it's their version of our double-pierced ears."

"I'm so glad I didn't have to meet men on something like Match or hook up with boys via text."

"Even as a single woman, I can't do the Match thing."

"I've decided to let her go to L.A. to meet him."

"They've never *met?*"

"He's a *friend.*"

"Is Torrick home?"

"He'd have stayed home if he knew you were coming to pick up Daniela. Before I forget, I was going to ask if you'd like to come over for Thanksgiving. We have open house. You might meet someone," Dianne half-teased.

"Thanksgiving? Yeah, sure."

"When I was Daniela's age, I had this fantasy in my head about how my life was going to be, with my Afro-wearing self and my Jackson 5 posters hanging on the wall. And don't forget Royal Secret. Loved that perfume."

"Mine was Chanel No. 5. Who didn't have fantasies?"

"I let *Right On!* magazine misguide me."

Phoebe laughed appropriately. "By the way…I got a call this morning." Phoebe dreaded going there, but she needed to get it over with. "From Gregory."

It was impossible for her to conceal being dumbfounded, but Dianne recovered swiftly by saying, "Gregory?" as if she didn't even know a Gregory—past or present.

"He said that you were trying to—what's the lingo?—friend him."

Dianne grabbed her knees with her hands and held them, her feet a few inches off the floor. "But why would he call you? Did you run into him while you were living in San Francisco?"

"No, but he managed to find me. I didn't really believe him when he said how he got my number, but…"

"I'm ready!" Daniela wore a cute cut-above-the-knee flare coat with her new iPhone in tow. "I figured you guys would want to chat, but Venetia's probably waiting on us."

"You're right. There's a lot to do. Dianne." Phoebe looked in her direction. "We'll see you at the brunch?"

Dianne stood, and with a slight brush of her hand, removed strands of hair from her face. "I'm so excited to finally see Venetia again."

After she walked them to Phoebe's car, Dianne went back into the house. When she closed the door and leaned against it, she felt a swell of emotions and covered her face in shame. *I can't believe Gregory called Phoebe!*

"I'm not too early, am I?" a young man said with dark good looks. He stood at the door, a woman next to him, dressed like a European.

"Nigel?"

"Yes." He entered the foyer. "And this is a friend of mine, Philipa Jerrod."

After handshakes, Philipa said, "Phoebe, is it possible for us to chat? I'm an author, and I'm working on a book…"

"Check out her blog," Nigel butted in.

"Why would you need to talk to me?"

"It's a book on past musicians. The book is focusing on the '70s and '80s. We can look back at music videos and cringe at the big hair and obnoxious shoulder pads…The music—let's say it was at least authentic."

"I agree with that."

Nigel interjected, "Philipa's father is—was Bradford Jerrod."

"They used to call him the white Al Jarreau."

Philipa laughed at the compliment lightheartedly. "They did." She flipped her bouncy, weed-blonde-colored curls off her shoulder. "I understand Dianne's also coming. It would be good to get together with both of you."

"The book is titled *Where They Are Now*," said Nigel. "I've read the introduction. It's going to be a fabulous read."

"The subtitle is *50 Songs and 50 Musicians that Influenced a Generation*."

"I'll think it over. By the way, Nigel. I enjoyed your book."

"Thank you."

"Look, why don't I take you in, and Venetia can give you the rundown on…"

The doorbell interrupted Phoebe.

"Do your thing. Philipa and I can find our way. I know the house."

Daniel greeted Phoebe when she opened the door.

"Hello," he said, holding a bottle of champagne. His look suggested he was unprepared for Phoebe welcoming him at the door.

"Hi." She herself bamboozled. "Are you…I don't recall your name on the guest list." He could know Venetia and she did a verbal invite, and thus there would be no RSVP.

"Jacqueline Daye invited me. Has she arrived yet?"

"Uhhh, no. But please, come in."

"Do you…live here?" Daniel asked.

"I'm staying in the guesthouse."

"I see."

Daniel was a man she met and talked to for all of ten minutes at the Blue Bar while she waited for Dianne to arrive. She hadn't anticipated hearing from him when he said he'd call her, and the fact that he hadn't called, her might explain why Daniel's body language came across as though he'd been caught red-handed.

The doorbell rang and she directed Daniel to go straight through.

"Phyllis!" Jacqueline said when Phoebe opened the door.

"My name is *Phoebe*."

"Really? And all this time I was calling you Phyllis. You're no longer with Media Cap, are you? Your café au laits were superb. You didn't learn that skill in America."

"Thank you." She allowed Jacqueline room to enter.

They walked through the front of the house side-by-side. Jacqueline said, "I love Venetia's home. It's...smart. European. That's the same painting at Dianne's!" She stood in the middle of the living room floor, staring up at the portrait of Venice. All the Venice and Cordia Street hits, framed records in the color gold, hung all over the room. Jacqueline's eyes became fixed on a photograph in stunning framework nearby. She walked over to the framed picture, and three young women in their early twenties were leaning on a sports car, posing flirtatiously at the camera lens. Jacqueline picked up the picture frame. The photo's coloring had faded; the clothes and hairstyles dating back several decades. "Wait!" Jacqueline turned to Phoebe. "*You* were in Venice! Phoebe! Phoebe Pleas."

"Hmmm, yes. Oh, and Daniel's here."

Out of habit, Jacqueline looked at her watch. "I'm not late, am I?"

"No," said Phoebe.

"You look smart, Dad."

Joseph felt stupid in the clothes his son picked out for him. Everyone and anyone would see right through him—this wasn't who he was. This get-up his son had him wearing was too jazzy, *too* young for a man his age.

"I don't know if I can sit through an hour with these clothes on," Joseph complained.

"You really are uncomfortable, aren't you?"

"What did I just tell you, Cornell?"

"Dad! Yo, you look hip. This is the problem: you act older than you are. What is it they say? Fifty's the new forty? The jacket complements your…physique."

"You mean it hides some of my large middle; that's what you mean."

"I didn't say that, but okay. Okay! If you're that uncomfortable, go ahead, change clothes. I'm not sure that chick you want to impress is going to dig you with the clothes you were wearing in the *last* century."

"Clothes *do not* make the man. And if a woman judges a man based on things like that—how he dresses—that's not a woman I want to know."

Cornell knew he wasn't going to talk his father down. He reached for his bottled water and finished it off. "This chick you—"

"I doubt she's a *chick*. Venetia wouldn't introduce me to a *chick*."

"Hey, my bad."

"You'd have to be shallow to care about what a man wears."

"You need to chillax." Cornell watched his father tugging at the jacket. "Okay, all right. Let's go upstairs and try to find something you believe is more suitable."

"Wait! Wait, Cornell."

He turned to look at his father and shrugged. "What?"

"I'll wear this. I can handle it for a few hours."

With a crocked grin, Cornell said, "Yeah, now you're talking."

Joseph decided the walk to Venetia's would do him good. The Street house was perched on a steep slope. He wasn't even half-way up the hill and he was winded.

When he rang the doorbell, he waited only long enough to take notice of the plump pumpkins strategically positioned along the stairway, and the gigantic stunning reef hanging on the door. When the door opened, there she was. That beautiful, classy lady Joseph couldn't get out of his mind. *This has to be Venetia's godmother, the woman she wanted me to meet.*

Caught short, Phoebe said, "Hello."

"How's it going?"

"Are you a guest?" *Phoebe, that was rude!*

"Yeah, for the, what's it called—book brunch."

Phoebe couldn't conjure up the man's name. There would have been no way for her to know that he would be a guest.

"Come on in."

Joseph followed behind her, and he took in the feminine smell of this woman. He liked a prodigious butt, but Phoebe's hips and backside still turned him on. She walked with confidence, and every step suggested she was making a statement. Nothing about her was modest, and perhaps it was the only thing that Joseph found off-putting. There was this intense independence about her, and Joseph himself was a bit insecure, especially around independent women. Hence, her autonomy struck him as too strong for his blood.

When they entered the room, there were a number of people standing around—some sitting, talking and laughing and drinking and nibbling on fancy food.

"The reading will be starting in ten minutes. Help yourself to ice tea, mimosa…"

"Mimosa? That's alcoholic, right?"

"Champagne and orange juice."

"I don't drink alcohol."

"Try the kale smoothie. Delicious!" Phoebe walked away before Joseph could respond.

He mingled about, all the while checking Phoebe out while she worked the room. He hadn't spotted Venetia. When Joseph reached for a bottle of water, he thought about how much the clothes cost him. He wanted to make a lasting impression on the woman Venetia had in mind for him to meet. If it turned out to be Phoebe, his new look didn't get even a reaction—not one iota—out of her.

Dianne must have changed clothes six times. Nothing looked right, or it fit too this or it fit too that. It's not as though she gained or lost one pound. Her weight was stable after both pregnancies. And the personal trainer—who was the only other man who'd seen her naked in years with the exception of a physician—thought she looked good, as he put it, "For someone my mother's age." Once she decided on something casual, something that wasn't over the top, her cell rang.

"Where are you?" a familiar voice greeted her.

"Jacqueline! I'm on my way. We need to go shopping. I'm like so tired of my clothes. Based on Daniela, I could use some of your tips. She thinks you're the fashionista of the year."

"We'll talk when you get here. Hurry!"

"I'm walking out the door."

In the car, Dianne checked her makeup in the visor mirror. "Okay," she said, taking a deep breath. "You can do this." She reached inside her purse and opened a bottle of pills, which her therapist had prescribed last week. Dianne avoided taking the antidepressant as long as she could. Yet, two days ago, she was in a crowded elevator and could sense herself starting to get antsy, and then she felt a hot flash coming. In the lobby of the building, she'd popped open the bottle and taken two. Once the magic pill took effect, she began to feel like her old self.

She pulled out of the circular driveway, steadily transforming into the Dianne she knew and loved.

"When can we meet? I'm excited to talk with both of you."

With a shrug, Dianne looked at Phoebe and then back at Philipa. "I'm open. I do have commitments, but I can make it happen."

Both women looked at Phoebe, who was reluctant to do the interview. She had said as much to both Dianne and Philipa. Phoebe said, "I'm not working right now."

"Why not tomorrow? Where do you live, Dianne?" Philipa asked.

"Not far."

"I'm by the university, on Twelfth. How about a light lunch or something?"

"Yeah, sure. I get out of church at noon."

Once again, both women looked at Phoebe. It was as though what she thought and felt hinged on what would happen next.

Although disinclined, Phoebe went along. "Sure."

"So two?" Philipa said.

"Two?" Dianne sipped her mimosa.

With a nod, Phoebe confirmed, "Two."

"I'll send both of you details. Thank you for doing this. I'm thrilled."

When Jacqueline saw Philipa walk off, she approached Dianne and Phoebe.

"You two have met?" Dianne asked.

"At Media Cap," said Jacqueline.

"Did you know Phoebe's the one who not only talked Cordia into being the voice of Venice, but she also wrote our first hit?"

Jacqueline never made the connection. All the while Phoebe walked around Media Capital assisting Chef, it never entered her mind that possibly, just *possibly* Phoebe had been successful in another life, but the downturn changed things. Even clients were conscientious about how they used consultants these days. A fiscal cliff loomed in the foreseeable distance. In a business like entertainment, and especially when the success was decades ago, it wasn't particularly unusual to fall on hard times. *What must that feel like: to be recognized all over the world and then end up temping as hospitality assistant?* The entire time she was at Media Capital, Jacqueline had no clue—Phoebe was *in* Venice, *and* she wrote their first single, which was the song that put the group on the map. Jacqueline still had the Venice album she'd bought at a record store back home. She would never voice it to a living soul, but she'd actually stood in front of a mirror, hairbrush in one hand, the other resting on her hipbone while she lip-synched along with Venice.

"How many mimosas have you had, Jacqueline?" Dianne teased.

"Only my third. I have to drive, you know."

"Oh, Phoebe. Jacqueline and I are spending next Saturday doing selfish stuff. Wanna come?"

"I don't want to be a third wheel."

"Oh, *puh-leez*. Join us. We can squeeze in a few hours at the spa. You know, mani-pedi, and I'd like a happy-hour massage. They serve wine. What's the name of that brow bar you go to?" she asked Jacqueline. "I want to check that one out."

"It sounds like a plan," said Phoebe. "By the way, how's Stefan's family?"

Jacqueline pursed her lips. "They are amazing people. And very close."

"And he was your best friend," Dianne said. "I know this was hard for you. When you came by the house…Jacqueline, I'm so sorry."

"Everything's starting to get back to normal. I'm glad I decided to come. This energy is just what I needed."

"Well, Daniel should certainly distract you." Dianne stole a glance his way. He was having a very engaging conversation with Nigel, the author.

"Are we extremely jaded at this stage of our lives? Am I the only one who looks back and thinks how great we were when we were parenthetically relevant? I read somewhere: the young steal the show. When I was young, I couldn't wait to be in my thirties. Like really *grown*. Life's transition…Remember how we tried to drink before we were legally able? Then, when we were legal but getting up there in age…Our ego wants to be carded, not our age."

"I'm defying age every step of the way," Phoebe declared.

"Oh, now that's a good attitude," Jacqueline chimed in. "Let's toast to defying aging." She held up her flute with a few droplets of mimosa left at the bottom of the crystal.

Optimistic, Dianne laughed, holding up her flute. They clicked their glassware together and each, without sharing with the other, felt a momentary bonding. And love.

Venetia broke up the evanescent connection, and stated, "We're about to start the book signing. You can purchase your book through Daniela in the sunroom, just beyond the kitchen. Nigel will sign them in the living room. Please start now. Nigel has a plane to catch. Thank you!"

Jacqueline said to Phoebe, her newest BFF, "I'll buy five books. Give them out to colleagues at Media Cap."

"How generous, Jacqueline. Good idea."

"Nigel has so much potential. His accent is so sexy."

Dianne and Jacqueline rushed to get on line; Phoebe watched them while nursing the last few drops of her mimosa. Of all the women Phoebe had met and knew in her lifetime, Jacqueline would have been at the bottom of the list of women she'd suspect Dianne to befriend. But as much as she hadn't changed in twenty-eight years, on the other hand, she had changed quite a lot. The Dianne Phoebe had met years ago was feisty, strong-willed, even conceited. When they'd returned to L.A. after Venice's first world tour, Dianne would order Perrier and Evian and her old friends, none of whom had ever traveled to Europe, hadn't even heard of the imported water back then. She ordered mineral water in their presence, Phoebe and Cordia decided, because she was a snob. They used to tease her because she'd grown up middle-class, but her mother always gave her daughters the best of everything. They lived in a section of Los Angeles with large, old homes and palm trees contoured each block, like statues. And the house they grew up in would go for a fortune. But they didn't come from money in the real sense of the word. Dianne's mother was a surgical nurse; and her father, a detective with the LAPD, was killed on the job. His pension provided them with security.

Daniel said into Phoebe's ear, "What is going through that mind of yours?"

When she looked into his hazel eyes, Phoebe had ideas about sleeping with him. Years ago, she was good at sleeping with a man strictly because she was attracted to him. She found it a challenge to resist Daniel's charisma. She told Venetia only a few days ago— there were advantages to getting older. One of them had to do with being wiser. But even more so, being selective, being less needy and desperate. The necessity to prove anything to anyone was no longer a subconscious reaction.

"I was watching my friend Dianne, and your friend Jacqueline."

"Let me guess. You're thinking they're definitely not two peas in a pod."

She laughed. "I'm actually glad you came."

With an arched brow, Daniel said, "Really?"

"You're a venture capitalist, right?"

"That's correct."

"I have this idea. This is not a good time to discuss it. But I'd like to run it by you. And I've started working on a business plan. I let someone read the first draft and she thinks I'm on to something."

"Those were her words, 'on to something'?"

"Those were her words."

"Do you trust this person's opinion?"

"She's young, but savvy."

"Why do you need me?"

"I'd rather let you see the business plan *and* meet with you to discuss it. That's all I'm asking you to do."

His eyes studied her closely. When they ran into each other at the Blue Bar, she was an attractive woman waiting for a friend. Daniel didn't look further than her attractiveness because he wasn't interested. Daniel invested his time wisely, and particularly when it came to women. He enjoyed doing business with women, so the woman he'd met while she waited for an old friend at the Blue Bar had his attention. Not to mention she wrote the lyric to "Plan B"—a song he'd danced to at high-school house parties.

"Okay," he said, sliding his hand into his trouser pocket. "I tell you what. Call my office." He pulled out a business card. "Set up a time with my assistant. Can you hold this?" Phoebe held his flute while Daniel pulled out a handheld and fooled with it for all of thirty seconds. He slipped it back into his pocket and retrieved the flute. "There. I've sent an e-mail to my assistant letting her know you'll be calling to set up an appointment."

"Like that?"

He finished his mimosa, and with a wink said, "Like that."

For years Phoebe heard, it's all in who you know. She never liked that line. Twenty years ago, she didn't *need* to know a living soul. When Dianne, Cordia and Phoebe started Venice, the group knew no one; they did everything on their own. They drove the highways of California and Nevada crammed in a sports car, often getting no more than an hour of sleep. Within eight months of working clubs around California and a few in Vegas and Tahoe, they met the man who eventually became Cordia's husband and negotiated Venice's first record deal. It was so simple back then. Phoebe could walk in a door and the world was her oyster. Slowly, gradually, that stopped happening. She wasn't sure when or even where she was when she began to sense it. Ever so slightly she turned, and caught Joseph flipping through Nigel's book. Venetia, unaware they had met previously, introduced them earlier. Phoebe had no idea Joseph was the man Venetia wanted to introduce her to. Why would she even think she'd be interested in Joseph? He was much too set in his ways.

When he looked up, his eyes roamed the room as if he were looking for someone to rescue him from the awkwardness that came with not having the edge to connect with vibrant people. Venetia was the only person Joseph knew. Phoebe hadn't seen him mingling or talking to anyone whenever he caught her eye. He was like the nerdy wallflower at the dance. Daniel reached in his pocket for his ringing cell just when Joseph looked directly at Phoebe. It was then she understood that he was there specifically because he was going to meet her. *He's lonely, and I don't do lonely.*

Dusk descended on the city. Torrick liked this time of day. Dianne called to say she and Daniela were going to stick around and help Venetia clean up after the brunch.

"So you and Venetia had some time to catch up?"

"Not really," Dianne said. "But we had a nice chat. Actually, staying behind after everyone else has left gives me the chance to spend quality time with her. We couldn't have had that same kind of time during the brunch."

"You sound good."

"I'm good, Torrick. We'll be home around eight."

While Dianne and Daniela were at the book brunch, Torrick and Henna went shopping at the mall and caught a matinee. Henna ran into a classmate who invited her to come along with some other classmates to her house to watch the latest *Twilight* DVD. Of course Torrick couldn't bring himself to refuse. A classmate's parent would arrange to get Henna home.

Since Dianne and Daniela were hanging out together, and Henna was overly enthusiastic about being with a group of classmates, Torrick decided to drop by the office and clear his desk. Not thirty minutes after he was settled into going over paperwork and approving invoices did his cell vibrate. Right at his fingertips, and so much so it had become an appendage. Torrick reached for it, and when he identified the caller, he cracked a wide smile. "Hello. Just approving some invoices. Where are you?" He listened momentarily. "Okay, yeah. Sure. See you then."

After several calls and arranging last-minute security for a client flying into the States from Prague, Torrick called it a day. He left instructions to his personal assistant and headed for the parking lot. After turning over the engine, he reached for his cell and called Dianne. Her voicemail greeted him and he left her a message.

The temperature had dropped over the past week. It was cooler than Torrick thought it would be. He adjusted the heating to low but opened the moon roof enough to let a breeze seep in. He turned on Marvin Gaye's "What's Going On" he'd downloaded from his playlist. Torrick was only fourteen when he first heard the *What's Going On* album. His older brother let him borrow it, and Torrick played it so much, eventually, the record player needle started skipping against the vinyl. Earth Wind & Fire was his favorite group of all time, but Marvin Gaye was the musical genius of his generation. His daughters had no idea the level of talent they missed out on. Their generation would never experience the gift and distinction of talent like Marvin Gaye's. His father had told him a few times: pay close attention to what shapes you. When they'd first met, music was the thing Torrick and Dianne had in common. His brother and friends were so jealous by the fact that he managed to take *the* Dianne Lewis out on a date.

He took in the cityscape. The sun left a bright splash across the horizon as it vanished to another part of the world. Torrick reflected on the connection he and Dianne had years ago. Daniela and Henna, in some mystical way, preserved their marriage. Without the girls, he wasn't altogether sure he could have held on to Dianne. He knew, for some years now, his wife was restless. She'd tried everything: getting caught up in a number of committees for non-profits, church functions for single women, teaching Bible study to young girls, and anything that hinted at a purpose. She'd spent the first ten years of their marriage raising Daniela followed by Henna when she came along a few years after Daniela. Dianne was a happy mother. She loved parenting. When she'd learned that she was pregnant, she'd had doubts about being a mother. She wasn't ready; and Torrick knew he wasn't the man she'd have chosen as a life partner.

If nothing else, Dianne had been an exceptional mother. She wasn't overprotective, and yet she was insanely attentive. So it should not have come as a surprise to him that when the girls were older and needed less of her time and attention, she'd feel a suspicious void. But something else was going on with her. After speaking with the pastor—although Torrick wouldn't dare divulge Dianne having allegedly caught a venereal disease—he made an appointment with his physician to determine if he'd been exposed to chlamydia. Still, Torrick hadn't been able to confront his wife. There had never been a good time in which to sneak it in. Some part of him was hoping she would come to him. He wanted to believe they had the kind of relationship in which she could trust him, despite anything. A longstanding marriage was tricky. On the one hand, complacency set in, and taking too much for granted was on the other.

He pulled into the quiet street and could see docked boats from a short distance, and tiny, sparkling white speckles garnishing the darkened sky. Torrick sought out a parking space on the street. He caught sight of a couple that couldn't be any older than mid-twenties walking a dog and it made him momentarily think back. He knew what that was like. When he and Dianne first had married, they lived in a small but charming Georgetown pied-à-terre with large windows. Seeing the couple in *this* neighborhood reminded Torrick of those very early days. Being young; being untainted by life choices, disappointments, setbacks, the unplanned-for and unpredicted—life. He watched the couple make their way down the sidewalk. He leaned in his seat. What was he doing? Why was he here? He could have made an excuse, or simply said over the phone it was a bad idea. Nothing good could come out it. When all was said and done, there would undoubtedly be heartache, regret. It was the odd thing about being older: mature choices could be as impulsive as those made in youth.

When she opened the door, Jacqueline had her cell to her ear. She held up a long index finger as if to tell Torrick to hold on, but motioned for him to come on in. He shut the door behind him. The condo felt warm and inviting. A delicate, sweet scent hung on the air, and a fire was burning in the living room. The curtains weren't drawn, so the city's skyline and the traces of an early evening full moon poured into the soothingly lit room. Homeowners burned energy so glowing lights sparkled across the bay. Torrick studied her closely. Jacqueline was a fascinating woman. She aged stunningly. As he best remembered, the men she had been involved with were often younger than her, but not boy toys. Jacqueline wasn't the type to pick up the tab for a man in exchange for male companionship. In fact, she was most likely the opposite. They had to be a rising star or already one; Jacqueline wasn't going to carry a man or be taken advantage of.

"Sorry," she whispered.

He crossed his legs, pressing his back into the sofa. Torrick waved his hand as if to suggest it was no big deal. He couldn't eavesdrop. Jacqueline was listening and the person on the other end was doing all the talking.

Torrick stood and walked to the kitchen and looked in the fridge. He grabbed a bottle of imported beer. After opening it, he rested against the counter. He spent days pushing Jacqueline to the back of his mind. Torrick wasn't the guy who spilled out his feelings to other men, except his older brother. Nor did he exchange stories about his personal life to colleagues; most were his employees. He always sought advice through his pastor, and in most cases, felt all the better in doing so. There was no way he could go to Pastor Stevens with this. That early evening, when he'd rescued Jacqueline from the rain, he couldn't have been prepared for what would eventually happen. Sleeping with her came as much as a shock to him as it did to Jacqueline. Once it was over, while they held each other, limbs entangled, body fluids staining her ivory white Egyptian cotton sheets, they each agreed it was a lapse in rational judgment. Although it wasn't something they discussed, they understood it in some innate way: it was one time.

Nonetheless, two days later, he found himself ringing her intercom.

She didn't answer, and he wondered if she chose not to answer. After all, Torrick knew the building was one of the top secured condos in the city. Every unit was highly digitalized with built-in screens whereby anyone at any entrance to the building could be seen on video. He was walking back to his car, deciding it was fate that she didn't answer if she was home, when Jacqueline called him on his cell. He lied about where he was. He didn't want her to know he'd made the impulsive move first. She asked if he had a window of time to drop by the condo. Torrick didn't ask why, but said he'd drop by around seven. When she let him in, just two days after they slept together for the first time, she rushed into him and their ravenous, fervent kiss landed them on the cocoa-colored carpeted floor. Her legs opened generously to him and Jacqueline succumbed to her good friend's husband: the rhythm of his body led her to an orgasm that brought tears to her eyes. Over the last year, her libido had subsided and she drew the conclusion that the multiple, and sometimes intense, climaxes from her younger years were a thing of the past. Being perimenopausal was a damn inconvenience. Her desires weren't nearly as concentrated in recent years. Even Torrick himself had been having trouble reaching out to Dianne. His physician had recommended Viagra at his last checkup. Pride—a very healthy ego more than anything—kept Torrick from filling the prescription. But on that first and faithful night, no sooner than Jacqueline began to caress his crotch did he grow stiff—he hadn't experienced a hunger so intense in a long while.

What were they doing? he asked himself, coming out of his distracting thoughts. He took a gulp of the beer. Jacqueline entered the kitchen and leaned beside him. "Torrick, what have we started? And how can we finish it?"

When Joseph got home, the hip-hop music blasting from his son's speakers didn't greet him at the door. The lights were out, which meant he was probably hanging out with one of his friends or with his girlfriend/potential fiancée/mother of his first unborn child. The timing was good; Joseph could use a moment or two to be alone. The brunch left him unsettled, and he never felt as old as he did this afternoon. After he left Venetia's, he took a walk along the path. It grew chilly and the lake, as still as a pane of glass, looked glossy and ink black. The day turned to various shades of night; the moon bobbed and weaved through smoky clouds. When the long and curiously hot summer faded, there was a good chance autumn would be fleeting. Once his knee started giving him trouble, he decided to drop by his friend's, the tax attorney who ran upward of five miles along the lake each morning, with his Porsche and barely thirty-something girlfriend. When Joseph rang the doorbell, he waited momentarily, but there was no answer. He wasn't sure if his friend was home since he most often parked his Porsche in the garage. Before walking back toward home, he looked up to see if he could find a speck of light.

Joseph looked in the fridge to see if he had anything good to eat. Venetia knew how to host; she'd learned that from her mother. But the food was too gourmet-ish for Joseph's blood. He wanted chicken wings or even some barbeque ribs. While he didn't expect Venetia to feed nearly thirty people prime steak, what about beef—meatballs, for example? Everyone was very aesthetic and intellectual and cool; drinking that mimosa, getting high from the champagne mixed with just enough orange juice to give the illusion of mimosa. The caterer wore skintight black slacks and an even tighter black blouse exposing too much cleavage; and those platform shoes—it reminded Joseph of the Commodores singing "Brick House." The tax attorney would love her. Maybe, thought

Joseph, I should have invited him to come along. The author, Nigel, was intelligent and smooth; that one had class. He was cultured with an accent from a country in Africa. Joseph bought two books, trying to help the brother out. Of course, Cornell thought *helping a brother out* was a line his generation came up with. His son suggested that "helping a brother out" was a meme. Joseph didn't know anything about a meme. He set his son straight: "Your generation borrowed that from my generation. This generation—what are they calling it, millennials?—whatever it is, couldn't comprehend what helping a brother out even means." Cornell came back with, "The baby boomers—the generation you think walks on water—might have changed America. But *this*—my—generation has reinvented the world!" Cornell could well be right about that. At any rate, Joseph figured Nigel had it hard trying to make it in such a competitive culture. These days it seemed nearly impossible to get anywhere. Everyone was vying for some kind of public attention.

There wasn't anything in the fridge worth heating up. It was a strange thing, but Joseph looked over at the answering machine. A red zero indicated no one called, or left a message anyway. He chuckled to himself about Cornell saying, "Now, Dad! Really? An answering machine in 2012!" Joseph supposed his son was telling him to, as they said back in his day, "get with the program."

Before he knew it, Joseph had climbed the stairs and without turning on a light switched on his computer. It would take a minute to turn on, and in the meantime, Joseph came out of those uncomfortable clothes—that in the end did nothing to better his chances with Phoebe—and slipped into something more comfortable. *Something more me.* He could hear the computer's hum. Cornell claimed it was too slow. Once he had on his house slippers, he sat in his chair and clicked the icon for Explorer. When the Internet was up and running, he clicked on his favorite porn site.

CHAPTER 9

Dianne couldn't recall the last time she was on this side of town. Not that she needed to be. The last time had to be when she'd attended a meeting at one of the hospitals on Pill Hill. It must have been over a year since she last made her way remotely close to where Philipa resided, and it was theoretically gentrified. She began to seek out a parking space when she turned off Twelfth. Her e-mail instructions indicated parking was tight. Even if it meant walking a few blocks, Dianne quickly pulled into an empty spot.

It was a chilly, gloomy Sunday. Dianne threw a faux sheepskin oversized scarf around her neck and blew warm breath inside her cupped hands. Hugging herself, she reminisced about that morning, before they headed off to church. When she was barely awake, Torrick entered her from behind. No foreplay—although the foreplay days were technically a thing of the past. Now and again Torrick would be playful; that was his idea of foreplay. On this particular morning, when she attempted to adjust her eyes to the digitalized numbers on the clock, her mind began to conjure up how the afternoon would unfold when Phoebe and she met with Philipa. And then she felt Torrick. It was as if a knife was at her throat. She lay motionless and pretended she was still asleep. In time, though, she could no longer pretend to be asleep, for she became aroused. When it was over, Torrick turned her face toward his and she was met with the intimate smell of his morning breath. He kissed her mouth and crawled out of bed. Within a moment, she heard the shower running. They didn't talk about it. She had no idea what came over him. Torrick was obnoxiously predictable. He stopped being spontaneous years ago.

"Two fifteen," Dianne read from the e-mail she'd printed out.

When she came upon the address, she stopped at the foot of the stairs. With critical eyes, she examined the house—small, simple, and one of the neatest and well-maintained on the block. The university was in close proximity, and many of the homeowners rented out rooms for students. But the block where Philipa lived, the houses were much closer together with no front yard, and each was similar in design: slanted rooftops and skylights.

A large wreath hung on the door—vibrant colors of autumn. It took Philipa no time to answer, like she was waiting for Dianne's arrival on the other side of the door. Dressed casually in mustard-colored jeans and a bulky, stylish sweater, Philipa sang, "Dianne!"

Like so many homes, it had the average-size living room, and a dining room spilled openly into the living room—no walls to divide one from the other. But Philipa was clearly artistic and had worked the layout in her favor with touches of vivid, bright hues. It had the feel of a loft. Old-World style—a lot of art on tangerine-painted walls, and a warm glowing fire burned in the fireplace. A large labyrinth was painted on the blemished wooded floor. Over-sized art books were stacked by the windows, which were too modern to be originals.

"I like your place."

"Thank you. Do you want me to put away your scarf?"

"Sure."

"Can I get you something? I have tea, or I have French cider."

"Oh, French cider sounds perfect. Thank you."

Dianne chose to sit in an IKEA-styled chair near the fireplace, which also faced the window and a house nearly identical to Philipa's across the way. The room exuded a balanced energy. When she turned her head slightly, Dianne caught sight of burning candles and a stunning alder wood table, finely crafted, set for their lunch. Anyone could walk through the door and feel something different, but likewise feel at home. Dianne swallowed hard, for she could see herself in this house. Like Phoebe, when Dianne was in her youth, she had a bohemian nature, too. But Phoebe was naturally free-spirited, and clung to hers. She loathed to admit it, but Phoebe made the most of it. Dianne hadn't lived on her own until Venice started making enough money so that she could find an apartment without having to rob Peter to pay Paul.

Cordia had called one day and said that she'd met this couple who needed to break their lease because they were moving out of the country. "You'd love this place, Dianne. It's so you, girl!" Cordia had said. "Where is it?" because to Dianne—and Vanessa, too— *where* mattered. They got that from their mother. "Sunset and La Cienega. It's in West Hollywood." Dianne broke speed limits to get there. When her eyes rested on the view—albeit smoggy— and the fact that she would have a 659 prefix, she didn't hesitate to take over the lease. They were living in and out of suitcases back then, so Dianne hardly lived there. But it was her first apartment, and away from the only home she'd ever known—the one she'd grown up in. At present, feeling at ease sitting in the adequate living room with unpretentious but stylish furnishings, she missed those days much more than she could bear right about now. She missed the not caring what the future held; she missed the risqué adventures she had embarked upon but came out safe and without any visible scars; she missed the discos and the nightclubs and the loud music and the smell of marijuana always reeking in the air;

she missed laughing out loud as much as she cried; she missed loving people and losing people and fighting over who would be the designated driver, and getting home no sooner than dawn adorned the sky. She missed—

"Here you go." Philipa held out a clear, oval-shaped mug.

"Oh!" Dianne used her pinky finger to dab the corner of her eye, and prayed everything she was feeling and everything she was longing for slipped right past Philipa.

"Would you like to see the introduction to *Where They Are Now?*"

Dianne wiped away the smudge—the imprint of her bottom lip—on the cup and said, "I'd like that."

Phoebe was in a good mood, despite not wanting to do the interview with Philipa. "How's Barry?"

"He's in New York right now. And speaking of which…"

Phoebe could feel her heart drop to her stomach. *Did Barry tell her about the conversation they had? Would he dare?*

"He's been approached to do a book. Remember, he covered Hurricane Katrina and the earthquake in Haiti. He has a lot of photography to share. Beautiful work, too."

"Do you still feel he's being…unfaithful?" When she turned onto Cherry, Phoebe caught Venetia's profile from the corner of her eye.

"Something's up. Either he's met someone or he's bored with me. We haven't had sex—well, I take that back; that's not true. When he was here, and when we were in L.A. But it felt—our sex feels off."

"Your sex life changes with familiarity. Sex won't always feel good. That's natural. Have you considered seeing other people? You're beautiful, intelligent and successful. You have so much going for you. You and Barry don't even live in the same city. That seminar you've planned for next year in London; you'll be there for a month. Where will he be, Libya, Syria? Is he someone you see yourself marrying?"

"You think it's tough to meet men in your fifties? You need to be in your thirties in the twenty-first century. The dating structure—look! My generation doesn't *date*; we live through each other online; we text each other dozens of times each day; we share 'likes' and hook up...Barry is one of the first men I met in my age range that I could be with *in person* and we talk. We connect."

"So you settle?"

"Barry isn't a *settle*. He has attributes I happen to appreciate."

"What's the address again?" Phoebe slowed on Philipa's street. Venetia referenced her cell. "Two fifteen. There it is."

Phoebe sought out parking. She turned off Philipa's street and onto the next street.

"There!" Venetia said. "You should be able to squeeze in there."

Once parked, Phoebe said, "Barely."

Philipa greeted them with a generous hello, holding a ceramic mug of organic tea. "Welcome!"

When Phoebe and Venetia entered the house, Dianne was surprised, although pleased, to see Venetia. "I didn't realize Venetia was coming."

"I thought she would benefit from our stories about Venice," said Phoebe.

They greeted each other warmly. Venetia mimicked the greeting.

"Have a seat," Philipa said.

"I love your place."

Philipa was flattered by Venetia's approval.

Phoebe and Venetia sat in the charcoal-colored sofa, across from Dianne seated by the fireplace.

"I thought we could chat a bit. After which we can eat. I made vegetarian chili and cranberry corn muffins."

"That sounds tasty," said Venetia. "Are you vegetarian?"

"When I want to be."

Everyone laughed.

"Potential clients introduce themselves by saying they're vegans, vegetarians, environmentalists, metrospiritualists, spent a year in India, and what they do for a living before even telling me their name."

"*Metro*spiritualists? These potential clients must live in L.A.," Philipa guessed.

"Most," Venetia confirmed.

"What can I get you? Espresso, tea, juice…"

"Try the French cider. It's delicious," Dianne suggested.

"Oh, that sounds divine," Venetia said. "I'll try it."

"So will I," Phoebe said.

When Philipa left the living room, Venetia leaned forward and embraced the warmth of the burning fire. She surveyed the room. "I like Philipa's style."

"I saw her father in concert. Yet another lost talent," Phoebe said.

Dianne whispered, "Is she and Nigel…?"

Venetia halted Dianne's words—"Nigel has a girlfriend. He and Philipa are colleagues and friends in the way people like that are friends."

"What does that mean?" Phoebe overreacted.

"Well, you know! Literati, culturati—they're all friends. And actors are all friends and people in the music business are friends. Can you really have that many friends?"

"On Facebook," Dianne said with amusement.

"See, you get what I'm saying, right, Dianne?" Venetia felt so happy.

"I get it, yes. When we were in Venice, we did the same thing. We befriended every stranger we met. From somebodies to nobodies to groupies to other people in the business we hung with at parties and discos. We even kissed female friends on the mouth," said Dianne.

"When you're in your particular bubble, there's a common thread. I'm glad I still have my best friend from high school. She was the only person that didn't treat me like Cordia Street's daughter."

"I feel that way about Jacqueline. And Phoebe, too, because we've reconnected." Dianne brushed a stray hair from the side of her face.

"Okay, here we go. It's hot," Philipa interrupted. After handing Phoebe and Venetia their drinks, she sat in a chair and crossed her legs. "I'm so excited to have you here. This is going to be an experience for our memoirs!"

The winding road was frustratingly endless to Torrick. He was running late. Henna forgot her cell phone, and his twelve-year-old had become obsessed with staying in touch with whatever her limited world was focusing on. While Torrick agreed to get her one, it was primarily so that she could text her friends, and to use in case of an emergency. But she, as well as Daniela, brought cell phones to the dinner table, and it increasingly annoyed Torrick. Not long ago, he'd snapped, "Can we please have a social media pause!" Daniela was meeting up with friends at the neighborhood Starbucks. Dianne was having a late lunch with Phoebe and some other people Torrick couldn't recall who. His trusting himself to have sex with her for the first time in some time flashed through his mind. He pushed it away; it was something he couldn't bring himself to spend time on, not right now.

When Torrick dropped Henna off at her best friend's, he headed for the freeway. A block from the entrance were road signs indicating detours due to road maintenance. Torrick elected to take an alternate route. His GPS was very reliable, and he followed it to the T. He had a window of opportunity to make some business calls en route.

He spoke into his Bluetooth: "I'm running about ten minutes late. Is that okay?" He laughed. Torrick admitted it to himself that morning, he laughed more, and felt more alive. He *felt* life; he wasn't experiencing it and tolerating it like on a flight with a teething baby who wouldn't stop crying and a bored kid kicking the back of his seat. Even when he was young, still single, taking the ladies out for a good time, he didn't feel like he was feeling these past few days. Deceit shouldn't feel this good.

Pulling into the parking lot, he asked himself how good did Dianne feel when she deceived him. Did she feel an ounce of remorse sleeping with someone potentially no more than a casual acquaintance, not someone she knew all that well? Had it occurred to her to use something to protect herself, and even better, to protect him, the man she chose to spend her life with? Did she in fact cheat on him? Without confronting her, Torrick could never know for sure. His wife was adrift, and her confusion was something she could not seem to articulate. At least not to him. She was no doubt going through what every person who was no longer *young* went through: questioning choices, and the big "What if?" And then there was Gregory, her first *real* love. It had been a long time since Torrick believed he was second choice. It took a few years after they married to finally feel as though Dianne loved him; when enough time had passed and he thought she might have put Gregory in the back of her mind. Torrick knew she had never been head over heels in love with him. Had he only recently begun to feel a taste of resentment, or had it always lingered beneath the surface?

When he walked into the small hotel with its out-of-the-way feel to it, he asked the woman at the front desk, "Your café, where is it?" With an open kindness, the woman pointed the way. "Thank you." Jacqueline was sitting at a table near an electronic fireplace. She was casually dressed in weekend attire and was fooling with her iPad. When he walked toward her, she looked up. "Good afternoon." He pulled out a chair.

"Good afternoon."

"Sorry I'm late. Henna, freeway issues—you know how it goes."

"I ordered a cappuccino. Did you want something to drink?"

"Sure," he said, looking over his shoulder. A waiter glanced their way and Torrick fingered for him to come to their table. "How did you find this place?"

"Stefan. He used to stay here sometimes. Once, about a year or so ago, right after his treatments, he stayed for a month. I drove up to see him every day."

"No one we know would ever be here, that's for sure."

She laughed; her heart felt as light as a feather. *How long can this last?*

"The strangest things happen. Even though it's fifty miles from where we live doesn't mean we won't run into anyone. We both have clients, don't forget."

"Good point." He looked up to the waiter standing at the table, his hands placed behind his back. "How about a beer? Do you have imported?"

"We do."

Jacqueline leaned into the table. "You don't have much time, do you?"

"Not much."

"I didn't book a room. I wanted to see you. That's all."

"Me, too."

"Torrick?" His eyes suggested, *Yes?* "I want you to know: I've never—and I do mean *never*—slept with a married man."

"I believe you."

The waiter returned with Torrick's beer, and left without uttering more than a few words.

"How do you feel about this? It has the potential to destroy your family." Jacqueline, unknowingly, reached for her cappuccino, holding the oversized cup in both hands. "There's no going back now. My relationship with Dianne—it can never be the same. We have plans to go shopping next Saturday. I don't see how I can spend the entire day with her now. Even yesterday, when we planned it, I felt awkward. Hopefully, Phoebe will come. It will feel less... Once you came over yesterday, something changed. I don't know what. But..."

"Look," Torrick butted in. "You're right. This has the potential to create I-don't-even-know-what in my life. The risk is colossal. How I manage it is not for you to deal with. You and Dianne— you have to figure out how you want to handle your relationship."

"If I up and cancel..."

"Don't cancel."

"Oh, and act like nothing's changed. Yesterday at the brunch was hard enough. But there were distractions, and a couple of glasses of mimosas helped, too. Besides, Dianne seemed very—like she was on something. Talkative, and laughing." Jacqueline replaced the cup on the dark wooded table. "I thought you two might have started working things out."

Torrick pushed the memory of his morning—having sex with his wife—out of his mind as quickly as it attempted to barge in and take over his entire way of processing his thoughts. Without question, he loved his wife. How he could be with her close friend— so intimate, in ways he hadn't been with Dianne—was something he didn't think he could answer so close to the experience itself. His life demonstrated to him, eventually the awakening would tap him on the shoulder. Still, the smell of his wife, and taste of her skin, the way she moaned softly when she came—

"Torrick?"

"Uhhh, yeah." He reached for his beer and took a good long gulp.

"We haven't gotten in that deep. But if…I can find a way to be less accessible to Dianne, but remain friends. Until we settle this… our indiscretion."

It was on the tip of his tongue last night, but he didn't tell Jacqueline that he suspected Dianne had been with another man. How often, when, where? He didn't have those details; he wasn't even sure if it was still going on. He doubted Dianne would have shared this with Jacqueline. He only thought of it on his drive to the hotel; Jacqueline also wouldn't have mentioned it to him if she was privy to such information. Had she betrayed her friend? No argument, she had. Yet Jacqueline wouldn't tell Torrick if she knew Dianne had cheated on him. It would give the appearance that she was justifying their behavior.

"That's why I asked you to come here. I wanted us to decide what to do. Together. Away from our lives. I thought we could agree on something. Whatever you decide, I can live with that."

She made it so easy and yet she made it nearly impossible to decide what to do. He didn't go for Jacqueline merely because the moment presented itself. Torrick had found Jacqueline dangerously attractive when he'd first met her when his family moved to the city and they naturally looked for a church. Dianne and Jacqueline met while volunteering for a church auction and hit it off straight away. Before they knew it, the Jameses had joined the church and Jacqueline had become like a surrogate aunt to their daughters. Torrick never looked at Jacqueline as anything other than his wife's hanging buddy. But he was definitely attracted to her. One weak moment and they ended up in an out-of-the-way hotel over forty-five miles from his home trying to decide whether what they started one week ago should continue. It was a ludicrous, redundant question!

"Torrick…" She reached for his hand. When his solemn eyes met hers, she had his answer. "Okay." She squeezed his hand and promptly let it go. "Do you want to have a quick bite?"

His full lips tilted upward, subtly. "Sure."

Joseph had just finished washing clothes when Cornell walked in. He'd heard his Jeep's engine roaring up the slight incline where his home was perched. *He always needs to make a grand entrance, that boy.* He put the last of the towels away when Cornell walked through the front door stomping dirt off his shoes and on the rug Joseph had vacuumed earlier. His father met him in the living room. "Son," he said.

"Okay, Dad. Give me the four-one-one." He pulled a knitted cap from his head and cracked a—what his sister used to call—pick-up smile.

"Stay with Zyn last night?"

"Yeah. She's getting fat."

"Please tell me you're using tact, Cornell. No woman wants to hear she's getting fat."

"Even if it's true."

"Especially if it's true."

"Any seafood spaghetti left?" He removed his coat and slung it over the arm of a chair.

Joseph frowned at his ill-manners. *Did we fail this boy?* "You gonna hang that up?"

"When I go upstairs, yeah."

"I think some's left."

"It's for real the second day. You eat yet?"

"I had a late breakfast."

"Late night?" Cornell mocked. "Are you going to tell me or what?"

"Come on. Let's go heat up that spaghetti. And we need to talk about why you haven't found a job and what you're going to do about Zyn."

Every single time Joseph set foot in the kitchen, with its modern appliances, he was reminded of his wife. She loved to cook. He'd had the kitchen redone for her fifty-second birthday. He hadn't seen her so excited in years.

Cornell reached for the spaghetti and Joseph for a pot.

"Dad, you do know we can heat it up in the microwave."

"It never tastes as good as it does when you stovetop it."

"Whatever!" He leaned against the counter and crossed his arms. "Dad?"

Joseph looked over to his son. "What?"

"So how'd it go yesterday? Based on the fact that you're holding back on me tells me it's not good."

"Well…" Joseph poured the spaghetti in the pot.

"Let me guess. You didn't make a move, right?"

"A move? You don't make a move on a woman like Phoebe."

"So her name's Phoebe."

"This is the kind of woman you have to ease into. The approach needs to be old-school, as you continue to call everything I do. I don't expect you to understand."

Cornell watched his father stirring the pot. "Okay, maybe I don't get it. Keep in mind I had nothing to do with when I was born. It's not my fault you wrote letters and I write texts. Or that I read about the news online and you *still* read about it on paper. Oh, yeah. Like I listen to downloaded music and you listened to AM radio. I had nothing to do with the outcome…"

"You can be cocky when you wanna be."

"Cocky? Really, Dad. Me, cocky?" His tone verged on facetious.

Joseph, mindfully, poured the spaghetti in two oversized bowls. After grace, they dug in. "Remember how you used to take Ritz crackers and make them into crumbs and put them in your spaghetti?"

He laughed, and the memory actually touched Cornell's heart. "Yeah, I do." He reached for a napkin to wipe his mouth.

They ate in silence. Cornell finished his meal and took the dish and rinsed it out. Joseph noticed the action at once. Since he'd moved back in, Joseph always cleaned up after his son. He didn't touch so much as a dish, and he left towels on the bathroom floor; it was so uncouth. Joseph cringed every single time he saw his son drink from the orange juice carton. Cornell leaned on the counter and reached for his cell, checking social media.

"Listen…" Joseph began.

"Just so you'll know, I got a gig. It's part-time. And I'm going back to school in January."

He turned to his son, his mind focused on whatever he was doing with his electronic device. "That's good, son. That's really good. Where'd you find a job?"

"It's at a start-up downtown. I'll be working in IT."

Joseph finished his spaghetti and went to rinse out the bowl. He massaged his son's shoulder, "I'm proud of you, Cornell. My intentions weren't to be so hard on you…"

"It's cool. Dad?"

Joseph wiped his hands with a dishcloth and said absentmindedly, "Yeah?"

"I'm not ready to get married."

In a solemn tone, Joseph said, "Then what are you planning to do? Do you love this girl, Cornell?"

"I I-I-like her."

"What exactly does that mean?"

He took a deep breath and prepared himself. "I can't marry Zyn."

"Can't or won't?"

"Both, I guess. I know I got her pregnant and even though I didn't plan it and she told me she was using birth control, I take responsibility. We—well, maybe I wasn't serious. When she found out she was pregnant, what? What…" he shrugged, "could I do? I feel trapped, but hey, I know what I have to do. I know you think I'm some loser of a son…"

"Stop it!" Joseph said, his voice sharp. "Stop right there."

Cornell, in the twenty-one years he'd been in the world, had never been so shell-shocked. To a degree he was nervous, and slipped his hands into the front pockets of his jeans.

"Don't ever—and you need to hear me good—apply the word *loser* to yourself. Don't ever under any circumstance use that word to describe who you are, even if it's flip. Do you hear me?"

Still reeling from his father's tone, he replied with a scarcely audible, "Yeah."

"Most of what you hear me say I say it because your mother and I worked hard to provide you and your sister with all that we could. We didn't make compromises so that you could waste your life away with nonsense. You think because a black man made it to the White House, it makes it easier for you? Hell, it might make it harder. I know you think I'm no more than a throwback…Well, this *throwback* put a roof over your head and those fancy clothes you wear on your back. That Jeep—it cost me a fortune. Your generation doesn't understand struggle. I mean *struggle*. Now, I love you. You're my flesh and blood and I'll stick by you come what may. Is that understood?"

"Yeah." But he had no idea where all this was coming from.

"You're not a loser. You're just a product of the society you were raised in. Nothing can change that. Heck, your grandfather didn't understand it when I came home from the Navy with tattoos. He thought that was radical." Cornell covered his mouth to suppress his laughter. "Does she know?"

"I haven't had the nerve."

"Then you're going to have to get some. Don't leave her twisting about in the wind. It's unkind to leave her thinking one thing when you're thinking something else, and just as cruel to say nothing at all. Whether you love her is beside the point. Whether she was using birth control is beside the point. She's the mother of your unborn child. You have to do right by her, because that's what a *man* does!"

"I will." Somber, he said, "You have my word."

Joseph rubbed his son's face; he took after his mother. "Good."

He was about to leave the kitchen when Cornell called out, "She doesn't deserve someone like you, Dad."

In the doorframe, Joseph turned. "What's that?"

"This chick—this lady…what's her name, Phoebe? You're too good for her."

CHAPTER 10

Venetia left for Los Angeles early. She was taking a six o'clock flight. When Phoebe entered the house, it was cold. She stood in the kitchen, looking out at the frosty morning. Now that she was no longer working at Media Capital, and her agency hadn't called her for another assignment, Phoebe was stuck in extreme passivity. Earlier she spent time on her business plan. She had been quite focused and diligent, but was now finding herself unable to concentrate on the charts and figures—something she wasn't necessarily good at. She needed to do more research. Still, she would call Daniel's assistant once she had a bite to eat.

The sky was dark, and it would rain. The dampness depressed Phoebe; the lack of sunlight even more so. At times it could be unbearable. For quite some time, she stared out at the morning. A bird was perched on the windowsill, and for how long Phoebe stared at it was unclear to her. It wasn't until she heard the garbage pickup that she blinked. Once she rushed through a bagel, she sat in one of the window seats and tried to calm her nerves. She wasn't good with idle time. She wasn't productive unless she had something to focus on. In the past, there were men and there was her planning and arranging events, which turned out to be a fortuitous career. It wasn't until she moved into Venetia's guesthouse that she realized most of what her life was about leaned on one or the other.

The afternoon at Philipa's should have been foreknown. In fact, Phoebe thought it wasn't the best idea, which was the reason behind her reluctance to be involved. But Dianne was enthusiastic about doing it. She needed to do this; that was clear to Phoebe the moment she began to talk about how everything came to be: Cordia, Dianne and Phoebe, and the way in which they'd met. While Phoebe thought Dianne's version was slanted in terms of detail, hearing her version was hilarious. The conversation started out lively and everyone was laughing and dabbing their tear-filled eyes. Venetia took pleasure in the girl-bonding and laughter. Philipa, taking notes and asking softball yet straightforward questions, was likewise having fun. Phoebe herself was put at ease.

When Philipa asked a question that Phoebe knew was inevitable, the entire mood of the afternoon shifted—the energy turned dark and somber. Philipa was poised in her chair, her leg crossed, her pen in her left hand, a classy notebook balanced on her lap filled with copious notes. She'd looked directly at Dianne and asked, "Why did Venice break up?" It was as if she already knew the backstory but wanted to hear it from the horse's mouth. The *real* story, however, had never really been known publicly. They all had made the decision to stick with the idea that Cordia wanted to go solo, which in fact was true. But *how* it actually came to a "break up" had happened in a strange sequence of events leading to one simple, distressful ending. Egos loomed quite large; feelings were bruised to the point of not ever being totally healed; good friendships were destroyed—and it all appeared to have everything to do with L-O-V-E.

Dianne acted as if she never saw the question coming. Phoebe knew that was absurd. Philipa's book was based upon *where* they *are now;* hence, the subjects of the book had been *known* at one point but were no longer *celebrated.* The book would naturally address *why* they no longer worked in the public eye. Dianne was intelligent; this pretense insulted Phoebe. Dianne threw her nose in the air and that I-grew-up-in-upper-middle-class L.A. thing emerged. While she went to Beverly Hills High, it *was* a public school. Nonetheless, Dianne always, always had this I'm-better-than-you air. It was why she'd married a man like Torrick; she could maintain the ludicrous charade. Unlike so many who had to work to earn a living, she could shop and have weekly manicures and pedicures. Her volunteer work, which Dianne was devoted to, made her seem less like a reality TV housewife.

"It was Gregory," Phoebe had blurted out. Dianne wasn't going to bring it up because it destroyed Venice. Dianne was delusional and Phoebe was ready to get rid of it—to get *it* off her chest once and for all.

Dianne had shot Phoebe a death stare. After a beat or two, her eyes had bulged. Yet there was a side of Dianne—she had this slickness that wasn't easy to detect. She'd chuckled with a sarcastic, "Gregory?"

"Who's Gregory?" Philipa had butted in, looking from Dianne to Phoebe, her pen in place ready to jot it all down. Despite painstaking research, the name *Gregory* never came up.

"Gregory…" Phoebe had begun.

But Dianne said, "Gregory has nothing to do with this."

"Dianne! Please." Phoebe had smirked. "Are you going to sit there and try to rewrite our history? You wanted to do this. Let's give Philipa the real story and not some fictionalized version of it."

"But Gregory isn't *why* the group broke up. That was her question."

"You actually believe that, Dianne?"

"It's *true!*"

"I won't sit here and pretend."

"Well, look," Venetia intervened. The moment was extraordinary, as it began to play out. "Why don't you both give *your* version. You know how that goes. People see things from a different prism all the time. Two people can witness the same accident, but if one is standing on the north side of the street and another on the south side, the viewpoint will be different. So…" She spread her hands. "Dianne, what's your side of it?"

Dianne pressed her lips together. "Cordia wanted to go it on her own. She'd learned she was pregnant. She was going to start recording a solo album…during the pregnancy. We were also in the process of choosing songs for our first Christmas LP. As you know, your father was our manager. He thought Cordia had the talent to cross over…You don't hear that term these days—*crossover.* Anyway, she could cross over, especially as a solo act. Besides, Phoebe and I were just background singers. We used to joke about it and called ourselves 'bookends.'"

Philipa was writing with such intensity her hand raced to keep up with Dianne's verbal emotions. She'd looked up when Dianne stopped talking. "So, where does Gregory fit in?"

"He doesn't. I mean, not in terms of why we broke up."

"But Phoebe," Philipa had said, "you disagree. Why?"

"I agree with Dianne up to a point. It's true that Venetia's father made subtle hints about Cordia going out on her own. But Cordia would never have gone solo without first doing a Venice third album and the Christmas album. The third LP was her way of giving us more leverage, more credit so we—Dianne and me—could segue into our own careers if we chose to remain in the business. Dianne's right: Cordia was the talent. She had the voice and charisma.

"But Gregory was fascinated with the music business and he began to intrude—he was trying to *manage* Dianne and telling her what we should and shouldn't do. He latched on…"

"Latched on? Phoebe, really!"

"That's how I saw it, okay, Dianne."

With an acerbic sigh, Dianne crossed and uncrossed her legs.

"Okay, so…Why do you see him as having something to do with the group breaking up?"

"Dianne fell deep for Gregory. She began missing rehearsals; she wasn't showing up when she was supposed to be somewhere. She claimed…" Phoebe paused, then gave Dianne a sidelong glance, "she wasn't the voice of the group and she didn't need to attend rehearsals and stuff like that. When she did show up, she brought Gregory and he was telling her what to do. I mean, I liked Gregory…"

"We know you did." Dianne's words had signified an innuendo.

Phoebe disregarded her. "But Gregory was in the way. He had a hold over Dianne. She did whatever he told her to do. She was distracted and Venice didn't seem to mean very much to her anymore. It was all about Gregory. She was obsessed!"

"Obsessed! That's a lie!" She was becoming pugnacious.

"No, Dianne. You were obsessed!"

"This was a man that I *loved*. How dare you sit there and suggest that—you believe that I didn't love Gregory?"

"It was a version of some kind of idea of love."

Philipa was intrigued and jotting down about every other word coming out of each of their months. Venetia found it all unpleasant.

"You have no clue!" Dianne hissed. "You've never loved anybody. You've never allowed yourself to love someone except yourself. You wouldn't know love if it knocked you down to the ground," she'd snapped.

Venetia, tactfully concealing her feelings, had wanted to say something, but she didn't know what *to* say.

Phoebe selected her words thoughtfully. "Cordia had a birthday party for Dianne. Dianne and Gregory had this argument at the party. I don't remember—I don't even think I knew what the argument was about. It got loud and it was nasty—name-calling, that kind of thing. I remember Dianne telling him to leave. But his car was in the shop or…I can't remember. Anyway, he always used Dianne's second car anyway, a TR6. Dianne said something about taking a cab and the argument became uncomfortable, and so ugly. Gregory said he wasn't going to take it—how Dianne was talking to him, and he called it quits! Words like that."

Phoebe went eyeball-to-eyeball with Dianne, and Dianne was antsy, outraged. She sat in the chair, her arms crossed stiffly over her chest. Phoebe resumed: "I offered to give him a lift. Gregory did have sex appeal. And magnetism. At least back then. He was always in a Members Only jacket." Phoebe half-smiled at the reminiscence. "I saw—even Cordia saw—the reason why Dianne fell for him. We used to say he had bedroom eyes. They were an unusual brown and cinnamon color. I could easily have dropped him off and returned to the party. But I enjoyed talking to him. He invited me up, and I thought it was because he needed to talk." She looked directly at Dianne. "I sincerely believed he was upset. And he claimed they were *over*. Anyway, I'll cut to the chase. We slept together.

"I wasn't overly surprised that two days later they patched things up. Eventually—and it doesn't matter how—Dianne learned about Gregory and me sleeping together and she lashed out at Cordia and said she was no longer going to be in the group because she didn't need us. Those were her exact words—*need us*. She was going to do her *own album* and Gregory was going to manage her.

"Cordia was hurt. She couldn't believe what I did and she even stopped speaking to me for a few weeks. It was awkward. It was a crazy time. Dianne broke her contract—our label even sued her.

But before she walked out on us, no one was speaking to anyone. Dianne thought Cordia sided with me and...That's really how the group broke up. We didn't do our third album and Cordia went on to record her first solo and the first single, 'Next Time Knock,' skyrocketed to number one; number one with a bullet as they used to say. She became a household name—armful of Grammys, AMAs and Soul Trains...I didn't see Dianne again until Cordia's funeral. Even then, we barely spoke to each other."

"Don't exaggerate, Phoebe."

"We *barely* spoke, Dianne. We were best friends for four-and-a-half years. The three of us did everything together. What I did to Dianne is unthinkable to me today." Phoebe only felt a vague ruefulness. "I was selfish back then. I betrayed a friend and I'm sorry for that."

Dianne sat across the room, her entire body went as rigid as a corpse, and she was visibly enraged; not upset, not sad. *Pissed!*

Philipa stopped writing and glanced over to Venetia who was sitting forward, her hands clasped together. She took note of her unease; it was as plain as day that she was hearing the details for the first time. Philipa wanted to end the silence hanging ominously over the room. She'd asked, "Where's Gregory now?"

"He lives in San Francisco." Phoebe darted her eyes toward Dianne. "And he's out, and has been for years."

Dianne, Venetia and Philipa each looked at Phoebe at the same exact time: eyebrows arched, mouths agape, and eyes bulged. They were stunned into silence. *Out* imbued the air like a perfuse perfume.

Dianne rushed to her feet and shouted, "Out? Like *out* of the closet? You're crazy. Gregory isn't gay! That's how rumors get started."

"That night we slept together, I asked him and he admitted that he was bi. Cordia and I even talked about it once. We thought he might at least be bi. It was his mannerisms. He was lean and stylish and effeminate. Back then, it was like being bi was a fashion statement, especially in L.A. I figured he might—*might*—be experimenting or something. During that time, before ballplayers started piercing their ears, there was this—I guess it was an unspoken rule: if a man wore an earring in his right ear, it meant he was gay. Gregory had a pierced right ear…"

"You and Cordia laughed—talked—behind my back!"

"We wanted to tell you, Dianne. But you were so toxically obsessed! Would you have believed us?"

"*Toxically* obsessed! You have such fu—nerve!"

"Dianne…"

"Where's my sheepskin scarf? I'm tired of this crap. I don't want to talk about this anymore. You know, Phoebe, you are such a bitch!" Dianne's eyes rolled to Philipa, who was taking notes and scribbling hurriedly. "Where's my scarf?"

She stopped writing, and by the look on her face, Philipa understood fully that Dianne was dead serious: She wanted to leave and she was through!

"I'll grab it."

"I really hate you!" Dianne was absolutely furious with Phoebe. "Do you have any idea how much I hate you for what you did? I thought we could be friends again because everything was so long ago, but the gap is unbridgeable. The only thing we're connected to is a past! I don't *like* you," she'd said, biting back tears. "You're malicious and cold." Dianne covered her face with a trembling hand.

Venetia was at the edge of the sofa, mentally debating whether to go and console Dianne, but everything about her body language suggested she wasn't in an embracing mood. "Here, Dianne," Philipa had said, holding out her sheepskin scarf. She wasn't going to attempt to iron things out. It was abundantly clear the feelings that were exposed went way too deep. Saying anything, Philipa trusted, would only make matters worse.

She'd reached for the sheepskin and walked to the door. And without saying good-bye, Dianne had stormed out.

A collective sigh had followed her dramatic exit.

Phoebe was brought back to the present by a ringtone. She reached for her cell nearby. "Hello. *Michael?*" She never expected to hear from Michael again. Even when he asked for her number, Phoebe didn't anticipate he would use it. She couldn't imagine the impression she made on him at the Mason over drinks. And after yesterday, and the words Dianne used to describe her, she suspected he, too, thought along the same line—that she was a *cold bitch.* "I'm good. No, not working. How are things at Media Cap…since Stefan's funeral?" Thoughtful, she listened to Michael momentarily. "Lunch? Okay, sure. What time? I'll be there."

When she disconnected the call, she stared at her cell for a few moments, curious as to why Daniel's assistant hadn't returned her call. She was bored and needed to be busy. Especially after what went down at Philipa's, Phoebe really needed a distraction.

Claire entered the spacious reception area and nodded to the concierge. A petite woman, with her back to Claire, held the ubiquitous Fran's Chocolates shopping bag. Claire said, "Excuse me?" The size zero woman turned and gave Claire a look that solicited, *who are you?* "You're here to see Jacqueline?"

"Yes."

"You're not on her calendar. Can I inquire what this is about?"

"I'm a client, and we're friends."

Her name didn't ring any bells. Claire even looked up her name in the client database to make sure. Jacqueline was in the Weekly Huddle and because this so-called client didn't have an appointment, Claire couldn't interrupt.

"She's in a meeting. Maybe I can help you. My name's Claire and I'm Jacqueline's assistant."

"Oh, a new one. I can't keep up," she said in a condescending tone.

"Well, I've been her assistant for over a month," *and I've never seen or heard of you.* "Would you like to come back? We can meet in her office."

The client took note of Claire's "I own this" attitude. *She definitely isn't like the last one, that's for sure. She was black with waist-long dreads, exotic, Stanford-educated and thought she was above getting clients coffee. She certainly didn't feel obligated to get Jacqueline her morning café au lait when she had legs to walk and could get it her damn-self.*

Claire thanked the concierge. When they headed back to the department, she asked, "Would you like something to drink? Coffee, tea…?"

"That delicious organic chai tea…that would be delightful."

They sat at Jacqueline's table. From Jacqueline's window, the air looked white, like static clouds. Racine, the client, alluded to the purpose for her unannounced drop-in.

"I'm sure Jacqueline will want to hear more about this, Racine. I don't know if she's going to like the whole I-can't-name-my-source bit, You know Jacqueline. Anyway, she has to leave for Chicago tonight. I'm not sure how much attention she can give to it. She's still playing catch-up."

"Oh, that's right. Stefan. He was such a terrific guy. I meant to—I need to send flowers to his family. He—was a friend. Can you be a jewel and get me his family's contact?"

Claire played around with her tablet. "Pen?"

The client pulled a pen from her designer handbag and reached for one of Jacqueline's personalized notepads.

Claire recited the address. "Let me ping Jacqueline and see if she can sneak out for a minute." Claire waited, staring at the screen with such attentiveness. The client frowned. "Oh yes. She's coming now."

"Oh, Claire. Thank you." *This Claire is so über.*

It took three minutes for Jacqueline to enter her office. In a pair of glasses and holding her cell phone, she said, "Racine!" Racine stood and greeted her with a gentle embrace, holding out the Fran's Chocolates bag. "Mmmm, thank you. But why didn't you call me?"

"I just, *just* learned about this. I need you to make some calls. I need air time. National air time."

"Why can't your agent handle this?"

"No, no, look, he's local. You have global contacts…I need to own this before, God forbid, Fox gets wind of it through whom-ever! Your contacts are first-class."

"Well, yes, they are, but…"

"You don't know the whole of it.….Jacqueline, this is my forty-seven percent. *My* forty-seven percent. I have to move fast."

"Claire, give us five, please."

Claire retrieved the iPad from the table. "Absolutely."

When she left the office, Jacqueline looked Racine straight in the face. "I need more than an elevator pitch. I need something buzzworthy."

"Jacqueline…Look, this could change the entire landscape of the election!"

"Don't be dodgy with me!" Racine wasn't budging. "You want me to put my backside on the line? We're going through some restructuring after Stefan left us. I can't afford to…"

"You have my word, it's huge. You're my media consultant, come on, Jacqueline. Mediate! Look, have Claire work with me. She said you have to leave for Chicago. *Your* name will make it happen. I need national. I was thinking *Good Morning America* or Anderson Cooper."

"I can make one single phone call and get you a spot on *Coffee with the Crew* as early as tomorrow. That's national. With what you've given me, it's not enough to get you on *GMA*, or *360*. The producers are going to need more than 'this is huge.' I need details, and sans the forty-seven percent drama, Racine. You're a local reporter…"

Once Racine told Jacqueline as much as she could without revealing her source, Jacqueline decided it was too risky to have Claire handle it solo, even while she had come to trust her. She didn't think she was ready for something of this magnitude. Racine was right: it had the potential to alter the election. "Claire!" Jacqueline yelled out. In no time flat she was walking into her office. "I need you to get Michael out of the meeting. Tell him it's a red."

"Red, right."

No sooner than she had one foot out of the office, Jacqueline said, "And Claire, when he arrives, I want you in the meeting, too."

Power-walking down the corridor, Claire could feel chills run up and down her spine. Making her way to fetch Michael, she grinned from ear-to-ear. *Dream Job No. 1 is so damn awesome!*

When she arrived at the condo, Jacqueline was pooped. She had all of ten minutes to grab her travel bag, take her multivitamins, fish oil and calcium supplements. When the phone rang, Simone's name popped up on the caller ID. Her nephew again. She decided against answering it. "He has to need money. He hasn't called me just to talk in five years. His habit will have to wait." She called for a taxi and was outside waiting for it when Dianne pulled up.

"Are you leaving?" Dianne asked.

"A presentation in Chicago. What's going on? You should have called. We could've met for a drink or something. This flight's the last flight out."

"I could use a friend right now."

"What is it?"

"Call me when you get back. We're still on for Saturday, right?"

Feeling awkward, Jacqueline said, "Sure." And to avoid dealing with Dianne, she said, "I'm keeping the taxi waiting."

"Have a safe trip—call me," Dianne urged.

The taxi pulled onto the freeway, and all Jacqueline could see was a sea of red lights leading out of the city. "Is there some kind of accident?" she asked the cabbie.

"I'll check."

Jacqueline caught Claire minutes before she was planning to leave. "I'm sorry, Claire. But I just realized I forgot the Power-Point presentation on my desktop. I forgot to save it on my memory stick. Can you forward it to me, please? Stefan's client is all about PowerPoint presentations. Oh, and reach out to Venetia Street. Gwen has a court appearance in two days. I'm going to need you to go to L.A. and do some hand-holding." Jacqueline listened. "Good, and what's the temperature in Chicago? That's cold." Claire actually cracked a joke and Jacqueline couldn't help but laugh. "See you Wednesday morning. And Claire? I appreciate how you handled Racine. Let me ask you. Where do you see yourself in the future...with Media Cap? Strategy? Huh, okay." No sooner than Jacqueline released the call and took a deep breath, her cell beeped.

Meet me at Trace. 7.

Jacqueline replied to Daniel's text: *On my way to the airport. Rain check?*

She leaned forward and asked the cabbie, "So, is this just traffic or what?"

"A slight fender-bender ahead. It'll clear soon."

Jacqueline leaned her head on her fist, and a sudden wave of sadness came over her. *How can I face Dianne?*

In the car Dianne called her therapist to see if she could squeeze in an appointment, but no such luck. Instead, she'd have to wait another day. The assistant so much as said she was accommodating Dianne by having her come in first thing the following morning, since the therapist generally didn't take appointments before eight. Dianne released the call. *Bitch!*

Dianne was a woman who for years lived a comfortable, joy-filled life. Outwardly, she had it so together. It was only a matter of time before that façade would be tested. She was actually relieved when Torrick had told her over morning coffee that he needed to go out of town and would be back in two days. Thankful because, when she'd told him about the afternoon at Philipa's, he was only half-paying attention, and when he'd offered feedback, it was as if he was blaming her for everything that went down.

"Where are you, Daniela?" Dianne said when her oldest answered the phone. "Where's Henna? Okay, I'm coming to get you. We're eating out, all right? Then put it back in the freezer!" She fumed. "Don't back-talk to me. Do as I say! I don't care! I'll be there in fifteen minutes."

Terence Trent D'Arby's "Sign Your Name" was playing on the radio when Dianne turned it on for nothing more than a distraction. She reached to switch channels. That song reminded her of the good old days; what Dianne defined as the Madonna decade. Or better, the days when she was young and saw the world through inquisitive eyes. Had she not met Torrick when she needed to go to D.C. on business during the Million Man March, it would be a wild guess what she'd be doing now. Prior to meeting Torrick, Dianne was working as a buyer for a major department store, and she was bored. Actually, she couldn't fathom what she'd be doing if she hadn't met Torrick and hadn't had the girls. He might have been conventional, but at least she had Torrick. The idea that she could end up like Phoebe—alone. Phoebe, and Jacqueline, too, had no inkling what it was like to worry over children, or have a good man to be a soft place to fall when the world looked insane and everything around her was falling apart.

Blindly, Dianne drove through the dark and damp streets. When last did she do anything with a present state of mind? Everything was sideways, out of balance. It all began, she persuaded herself, when she ran into Phoebe. Her big sister attempted to remind her ever so gently that she'd slept with the personal trainer *before* she ran into Phoebe. "Come clean to Torrick," she'd said in their last conversation. "You might be surprised how much it will clear your conscience if you do."

Dianne decided there was no need to *come clean*. It was over. Done. Torrick needn't know. She'd had a lapse in judgment one time in her entire marriage. She'd slipped, lost her way. *One time!* She was confident it would never, ever happen again. The shame that came with it; the way the personal trainer treated her in the Safeway parking lot—she couldn't imagine being so lacking in good judgment—not like that—ever again.

Dianne pulled to the curb in front of the house and blew the horn twice. Henna opened the door and waved. When they jumped in the car, Daniela said, "When's Daddy coming back?"

"Day after tomorrow."

"Where are we going, Mama?" Henna asked, buckling her seat belt in the backseat.

"What are you hungry for? How about SoJo's?"

Dianne pulled out onto the street. Daniela said, "Why are we eating out on a weekday? What's going on?"

"I didn't feel like cooking. Since your father isn't here, I thought we could go out. It would be...different."

With a frown, Daniela looked at her mom. "Are you okay, Mama?"

"Why do you ask that, Daniela?"

She shrugged. "You're freaking me out." Her eyes dropped to her cell in her hand.

"If you want to go to L.A. for the holidays, you better show me some respect."

"What?"

"Don't *what* me!"

"Excuse me."

"*Excuse* me? I don't think I like your tone!"

"I just said..."

"Shut up, Daniela. I'm really not in the mood."

"Obviously," her oldest said beneath her breath.

Dianne pulled to the side of the road. When she unbuckled her seat belt, she slapped Daniela across the cheek. "You are too grown!"

With her hand covering her cheek, Daniela was thunderstruck.

"Mama!" Henna cried. "Stop it, please!"

Dianne looked over her shoulder. "Stay out of this," she instructed her youngest.

"I wanna go home."

"If we go home, you can't eat!" Dianne threatened Daniela.

They held each other's eyes for quite some time. Henna put an end to the silence that hung like an indescribable order within the interior of the car. "Mama, are you sick?"

She looked at her youngest in the backseat. "What—no, I'm not sick," she hissed.

"What's chlamydia?"

"Chla—" The word got stuck in Dianne's dry throat. *Why would she ask me that?* "What are you talking about, Henna?"

Daniela, with a frown on her face, was bewildered.

"I heard you say you had chlamydia. Daddy said it wasn't anything, but I think it is and he just didn't wanna scare me."

"You talked to your father about chlamydia? When was this, Henna?"

"I don't know."

"Think! When?"

"A few weeks ago, maybe. I don't remember."

"How did…when did you hear me talk about chlamydia?"

"You were on the phone."

"You have chlamydia?" Daniela recoiled. "How?"

Dianne leaned in the seat. Swiftly, she saw everything that mattered slipping away in front of her eyes. *Why hadn't Torrick mentioned this to me?*

"Mama? That's like an STD!"

Dianne flat-out lied: "I've never had an STD."

"What's STD?" Henna chimed in.

Dianne looked at Daniela. In her daughter's eye was utter contempt.

With her arms crossed, Daniela said, "I'm not hungry. Anyway, I need to finish my homework."

With pursed lips, Dianne put the car in gear and headed home. The drive was bitter silent, and the only sound that could be heard in the interior of the car was the discernible sound of tire treads against the asphalt.

An hour later, she waited for Torrick to return her call. She'd called twice; each time it went into voicemail. Nervously, she dialed her sister. When Vanessa answered, Dianne said, "Torrick knows."

While Jacqueline was taking a shower, Torrick ordered room service. He needed to break down and check his messages. Only his right-hand man knew where he was, so if an emergency arose, he would contact him immediately. Torrick intentionally turned off his cell, something he rarely did, in case Dianne did call. She was so far inside her own head these days, she wouldn't be bothered with him unless she had to. Just that morning, she'd paid little or no attention to what he was saying to her. She stared strangely, slurping her tea. Torrick had snapped his fingers in her face and she'd jumped, saying, "What?"

Even while sitting on the flight to Chicago, he knew this was wrong. What he and Jacqueline were doing went against everything he stood for in this regard. Their lust crowded out all other consideration. He knew men who cheated on their wives and they did it so cavalierly. Once, about a year ago, he and one of his security personnel went out for a lunch meeting. They'd known each other while they both worked for the agency. When Torrick started his private security business, he was the first person he'd hired. He knew his wife. She and Dianne occasionally had lunch or went shopping—whatever it was they did together. While Torrick and his employee lunched, a young woman approached their table, bent over and kissed his employee on the mouth. Torrick had no idea what was going on. They exchanged a few words—nonchalant, familiar. He introduced the woman to Torrick, and when she'd walked away, his employee told him he was seeing her "on the side."

A phrase Torrick hadn't heard in years—seeing her *on the side*. When he thought back on it, it sounded so dated. "Why, man?"

Torrick had asked him. He'd replied flippantly: "Why not?" That afternoon he understood something he might well have only vaguely paid attention to in the past. People he passed on the street, and the faceless people he talked to on the telephone—they could be having affairs. It was strikingly common, and yet Torrick had no clue until he became one of those people seeing someone "on the side."

Was that what Dianne did: Saw someone "on the side"? Was she still seeing him?

They both—he and Jacqueline—decided at the out-of-the-way hotel that they would stop and not look back. In the parking lot, they agreed they'd continue to throw each other business and maintain a friendly disposition at church or whenever they ran into each other in public. But when he kissed her for what was meant to be one last time, it—she—felt good; she felt timely. Fifteen minutes later, they had a room and spent the remainder of the afternoon in bed. He always thought cheating was something one thought through carefully. The idea that it *just happened* sounded so cliché-ish. Things—especially an affair—didn't *just happen*. People chose to make things happen. Either consciously or based upon a mindless reflex, people chose.

But Torrick knew he hadn't chosen for Jacqueline to run out of gas. He didn't choose the events that unfolded when he gave her a ride home. A sensible man, he thought about it on the plane: he could have arranged to have his tow service come to assist her and left it at that; except at the time, he didn't see himself ending up in bed with her. He saw his wife's friend, a fragile woman, sitting in her car and feeling alone. A friend had died. It was a moment that, in the course of an ordinary day, would never, ever have happened.

So when he stepped into a taxi at O'Hare, to rendezvous with a lover at an overpriced hotel, he got it: it could *just happen*.

CHAPTER 11

"Well now," said Joseph. "We keep bumping into each other. This couldn't be random."

Phoebe looked at Joseph. Whenever she ran into him, she winced. He was bothersome, and quite frankly, she didn't care for him. That damn grin, and the undeniable fact that he was attracted to her, left Phoebe exasperated.

"Hello." Phoebe managed to find her lighthearted voice.

"Mind if I sit?"

Yes, I do. "Sure."

"I like this bakery and café. The freshest bread in town. Haven't seen you here before."

"The weather invited me in."

"Can I get you anything?" a waitress interrupted.

"Why not? Coffee," said Joseph.

"I forgot your name."

"Joseph."

"Oh, right." She looked down into her mug, wondering how she could get up and leave without being transparent. Then she considered what about this man unnerved her. Venetia had said, "He's a *good* man. No, he's no Denzel," she'd joked. "But I've known him since I was a child. I babysat Cornell and Christine and I played together. When his wife passed away, Mr. Morgan changed." Recalling that, Phoebe attempted to appreciate, if not respect, that basic knowledge.

"So, tell me. Why did you leave California?"

"I needed to get away."

"I know you aren't married, because Venetia wanted me to meet you. Now I'm not being nosey, but did you leave California because of a man?"

"Excuse me?"

"You know, that *is* often the case. Not always, but generally people lose perspective because of job burn-out, a troubled relationship, or both. Our lives are fueled by intimate relationships, our work, our health, or money. Our children. Let one become a problem or change in some way, it affects us. We don't change our lives unless we have to. That's just human nature."

"Here's your coffee," the waitress said, slipping a check on the table.

"Thank you, young lady." Joseph reached for a packet of sugar and tore it open. While stirring, he looked directly into Phoebe's eyes. "You don't have to talk about it. But feel free. I got a good ear."

Discreetly, she rolled her eyes.

Joseph slurped his coffee demonstrably, studying Phoebe. His first impression of her was that she was strong and independent and sure of herself. Those attributes were as perceptible now as they were the first time he ran into her on the path. Yet, with her seated directly across from him, he sensed her vulnerability.

"He's married, isn't it?"

Phoebe's eyes met Joseph's. "You're insightful."

"Oh, thirty odd years with the post office, you meet a lot of folks. Across the counter…People like to talk to strangers. Share details they might not want to tell those familiar with their story. They can go on and on. If there was no line, customers got really care-less with information."

"When we met he was separated."

"Being separated doesn't mean divorced."

"I wouldn't have invested in the way that I had if he was still living with his wife and children."

"So he moved out, is that what you're saying?"

"Yes, of course."

"Why of course?"

"I wouldn't have gotten involved with a *married* man."

"But he *is* married."

"He's separated."

"And *married*."

Phoebe wasn't in the right mood to squabble with this man she didn't give a damn about.

"Until a man *leaves* his wife, he's still married, and committed, to her. Until he gets the papers that indicate that his marriage has been wiped clean…separation—that's a technicality."

"I don't get involved emotionally with men that are married."

She's headstrong. Joseph couldn't reason with her. She wasn't going to see her relationship with that man in California as an affair, not while they were sitting at the table. Why did intelligent women make such bad choices?

"I didn't realize you were in Venice, but I should have. You're no more than an older version of your younger self. Venetia said you wrote the lyrics to 'Plan B.' That's the one song by Venice I remember the words to."

"So what's your story, Joseph? You're a widower; you have two children and took early retirement. Venetia told me. You seem like a decent guy. No woman in your life?"

"They don't make 'em like they used to."

Phoebe laughed. "Are you looking for someone Venetia's age?"

"Oh, no. I need someone who understands the political ramifications of Viet Nam, not Iraq. I need someone who *understood* what Camelot was all about, not someone who relates to that *Gwenology*. Someone who was born before King and the Kennedys were assassinated and before they could change the whole landscape of American history.

"You see, I remember exactly where I was when each of those men was shot down. I was a kid, and despite the fact that I was too young to understand the impact of their deaths, I knew in a kinda natural way that their deaths would impact my life somehow. I saw how their deaths affected my parents. Especially King. No woman under forty could possibly relate to that."

"It's not easy to trust modern culture."

"I worry how this world will affect my grandchildren. Will they live just for personal satisfaction or will they chase a life of purpose? Culturally, I think we're on the wrong side of history.

"Well, that's strange. Snow flurries."

Phoebe took in the white dots adorning the night air. With a touch of warmth in her heart, she observed passers-by tucked in pea coats and scarves and knit caps. When she spent a few years in New York, Phoebe looked forward to snow.

"Don't see this in L.A."

He's actually a kind man. "No, you don't."

"Hey, let's finish up. We can walk home together."

The moon dodged between smoke-colored clouds. In silence, they walked about a block before Phoebe said, "Do you have arthritis?"

Joseph looked over at her; he hesitated. "How'd you know?"

"My grandfather has rheumatoid arthritis. Do you want me to walk up to the house and get my car?"

"I can do this slope." His voice was laced with pride.

"You sure?"

"I'm sure. Thanks, Phoebe."

He was modest and proud. A strange combination Phoebe didn't particularly find attractive in a man. But he was decent and kind, which any woman could revere.

When they reached Venetia's, she said, "Do you want to come in for a minute? Rest your knee?"

He looked to be considering it, but eventually said, "Sure. Probably should get off it for a minute."

The guesthouse wasn't visible from the street. The Streets' tri-level house, with lots of windows that offered extraordinary views of the lake, sprawled over a hill—was a jewel of a place. The guesthouse, small and quaint, was set on a slight incline. The flurries turned to rain which made the stones, leading to the guesthouse, slick. Joseph took painstaking steps to avoid slipping. Momentarily, he stared at the tree planted in reverence to Cordia. It was taller than he would have expected.

When they entered, the guesthouse was cold. Upon giving the room some light, Phoebe turned on a space heater. "It gets warm quickly. Take a seat."

Joseph went for the closest chair, which was too soft. He practically flopped in it and had to adjust himself.

"Can I get you something? A glass of water or..."

"I'm good. That coffee was mighty strong. It'll have me up half the night."

Once she sat, Joseph watched Phoebe closely getting comfortable in the small sofa, curling up at the corner hugging a cherry-red chenille pillow. He knew it in his gut that there was no hope for him with this woman. She was out of his league even more so than he at first realized. It came out before he was aware he said it: "You don't have children?"

For years Phoebe felt analyzed because she *chose* not to have children. By both men and women. At a certain age it was something you did in life. Even if you didn't get married, if you were a whole woman, you gave birth. No one considered that it was possible you couldn't have children. No one ever took into account some of the other underlying reasons, which were plentiful.

"No." But then Phoebe caught her words. "Well…"

"You were going to say?"

A car alarm went off in the otherwise silent night and the sound went on for quite a while; it distracted Phoebe.

Unguarded, and in a small voice, she said, "I did have a child."

"Was there some kind of incident?" He rubbed his aching knee with the palm of his hand.

Phoebe pulled at a corner of the pillow. An unacquainted melancholy rose in her chest. "I had a girl. I gave her up for adoption."

Joseph, his back rising straight as a board, wasn't anticipating anything like what he'd just heard. Hearing those words drip from her lips struck him: how the distinction of knowing and not knowing details about a person's history made all the difference. It took little to judge a person's character based on minute facts: what they did for a living; their religious affiliation; the clothes they wore or the cars they drove. Even worse, to determine their life story based on attitude or looks. Everybody had a story; one of depth—euphoria and suffering.

"There are probably good reasons why you made that choice."

"No one knew about this. Except Cordia. My mother never knew that I had given a child up. She didn't see me for over a year so she didn't even know that I was pregnant."

"Why did you do it?"

"It's easy to look back now and say why I did it. But at the time I chose to do it because I was very selfish and…"

"I don't see you as selfish."

"But then you don't know me."

Joseph agreed.

"Do you remember meeting Dianne at the book brunch?"

"She was also at Cordia's tree planting ceremony. Who could forget those cheekbones? You weren't there, at the tree planting. Why?"

"I was living in Sydney at the time. I missed my flight. I cried for days. I desperately wanted to be here."

Phoebe was wordless, solemn.

"Why'd you ask about Dianne?"

"When we were in Venice, she was crazy about this man, Gregory. It wasn't so much that Gregory had broken us—broken Venice up, but he helped get us there. We would have eventually broken up, but Gregory really was the instigator. We would have done another album had he not…"

"Did he ruin friendships?"

"The question I've raised a few times over the past week is whether it was a friendship to begin with. It took a while for our friendship to be truly tested. Friends have your back. They keep you grounded and call you out on things. They talk to you and *hear* what you have to say. They love you in spite of. They might judge, but they make sense of it. They agree to disagree.

"Dianne and I didn't have that kind of bond. We were—you know the loose term—*girlfriends*. Our friendship was based on timing. Synchronicity—for a season or a reason. But when we ran into each other after so many years had come to pass… We met for drinks not long after I moved here. Sitting at the table talking to her, I knew, if we were to have met in present time, in our fifties, we would never have started a friendship. We no longer have anything in common.

"That's the sad part. Because I always liked her and always thought about her through the years. I *cared* about Dianne and wanted her to be genuinely happy. But when I sat and talked with her, I saw her…"

"First, you two were young. I've lost touch with some of my buddies I'd known for years. We gradually lose touch with friends from our youth because our lives go in opposing directions. The more responsibilities we have, the less time…"

"I suppose so."

"Then, well, Venice might have made you appear as if you had more in common than you did. Surely becoming popular record-ing stars and traveling all over the world—you bond when you have something big holding you together. But you maintained a friendship with Cordia, up to her death. Were you two closer?"

"Actually, I was closer to Dianne than I was Cordia. But Cordia and I grew very close when Dianne broke her contract and left Venice. Cordia became my best friend. It's how I became Venetia's godmother."

"How does all this relate to giving your girl up for adoption?" Joseph figured the two were linked somehow. Or Phoebe changed the subject to avoid talking about the girl she gave up for adop-tion—a decision that, in hindsight, was impetuous.

"Gregory."

"Oh, yes, Gregory. Is there more to Gregory?"

Phoebe replied in a quiet voice, "Yes."

Joseph stopped rubbing his knee. Ever so slightly, he leaned forward. "Let me guess?"

"You think you can?"

"Possibly," he said. "Gregory was Dianne's boyfriend, right?" Phoebe nodded. "And…Did something happen between you and Gregory?"

"Dianne and Gregory had a fight. They supposedly ended things, and I'm not sure if I believed the breakup was really genuine. But…"

"He's the father, isn't he?" Phoebe swallowed tears. "You couldn't raise that child. The guilt was too great."

"Cordia said to abort it. That I would regret adoption more than abortion. I couldn't do that. I couldn't," she said, shaking her head. "I'm not really sure if it was a moral decision, but I couldn't abort the child. Every now and then I find myself looking at a young woman who would be her age now. I look to see if there's a trace of me in her. If she has my height and body type and hair texture, my skin color and think…I look, deeply. *Is that my child?* I ask myself. About three years ago—and it was an unconscious thing, really—I began to wonder if I should try to find her. For such a long time, it was never an issue. I didn't give it that much thought. Frankly, for years I didn't even care."

"There are consequences to choices, aren't there?"

"Oh, don't I know it. At the time, when you're young and don't have the knowledge or maturity that comes with being older… You can't know how much your choices influence your fate."

"You should consider trying to contact her."

"I…"

"Are you afraid, Phoebe?"

"Not necessarily afraid."

"You never told this Gregory dude?"

"He cared as little for me as I cared for him. I can't imagine doing something so insanely stupid now. I didn't even really *like* Gregory as a man."

"The child was born in L.A.?"

"Yes." Phoebe nodded.

"Phoebe?" Joseph's voice was solemn. She looked at him, traces of subtle tears hung in her eyes. "Find your daughter. Make peace with it."

Calmly, she said, "Yeah," and bowed her head.

When Joseph left some half-hour later, Phoebe stared into the void. Interrupting a person's life that way—she didn't think she could do it. If it were her, she would be loaded with questions and needing answers to fill in every single blank that left her life with ellipses. More than anything, she would want to know who her father was.

Torrick was in a taxi and leaving the hotel when his ringtone alerted him that Henna was calling. "O'Hare," he told the cabbie. "Henna?" Torrick frowned. "What's wrong? Why are you crying? Henna, calm down. Where are you right now?" Torrick clutched the handheld tightly. "Where's your mother? Sweetie, you need to calm down. What?" Torrick's voice went an octave higher than his general monotone. "I'm on my way to D.C., baby." With an uncontrollable heave, he said, "Has Daniela left yet? Okay, okay, baby. Go to school. I'll handle it." He covered his mouth and his mind went from one thing to the next.

He knew Jacqueline was probably giving her presentation right about now. He couldn't reach out to her. Torrick needed to settle down. His head was all over the place. He searched in his contacts and decided Pastor Stevens was the best decision he could make right about now. His wife answered on the second ring and Torrick asked if he could speak with the pastor. "I see," he replied when the pastor's wife told him he was out. "Listen, I'm traveling and I'm concerned about Dianne. Well, I don't know. She's been distracted lately." Torrick looked at the cabbie through the rearview mirror. When their eyes met, the cabbie diverted his eyes abruptly. "Is it possible that you pick up Henna? I really appreciate it. She gets out at three. That's right. Thank you. I appreciate this, I really do." When he finished the call, Torrick bowed his head.

He was in so deep with Jacqueline. He wanted to be with her; he *liked* spending time with her. He knew he needed to give it up and pay more attention to his home life. He wasn't even sure how, or even when, but he and Dianne were losing each other. They had been happy for some years. Of course, which happened even in the best of marriages, they became each other's routine. Sex, on some level, verged on perfunctory in a long-term marriage. He couldn't recall the last time they'd gone out together and did something fun. Not without the girls. It could have been the Beyoncé concert last year, but Torrick couldn't really pin it down concretely.

When he returned from Washington, he'd need to have a serious talk with Jacqueline. They each made an effort to end it. Or were they kidding themselves? What they started was as a result of desire and timing. They never acted on it previously. But their clandestine relationship could easily have happened a year ago, given the right circumstances. He stared blindly at the Chicago skyline subtly drifting from view, and he asked himself did he want to end things. It wasn't so much about being ready. It was quite possible he wanted to be with Jacqueline. And end his marriage? Torrick couldn't conceive of it; when he looked at his life, he saw it *with* Dianne. But slapping Daniela? Nearly running down a deer? Allegedly getting involved with someone that gave her chlamydia? Having fights with Phoebe over triviality? Being distant, moody. *Hell, what was the therapy for?*

What could Daniela have possibly done to deserve to be slapped? Between the two, Daniela was the more obedient child. Mature for her age, she hardly, if ever, gave them trouble. They could depend on her. Quite conscientious for her age, she did what she was told eight times out of ten. Henna got bored easily, and had a way of holding on to secrets. Quiet as it was kept, she was his favorite. But Torrick anticipated more trouble coming his way when she was older.

"What airline?" The cabbie interrupted Torrick's erratic thoughts. "American."

"Those pills aren't working. I'm jittery, and I'm too fucking emotional. Do I need to look into hormone replacements? Why is coming here not working? Hell, you aren't cheap!"

"Dianne, please have a seat. You appear upset," the therapist said.

"You think?!"

The therapist took one step and attempted to reach out to Dianne standing in the center of her office. She was shaking, and while there were no tears, her eyes were bloodshot.

"What's wrong with me?" she screamed. "What the hell is happening to me?" she cried out. "I slapped my daughter. I *slapped* her. I've never laid a hand on her. You tell me, doctor. What the hell is going on?"

"Dianne, please. Sit. We need to identify your stressors."

She sniffed her runny nose and balled her trembling hand into a tight fist. She took the nearest seat. The therapist reached for a chair and pulled it close to Dianne, extending her a Kleenex. "What has happened?" she asked in a voice that was naturally but annoyingly calm.

Dianne blew her nose. "What must my children think of me? What?" She pressed her hands together and placed them against her lips, prayer-style.

"Where is Torrick in all this?"

"He's—he had to go out of town on business. I don't want him seeing me like this. I have to get it together, do you understand? I can't—I *can't*—let my children see me like this."

"Dianne…" The therapist touched her knee gingerly. "How many pills have you been taking? Are you following my instructions?"

"I don't know. I'm out."

"Then you're overmedicating. You shouldn't be *out*."

There was a beat of silence. The therapist placed both of her hands on Dianne's knees. She saw the dark circles under her eyes. *Insomnia*. Her lips quivered. She was going to fight it every step of the way. She was stronger than this. Whatever brought her here, she would make it right and leave with her head high, the therapist assessed.

"Why did you slap your daughter?"

"I'm not sure what came when. We were going to get something to eat. Henna asked me if I was sick."

"Why would she ask you that?"

"She thinks chlamydia means I'm sick."

"Are you saying Henna knows about the chlamydia?"

She answered with a slight nod of her head, her eyes downcast, but her eyelids fluttered.

"How?"

"I...She said something about hearing me talking on the telephone. It could only mean she overheard something I said to my sister. She's the only other person that knows, except you. The personal trainer blames me. He told me I gave *him* chlamydia. And that can only mean that Torrick gave it to me." Her laughter was sarcastic. "You see, I don't know who did what and what is what. I'm not even sure. My husband could've given it to me. The personal trainer put that in my head and now I think Torrick's been sleeping around. Two months ago, I would never have considered that."

"Do you, Dianne, believe that Torrick is the one who gave you chlamydia?"

She shook her head.

"Do you believe he's being unfaithful?"

She shook her head.

"Then you have to stop considering what the personal trainer said to you. He needs to put it on someone else. If he didn't get it from his partner, that means he got it from a third party and not you or his girlfriend. He doesn't know how he got it, so he's putting it on you."

She sniffed her nose. "Torrick knows."

"What, that you had chlamydia?"

With a nod, Dianne answered the therapist's question.

"You told him?"

"No," she said quietly.

The therapist took Dianne's hands into hers. "How?"

"It was Henna."

Startled, the therapist said, "Henna?"

"When she overheard my conversation, she thought I was sick and she asked Torrick what exactly is chlamydia."

"But he never mentioned it?"

"He never even hinted at knowing."

"What else has happened?"

Years ago, she was a beautiful woman, thought Dianne.

A tear sat at the corner of Dianne's eye. She used her forefinger to absorb it. "Remember I told you about the book brunch. Well, there was an author there who's writing a book on musicians from the seventies and eighties. A where-are-they-now something or other. She wanted to interview Phoebe and me. I honestly had no idea how much I resented Phoebe until Sunday. I knew that Gregory was a sensitive subject with me. But talking about that time in our lives…it was difficult. I never want to see her again. I want nothing to do with Phoebe."

"Forgiveness is so important to your emotional well-being, Dianne."

"That woman needs to kneel and kiss the ground."

"Do you realize how you collude in your own suffering? T.S. Eliot wrote that the end is where we start from."

"What does that mean?"

"I'm going to let you consider what it means. But consider this, too: You are constantly feeding an old issue. You have unconsciously built a trap."

"I don't feel trapped."

"Some part of you believes that you got cheated."

"I wouldn't rewrite my story. I like my life."

"You are comfortable with your personal myth?"

She retrieved her hands and leaned back in the chair. "You have a way with words, don't you? I feel blessed to have Daniela and Henna. They're the best thing that's happened in my life."

"And Torrick?"

"I love Torrick."

"I believe you do. But I also believe—after talking to you for weeks now—there is something you need but aren't getting, either from your marriage or from life."

"You think this because I chose to sleep with another man?"

"You are preoccupied with your past. And you are clinging."

The therapist watched Dianne turning her wedding band around with her fingers over and over until it no longer served a purpose. She looked straight into the therapist's eyes and said ever so calmly, "Phoebe claims Gregory's gay."

"Gay?" But the sound of her voice revealed nothing specific.

"I've been in love with a gay man all this time. How ridiculous is that!"

"So he was never available to you, was he? God works in the strangest ways, Dianne. In an unforeseen way, Phoebe saved you."

"It's not like she meant to save me."

"It may have been fated; something the universe had a hand in. We will never know. You met Torrick, and you have said enough times in this office that you are blessed. Do you really believe that you are blessed?"

"I'm not following you."

"Anyone who believes in a Higher Being would most likely say they are blessed. Being blessed is more an experience. When you say you're blessed, how does that look to you? Is it because you have a wonderful home and live in a safe neighborhood? That you are physically well, as are your children and husband? You aren't struggling, or facing hardship of any kind like so many are right now? Is that what blessed means to you? Would you feel equally blessed if something happened to Daniela, or Henna? What if your security was snatched from under you and you had to start over? Like Phoebe. Would you still consider yourself *blessed?*" The therapist watched Dianne closely. She began to shrink in her chair. Her patient didn't come here to talk about being blessed, despite the fact that each time she visited her office, the therapist was aware that Dianne referred to herself as blessed. She was there solely because her life was falling apart and she didn't know why and she couldn't control the out of control-ness of what was happening to her. She couldn't make sense of her *blessed* life. "Dianne, time will find you out."

"What does that mean? The personal trainer will always follow me around like a shadow?"

"It's much more complicated than your decision to sleep with the personal trainer. You see, the brain constructs our reality, and our hearts have a way of believing what our minds cannot seem to rationalize. On a conscious level, yes, you have an awareness of being blessed. What you are lacking is the emotional connection to that belief; the genuine *feeling* of being blessed.

"You have traveled the world and led a glamorized life. Even experienced years of public persona. You ate at some of the best restaurants and flew on the Concorde. So many people—especially these days—would give anything to have experienced your life. In your still young life, you've managed two *blessed* lives: one of excitement, exposure, and traveling the world, and then the life of wife and mother. That is an amazing story. Your life is indeed a blessing. And yet you feel something is wrong. There's something missing. Your attention—your focus—is elsewhere. Why is it so difficult for you to embrace *this* moment? To live in *this* moment?"

Dianne lowered her eyes.

The therapist said, "I think you're ready to do the work you came here to do. I want to help you. You're ready now."

The presentation put a strain on Jacqueline. Stefan's client base was primarily made up of corporations, and since his passing, she, along with Michael and another consultant, was holding the hands of those clients who brought Media Capital substantial revenue. Until it was determined who would take over Stefan's clients, Jacqueline had to play nice. But she loathed working with men running Fortune 500s. It wasn't her thing. She was so much more comfortable, not to mention effective, with one-on-ones.

When she arrived at the office for the presentation, it occurred to Jacqueline that she didn't have her laptop. She called Torrick before calling the Town Car driver to have him check to see whether she'd left it in the room, and he informed her that it was on the table, still open to the presentation she was working on prior to leaving for the meeting. That was something Jacqueline never, *never* did in all the years of working as a consultant. She made it in a cutthroat business by being organized, driven, a smooth talker, and had the skills to work a room with her often irresistible allure. Her looks, no doubt about it, didn't close any doors. Yet in the business she was in, looks alone couldn't seal the deal. Moreover, at her age she was competing with young women straight out of college having grown up in an intense mediated culture. In her college days, Jacqueline couldn't imagine an online university. Here she was now, competing with the likes of Claire, her assistant. So when she left the laptop and wasn't particularly comfortable in doing the presentation—not to mention standing in a boardroom before a group of people she needed to impress and persuade—she knew she wasn't going to be on her game. Not like she was three, five years ago, prior to people referring to her as *ma'am*. Torrick had given her a pep talk and convinced her she'd knock it out of the park. Jacqueline left the hotel room feeling better because he'd managed to get her adrenaline flowing.

Still, forgetting the laptop was a sign. She was slipping. She dreaded calling Claire, who most likely hadn't gotten in the office yet, to ask her to forward the presentation so she could download it from her electronic tablet. It showed a lack of professionalism, and it would be the second time Claire had to forward her the presentation in less than twenty-four hours. When Claire answered, Jacqueline was relieved. She was only too pleased to forward her the file.

After all was said and done, Jacqueline felt good following the presentation. She called Michael and briefed him. While she waited in the hotel lobby for the hired car to take her to the airport, Jacqueline checked her voicemail messages. Gwen's father was requesting she be at Gwen's court appearance the following day. There was no way Jacqueline could fly to L.A. with what she had on her plate. She called Gwen's father and they talked briefly. He inquired if she could recommend security for Gwen; he didn't like the *so-called* security that was hired by her manager. "I'll see what I can do," she'd told him. "But my assistant, Claire, will have to take my place. You'll need to trust me."

"Venetia Street."

"Perfect timing; it's Jacqueline."

"Hi, Jacqueline. How's everything?"

"Good. Tell me, are you going to be in L.A. tomorrow?"

"I'm here now. What's going on?"

"Gwen's hearing. I know you've made several attempts to reach out to her and she's rebuffed you. But this hearing is important. It's the difference between serving time or a hefty fine, probation and community service."

"Tell me, Jacqueline. Could Gwen handle time in jail?"

"Absolutely not. She throws off that diva persona on television, but she's a daddy's girl to the core. She's never had to do any heavy lifting. When she got that reality TV show, it only made her less accountable to go out and do something of, well, depth. I feel a certain obligation to help her, but I'm leaving Chicago and I have to be back in the office tomorrow. My assistant, Claire, is going to fly into L.A. and work the media."

"I don't have to warn you, it's going to be pandemonium."

Jacqueline rolled her eyes, and the idea of having Claire take this on gave her pause. Would it be too much for her, especially on such short notice? It would be the first time she handled something of this magnitude. Although, while Jacqueline took days off to mourn Stefan, Claire was awesome.

"Her father's requesting additional security."

"I was going to suggest that."

"Is it possible…?"

"I'll reach out to her again. What would you like me to do? Prep her?"

"Exactly."

"What about her attorney? We were at SC at the same time. Brooke Richardson?"

"Kent Richardson's daughter? I heard she went to Georgetown."

"She definitely went to USC. She received her J.D. from Boalt Hall. She's a lefty."

"Kent Richardson…Well, I knew he was at Vanderbilt, but got his masters at Stanford. Okay, so can you reach out to her?"

"I'll get back with you."

Jacqueline called Torrick's assistant to request extra security for Gwen's court appearance. Ordinarily, she would have contacted Torrick directly, but she decided to go through his assistant instead. She was polite, professional, and said she'd discuss it with Torrick's director of public-profile security detail and have it arranged.

When she hung up, Jacqueline studied her watch and wondered where her driver was. She couldn't miss the flight. No sooner than she decided to call Claire to find out what was going on, her cell rang. "Hi." She grinned from ear-to-ear. "I'm waiting on my car. I wish I could be in D.C. with you. I love Washington this time of year. What's happened?" Jacqueline caught sight of her driver entering the hotel and she rushed to her feet, waving to get his attention. He acknowledged her with a professional nod. "What's going on with Dianne, Torrick?" she asked, walking toward her driver. She listened attentively. "She's in therapy? She didn't tell me that." They walked out of the hotel entrance and to the parked Town Car. "Should I talk to her? Okay, call me."

On the way to the airport, Jacqueline could feel butterflies in her stomach. For several weeks, she and Torrick stole as much time as they could muster in order to spend time together. Not every encounter was sexual. Sometimes they talked and laughed—their conversations were animated, vivid. Typically, they ate delivered meals; although once they chanced it and walked to Whole Foods. It was a dry night and the air was crisp and clean; vivid stars ornamented the ink-blue sky. They piled cartons with all types of veggies and meats and salad. They bought so much prepared food Jacqueline had two days' worth of leftovers.

She knew it could not last. When she talked with her mother a few days after she started formally *seeing* Torrick, she warned her daughter that her heart would be broken. What Jacqueline admired about her mother—she herself lacked it—was her sense of non-judging. Growing up, she looked up to her mother and used to pray to turn out like her. She knew that her father had cheated on her mother which eventually led to her leaving him. Jacqueline's mother, style-conscious and dignified, told her once, "Your stepfather is a beautiful man." Jacqueline said back to her mother, *"What?"* Too young at the time to comprehend the meaning of those words, now though, having spent blissful weeks with Torrick, she understood exactly what her mother was trying to tell her. But the distinction: Jacqueline was sneaking around, and Torrick was lying to his wife, and she backstabbing a good friend—the deceit of it all. Jacqueline was never good at being second or third. It wasn't *the* reason why she wasn't big on being involved with married men. But it was *a* reason. And she ended up—despite avoiding it all her adult life—in love with a married man. There, the truth was out in the open: she was without question *in love* with Torrick.

She covered her face, feeling shame and sadness in chorus. *How did I let this happen?*

"There's a slight delay up ahead, Ms. Daye. But you should make your flight."

In a quiet, mechanical voice, Jacqueline said, "Thank you."

Now, Torrick's domestic life—his wife, their children—was starting to spill over into the life they had been sharing. Another reason Jacqueline couldn't get caught up in a married man—his baggage, his *other* life. It was messy. Intellectually, she knew only two things could ever come from it: he'd leave his wife, or it would end with his choosing his wife over her. The idea of that was always unbearable. *What would Stefan think of what I'm doing?* He would be the first person she'd go to to discuss something like this. While she didn't share all the details of her intimate life with Dianne, this might have been the one time she would seek her advice. Jacqueline had nowhere to go with this. She had no one to talk to. A friend, a confidante. There was no one.

She told herself as soon as what they shared interfered with his life with Dianne, she would end it. Sadly, painfully, it was what she had to do. Forgetting the laptop was something she would never have done if Torrick hadn't come to Chicago to spend time with her. Every man she'd been with over the past decade never once distracted her to the point it diverted attention away from her working life. They were never compelling enough to sidetrack her. Daniel wasn't solely intellectual curiosity to Jacqueline; he was physically very attractive. Had she not started something with Torrick, perhaps he would now be her lover.

From the moment she stepped out of the Town Car and went through security and stood waiting for the plane to board, Jacqueline couldn't surmise why Torrick had put a spell on her. By the time she slid her key into the condo lock, she decided it was precisely because he wasn't attainable. Once inside the semi-dark condo, she rested her body against the door and regret overcame her.

CHAPTER 12

There was not one thing to wear in her closet. Phoebe needed to pull off a professional look as best she could with what she had to work with. Yet the clothes she'd brought with her from L.A. were not quite it. *Darnit!* She couldn't justify going out to buy something new. Phoebe reached for the remote control; television would distract her, at least momentarily. She turned the volume up. Paparazzi swarmed a street with palm trees leaning toward the wind in the backdrop. Phoebe could discern the sound of cameras snapping. Videographers clashed into one another and into a mass of onlookers—it was mayhem. Fans—in the dozens—were screaming the name "Gwen!" and holding posters stating "We Love You So Much, Gwen," and "We Are Here For You, Gwen!" The star of *Gwenology* was being escorted into the courthouse; she struggled to get through the chaos.

Is that Claire? Phoebe cracked a facetious grin. Two months ago, she was answering phones at Media Capital. She went from that to a celebrity handler? Between the Beverly Hills police and the impressive security detail surrounding her, one would have thought Gwen was royalty. It took forever to get her from the chauffeur-driven vehicle and escorted into the courthouse. Phoebe never saw a *Gwenology* episode, but to have not heard about Gwen, one would have to be in a coma or six feet under. She didn't know enough about her as a person or what she did before she got the top-rated reality show. Prior to leaving L.A., Phoebe had heard about her drunk driving escapades and at least one hit and run, which was abruptly changed to something else—like a "misunderstanding," and the person allegedly hit by Gwen recanted her story to the press. *Rumor had it, she was paid off.*

Phoebe pressed mute; she couldn't bear it. A respectable cable network felt the conscious influence of ephemeral trivia. They spent valuable airtime on something as inconsequential as Gwen making a court appearance. Since the president was reelected, the cable networks had to resume their repetitious programming.

"We're not doing one more thing for this young woman until she signs an exclusive. Frankly, I don't like her and we should wash our hands of her. By end of business, if she doesn't sign the new contract, drop her. She's a liability."

Jacqueline muted the television and slipped off her glasses. Michael stood in the center of her office, and he looked exhausted. Everybody at Media Capital was exhausted. The hours were long; the work stressful. Stefan left things in remarkably good order, but his absence was deeply felt.

"Michael, calm down."

"No," he snapped, and something he never did with Jacqueline. "This appearance…What, extra security, a life coach? I know Gwen is a personal friend, but Jacqueline, I draw the line on this."

"I hear you. I agree." She dropped the remote control on a stack of papers. "I'll fly to L.A. next week. I'll have a one-on-one with her personally. Her manager blocks me, her father. I have a sneaky suspicion they're, well, you know."

"Sleeping together?" Michael chuckled. "Find a way to change the narrative on Gwen."

"To change the narrative means to alter her popularity."

"We're not babysitters. We've got Anthony Perez's attorney working with legal—a cop killer *and* drug smuggler who likes to social-network! I feel we're going in the wrong direction. Work something out with Gwen's people."

When he left the office, Jacqueline tuned the volume. She was proud of Claire; she did a fabulous job. She'd never seen the outfit she was wearing, which had J. Crew written all over it. Discreetly fashionable, it didn't clash with Gwen's just-perfect black dress— a bit tight but tasteful—and a chiffon pashmina wrapped loosely around her toned arms; her reddish-blonde hair pulled back in a ponytail; and thank the Lord, peep-toe, six-inch heels. Her incessantly talked-about look, which included every type of plat- form on the shoes market, and signature oversized gold hoops, the hoodie, false eyelashes and glossy lipstick, would be a tad bling for this appearance. It was crucial; the difference between jail time and freedom. Standing before a judge that was already *up to here* with Gwen, she needed to impress him and demonstrate that she took this thing seriously. What's more, she needed to show some respect. Venetia was worth every penny. If she could talk Gwen into that outfit, her reputation preceded her.

"They're still talking about this?" Phoebe turned off the television. She assumed if one cable network was following the Gwen court appearance, in all likelihood, the others would be, too. She still hadn't decided on what she could wear to the interview. She went rummaging through Venetia's closet, but she had to face it, Venetia's clothes—while fashionable and chic—were simply too small for her. Venetia had to be no more than a six. Phoebe was an eight. Venetia wore her clothes close, which meant anything in her closet wouldn't get past Phoebe's hips.

She slipped into a pair of jeans, straightened the guesthouse, and headed for the mall. There was no parking available on the street. Finally, she broke down and parked under Barnes & Noble. She'd pay the outrageous parking to avoid wasting any more time. She'd come to learn, sometimes it was best to spend the extra cash, since time itself had a way of calculating into money somehow.

It was love at first sight—the attractive clothes hanging on the racks at Nordstrom that Phoebe couldn't afford to spend her money on, but wanted. Or did she fancy them strictly because they were out of her reach at the moment? She needed to use the toilet and afterward she'd head to the Rack. "The restrooms?" She stopped a woman she identified as an employee.

"Right through there," she offered courteously.

Making her way in the direction of the restrooms, Phoebe was drawn to the café. She decided to steal a look at the menu. "Hello," she said to someone passing with plates of yummy-looking salads. *Mmmm*, she thought. "Your menu," she asked someone behind the cash register.

"Right there," said the cashier in a patient voice.

She stepped away from the area where people were standing on line to pay for their meals. When she turned her head, Phoebe spotted Jacqueline Daye at a table near the opened French doors adjacent to the skybridge. She was with—it was Dianne. Phoebe stopped dead in her tracks. She couldn't go to speak to Jacqueline with Dianne at the table. She had no idea what would happen. Dianne's intense fury toward her—no telling what she'd do. The look she gave Phoebe when she stormed out of Philipa's—if looks could kill, Phoebe would be a corpse. She returned the menu to the slot and decided she could grab something at eBar.

While browsing through outfits in the Rack, she flashed back on her lunch with Michael. When she took the elevator to the top floor of the tallest building in the city to have lunch with him at a reservations-only restaurant, what came to mind was that she made an impression on him that totally slipped past her. Or he mistook her indifference as playing hard to get. *Perhaps he was used to dating younger women. Women in their fifties didn't play hard to get.* While their drinks at Mason House ended civilly, there was nothing in it that suggested she was interested in him.

He hadn't arrived when Phoebe was greeted by the maître d'. He seated her by the window. On a clear, sunshiny day, the view would be stunning. But it was chilly and wet; quite typical of the region. Phoebe ordered mineral water and tried to stay in the moment. Not that she was nervous necessarily, but she was feeling insecure. She didn't know why.

"I apologize for keeping you waiting." Michael pulled a chair out and sat.

"I worked at Media Cap long enough to get it."

"I live in a strange world."

Why am I here was at the tip of her tongue, but Phoebe chose to allow the lunch to unfold naturally.

The waiter approached their table and Michael ordered a drink. He rested his forearms against the table's edge. "Thank you for accommodating me. I had a meeting in the building so I thought lunch here would be convenient."

"Sure, that's fine."

Michael averted his eyes from Phoebe and to the heavily suspended clouds. For a split-second, he lost his power to speak, as if her presence—strong and palpable—threw him off. "I have a client who's in the beginning stages of preparing for a major fundraiser. It'll be high-profile and a lot of influential people will be in attendance. During our conversation, he happened to mention that he was in need of someone with stellar event planning skills. I thought of you."

Surprised, Phoebe said, "Me?" as she pointed her finger at herself. "Yes, you."

So caught short, she lost all sense of thought. She took a sip of her mineral water and finally said, "Why?"

"Hospitality assistant was beneath your talent. This opportunity would never be something you could learn about on the Internet. It's not one of those copious opportunities. It's the type that can only be gained by who you know. Maybe social media, it could slip through. But even then to get to my client or the people who work directly with him? Nearly impossible. He's looking for someone who comes highly recommended."

"Did you recommend...mention me to your client?"

"I told him I knew someone and suggested that he meet with you."

The waiter interrupted without saying anything but placed Michael's drink on the cloth-covered table. Michael, without looking at the waiter, thanked him and reached for his glass.

"Would you like to see menus now?"

Michael told the waiter to give them five.

"So what do I need to do?"

"I'll contact him and let him know you're interested. I take it you are?"

"Very much so."

"If he wants to meet with you, you'll need to be ready because he's leaving for London tomorrow night. And you'll need to raise an eyebrow. He's not an easy man to make an impression on. It's like a Hollywood pitch—you'll have only a small window in which to persuade him."

The pressure was on Phoebe not only to impress Michael's mysterious client; likewise, she needed to walk into that meeting with everything she had. She had to break down and buy a suit she shouldn't be buying. She wanted this chance. She needed to get her life back on track.

"I forgot how much of a bitch she can be. A damn backstabber!"
Jacqueline replayed those words in her head. Seated on the loveseat in her office trying to concentrate on what was in front of her, her mind was so far away from everything that just a month ago shaped her full and hectic life. She wasn't in denial that her work came first. Everything else took a backseat. Jacqueline blinked, reached for her reading glasses and tried yet again to stay focused. Within a minute, her mind reverted back to her lunch with Dianne. She looked tired, as if insomnia deprived her of sleep. Although it was cute, Dianne wore a cap; something Jacqueline couldn't recall ever seeing her wear before. In some ways she looked younger, more childlike without makeup, except a subtle, mocha-colored lip-gloss. While they sat in Nordstrom's Café, Jacqueline sensed that Dianne was under mysterious pressure. Since she'd known her, Dianne was about appearances; and it wasn't as though Jacqueline didn't care about public impressions. She'd be the first to admit it. By chance, that was the initial connection. Jacqueline's career depended on how she presented herself. She was no longer that thirty-year-old that made heads turn when she entered a room. While perspicacious, she was no longer on the cutting-edge and her career now had a shorter shelf life. It took more time to negotiate a deal. The way business was conducted had indeed changed. Still, Jacqueline knew the phone didn't ring as much as it once had because she was middle-aged; it didn't matter how good she looked. Ten years ago, she could make things happen quicker, easier.

Jacqueline not once had this deep need to have what Dianne had—being a mother and a wife. Despite her labels, Dianne wouldn't be caught dead in running shoes and designer work-outs browsing the aisles of Trader Joe's, or doing coffee with other mothers as they gossiped about troubled marriages or who needed liposuction! Dianne was a proud mother; likewise she was a former Venice girl. In sly ways, her friend reminded Jacqueline that she was getting older and her biological clock stroked midnight a decade ago. Men in their age group were looking for women half the age they were, and she would be lucky to find someone to be with in a *real* relationship. *Real* relationship—those were her words. As if to suggest Jacqueline was past the stage in life of having a *real* relationship. Jacqueline always suspected that Dianne thought she slept around just to be with someone. She failed to know details about Jacqueline's love life because she never bothered to inquire. Yet Jacqueline didn't sleep around with random men; she wanted love, not superficial comfort. She had standards; neither high nor low. Not even demanding. She simply refused to settle so not to be alone. There was a time when she did consider a family. Yet the years attempting to get past the proverbial glass ceiling came and went so suddenly. When Jacqueline was trying to make a name for herself, a child wouldn't only have gotten in the way of that, but would also have been slighted in some way. Besides, no man had given her what she needed in a relationship in order to go so far as marriage.

Until Torrick.

"So how are you and Torrick?" Jacqueline asked. She had a consuming need to know. Their lunches arrived, and she was struck by her audacity to even inquire; she'd never done such a thing in the past. She needed to know whether Dianne sensed that her husband had strayed. She'd bragged enough times over the years about how her man was the faithful type and that she never had to "worry about Torrick."

"We're like ships in a dark night, out at sea." She stared at her wedding band—traditional, gold. "Maybe you were on to something—by not getting married."

Jacqueline asked too emotionally: "What do you mean?"

"Look," Dianne said. She reached for her water to wet her tongue. "I can't talk marriage, and especially about Torrick right now. It's…" She looked so exhausted. "Are we ever going to do our spa-day and go shopping? Daniel must be taking up all your free time. When was the last time we did hot yoga? You know, I was thinking of checking out Botox."

"I might have a conflict—did you say Botox? Dianne!"

It was the first time Jacqueline saw her laugh over lunch. "Well…"

"Black doesn't crack, you know that! Anyway, I'll text you and let you know if this weekend will work. Will Phoebe be coming with us?"

"I didn't tell you?"

"Tell me what?"

"Oh, I didn't get a chance. You were on your way to Chicago. Do you remember that woman that was with Nigel, the author?"

"The white woman with that so-sharp dress? She asked for my business card."

"She's Bradford Jerrod's daughter."

"Oh, really. I'll need to check to see if I kept her information."

"And she's writing a book…"

"Dear God, who isn't writing a book? It used to be such a well-guarded profession. It required—what?" Jacqueline shrugged. "Now anyone—you, me—can write books!"

"Nigel's book is good."

"Oh, I agree. I'd like to arrange a European tour for him. I have good contacts across the pond."

"Philipa—that's her name—she's writing a book on musicians

from the seventies and eighties. She wanted to talk with me and Phoebe because she's doing a chapter on Venice. We—Phoebe and me; and Venetia was there—met her the day after the book brunch. It turned out to be the worst day of my life. I despise Phoebe. You remember me telling you about Gregory? She claims he's gay. She—Phoebe's so faux."

"Was she 'so faux' when you were in Venice?"

"She was *always* faux. Now she's an old maid; a has-been without a man or a career. You know, her house is in foreclosure. It was such a cute California bungalow. Now she doesn't even have a place to live. She squandered all of her money. Two-faced cow."

"Jacqueline?"

Jacqueline looked up from her paperwork. Claire was standing at the edge of the loveseat. "What's up?" *How long had she been standing there watching me—reflect?*

"The judge made his ruling. Gwen's getting probation, community service, and being fined thirty-five hundred."

With a sigh of relief, Jacqueline said, "Thank you, Claire. Good work, by the way."

Claire was flattered by Jacqueline's compliment. "Thank you."

When Jacqueline got home, she was greeted with two voice-mails from her heroin-addicted nephew. She made a mental note to call her half-brother—let him pay for his son's habit. Jacqueline drew the line; she was no longer going to be her nephew's enabler. Another message was from Torrick. At once, Jacqueline went into insecure mode. The *other* woman mode. The *mode* she dared never to be in because it was precisely what being with a married man entailed. A week ago Torrick would never have called her land-line. She vaguely remembered giving him the number. He knew the best way to reach her was to call her cell. A year ago nothing about her or her life suggested she could be in such a strange and seemingly powerless position. Jacqueline planned her life to the T. Rarely was she met with unforeseen surprises that she herself hadn't in some way mindfully orchestrated. She had become precisely what she loathed in other women.

"Joseph? Hey, good to see you. Come on in," his tax attorney friend said. "I was about to head to the path."

They arrived into a spacious living area with a plasma screen nearly the size of the wall it was mounted on.

"You've redone the place," Joseph said.

"How long has it been?" The tax attorney reached for his trainers and slipped each one on.

"Well," Joseph said, taking a seat. "I'm not sure."

"So what are you up to?"

Joseph pressed his elbows to his knees. "I was thinking about getting on a program. Doctor says I need to lose a few pounds."

"Any serious health issues?" the tax attorney asked, relaxing in the chair, his arms resting loosely on the armrests.

"No, no," Joseph said. "Blood pressure's a little up, but I've cut back on some things. We aren't as young as we used to be."

"But it's lifestyle, my friend. As long as you maintain a level of moderation, you'll be fine. Have you considered someone yet?"

"Huh? Oh, you mean a personal trainer? I thought you might be able to recommend someone."

"I could do that, sure. I used to work out at this gym over there off Eleventh. Right next to the Jamba Juice and Safeway? There's a guy—I don't recall his name. Black guy, good-looking, in terrific shape. I think I have his card. I can check if you'd like." The tax attorney was on his feet before Joseph replied.

"That'll be good."

"Hey, have you met someone?" the tax attorney wondered, stopping at the edge of his living room which led to another part of the house not visible from the front room.

Ill at ease, and later he would ask himself why, Joseph said, "Nothing like that. Why do you ask?"

"Not that health isn't a reason. But what generally inspires us to get in shape is ego. We start to notice how women pay less attention to us. Especially when we get that middle," the tax attorney candidly spoke. "It ages us. But these days—science is a beautiful thing—cosmetic intervention can visibly stop the clock. Let me see if I still have that card."

Of course Joseph was inspired to take a closer look in the mirror, especially after spending time with Phoebe. She had no plans of staying in town. He figured if he had time, he could show his good side and she'd soften up, grow to like him more. But that was false hope. Even his son said he needed to get back out there and try to "find someone." He'd recommended he go online to one of the dating sites—MiddleAgeSingles.com. Joseph visited the site, but he didn't join. For one thing he didn't have a photograph to upload; and quite frankly, the whole online dating idea didn't appeal to him. Besides, Joseph wanted to meet a woman the old-fashioned way. "Dad, you have to come up out of the twentieth century. You'll never meet someone buried in the house. And you claim the women at church just want a companion or something. You *need* to get online!"

"I can't believe I still have this. I wrote down the date we met. A thing I do," said the tax attorney, coming back into the living room. "Here you go. I'm not sure it's still a good number. The date on the back was just under two years ago. But give it a try."

Joseph studied the business card with a judgmental eye. "He has his picture on the card."

The tax attorney started stretching. "Branding they call it."

"Hey, what do you think of online dating?"

He bent over, his fingers dangling, and just short of touching the spotless carpet. The tax attorney said, "I tried that; I didn't give it enough time. There's always speed-dating." He began stretching his legs by grabbing his foot with his hand from behind.

"I heard of that," said Joseph. "But I thought that was for young people. You know, like Cornell's age."

"How's Cornell by the way…since he moved back home?" The tax attorney started doing crunches.

He's in really good shape. "Going back to school next semester and found himself a part-time job."

"There's a sense of pride, a sense of meaning and purpose, in doing a day's work. He's a smart kid."

"Yeah," Joseph said, his mind drifting to and fro.

"Hey, if you're interested in speed-dating, they have one for seniors. I can e-mail the website to you."

"Seniors?" Joseph frowned.

The tax attorney looked over at Joseph sitting in the chair. He hadn't noticed just how much weight Joseph had put on since he stopped working, or was it when they stopped playing racquetball once a week? His RA was a factor; the tax attorney recognized that. While it wasn't easy to lose weight at their age, there was no excuse for him to let himself go.

"Look, I met a really attractive woman and we went out a few times. She was an eye-stopper. A yoga instructor. Tight ass for fifty-six." The tax attorney thought Joseph needed to ease back into the scene. He'd known him for quite some years; he didn't see him doing online dating. Speed-dating, on the other hand, might raise his self-confidence again.

"Well, maybe." Joseph struggled to his feet. His weight made it difficult; he couldn't jump to his feet like some spring chicken.

"I'll even go with you." It was clear Joseph wasn't up for it. Perhaps if he went along with him, Joseph might feel more comfortable. "I'm seeing someone, you know. But these things are good social settings. A little conversation, a little laughter. It's harmless."

"Yeah, well…"

"Call that trainer. See if he's still taking clients."

They started walking toward the front door.

"You 'bout to go run?"

"That's right."

When they reached the corner at the foot of the hill, the tax attorney started jumping and jogging in place, showing off.

"We'll talk!" the tax attorney said, and trotted off toward the path.

"Sounds good!" Joseph called out. He watched the tax attorney running gracefully toward the lake. Observing him running effortlessly, Joseph felt defeated. *I'll never look like that again.*

CHAPTER 13

Pastor Stevens rushed in, his Holy Bible clutched in one hand. "So sorry, Torrick. My meeting ran over. A couple came in for pastoral counseling prior to taking their vows. It's so important to know if you're making the right choice. Sometimes..." He placed the white, oversized Bible on a desk. "You just don't know." He took a seat, and as a courtesy, Torrick began to stand, but the pastor said, "Don't bother."

"Thank you for seeing me on such short notice."

"I got nothing but time for you, Torrick. All you've done for the church."

"You give me too much credit."

"Actually, I don't give you enough. And neither do you. But let's not fuss over this. I'm guessing you're here about little Henna. And Dianne." Unconsciously, he was wringing his hands. Pastor Stevens took notice. "Everything will work itself out. You can trust that. We face troubled waters now and again. The broken places—that's when light finds its way in."

A tolerant man, and one who believed in the Divine, Torrick wasn't in the mood. He respected that Pastor Stevens was, after all, a man of God. It was his way to go on about faith and trust and patience.

"Let me ask you, Torrick. Are you still unfaithful?"

His head low, his voice hardly audible, he admitted that he was.

"Little Henna's confused. Now, Mrs. Stevens worked it out with her. She explained that Dianne wasn't ill and that Henna overheard a conversation and took it out of context. That she didn't have all the facts. That seemed to put her mind at ease. Now Dianne," the pastor said. "She's another story. You know I'm partial to therapy. Sometimes you need to…well, have faith in science. But…"

"Dianne's all over the map. I really believe it has to do with menopause."

"She's menopausal?"

Torrick nodded. "Pastor, she feels…irrelevant. The girls are self-sufficient, something she taught them. Like her, they're independent."

"It sounds as if Dianne doesn't believe she has a purpose."

"It's natural to feel purposeless at times."

"Well, if you're serving your own ego instead of serving the Lord, you'll eventually feel a lack of purpose. Now I know Dianne as a person, so…Are you prepared to stop seeing this other woman?"

Torrick swallowed hard. He'd avoided Jacqueline since he left Chicago. And he knew that she knew it. She was no fool; far from it. She deserved better. It wasn't fair to put her on the backburner. "I haven't seen her or talked to her in two days."

"Two days, huh?" The pastor lowered his eyes to his clasped hands. "Are you prepared to end this, to walk away? And in doing, work on your marriage?"

"I—"

"It can't work if you aren't *ready*. You need to be ready to come back into your marriage; fully and completely prepared to let this other woman go. But if you aren't ready…"

"I'm ready. But…"

"Oh, now there goes that qualifier! Is this *love*, Torrick?"

"It's not strictly physical. It's too complicated to…I care about this person. As a woman, and as a friend. And yes, as a lover."

"You don't want to hurt her?"

"From the moment this thing started, she understood there was the potential for her to get hurt."

"She's a mature one. There's self-respect involved here. Don't abuse it, Torrick."

"She's a realist."

"Are you telling me that if you end this, there'll be no repercussion from her end?"

"She'll be hurt; there's no getting around that. But will she?… She would let me go. She understands what's at stake." With downcast eyes, he said, "I think I love her."

"Oh, Torrick." Pastor Stevens hadn't anticipated hearing such a declaration, and with conviction. Temptation had its mystery. Torrick wasn't the first man who sat in his office because he cheated, and didn't honor his vows. "Do you see yourself with Dianne? You need to reach inside your soul and know for sure. You can't be faithful to your wife *and* be faithful to your lover."

"I love Dianne."

"What kind of love is this you're feeling for the other woman? Are you sure it's not lust? Sometimes we fail to recognize the difference."

"Of course it's lust." He chuckled. "But I'll have her back under any circumstance. She's not just a lover, but a friend."

"Torrick, my brother. You're a man in crisis."

While she sat waiting to be escorted to meet with the man that had the potential to change her life, Phoebe was anxious. In all her years of working, not once had she felt such butterflies. She sat trying to bring any prior incident to mind, and there was only one: the evening Venice opened at the Troubadour in West Holly-wood. Earlier that day they went to Fred Segal and purchased new pairs of recycled blue jeans outlined with rhinestones, and tube and halter tops from Ohrbach's. Then they drove to the Crenshaw District and waited three hours to get their hair done. Backstage they were intensely nervous; Cordia more so than Phoebe or Dianne. After all, the night's performance rested more on Cordia's shoulders than it did theirs. But Phoebe was similarly scared. They had played a number of clubs, but the audience was familiar with them as a group. They had made a name for themselves in L.A. The crowd that supported them was likewise the crowd that they often clubbed with, and mingled with at house parties. But the Troubadour catered to a different clientele, and it undoubtedly gave Venice exposure on another level altogether. Once they were onstage, the most they could see were the flames from cigarettes—from the stage it was as if looking out at a black sheet, and cigarette smoke swirling into the air. They opened with Chaka Khan's "I'm Every Woman"—the audience was receptive. Then they broke out with the Pointer Sisters' "Yes We Can Can" and the crowd began to exhibit animation. But when the strobe light came on and Cordia's alto, but high-hitting-note voice eased into "Don't Let the Sun Go Down on Me," disquiet was replaced with exhilaration. Before they could get through the song, they had the crowd on their feet singing along with them. From that moment onward, they performed that first set with adrenaline they were completely unaware they even had. When they started Venice, they sang, danced and had a lot of fun being singers. They did it for excitement, not believing for one minute they had the potential to one day become *known*. Yet that evening at the Troubadour, which was Venice's defining moment, the feelings were visceral to Phoebe: it wasn't a matter of if but a matter of when they would make it. They would play the Universal Amphitheatre, the Hollywood Bowl, and Madison Square Garden.

"Ms. Pleas?"

Phoebe looked up and into the cinnamon brown eyes of a classy young woman about Venetia's age. She wore a nicely fitted suit, casual but business. Her hair, falling just past her shoulders, was a deep dark brown, and her skin the color of rich hazelnut. A pair of diamonds—one karat—dangled from her ears.

"Yes." Phoebe came to her feet.

"Brooke Richardson." She extended a firm hand.

Phoebe and Brooke were identical in height. When Phoebe let go of the young woman's hand, she felt a warmhearted sensation. Something shifted in her body; something so intense it struck Phoebe.

"I'm going to escort you to Kent Richardson; he's my father. He's the one you'll be interviewing with."

Phoebe tugged gently at her jacket, cut sharply just above her hips. The suit cost an arm and a leg and then some; upon choosing to buy it, she decided to look at it as an investment.

They were walking toward a bank of elevators when Brooke said, "This is totally unprofessional, but when my father told me he was going to be interviewing someone from the group Venice, I was curious. I asked if I could come and greet you."

Brooke pushed a button to call for the elevator.

"Why?"

"I have the Venice *It's a Simple Question Tour Live at the Olympia* on my playlist."

"Playlist? I didn't realize Venice music was downloadable."

With a happy laugh, Brooke said, "Oh, please don't tell me... You are kidding, right?"

"It's my past. And a lifetime ago. I wrote three, no, four songs that we sang on the *Simple* tour. At least two we sang at the Olympia."

They were in the elevator when Brooke said, "I'm an entertainment attorney. Who is your publisher? I can get you any unpaid royalties. The record business can be like a snake in the grass."

"I would need to dig out my contracts…"

"Before you finish speaking with my father, I'll give you my business card. We should talk." They stepped out of the elevator and Brooke held out her hand. "This way."

They arrived at a suite at the end of the soothingly lit floor, and Brooke used a keycard to enter. Decorated in silver and gray, the high ceiling gave the suite depth and character, and soft cloud-hued carpet made Phoebe feel as if she were walking on air. A tall man, topping six feet, stood with his back to them. He was by a table with a half-dozen laptops and bottled water.

"Wait here, Phoebe." Brooke walked toward the tall man, and as she met him, he turned to greet her. Phoebe saw him look her way. At the moment nothing else mattered except to make an impression on him. The tall man who looked in charge—Phoebe wanted to be at the top of his list of candidates to plan the major fundraiser he was in the throes of putting together. She'd gone online to read about the fundraiser. The website was very organized and the facts and figures were impressive. Each member of the board had a laundry list of career achievements.

Brooke stopped only briefly before heading out of the suite. "Can I get you something?" While her throat was as dry as a bone, Phoebe declined. "Have a seat. Good luck to you, and here's my card." She handed it over to her.

Phoebe thanked Brooke and slid the card in her jacket pocket. She went for the closest seat. She studied Kent Richardson talking spiritedly to someone on a cell phone. He was too far away for her to snoop.

"Sorry to keep you waiting," the tall man greeted Phoebe a few minutes later. "I appreciate your allowing me to meet with you on such short notice."

"It's nothing."

He reached for Phoebe's résumé and only perused it fleetingly, as if he'd already studied it with care but was merely recalling some basic information in which to question her. "You managed Rules in San Francisco. I take it you know the owner?"

I used to sleep with him and we lived together in his Pacific Heights townhouse was at the tip of her tongue. "Yes."

His eyes lingered on Phoebe for a moment. Naturally, smoothly, he referred back to the paper he was holding. "The Heroes Awards—quite an event. Impressive. And Windows by the Pacific...Oh, that was a boutique hotel in Pacific Palisades, wasn't it?"

Phoebe's throat was so dry and she could really use a drink of water. Suddenly, she felt a wave of heat as if her face was on fire. *Hot flash?* Now? Oh, no, no, no! She managed to find her voice. "Yes." She could feel beads of sweat along her hairline. Did Kent Richardson notice?

"They were bought out by...a chain hotel. I forgot who purchased it. I actually had my eye on it once. It was an enchanting hotel." He looked up at her. "There are gaps. The reason?"

"When the hotel was taken over, we were all let go."

"You started out as catering manager and then for...let's see; in just over a year, you were promoted to director of events. Uh-huh." He flipped to the second page. "And you were director of events for...just over a year?"

"Correct."

His demeanor was somber. He placed the résumé beside him on the settee. "So tell me, since Windows by the Pacific closed, what, two years ago—what have you been doing?"

"I did some contract work. A few small clients, and of course the Heroes Awards."

"And the last one?"

"It was an event held on the Sony Pictures lot. Galinda Childs..."

"I know Galinda. I recall that event. Yes, it was for breast cancer. You'll have no problem if I speak with Galinda?"

"Feel free."

"Michael spoke highly of you. He said you worked as hospitality assistant—something to that effect, at Media Capital."

Although she was paying very close attention, and hanging on to each and every word Kent Richardson spoke, Phoebe found herself attracted to him. His salt-and-pepper hair and a closely shaven beard blended handsomely into his deep mahogany complexion. She guessed he could be older than her, but he didn't look it. He was in good shape, and dressed impeccably. He didn't wear a wedding band, but he did have a daughter. Divorced, widowed?

She caught the last part of his question: "To L.A.?"

"I'm sorry, can you repeat that?"

"Would it be a problem in returning to L.A.?"

"L.A.?"

"The individual that takes this opportunity will need to be in L.A. It's roughly six, seven months of intense work. If you worked with Galinda Childs, you can handle it. This event is going to be monumental. Names that dominate in this country—from politicians and entertainers to businesspeople—will be attending. The candidate will have people working under her or him. It will require the person to be on-call. Phoebe," Kent Richardson said, leaning forward, "this is a demanding gig. You have to be thick-skinned and manage in an extremely fluid and oftentimes ambiguous environment."

Phoebe wondered if he was suggesting the opportunity would be too much for someone her age; as though she was set in her ways and couldn't be open to constantly shifting situations. Self-conscious, Phoebe wet her lips. She hadn't handled something of this magnitude before. As director of events with Windows by the Pacific, the biggest thing she'd managed was a film crew shooting on location at the hotel for two weeks. While she hadn't managed a team, Phoebe directed multiple projects consisting of six people. Was she up to this task?

"I am all about challenges," she blurted out with remarkable conviction.

For what felt like minutes, but lasted no more than five seconds, Kent Richardson looked into her eyes, as if the answer to any lingering questions rested inside them. "Okay," he said, and his lips—full and moist and luscious—curved ever so slightly, exposing cosmetically whitened teeth. Standing, he said, "I'm leaving for London in a few hours. When I return to the States, I'll be making a decision."

Phoebe stood, too. Somewhat nervously, she situated her hair behind one ear. They shook hands at the door, and Kent Richardson's hand felt softer than hers. He never did hard labor in his life. *Who is this man?*

Calmly, she made her way across the hotel's lavish lobby, crowded with people, some seated at the nearby fireplace talking, drinking wine or liquor to loosen up after the stress of a business day. She pulled out her cell from her pocket. Phoebe went to retrieve her coat at the coat check and rushed out into the cold early evening air. The streets were bustling with after-work foot traffic—people making their way to bus stops or coffee bars or lottery kiosks and restaurants or stores to shop. "Venetia," Phoebe said, trying to make her way through a crowd of disconnected souls, "I need you to call me. Soon as you can."

In the car, Phoebe pulled out Brooke Richardson's card. *Have we met before?*

"Hey," Torrick said. He was wide awake. In fact, he hadn't slept a wink. "Daniela is on me about going to L.A."

"Yeah," Dianne said, half awake. "For Christmas, I know."

"No." Torrick yawned. He was checking e-mail from his hand-held.

"What do you mean, no?" Dianne peeked from under her fluffy pillow. She stretched her legs, her toes and fingers; something she did every single morning before rolling out of bed.

"She asked me last night if she could go for her birthday."

Frowning, Dianne fluffed her pillow and slipped it back under her head. "For her birthday? She didn't mention that to me."

"You have been…sorta remote. She probably didn't want to overwhelm you with information."

"What exactly does that mean?"

"You've been preoccupied. She thought coming to me would get a quicker response. She said she tried to ask you days ago, but you weren't really listening."

"When was this?"

Torrick rested against the headboard. He let his forefinger glide up and down his touchscreen. "I'm not sure."

Annoyed, Dianne snatched the device from Torrick's hands. "Will you for once give me your undivided attention!"

Rubbing his eyes, he said, "Dianne, give me my phone back." He held out a limp hand.

With his phone camera, Dianne snapped a photo of her husband. "Dianne!"

She slipped the cell inside her underwear. "Come and get it!"

Torrick sighed deeply, and tossed the bedding off him. "I have a staff meeting in less than an hour."

Dianne texted Daniela from Torrick's phone: *Peet's Sumatra? Thx Sweetie.* If she was on time, she was already downstairs having breakfast while fooling around with her iPhone Torrick broke down and bought her a few weeks ago. While lying in bed, Dianne reminisced her own youth. She wouldn't have wanted to grow up in such intense cultural pressure; the severe pace. She wouldn't have wanted to be in Venice while the ethos was so chaotic, rushed; yet it was easy to say in hindsight. She felt sorry for young women exposed to a public persona and a generous bank account these days. It was intense in the late '70s and into the '80s. Now? Thinking about it deeply, Dianne wouldn't want any other childhood. She especially liked her teens. Growing up in Los Angeles and attending Beverly Hills High and having the friends that she had and the experiences that shaped her personality—she honored that time in her life. Nothing about it she would want to edit. She couldn't say the same about her adult life. Back then, when she was Daniela's age, things were reasonably straightforward. She liked using payphones and waiting for letters from Vanessa to arrive in the post when she went off to San Jose State. She felt blessed that she was able to acquire emotional intelligence through the experiences in her life instead of relying so much on uncensored information and tweaked, and often distorted, historical facts.

Dianne climbed out of bed and went to her laptop to check her calendar and placed Torrick's phone on the table. She slipped on leggings and one of Torrick's worn UC Davis sweatshirts while her laptop turned on. Torrick was in the shower when she went to freshen up—exfoliating her face and brushing her teeth. When she returned to the bedroom, she heard a beep from Torrick's phone. Dianne never touched Torrick's cell. It was used almost entirely for business and she never crossed that line. An impulsive urge made her pick it up. Jacqueline's name was at the top of his messages. If she opened it, he would know that she had fooled with his phone. *Why would she be texting Torrick?* With a curious look, she studied the cell in her hand, and she was so bloody curious. She replaced it, but stared at it on the table until the water from the shower stopped. She snapped herself away and checked her calendar. *Two appointments?* Well, the second one was close to the pharmacy. She definitely needed to get her medication refilled.

When she made it downstairs, Henna was finishing a bowl of granola. Daniela was spooning fresh blueberries into her bowl of steel-cut oatmeal, her earpods plugged into her ears. She hummed to something she was listening to on her iPod.

"Good morning!" Dianne said, in the most chipper voice she could muster.

"Hi, Mama," Henna said.

Dianne tapped Daniela on the shoulder and kissed her cheek. She was hoping her daughter would take it as a truce. She was still giving Dianne the cold shoulder since the impulsive slap.

Her amiable look was genuine; Dianne knew when Daniela was faking it. "Hey, Mama." Daniela bumped her hip against Dianne's playfully.

Dianne reached for orange juice in the fridge. "I hear you're wanting to go to L.A. for your birthday."

"You talked to Daddy?"

"He mentioned it. Did we discuss this?" Dianne hoped that her tone wasn't making any accusations.

"It was a suggestion at the time. I really want to go, Mama."

Dianne poured a glass of orange juice and hadn't noticed the smell of Sumatra brewing until she actually saw it across the counter. Dianne hugged her daughter's tiny waist. "Okay. But can we celebrate here, too?"

"That's cool."

"How about your best friend Kyndra and Henna and me and your father and Jacqueline—she'd come. We can go to Cheesecake Factory, your favorite."

"It's Henna's favorite, Mama."

"Oh, so you're too grown for the Factory now?"

Henna washed out her bowl and placed it in the dishwasher. She hugged her mother and said, "I gotta catch the bus!"

"The Factory's okay. I don't mind."

"Good morning, Daniela!" Torrick said. He reached down to kiss her on the cheek. He poured a cup of coffee.

"Hey, Daddy." She slipped her earpod back in her ear. "I'm eating in my room. Can you drop me off?"

He leaned against the counter. "Ten minutes?" Torrick said.

"I'll be ready."

"Thank you. I have to shower *and* I have to be at a meeting in the opposite direction at eleven," Dianne said. "I thought Kyndra got her driver license and drives now."

He slurped his hot, strong java. "Kyndra's getting a car for Christmas. Her father told me."

"A *car?* Well, you know what that means."

"Yep!" Briefly, Torrick studied his wife, trying to ascertain her mood. She moved around the kitchen, humming and cleaning up after Henna, who always managed to drop something on the floor or on the table. He used his remote starter to rev up the SUV's engine.

Minutes later, Torrick stepped in the already-running SUV. While waiting for Daniela, he reread Jacqueline's text. He couldn't put it off any longer. He would need to speak to her. Torrick blew his horn, reminding his daughter that he was waiting. Two minutes later, she jumped into the SUV and Torrick pulled out of the driveway. At the stop sign Daniela said, "Mama was in a good mood."

Torrick winked, but he was thinking quite the opposite.

Something's not right. Jacqueline stood at the elevator doors, waiting for Michael. *What did I eat?*

"Hi, excuse me," Jacqueline said to the concierge.

She grinned ear-to-ear. "Hi, Jacqueline."

"When Michael comes up to the elevators, would you let him know I went to the ladies?"

"Absolutely!"

Jacqueline leaned over the toilet, for she was certain she was going to be sick. A little something came out. *Oy*, she thought, Thai. It was never the best thing to eat as a leftover. Even from Wild Ginger. Nothing else would rise beyond her throat. She flushed the toilet. No sooner than she made it to the sink to wash her hands, Jacqueline felt sick again. Before she could pivot and rush to the toilet, she collapsed.

Shortly thereafter, a colleague entered the restroom and discovered Jacqueline passed out on the floor. She dropped to her knees. "Jacqueline! Jacqueline!" she cried out. "Jacqueline?"

Jacqueline moaned something, and the colleague tried to make out what she was saying.

"Ohhhh," Jacqueline said, starting to come to.

"Jacqueline—you blacked out!"

"I...Did I?"

"How long have you been lying here? Jacqueline!" the colleague spoke up. She felt her head, but it was normal. "Are you able to stand?"

Brushing her hair off her face, Jacqueline sat upright. "What happened?"

The colleague helped her to her feet. "You were out of it. I think we should call someone..."

"No, really. I'm borderline anemic. Plus, I'm not eating right."

Gingerly, the colleague placed her hand on Jacqueline's back while Jacqueline pressed her hands against the basin. With her head bowed, she swallowed hard and her mouth was so, so dry. "Oh, boy."

"Look, are you going to be able to sit through a two-hour meeting? This is a very important account."

"I know." She dusted off her black designer lacks. "I'll grab a Pellegrino to flush it out. I'll be fine, really. Please, it's okay."

Her friend and colleague looked Jacqueline straight in the eye. "Flush *what* out?"

"It's my iron." Jacqueline didn't know what was wrong. It could be her anemia, but she'd never blacked out before. She straightened her crisp white shirt and tucked her glossy hair behind her ears. "Michael's waiting for me. Tell him I'll be right there."

The colleague reached for Jacqueline's coat and iPad on the granite counter and handed them to her. Apprehensive, she studied her face. "Are you sure you don't want me to go in your place?"

Someone entered the restroom and pleasantries were exchanged. Jacqueline whispered, "I'm fine now. Really."

They shared a gentle embrace, and the colleague left to go brief Michael. Fleetingly, Jacqueline studied her reflection in the mirror. She rummaged in her bag for the can of Evian facial spray. After refreshing her face, she dabbed it with a paper towel. When she heard a toilet flush, she slipped on her coat and rushed out of the restroom. Waiting for the elevator, she tried to shake off what had happened. Jacqueline never got so much as a cold, let alone the flu. She was blessed with good DNA. Both of her parents' parents lived long lives. At 101, her great-grandmother walked upward of three blocks, daily. Jacqueline could easily celebrate her one-hundredth if she stayed in shape and maintained a healthy diet. Save for the occasional headache brought on by stress, Jacqueline couldn't recall the last time she was bone-tired, or sick.

She stepped out of the elevator and headed to her car when she received a text from Daniela, inviting her to come to her birthday celebration a week from tomorrow. "Oy," she said, standing at her car. She used the remote to unlock the car and stepped in. She thought twice before responding. As honored as she was for Daniela to include her, it would be dreadfully awkward for her to sit through an entire evening with Torrick and Dianne. She'd cancelled shopping and spa-day twice, and now to find an excuse not to attend Daniela's birthday party? *How can I do it?*

Phoebe looked around attempting to seek out Daniel. A fleeting thought ran through her mind: how strange things turned out. While she was waiting to find out whether she would get the contract to work with Kent Richardson, Daniel's assistant called and arranged for her to meet with Daniel at the Blue Bar. For over a week, she waited for Daniel's assistant to phone her; and now, when she had the potential to get absorbed in a high-profile project, Daniel's assistant called and said, "Send me a PDF copy of your business plan so I can prep Daniel. Make sure you bring a hard copy to the meeting."

She decided against ordering anything. Phoebe wasn't sure how long she'd be meeting with Daniel. Maybe he would flip through her plan and say something like *I'll be in touch* and not even grab a table. She leaned against a wall, waiting. She thought she saw a familiar face. Phoebe knew that woman seated alone, a glass of white wine placed on the table in front of her. From?—Gloria, TA. Media Capital.

She walked over to the table. "Hello, Gloria."

"Hello…" Gloria's expression suggested she wasn't exactly sure who Phoebe was.

"Phoebe. I temped at Media Cap. Hospitality assistant?"

"Yes. How are you?"

"Good. Thank you."

"Are you meeting someone?"

"In fact I am. Hopefully, it'll pan out to be a business deal."

"Have a seat."

They chitchatted for a few minutes. Gloria apparently had several drinks before Phoebe spotted her. She began to discuss her personal life: A painfully failed marriage which led to a hostile divorce; and she was paying *him* alimony. Phoebe couldn't conceive of how that could happen to a woman in the twenty-first century. A woman like Gloria was educated, savvy. She listened long enough to see how glum and lonely Gloria sounded. This wasn't the same Gloria she'd met in her office when Phoebe first came to town and got that temp job through the Next Generation. The Gloria she'd met her first day at Media Capital appeared, on the surface anyway, on top of it. *We all have façades.* She took small sips of her wine, and finally drank enough to talk freely. She explained to Phoebe why she was sitting alone at the Blue Bar. A friend of a friend had set her up on a blind date. It was meant to be a brief "intro" over drinks. The man hadn't shown up. In fact, Gloria had been waiting nearly an hour.

Phoebe thought, *I'd have been gone in ten, fifteen tops.*

"It doesn't get any easier," Phoebe warned Gloria. "You think the forties are hard. Don't be alone in your fifties."

"After you left, word got around Media Cap—you were *the* Phoebe Pleas from the group Venice. If someone like you can have problems…I need to change what I like about men. I'm so tired of this, Phoebe."

Phoebe's phone rang, and it was Venetia. She decided to answer. "Yeah?"

"Sorry it took so long. I have e-mailed you some information I gathered on Richardson. By the way, he's divorced. His daughter's an entertainment attorney."

"I learned that much online."

"Yeah, but did you know she's Gwen Jackson's attorney? *Gwenology?*

Also, she's adopted. Richardson and his ex-wife have no other children."

"Okay, good. I'm at the Blue Bar. We'll talk. How much longer are you going to be in L.A.?"

"I'm waiting for Barry. He'll be in tonight. Maybe by the weekend."

"See you then."

Phoebe felt a touch of simpatico for Gloria. She looked visibly crestfallen. Phoebe could relate. She'd been there enough times to feel her pain. "Listen, I know someone…he might be a bit older than you'd fancy. But he's a really decent man."

"I know I'm rather mature for the traditional bad boy. But a *decent* man? That's code for boring."

Phoebe had to laugh. "I wouldn't call him boring."

"Well…"

"You can meet. There's no commitment. I can take your number and have him give you a call. Or vice versa if you prefer."

"Okay, Phoebe. Why are you pushing him on me? What's wrong with him?"

"Nothing. Well, he can afford to lose a few pounds. You know who he kinda looks like? Steve Harvey without the dimples. He's… let's say *middle*-school, but he's actually charming."

With a smirk, Gloria said, "*Middle*-school, charming?"

They laughed as if they each agreed "charming" was one of those *code* words.

"Would it really hurt to go out and have a nice dinner with a charming man who's…mature? I've had my share of immature. They don't show up and they aren't responsible. They're agenda-driven. A mature man wouldn't be disrespectful."

"See, there you go," Phoebe agreed, taking pleasure in talking with Gloria.

"Phoebe?"

She looked around and there he was, Mr. Fine Himself. As a courtesy, Phoebe introduced Gloria and Daniel. She told Gloria she'd call her at Media Capital to "set something up."

"I'm sorry for being late. Traffic in this town is getting worse than the traffic in L.A."

"Your timing was perfect. Besides, you're doing me a favor."

Daniel asked the host to find them a table. "Did you bring your business plan?"

She handed it out to him.

Daniel excused himself and took a call. Gloria passed through a crowd of people waiting for available tables. She put her hand to her ear in a gesture that suggested she was making a phone call and mouthed the words *call me* to Phoebe.

Phoebe pantomimed back, *Will do*.

"Sir, there's a table ready," the hostess said to Daniel.

Phoebe watched closely while Daniel studied over the business plan, and she thought if Jacqueline was sleeping with him, she was damn lucky. And then something which never once occurred to her before hit her like a glass of cold water thrown in her face. If it had occurred to her, it had been so long ago. Daniel was doing this for her because she was one of Venice. How many times had being a Venice girl opened a door or altered her course, and long after Venice was no more than a nebulous afterthought? For days she was concerned that she hadn't made the right impression on Kent Richardson. She was aware her background didn't come with the most distinguished credentials. But as she sat across from Daniel, Phoebe began to feel a renewed trust that she'd be hearing from Richardson after all.

It had been some time since Joseph had made his way on this side of town. It was highly influenced by urban achievers, with their twenty-first-century careers in high-tech and new medicine and the like. Cornell had shared a place with a friend for a while, not three blocks away. For decades the quaint community was shaped by middle-class homeowners; yet the area had lost some of its allure in recent years. Random homes looked rundown and weren't maintained. The boulevard that divided the haves from the have-lesses attracted a mixture of the partially homeless and slackers hanging out at bars and clubs and anything opened late into the early morning hours. Joseph managed to find a parking space on the street. That was another thing: back in the day, parking wasn't a luxury. These days you couldn't pay someone off for a parking space—the streets were crammed because of the influx. Now they had machines that print out parking permits that must be showcased in the window of the vehicle. When he used to come over in this area from time to time, he slipped a quarter in the parking meter and it lasted for an hour. Popular imagination made everything so complicated now; Joseph tried to make peace with it, though it continued to be a challenge for him.

He walked into the gym. He was on the lookout for anyone who might look like him: out of shape and middle-aged. There was one gentleman, a member of the gray society, but fit. His skin was wrinkled, but he didn't have a bulge. Joseph was to meet the personal trainer his tax attorney buddy recommended. He looked around for someone to assist him, but everyone looked so busy, so preoccupied. He began to notice several people walking around with T-shirts that endorsed the gym, so that meant they could help him out, and point out the personal trainer he was to meet up with at eleven.

"Excuse me," Joseph said to a young man rushing by.

"Be right with you," the man said, stopping to talk to a toned and attractive young woman. She slung a towel around her neck and giggled like a teen-ager. They talked a good two minutes before they each departed, but the young man who told Joseph he would be right with him went the opposite way. He either forgot or he didn't care.

"Uh, excuse me," he said to a young woman making her way toward him. She, too, wore a T-shirt endorsing the gym. "Do you work here?"

"Yes."

"Can you help me?"

"Sure," she said, making no attempt to conceal looking at her watch, as if Joseph was taking up too much of her time.

"I'm looking for…"

"Jane, hi," someone butted in. "I'd like to pay my bill for next month. No one's at reception. I'm in a bit of a hurry…"

"No problem. Excuse me," she said to Joseph, and off went the two women: the one needing to pay her bill, and the other one who worked at the gym. Joseph could take her snub one of two ways: she didn't want to be bothered with him because he was a black man, or she didn't see any future investment in an old, overweight black man. Joseph felt ignored, dejected. He turned on his heels to leave the place. Who wanted to give up their money to an establishment like this? Disorganized, partial. The gym's employees weren't trained too well. If they wanted his business, they wouldn't treat him with such flagrant disrespect.

He made his way to the front of the gym and caught sight of the woman wanting to pay her bill. She was being assisted by another young woman; not the one Joseph was trying to talk to when the woman with the unpaid bill butted in on them. He was making his way through the automatic doors when a handsome man, fit, with a shaved head and holding a helmet bumped into him.

"Sorry," the man said. He slipped off his shades—the sun hadn't made an appearance in three days. With his gym bag slung over his shoulder, he was on his way. Joseph had reached the sidewalk when the young man called out, "Are you Joseph Morgan?"

Joseph stopped, and with an annoyed look on his face, replied, "I am."

"Hey, Trey Bradshaw, the personal trainer. Sorry I'm running late. My last appointment was late and you know how that goes."

"Yeah, I do." They shook hands. "You work at this gym?"

"Well, I don't work *for* the gym. I lease time on the equipment. It's a new thing gyms are doing these days. Overhead, that kind of thing. I teach rock climbing over at World Sports, and when I can get it, I stunt."

"What's stunt?"

"Stunt work. You know, for films, television."

"That's dangerous, isn't it?"

"Yeah, but I like living dangerously."

"How do you have time to do all this *and* have a life, too? When I was your age, we called that having too many irons in the fire."

The personal trainer's mirth was exaggerated. "Were you leaving? As I said…"

"I understand." He was a courteous young man, trying to make a living, working all kinds of jobs to stay afloat, or to get ahead. Joseph couldn't fault him for that. Booking clients too close to one another—it happened; people got caught in traffic and once a client was late, everyone else would be pushed back. It happened at the dentist office every six months.

"Would you like to come in? It'll take roughly fifteen minutes since it's only a consultation." The personal trainer looked Joseph over without being too obvious. "Would you…"

"Why not? Sure." He headed back inside.

"Any medical issues?…"

CHAPTER 14

When Torrick greeted Jacqueline at the door, he looked tired and stressed. He attempted to lift the corners of his mouth, but his body language didn't match his expression. Jacqueline caressed his face, and for the first time noticed that he had a pierced ear. *When did he start wearing an earring? He certainly didn't wear one when he worked for the agency.*

He let go of the door knob and grabbed Jacqueline by the waist and embraced her with—there was no other word for it—love. "Oh, you smell so good." She felt *loved* when he squeezed her. Torrick kissed her neck, her cheek. He traced her teeth with the tip of his tongue. Her mouth opened wider to receive his tongue, which had the subtle taste of a *curiously strong* breath mint. Jacqueline nearly went limp and could feel a pulsing sensation between her legs. When she cupped his face into her hands, she could see the strain their relationship put on his life. If he walked out that door within the next ten seconds, Jacqueline would begin immediately making peace with it. In the beginning, the first weeks anyway, she took great pleasure from being with Torrick—the confluence was a respite from the relentless activity that entirely consumed her day. The gratifying sex, the attention, and truth be told: the clandestine nature of their relationship—it kept it exciting, on edge.

"How are you?" she asked.

They stepped away from each other, their fingers intertwined. "I've missed you."

"I've missed you, too." She took him by the hand. "Come on, let's sit."

Once they were relaxing on the mushroom-colored sofa—Jacqueline in the corner, her legs tucked under her, and Torrick a few inches away—they sat quietly for a good while. The room was alight with burning candles. Finally, Jacqueline said, "Daniela wants me to come to her sixteenth birthday celebration."

"She asked me if I had your number."

"I was touched—so touched, Torrick. And it would be difficult for me to turn her down."

"You can't turn her down." He reached for her hand and held it lovingly. "She wouldn't understand. If you were out of town or something…And Dianne wouldn't understand it either."

"I can arrange to be out of town if that would be…"

"You have to show up. Look…" He met her gaze purposefully. "Maybe because I'm feeling sorta guilty that I think if you don't show up, it'll be because we're…"

"Don't be ridiculous, Torrick."

"I'm in a quandary here; you do get that."

Jacqueline, reluctantly, nodded as if to agree.

"My relationship with Dianne is complicated right now. Even before this happened, we were one foot shy of being—our relationship was tenuous, at best. But being with you has made me see my relationship with Dianne differently. I don't know that I would be contemplating leaving her if we had never…"

"You would leave Dianne?"

With a shrug, Torrick said, "I don't know what I'm thinking right now. I know that I *like* being with you. I like our time together. But what does that mean, really? When a man is married…This is something I've never done." Pensive, Torrick stared into the flames of the burning candles. "I know I was a choice for Dianne and not *the* choice. That probably happens to a lot of people."

"I'm sure it does."

"I've asked myself—but it's only been since we started this—if she hadn't gotten pregnant would we have married."

"And if you hadn't, the likelihood of us ever having met…"

For a long while, they sat in silence. Torrick turned his body toward Jacqueline and rested his arm on the back of the sofa. With his fingers clasping hers, he said, "Please come to Daniela's party."

"How can I refuse you?"

When Dianne pulled up to the curb, Daniela wasn't standing outside Starbucks. Prior to leaving the house, she'd received a text from her oldest: *ride @ SB Yesler.* She explicitly had instructed Daniela to be *outside* because she would barely have enough time to pick her up, drop her off at the house and get to her therapy session on time. She checked the text to make sure she was at the right Starbucks. Parking was horrible this late in the day. From where she was parked, she couldn't see Daniela or Kyndra.

Starbucks was crammed, and one of a hundred versions of "Hallelujah" played vociferously. She squeezed through the crowd and managed to make her way to the back amid a group of people. Several people sat at pushed-together tables holding up cake pops, and began to sing "Happy Birthday to You…" Dianne smirked at their obnoxious joy. Daniela was sitting in the back. *Alone?* When Dianne approached her, she looked up with sad eyes laced with fresh tears.

"What's wrong?"

"Kyndra!"

"What about Kyndra?" Dianne sat in the accompanying chair.

"We had a fight."

"Over?"

"She called me fat!"

Dianne was amused by her daughter's lugubrious experience with her best friend; however, she decided not to make light of it because Daniela was visibly upset. Although she knew that girls her daughter's age could only relate to the latest mainstream ideas—e.g., skinny being the new waif—Daniela was slender with long legs, a tight tummy and cute inverted navel. She developed breasts early, and they were full compared to Dianne's at her age. She wished she had been as food-conscious as her daughter. Unlike Dianne, who at sixteen lived off fries and vanilla shake from McDonald's, Daniela didn't eat at fast-food restaurants. She didn't obsess over being thin as floss—that was no more than a commercial fantasy anyway. Dianne reached across the small table and held her daughter's hand. "I know you won't believe me because at your age, I wouldn't have believed my mother either. But you have to trust me on this one, Daniela. *You* aren't fat!"

"I know I'm not fat."

"So—"

"It was such a mean thing to say. Especially since Kyndra is one size bigger than me."

"How did all this start anyway?"

"We were talking about cheerleaders and I don't know…all of a sudden, Kyndra said I couldn't be a cheerleader because I was fat."

"But you know that's not true so why are you really upset?"

"Well…"

"Tell me."

"You know the boy I like in L.A.?"

Quietly, Dianne responded with kind-hearted skepticism, "Yeah."

"She told me that he said I was fat on Facebook."

"He's never actually met you so how would he know?"

"He's seen pictures; we Snapchat."

"No sexting, you promised!"

"Mama! I know! Daddy and his obsession with security…I know he checks my laptop!"

"How would this boy know you're fat? I've seen your photos on Facebook. They're mostly above-the-waist."

"I don't know."

"Do you want me to talk to Kyndra's mom?"

"*No!*"

"Best friends fight. It happens."

"Like you and Phoebe?"

"Well, that's different."

"Why's it different?"

"Phoebe and I stopped talking years ago. A lot's changed. We experienced a pseudo-reconnect. Listen, Kyndra's jealous. She's a pretty girl, but there's so much more to you, Daniela. Personality— and you have this aura."

"Aura?" She grimaced.

"Trust me, one day you'll appreciate having a special aura."

She giggled. "I don't know, Mama."

With a napkin, Dianne reached across the table to dab away the small tear hanging below her daughter's eye. "Trust me."

"Why would you think Kyndra would be jealous of me? She's popular and pretty and has a nice shape. This aura thing is totally mature—unrelatable."

"Well, you're right. She won't relate to *aura* in the way I'm using it. It's your essence, and on some level she senses something about you and it intimidates her."

"Intimidate?"

"There's more to a female than attractiveness. Men—boys, they aren't attracted to just your looks. They're attracted to something you exude."

Dianne could tell Daniela was feeling—different. She was so proud of her. She was smart with excellent grades, she wasn't into drugs; she and Torrick were certain about that. They trusted her enough to let her go to L.A. to meet the boy she'd been social networking with for several months.

"Since I'm here, I think I'd like a Bliss Bar. Would you share one with me?"

"Great, Mama. It's like the most fattening thing on the menu."

"But if we share it…"

"Uuugh! Okay," she said, her mouth softening, the corners elevating just enough.

Dianne stood. She touched her daughter's face and said in a confident voice, "Trust me, Daniela, this will pass. She's coming to the party, right?"

"Well, I don't know if I want her there. She just walked out and left me here. She knew I needed a ride."

"Remember she loves you and resents you at the same time. Give her a pass. I'll be right back."

Dianne was pressed for time, so Daniela said she didn't mind waiting for her mother in the reception area while she had her appointment with her therapist. When Dianne told her therapist about Daniela's experience at Starbucks, the therapist asked her, "And you felt needed then, didn't you?"

It hadn't occurred to Dianne. "I guess I did."

"Good," said the therapist. "Based on our conversations here, and meeting your daughter, I have to say this, Dianne: you have done an excellent job raising your daughter."

"Yes, I know."

"But some part of you doubts it."

"No, I don't think so."

"How are things with Torrick?"

When she looked through the peephole, it was Philipa, and Phoebe was conflicted on whether to open the door. But it was clear she was home. The lights were on. She opened the door and greeted her with a spurious look of surprise. "Philipa?"

"Hi, Phoebe. I'm sorry to drop by without calling, but I didn't have your number. Do you have some time to spare?"

Every bone in her body hesitated, but she said, "Sure, come on in."

Phoebe offered Philipa something to drink and she said a glass of wine would be "blissful." They talked casually for a few minutes before Philipa explained the purpose of her visit.

"You have my word, Phoebe. I won't write about the experience at my house. The whole thing left me somewhat disconcerted. My book's not about gossip. It's strictly a historical sketch of the subjects of the book—what have they done with their lives since they left the public domain. Most importantly, it's a sort of reverence to their talent, which had impact on music as well as the shaping of current pop culture. MTV, BET—the landscape of American music changed because of Michael Jackson's *Thriller*. Venice had a hand in that, too."

"I didn't think that you'd write about it in your book. I didn't pick that up from you."

"I don't want to take up too much of your time since I dropped by unexpectedly. But I did want you to—if you could—fill in some holes as far as Cordia's concerned. There's enough to go on from the Internet, but much of what I read on the Internet I consider second- and third-hand information. It can be true, but once a story starts traveling through various forms, it gets slanted. You were there. I take it you're less emotionally invested in that time in your life than Dianne."

Phoebe drank her wine. "You're perceptive."

"Can we talk about Cordia? Are you comfortable with that?"

"I can always talk about Cordia."

Philipa took a sip from the wineglass. She was a poised, stylish young woman—even the way she crossed her legs. "I understand she was an angel."

Phoebe nodded slightly. "For a long time, I obsessed over why it had to be her. She had so much to live for. Her career was going so well. She'd just released her latest album. She had an adorable young girl—and her marriage was still solid, which said something because the business…Well, you know." Phoebe looked directly at Philipa. "She was happy. I don't mean like she had to depend or lean on something in order to be happy. She embraced life without feeling it owed her anything.

"I even wished it was me instead of her."

Hearing those words startled Philipa. "Why do you say that?"

"She had a lot more to live for."

"I remember feeling something similar about Princess Diana when she lost her life in Alma tunnel. I was at the Sorbonne and dropped out. It was a low period. I take it, like me, yours passed?"

"Eventually.…Venetia's a lot like her mother. If you need a reference point where Cordia's concerned, study Venetia. They attract people because they each have this indescribable grace. They make you feel special in their company.

"Dianne and I had quite a few arguments over the years. On the road, when we were spending too much time together in small spaces, we really didn't get along. I think in the end, when I can look back now, I might never have befriended her had Cordia not started the friendship between us. Let's say someone named Jill stopped that argument that day at the gas station. Dianne and I would have gone our separate ways. We'd most likely have never seen each other again."

"And there would never have been Venice, and I can't imagine that. How did you end up moving to L.A. from Albuquerque?"

"I wanted to get on *Soul Train* so I applied to schools all over Southern California. Being on *Soul Train* was a big deal back then."

"Cordia used to be a regular on *Soul Train*."

"How did you find that out?"

"It's not something I read about. Venetia mentioned it to me."

"Cordia was friendly with Don Cornelius, the creator of *Soul Train*. She managed to get me on once. A lot of good memories surrounded my first couple of years in L.A. You know, when I look back now, I realize how quickly things happened for me. If I had to wait for something it didn't take long. Once we opened at the Troubadour, doors flung open for us. Within eight months, we had a record deal. I'm not sure if that really happens today. Well, there's *American Idol*. We'd known each other roughly eighteen months when the *Plan B* album dropped. Within three months of its release, we were an international success. *Plan B*—six times platinum…Thirty years later, I'm sitting around waiting on calls from possible business prospects. It feels like there's so much more at stake. The quickaholics that we've all been forced to become, it's strange because it takes much longer to make things happen. I loathe waiting for someone else to make things happen for me. My mother says I lack faith."

"I lack faith, too." Each nursed her drink in silence. "Where were you when you learned about Cordia?"

"In Lisbon. I'd moved there with a boyfriend. I was wandering around Europe, confused, not knowing what to do with my life.

It had been some time after Venice broke up, but I was clueless what to do. I had no long-term goals. It takes time to resume a life of normalcy after experiencing something like Venice.

"I met this man—boy, because he was younger than me—at Georges Pompidou Centre. He couldn't speak French and needed directions. He claimed he was pickpocketed in Rome by a swarm of gypsies so he had no money. I trusted that story. Three weeks later, we moved to Lisbon and rented an apartment by the week. Not three months after we were there, I woke up and he was gone. He just split. He didn't steal from me, but I felt used. Eventually, I started meeting people through the American church. I needed something to do with my time. I met this American couple—they became filthy rich through this pyramid scheme. Gradually, I started arranging their life—organized their travel, parties...It was really fun. A group of us were all sitting around talking about America and how we loved being elsewhere but missed things American not accessible in Portugal. CNN was on, which is something I began to rely on when I lived in Lisbon. They were showing the crashed plane. You could still see the smoke and fire, and when someone turned up the volume, the reporter said it was Cordia Street, her husband, members of her band and the pilot—they all perished.

"I managed for years living a really fast life without getting caught up in the drug culture. That's not easy to do in the entertainment world. But someone—I don't even remember who it was—gave me something. They wanted to calm me down. I was so hysterical."

Quiet tears collected in Phoebe's eyes. Philipa could feel a lump rising to the top of her throat. Her father, likewise a notable musician, died a startling death.

They talked another hour, and then Phoebe walked Philipa to her car. When she drove off, a taxi pulled to the curb. Phoebe turned to find Venetia getting out, dragging her luggage as if she were beat. "Hey!" Phoebe called out. Venetia looked dreadfully sad. "What's wrong, Venetia?"

She covered her face.

"Venetia, what?"

She wiped away the tears resting on her cheeks, and took in a deep breath. "Barry's going back to the Middle East. Why would he go to Gaza?"

"Oh, Venetia…"

"He ended it."

"End—?"

"It's—we're over."

The personal trainer suggested Joseph work up to taking one lap around the path. In Joseph's mind, that seemed nearly impossible. The personal trainer strongly urged he get a kneepad. Joseph was surprised himself when, after his first session with the personal trainer, he stopped in a Walgreens and purchased something highly recommended by the friendly pharmacist and it worked. The day's hue changed a half-dozen times. Joseph attempted to get his son to come join him on the lake, but Cornell, naturally lean—his mother's side of the family—was in good shape.

Making his way around the path, he reflected back on something the personal trainer had said to him. "Start noticing people you'd like to look like," he'd advised. "You know, like get an image in your head. It's not a point of trying to *look* like those people. Use them as your muse, something to aspire to." A few days ago, right after he'd met with the personal trainer, Joseph ran over to Target to grab a few things. The personal trainer's words started working without Joseph even being aware. But it was the opposite of what he'd suggested Joseph do. His eyes traveled to every overweight person he saw in the store. Men and women. He found himself comparing his abdomen to other men, and their balding heads to his. One day out of the blue, Cornell said to his father: "Dad, you ever thought about going all the way?" Joseph didn't know what Cornell was getting at. "You know, like Samuel Jackson, Bruce Willis? They're senior citizens, and they're smooth. The ladies love them. Shave off the rest of that hair. It could take a few years off."

Joseph had come back with, "I don't have a problem with my age, Cornell."

"I'm telling you the ladies love shaved heads. They think it's sexy."

By the time he made it to where the bridge separated the path, Joseph was too tired to walk all the way back. He might have been too ambitious his first time out. He'd done better to build up his momentum.

He walked nearly halfway back before he needed to take a seat on one of the benches that outlined the path. Generally, there was someone out running, walking their dog, a nanny pushing a carriage. But the curiously cold weather kept even the diehards at bay.

Joseph wasn't sure how long he'd been sitting there when Phoebe tapped him on the shoulder. "I thought that was you."

Seeing her always did something to Joseph. He felt as if she was something the spirits delivered his way; like a second-stage-of-life kindred spirit, despite whether he believed in that sort of thing. Something happened whenever he saw her. While his heart felt light, it was how his manhood stirred whenever he was near her; he never pretended otherwise. She sat next to him on the bench and Joseph wanted to reach over and kiss her in a way he hadn't kissed a woman in years. There was this disturbing hunger he had for this woman and he began to resent her for it.

"Are you okay?"

"What brings you out here on this cold day?"

"I was headed for the market when I thought I saw you sitting here. I wanted to make sure you were okay."

"Why wouldn't I be?" She was beginning to piss Joseph off. He couldn't have her and yet he wanted her in a desperate way. Her very presence did nothing but remind him of all his failings—his weight, himself, losing touch with life. She reminded him of this every single time he saw her.

"Would you like a ride home?"

"I'm good."

"Are you sure?"

"I'm fine!" He didn't mean to snap.

Phoebe, without meaning to display it, was aghast. She was unsure if she wanted to even bring up Gloria, Media Capital's TA director she ran into at the Blue Bar. Should Kent Richardson make an offer, she would be leaving soon, so she might not have the opportunity to see or speak with Joseph again. She decided to take a chance, despite his mood.

"Listen. There's someone I'd like to introduce you to."

With a frown on his face, Joseph said, "Excuse me."

"I'd like to introduce you to someone."

"Who?"

"A woman."

"And why are you wanting me to meet his woman?" he said in a crisp, pointed tone.

Phoebe detected a side of him she was not exposed to previously. When they ran into each other at the bakery and café and walked to the guesthouse and talked for well over an hour, she felt comfortable enough to tell him about giving her child up for adoption. She'd never shared that with men she'd been quite intimate with. Now, she wasn't sure if he was in a bad mood or she said or did something that offended him. Phoebe knew she had been more than gracious to a man she understood was attracted to her. She had come to see that he was decent, caring. Venetia was right: *he's a good man.*

"She works for this media consultant firm downtown. I know her only casually, as I know you. But I ran into her a week or so ago and I thought of you. She's a successful woman. Good-looking, and divorced. Forties. I'm not sure of anything else when it comes to her personal life. But I really do think you should meet her."

Regardless of the writing on the wall, Joseph *wanted* Phoebe. He had lost interest in relationships when his wife passed on, but periodically he'd go out to dinner with someone from church. He was never captivated or interested beyond a casual dinner on occasion. But the moment he met Phoebe, she opened him up again. She got him curious. He even went so far as to start working on losing a bit of weight. If it meant he could be with her, he'd shave his head as Cornell once suggested. He *wanted* Phoebe. He didn't want this Gloria or whatever her name was.

"There's no commitment in meeting casually for coffee since you don't drink. I think, Joseph, if you start making the initiative, it'll come back to you."

"What would come back to me?"

"Being around women and feeling comfortable with them."

"Are you suggesting that I'm *un*comfortable with women?"

"I saw you at the book brunch. You were out of your depth. You felt completely out of place. That's because you need to get back *out there.*"

"What does that mean: *out there?*"

"Socializing."

"I was never some social butterfly."

"Can I set something up between you and Gloria?"

"Let me think about it."

"Okay." She came to her feet. "Now, let me take you home."

By the time they reached Phoebe's car, Joseph had shaken off some of his animosity. "I can't fit in this little thing. It's not even a real car."

With laughter, Phoebe said, "You can fit in."

Once buckled into his seat, and feeling claustrophobic, Joseph said, "What they call these, Hybrids?"

CHAPTER 15

"Good morning, Claire. You're in bright and early."

Jacqueline and Claire hadn't become *homegirls* by any means; still, Jacqueline had come to respect her assistant. When she first made the decision to hire her, it was for no other reason than business. She desperately needed an assistant and Jacqueline was impressed with how she functioned under pressure without a strand of blonde hair out of place. Were it not for the Gwen mishap, she might never have given Claire a mere sidelong glance. She apologized for the mishap, made no excuses. Claire owned it. Jacqueline needed a rock star and Claire fit that bill. When she took time off to mourn Stefan, Jacqueline remembered saying to Claire, *impress me*. Not that she expected her to knock her off her feet, but yes, Claire made an impression on Jacqueline. And when she'd mentioned it to Michael over coffee a few mornings ago, he'd told Jacqueline: "You must be getting soft in your old age."

"I have an appointment away from the office. Pastor Stevens is not on my calendar...You've heard of Pastor Stevens? Oh, okay. Well...yes, I attend his church when time allows. Yes, I'm a member," she affirmed. "But listen, he's supposed to be coming in at nine. Could you do the usual? And I would suggest that you do a search; nothing time-consuming. I'm not ready to present him to the Huddle. Well, he's certainly high-profile in this city, but he's about to publish a book and Lord, do we need one more Creflo

Dollar, or T.D. Jakes? Being a man of the cloth—do they really need multiple media platforms?" Jacqueline joked. "I said I'd meet with him, but before I present him to the Huddle, I'd like to see what I can do for him." Jacqueline rushed into her kitchen and rinsed out the teacup and placed it in the dishwasher. Hurriedly, she gathered her accessories that were already laid out where she'd placed them earlier. Slipping into her black suede heels, she butted-in on Claire. "Excuse me?" She listened, confusion outlining the tender grooves that her forty-eight years had produced. "Dr. Hugo? I don't think so. All we need is another Dr. Somebody on TV. Dr. Phil, Dr. Oz, Dr. Drew…enough! No, I'm not interested in meeting with Dr. Hugo! Claire, liaise with Rowena in Image. She might take an interest. Make Pastor Stevens feel at home."

"Why so much traffic!" Her cell rang and Jacqueline knew if she answered, it would slow her pace. No one was really effective trying to do three things at once. But to say it aloud would suggest that they weren't ahead of the curve. "Jacqueline Daye!" Her face softened straight away. "Torrick, hi. Oh! What's that? You're break-ing up. The party's where? I can't hear you. If you can hear me, text me details." She made a sharp right-hand turn, and inside of the middle of the block pulled into an underground garage.

"Good morning, I have an eight o'clock, Jacqueline Daye."

"Good morning, Ms. Daye. Please sign in and I'll need your medical."

After producing the necessary information to the medical assis-tant, Jacqueline took a seat nearest to the door she'd have to enter when her name was called. She didn't bother to reach for a maga-zine; she didn't have time to wait that long. She noticed a woman across from her, very pregnant, reading *People*. When she looked closer, she could see that Gwen, along with several other high-profile reality TV personalities, was on the cover. She was about to reach for her cell when her name was called.

She was escorted to an examination room and told to strip and put on a smock.

Jacqueline waited six minutes. Her doctor knocked, paused, and entered the examining room. Jacqueline had been coming to her since she'd moved to the city a decade ago.

"Jacqueline, good morning." She shut the door. "It's good to see you as always. You're looking healthy. I'm not supposed to see you for another four months."

"Good morning, Sylvia." Jacqueline sat at the edge of the examination table.

The doctor washed her hands and asked, "Any problems I need to know about?"

"Well, I've been really tired lately. And…" She didn't want to admit to it, but she needed to so that her doctor could properly diagnose her. "A little over a week ago, I blacked out…fainted."

The physician was wiping her hands with a paper towel and halted. "And you waited over a week to come in?"

"It…I didn't think it was that serious. I was overworked so I thought…"

"You first came to me when you were, what, thirty-nine? You're short of fifty. Did you drive?"

"Yes, why?"

"Well…let's do some tests, shall we?"

In a somber voice, Jacqueline said, "Sure." On her back, all she could do was think about Stefan. It was natural when someone close was diagnosed with cancer, some part of you wondered if your number was coming up eventually. That disease knew no bounds.

Fifteen minutes, later Jacqueline was sitting in her doctor's office waiting. So many things went through her head. She couldn't stop thinking about Stefan when he first told her he had cancer. She didn't dare show how scared she was, not in front of Stefan. But later that day, on her way home, she had to pull over as a cloak of grief drew tightly around her. And then she broke down in uncontrollable sobs.

"Okay, Jacqueline," the doctor said entering, putting an end to Jacqueline's mental chatter.

She looked closely at her doctor, whom she trusted, trying to detect any clues in her face. Her head was down, and she was studying paperwork. Jacqueline began to think she had something dreadful to say and was trying to find a way to say it. Yes, she was a professional, as was Jacqueline, and she knew Jacqueline could handle any bad news. Nonetheless, they were on a first-name basis and had even once shared a taxi to the airport. *She doesn't know how to tell me something is very wrong.*

"Okay," the doctor said. "I'll need a few days for the results of your blood tests. Oh, my colleague failed to note...When was your last period, Jacqueline?"

"My last..."

"You *are* still menstruating?"

With a slight nod, Jacqueline confirmed.

"Brace yourself. You're pregnant."

"Wha—Dear, God. I'm...That's still biologically possible?"

The information the doctor just shared with her patient was neither good nor bad news. Visibly, she appeared to be in pure shock. "Yes, it's biologically possible for a forty-eight-year-old to still get pregnant. I see from my records dating back—you told me you had an abortion when you were..." She referenced the notes fleetingly, "Nineteen."

The doctor could barely hear Jacqueline. "Yes."

"Pregnancy at your age comes with increased risks."

"What are the risks?" She couldn't believe she even asked.

"Naturally…Well, a preterm birth."

"Down's syndrome…"

"Absolutely!"

"I…" Jacqueline's mouth was suddenly dry. "I can't have this baby, Sylvia."

The doctor leaned her forearms against her cluttered desk. "What are you saying? You want to terminate? Listen, Jacqueline, you need to think about this. Yes, it can be a high risk, but we can do all the necessary tests to make sure…"

"No, no," she shook her head, "you don't understand. I *can't* have this baby."

Confused, empathetic, the doctor asked, "Why?" She watched Jacqueline sitting on the other side of her desk looking as vulnerable as a child lost in the park. She'd never seen her fragile. Jacqueline, to her credit, worked her butt off. It cost her—a husband, children. So many career-driven women found themselves in the same dilemma, or they started a family but were conflicted or buried their remorse in their long hours at the office. Not once, in all the years she'd come to know her, had she seen Jacqueline remotely weak. With a face that defied aging, she walked in and out of the doctor's office with the latest fashion and wore them well. Her hair—never out of place. Both her toe and fingernails were always polished and looked freshly manicured. Outwardly, she was someone you envied because she carried herself with so much strength and dignity. To see her like this—

"He's married."

The doctor thought she heard her correctly, but wanted to be sure. "Sorry," she said, looking over her eyeglasses resting below the bridge of her nose.

"The father. He's married."

The doctor wasn't exactly sure what to say. As a professional she needed to explain what this meant to her patient. "You're using a diaphragm for birth control?"

Jacqueline's voice was as low as a whisper. "Yes."

"Do we need to refit you?"

With a shake of her head, she said, "No."

"Then…"

"It happened so quickly. I wasn't prepared."

"You aborted a child when you were nineteen. Why?"

She caught a tear before it slipped from her right eye. "I was raped. My mother wouldn't let me keep that baby even if I wanted to. Besides…Anyway, that's why."

The doctor took a deep breath, and with care in her voice, said, "Let me recommend that you think this through for a few days. Then we'll talk."

"There's nothing to think about. It's out of the question, Sylvia. *Please.*"

It took several seconds to speak. "Sure, fine."

Blindly, mindlessly, Jacqueline drove straight to work. Once she parked in the underground, she used her rearview mirror to check herself. There was slight puffiness under her eyes, but otherwise, she looked typical.

Without her usual cell to her ear, the *Wall Street Journal* under her armpit, she rushed past the concierge with a barely audible "Morning!" and making her way to her office, spoke to Claire. Claire, trailing behind her, kept tempo with Jacqueline. "Where are we?"

"Pastor Stevens is here."

Jacqueline tossed her coat. Claire watched the action, stunned. *Something's up.* "Where is he?"

"Michael came looking for you about three minutes ago. He saw the pastor waiting in your office and decided to take him for a coffee in his office." "Office" sounded like a question.

"Oh, you can count on Michael. Okay, so…"

"He's got quite the following. The dossier, Jacqueline, is on your desk." Claire reached for the profile and handed it to her. "Amazing. You might be wrong."

"Wrong?" The question translated to *me, wrong?*

"He's got a world base. It's not only local."

"Seriously? Pastor Stevens?"

Claire said, "Pastor Stevens, yes." *Pause, Claire.* "He has millions of likes on Facebook and equally as many Twitter followers."

Jacqueline flipped through the dossier Claire compiled—and she did this while she was at the doctor's?—and it stunned her. "Claire, this is brilliant."

"Thank you. I forwarded you YouTube footage on the pastor."

"Good. Oh, Claire?"

"Yes."

"There's a *People* on the stand. Gwen's on the cover. Can you fact-check the article, please?"

"On it."

Jacqueline sat. She held out her hands. They trembled. She had to go to Michael's office, but she couldn't go in there like this. *God, forgive me, and please, please show me the way.*

Phoebe had been waiting for not only Daniel to get back to her, but to hear back from Kent Richardson, or his people. The waiting was a strain and she wasn't good at waiting—it was enough to drive her insane. She felt like the last few years of her life were on hold. Before she called her married lover to *feel* something else, she cleaned the guesthouse to avoid doing something she would later regret. She refused to call Daniel's assistant, and as much as she wanted to, she dared not pull out Brooke's business card. Phoebe could easily say she was calling to discuss potential in arrears royalties, per their conversation when first they'd met. Dusting around the windowsill, Phoebe noticed Venetia sitting out on the porch-styled bench, staring at the naked tree she'd planted in reverence to her mother, Cordia. Some part of Phoebe wanted to go out to see if she was okay. Then another part of her knew she'd be intruding. Barry's decision to return to the Middle East was strictly related to what he did for a living; yet his decision to end things with Venetia was something Phoebe knew at least indirectly she'd had a hand in. Eventually, she'd need to tell Venetia about the conversation they'd had. She'd lived long enough to know that it would eventually come back to haunt her should she choose otherwise.

When her cell rang, Phoebe ran to answer it. The number was the last number she wanted to see on her phone, and for over three months she tried hard to avoid him, but on two occasions she broke down. Only minutes ago she felt the urge to hear his voice. "Hello." They talked briefly. She chose this moment. Phoebe said, "Please don't call me again. Ever! *Please.*" When she released the call, she couldn't believe how easy it was for her to say it. Joseph had been right: as long as he wasn't divorced, her lover was still married to his wife. His not living with his wife didn't alter that reality. He'd hemmed and hawed for so many months about the whys of not divorcing his wife. One being financial. *Out of bitterness, she'll take me for everything she can legally squeeze out of me.* Oh, then there were the children—sixteen and fourteen. Those were the excuses every woman heard who involved herself with a man who couldn't—*wouldn't*—leave his wife.

"Hey, you," Phoebe said, sitting next to Venetia.

"Good morning." Venetia held a cup of something warm; steam swirled from the cup. She continued to stare out at the tree, almost hypnotized.

"What's going on? It's cold out here."

"Yeah, I know."

"About Barry…"

"If you don't mind, I don't want to discuss him. Really, I don't."

"But…"

"No, seriously. Please."

She is way too calm. Phoebe was in an uncomfortable quandary. She wanted to confess; there was no question in her mind that Barry broke things off, at least in part, because of the conversation they'd had. To what degree did it persuade him, she wasn't certain. Was he in fact gay but still struggling with his sexuality? That, too, Phoebe couldn't say. But she couldn't afford to lose Venetia's trust. She needed her in her life. When Cordia asked her to be Venetia's godmother, she'd made a promise to Cordia she would always, *always* be there for Venetia—carpet ride or by foot, she would get there.

"Philipa wants to have a photographer come and take a few pictures of the tree. She wants my permission to use lyrics for the book."

"From which song?"

"Promise Me."

Phoebe suppressed her gasp. She had written the lyrics to that song, but as a gift permitted Cordia to have the credit. Other than Cordia's husband, no one else knew, and Phoebe would never tell another living soul. It wasn't as if she didn't receive monetary gain for the use of the lyrics. Cordia wanted—needed—a song that would put her back on the charts. She felt her status ebbing. Still making good songs and managing to rise on the charts, she struggled to retain relevance that brought her such success years before. There was a time when she was depressed about it. Such was the irony of life—"Promise Me" stayed at number five during the first leg of Cordia's world tour. It immediately reached number one and hung there for six weeks in consequence of her death. The album sold nearly 13 million copies worldwide.

"Are you okay, Venetia?"

"Where are we having Christmas? Here, L.A...."

"I think we should do it here. Your grandma's assisted living facility is here. We can bring her to the house and let her open gifts. You know, like you always do. How about we invite some of your clients? Nigel's local. Then, perhaps Philipa. I like them."

"Should I put the house up for sale?" She asked it quite perfunctorily, as if she was asking someone to give her the time.

"Why would you want to put the house on the market?"

"I don't know. Mother loved this house. Our house in Benedict Canyon was half this size. When I decided to sell it, I got a good price. It's a different market now, though. This is where she was born and raised. Mother liked L.A., but this was home to her. Her safe haven, away from that life—music, drugs, recklessness. My mother loved music, but she didn't care for the life. She was grounded. Father would follow her to the end of the earth. So he agreed to buy the house. When they left us, Grandmother moved in it and became my guardian. I was just starting sixth grade. Grandmother said, 'I want you to have a normal life, Vennie.' You know she calls me that, right?"

Phoebe wrapped her arm around Venetia with deep compassion. "Yeah, I know."

Silently, they stared at the tree; each experiencing different emotions, sundry thoughts.

When Dianne saw that the call coming into her cell was Torrick, she excused herself from the conference room and said bossily, "Don't tell me you're still in San Jose!"

"I'm at the airport. There was a delay."

"If you miss Daniela's birthday like you've missed at least ten of them, I will never forgive you." Two people were passing her in the hallway where she was talking to Torrick. Dianne offered them a forged smile and continued: "This means a lot to her. She's sixteen today!"

With his handheld propped on his shoulder, Torrick pulled a ten-dollar bill from his wallet and handed it to the salesperson. "It's a two-hour flight, Dianne!"

"Don't miss this birthday party. I mean it, Torrick!"

He reached for his sandwich and told the person behind the counter to keep the change. In a quick pace, Torrick pivoted between lackadaisical travelers to make it to the gate. "There's no reason the plane should be delayed; I'll be there in time."

"You had better!" Dianne ended the call.

After the meeting, Dianne headed for her car. If one thing went wrong, she'd blame it all on Torrick. He hadn't lifted one finger to help her. While he was preparing to leave for the airport the day before, she made mention of him not helping her with the birthday celebration. Torrick said, and in a tone that literally knocked Dianne off her feet, "I wrote the check, didn't I?" Torrick hadn't written out a check in years; they used debit or credit. But she got his point, and heard it loud and clear.

Moving through light late-morning traffic, she kept hearing his words. Even the night before, his words had stayed with her and she couldn't get a wink of sleep. The pastor's wife had phoned her that morning, inquiring how things were. She couldn't believe that Torrick had called the pastor's wife to pick Henna up from school while he was back East, in Washington. And how dare Henna betray her, calling her father to tell him she'd slapped Daniela. Even now, with time bridging the incident, Dianne was still bothered by it. She continuously held fast to things that no longer mattered. Her therapist so much as said so. "You're clinging to an outdated persona," was what she'd said.

Unaware of it, but Dianne was starting to resent that she had to rely on Torrick so much. All the years they were together, he never so much as mentioned "writing out a check"—and the fact that he said it meant something was up! He was separating himself from her. *Are we having financial issues I know nothing about? Why would he say something so insensitive?* When she mentioned it to Vanessa, she asked if it was possible Torrick was involved with someone else.

"What do you mean? Like having an affair?"

"Well, yeah."

"Remember, I thought he was. But I think I thought that only because that damn personal trainer pretty much convinced me that *I* gave him chlamydia. I hadn't been with anyone else. I'd never cheated on Torrick before. This meant if the personal trainer was right, Torrick had to give it to me. Which meant he had to be sleeping around."

"Remember what you told me when you were here? You married him because he was *safe*."

"And I was pregnant."

"Well, that too."

"I wish you could be here for Daniela's birthday."

"Look, let me see if I can get some time off. I can use my frequent flyers and come home."

"You mean meet up in L.A.?"

"Yeah, why not? It's such a busy time at work during the holidays;

I won't make it for Christmas. But I want to see my daughter anyway. It's been four months. Let me check on it."

"Oh, please do! I can fly down with Daniela. I was going to let her be Miss Grownup. Let her fly on her own. But it would be good if all of us…"

"I'll make it happen."

After that conversation, Dianne couldn't stop thinking about how differently Torrick was behaving of late. She couldn't necessarily pin it down. He wasn't the same. But an affair? She wouldn't say he wasn't capable, but sneaking around and secrecy wasn't his style.

On the flight, Torrick was restless. Normally, he would have arranged to have an aisle seat, but first and business class were full and he had no choice but to take the window. He played it too close too often. Meeting with a high-profile software developer to strategize security on trips to Seoul and Tokyo took longer than he anticipated. It was a major client which required him to meet in person. Yet the client held him up for an extra hour; thus, he'd missed his already-arranged flight. It was a popular route with up to five in- and outbound flights daily. Still, he had to do some fast talking to get on this flight, which would get him home just in time for Daniela's birthday party.

"How are we going to handle this?" Jacqueline had asked.

"Be yourself."

"It's easy to say than to do."

"Other people will be there."

"How many people?"

"Eight, I think."

"Do I know these people?"

"Act normal."

When she said, "Oh, you mean my new normal," Torrick laughed. He *liked* Jacqueline. That's why he'd risked everything to be with her; and Torrick knew it was risky from jump. He hadn't managed to picture himself outside of a life without Dianne. Even when he had fallen for Jacqueline, he saw no way of leaving the woman who had brought him two precious and irreplaceable blessings: Daniela and Henna. Yet when he last saw Jacqueline and they made love, the scent of her, the intensity he felt being inside her, and the very essence of who she was as a woman, he was prepared to leave Dianne. This was no school-boy crush. He'd had plenty in his youth. It was a salient fact; the feelings for Jacqueline weren't frivolous. There seemed to be something natural about what he felt. As though it was the route his heart was destined to take. When the pastor asked *when* was he going to end the affair, Torrick told him, and in a firm voice, "I'm not sure I can."

"Oh, baby girl, I miss you." Joseph had just finished putting away the dishes when his daughter called. They often spoke four times a week, and their conversations generally lasted about thirty minutes. Joseph lived for those talks. "I can't wait. Cornell? No, he's out. You can try and reach him on his cell phone." They talked a good fifteen minutes before Christine told her father she had to go. While he sat reading the paper, he kept hearing Phoebe's voice in his head: *Being around women and feeling comfortable with them.* From the moment he crossed paths with her, he had been completely comfortable with Phoebe. Why were two people who clearly had things in common, and when someone had such strong feelings for them, that they were not *meant* to be? It made no sense to Joseph.

When he met his wife, they hit it off *like that*. The rhythm of their relationship was as natural as breathing. They complemented each other. Their first date, Joseph took her to a Prince concert. He impressed her with second-row seats, and the concert, which opened with Sheila E., was sold-out. Reflecting back on it now, Joseph forgot how loose he was in those days. On their second date, he'd taken her to a basketball game; Larry Bird and the Boston Celtics were in town. The seats were excellent—courtside. A friend and coworker at the post office had season seats. Afterward, they went to his small apartment, unassuming but clean and neat, and he had sex with her for the first time.

He flipped the page of the newspaper. *I'd known her less than a week.* The idea of that blew Joseph's mind nearly thirty years later. Aging had that effect on one's life. If his daughter had the exact same experience now, he would find himself bothered by it—her going on a date with a man and sleeping with him within a week of knowing him. Joseph would want her to get to know him better. It's what fathers hoped for when it came to their daughters.

There was no way that Phoebe didn't know how Joseph felt. He'd made it clear, he was sure of that. Still, she wanted to introduce him to some woman named Gloria. Thinking back on their conversation at the path, Joseph realized how defensive he had been toward her. *And why are you wanting me to meet his woman?* The tone he'd used with Phoebe; surely, she was uncomfortable but had discovered a way to disguise unease over the years. He hadn't meant to be so put off by it. Frankly, he was both disappointed and unprepared, although he wasn't exactly sure which dictated his emotions.

He'd discussed Gloria lightheartedly with Christine and she made some remark about going for it! *Go for it!* Cornell, just as he was walking out the door, said, "Dad, you look like you might have shed a few pounds." Joseph put the newspaper down and looked out at the sun forcing its way through a corner of the gray sky. For quite some time, his mind wandered to and fro. He leapt to his feet and headed for the telephone. He stared at it resting in its carriage. *Go for it!*

"Oh, what the hell."

CHAPTER 16

Jacqueline couldn't find a parking lot nearby that wasn't full. The streets were a dead-end as well. It was an omen she told herself. She had no business going to the birthday celebration to begin with. Jacqueline knew she was fully capable of putting on a front; she did it every day. Torrick was a different story. The fact that he'd managed to keep their relationship a secret was beyond belief. Well, then there was Pastor Stevens. When Torrick told her he'd gone to the pastor for counseling, Jacqueline looked at him, her mouth agape, taken totally aback.

"You went to the *pastor?*"

"He's my spiritual adviser."

"Torrick!"

"I didn't name you. He wouldn't ask that kind of question anyway."

"You should never have told him."

"This whole thing...a year ago, six months ago—hell, three months ago, I wouldn't have conceived of doing something like this to my family. I needed to confide in someone."

So of course Jacqueline couldn't imagine Torrick being cool under this kind of pressure. He'd been with the Secret Service for nearly ten years and could handle *that* kind of pressure. But sleeping with another woman, whom he had fallen in love with—it was too complicated; a cloak and dagger much too close for comfort. Amazingly, they hadn't been discovered. Much of their time was spent at her place. A few times they publicized their relationship, but they had always been in faraway places to avoid running into anyone they knew in town. They chanced dining at a Chinese place, a dive in the International District, because Torrick had a taste for the restaurant's deep fried oysters. Nowhere was 100 percent safe. When Jacqueline made it to O'Hare last month after that stressful presentation in Chicago, on her way to the gate, she ran into a client. Even then Jacqueline thought it was only a matter of time.

When she turned onto Ninth, a car was pulling out. Jacqueline stopped abruptly and backed into the tight space and entered Josefina's six minutes later. A friend of a friend of a friend from Lafayette owned it, but Jacqueline never had intentions of ever dining at Josefina's. It had that must-try reputation; the clientele, bourgeois. A young woman approached Jacqueline. "The James party," she assumed.

"Yes, that's right."

She was escorted to the back of the restaurant where the James party would be seated. Jacqueline noticed Daniela with several other girls talking and laughing nearby. The hostess said, "Right this way." At once Jacqueline saw Dianne and Torrick standing together, holding glasses. They were a good-looking couple, and comple-mented each other. When she'd first met them, Jacqueline admired the Jameses. Of all the couples at church, Dianne and Torrick had the strongest marriage—it was a poignant paradox. With their attractive daughters in tow, they were treated like royalty, espe-cially since Torrick did a great deal for the church. Tithing, of course; but his company offered security at no charge, and he'd done his share of hauling senior citizens around and organizing functions for the single men in the congregation. She'd always liked Torrick. He had noble qualities. Still, Jacqueline hadn't been attracted *to* him; first and foremost because he wasn't available.

The hostess said teasingly, "Dianne James is practically flagging you down." Jacqueline took notice of Dianne across the room, waving her hand, the gesture suggesting *here we are!* "Thank you," Jacqueline said to the hostess.

Dianne greeted Jacqueline with an embrace.

"I love that dress. Where'd you get it?"

"I believe I snatched it from some woman in Kate Spade. It's the only one they had in my size."

"I can see you now. We have to promise to get together and go shopping. After you cancelled our plans yet again…If I didn't know you better, I'd say you were avoiding me."

"Dianne!" Jacqueline didn't know what else to say. "Mr. James, you are *wearing* that suit."

"Thank you." His voice was natural, cordial.

"So how does this work? Did you guys rent out the entire restaurant, or what?"

"We're waiting for everyone and then we'll take our seats at two tables."

"How many are coming?"

"It started out as ten and grew to thirteen. First it was a few friends from school, then two from church, and then…"

"Henna wanted to invite one of her friends," Torrick interjected.

Jacqueline looked over her shoulder at Daniela and her friends huddled nearby, sharing their updates and whatnot. Each one of them wore cute clothes from the trendy stores for girls their age. Two boys stood with them, behaving rather standoffish, their body language implying they were too cool to be at a party with adults.

The hostess approached. "It appears everyone's arrived."

While Dianne went to gather everyone, Torrick said to Jacqueline, "I appreciate you coming. I know you'd rather be anywhere but."

"I can handle it. When can I see you?"

Walking toward the tables, Torrick said, "I'll text you."

Once everyone was seated, the hostess announced that appetizers would be served. She asked if anyone wanted to order anything from the bar. Dianne looked to Jacqueline. "Your usual?"

"I'm driving, so…"

"Like that has ever stopped you," Dianne taunted. "Maybe a Bloody…?"

"Mineral water with a slice of lemon," she spoke directly to the hostess.

While they waited for their meals, Dianne arranged it so that Daniela would open her gifts and share what she'd received. Each gift had a delightful surprise, and Daniela was deeply touched by everyone's generosity. When she arrived at Jacqueline's gift, she was elated by the small, mysterious box. She shook it, and something rattled inside. Daniela slid a very chic greeting card from the envelope, and a gift card from Neiman Marcus accompanied it.

"Wow!" Dianne said.

"Can I use it online?"

"Use it when you go to L.A."

Dianne said, "Perfect idea. I can take you to the one in Beverly Hills."

"Are you going with Daniela to L.A.?"

"Vanessa's going to meet us there. I thought it would be good to hang out—the four of us. Vanessa's daughter at San Jose State's coming, too. You met Carmel."

Daniela opened the decorative box and a pair of earrings was wrapped inside olive-colored tissue paper that duplicated the gift box. "Oh, Jacqueline. These are so cool." Her friends examined them and offered ideas about what clothes would look best with them.

"And Daniela?"

With a wide grin on her face, she said, "Yeah?"

"I've arranged for you to meet Gwen Banks. A limo will pick you up and take you to the studio where she shoots some internal scenes for the show. Afterward to her house in Hollywood Hills. She's having a casual dinner party. I'll give Dianne the details."

"Oh, my God! *Oh*, my God!" Daniela said. "Daddy, Gwen!"

Several of her friends chimed in and were excited by the very idea that Daniela was going to hang out with Gwen. *At her house in the Hollywood Hills!* When Jacqueline snuck a look Torrick's way, slyly, he winked. Dianne pantomimed *thank you* with tears in her eyes.

Following dinner, Jacqueline made excuses that she needed to leave; she'd sat through dinner and endured it passively.

"You've barely touched your meal. Are you all right, Jacqueline?"

Jacqueline was on her feet, and walked over to Dianne and brushed her cheek against hers. "I'm so overwhelmed since Stefan..."

Dianne squeezed Jacqueline's hand. "You have to really miss him. Call me."

"Daniela!"

She stood and rushed into Jacqueline, thanking her profusely for her gifts.

"Torrick, walk Jacqueline to her car. She's parked on the street."

Before Torrick could get to his feet, Jacqueline halted him with, "There's plenty of foot traffic. Please, enjoy. Love you," she said, and off she went.

Dianne told Torrick, "She's seeing someone. She should have brought him."

"Seeing *who?*"

"That venture capitalist. Daniel Terry."

Venetia ran so hard she could barely breathe once she stopped, bent over, and caught her breath. The day wasn't nearly as cold, and she was trying to stay focused on her work and moving into a new phase in her life. Alone. She admired her godmother, who had been in and out of relationships and during her dry spells, as Venetia chose to call them, there was something about her—she didn't fear being alone. As if, in losing a lover, she could be selfish, and she could devote more time to herself again. Venetia had cried enough tears over the past weeks that she felt certain she had none left. Since her college days, she only had three serious boy-friends, and that included Barry. She spent three years with a boy right out of college. They traveled through parts of Egypt and spent a week in St. Petersburg. She thought they were going to get married. He never proposed. Like many young women who loved so deeply, Venetia assumed it would lead there. As much as she admired Phoebe, she didn't want to end up like her. Alone. Sleeping alone, or with a random lover. No children to love and to be loved by. Venetia didn't want to know that kind of emptiness. In so many ways she admired Phoebe because she chose her path tenaciously, and whenever things went badly, she didn't blame. She accepted the fate of it and did her best—and with such dig-nity—to move on.

Venetia knew she wasn't that strong, that determined, that focused. Not when it came to her personal life. She was more dependent on a relationship than she realized. The second man she fell for was a music producer she'd met after she attended the Grammys. Someone threw a party at Spago and she tagged along with a group. He was older, and she had loved him more so as a father figure than as a *man*. Eventually, he went on to the next pretty young thing and Venetia was devastated. She went away for a long while, until her grandmother required care. When she met Barry while having drinks with friends at Busboys and Poets in D.C., their relationship happened fast and hard. They took the Acela back to New York and became completely inseparable. After weeks of talking a lot and eating out and sharing books and seeing films, they flew to Montréal and stayed three days, turning off their cell phones. Barry was intensely sexual and Venetia grew as a woman being with him. She became more at ease with her sexuality. Because he suggested it, she had a threesome with Barry and a very close male friend of his. Venetia was unnerved by the whole idea, but she was so hypnotized by Barry and wanted to please him. Her mistake was sharing it with Phoebe who asked her an odd question: "Who did what?" Venetia regretted sharing the experience with Phoebe to the day.

And now, as she looked back on that experience, she realized there were insinuations nudging at her. When she made a decision to be with someone, she was with them completely. Her experiences taught her to make compromises. Venetia sat on a bench. She caught her breath and realized that she was crying. She'd been running so hard along the lake; her heart was beating so fast, and she was gasping for air. She was sweating and panting when Joseph touched her shoulder. "Venetia? Are you all right?"

Venetia wiped her face in the fold of her arm and cleared her throat. "Yes, I'm good. How are you, Mr. Morgan?"

He sat next to her on the bench. "You sure you're all right?"

Her voice was low and solemn. "Why?…Yeah, absolutely."

"Well, I have to say, I thought you'd been crying."

"Probably sweat," she fibbed. "So tell me, what's the latest on Cornell?"

"Going back to school in January. Got himself a part-time job downtown."

"I knew it would work itself out. Cornell is a great guy, and he's smart. After all, he's a Morgan."

"Christine's coming home for the holiday."

"We keep tabs on each other through Facebook. It would be good to catch up in person, though."

For a short time, they sat quietly.

"Hey, I have an idea. Phoebe and I are going to bring Grandmother over to the house for Christmas. She would love it, I know. You and your family should join us."

"Oh, really. Well…And Phoebe's going to be there?"

"She'll be there. Now I understand she's tried to set you up."

"Oh, right. Gloria. We've e-mailed a few times. But…"

"You aren't feeling her?"

Joseph's laughter was inflated. "It's not a matter of not, as you say, feeling her. I guess I've been out of the game too long. She's probably waiting for me to do something."

"Like what?"

"Invite her out or something. Our e-mails have been friendly and we've found some things we have in common. But…"

"I'm going to tell you something and I hope it won't offend you."

"You certainly have my attention."

"You know Phoebe's not staying here, right?"

"She said as much."

"And…well, Mr. Morgan…"

"Call me Joseph. It's fine."

"Okay, Joseph. When I first suggested you two meet, I thought you could maybe just hang out. You know? Go to a movie, or have dinner. Something friendly."

"What you're trying to say—there's no hope for me as far as Phoebe."

"In a manner of speaking? Yeah."

Venetia was a lovely, strong and independent young woman with heart and spirit. Joseph carefully observed how she'd handled her parents' death. There was a time when she was aloof, but then became more outgoing. Yet there was always something inexplicable about her. She *was* an only child.

"That Christmas idea sounds like fun. I'll mention it to Christine and Cornell. You know, he's gone off and got his girlfriend pregnant. Although I'm not sure if she's an ex-girlfriend or what. She might well have been planning to…"

"She's welcome, too. And by the way, you can even invite Gloria."

They both broke into a hearty laugh.

Somber, Venetia said, "Thank you."

"For what?"

"Your timing."

Phoebe hadn't heard from Daniel, nor had she heard from Kent Richardson; accordingly, she withdrew into herself. When Richardson said that the opportunity required her to be in L.A., she trusted the entire thing was fated. But now? Not having heard from Richardson or his people troubled her, and she became depressed, her thoughts dark; her hope vague. More times than she cared to ever admit to herself, she picked up the phone and called Daniel's assistant, but was told Daniel was out of town on business. Moreover, his assistant said she wasn't privy to where Daniel stood in terms of Phoebe's business plan, but that Daniel would "reach out to her" upon his return. It was one of those bridge-over-troubled-waters days.

Phoebe was never good at being in limbo, and this feeling felt strangely déjà vu-ish. Being here, in this place, reminded her of her neighbor. At three-fifteen in the morning, she began to howl at the night, like a wounded animal. Several disappointments had hit her in one day she'd told Phoebe over wine only hours before: her boyfriend of three years fell in love with his daytime soap costar and moved out; and she learned that her contract with a studio where she was a producer for a nighttime TV show was ending because the program was being cancelled; her dog had gone missing. Phoebe wanted to go into the early dewy air and save her neighbor from herself. She chose otherwise, and waited for her to stop howling.

Being stretched between the known and the unknown, the waiting—it was a pervading sense of unease she couldn't manage to shake. And there was nothing to distract Phoebe. She phoned the Next Generation to see if there was work, but they'd said flippantly that they would "reach out to her" when something with her skills came their way. *Reach out to her.* That was the exact phrasing Daniel's assistant had used. From where it came she cannot be sure, but over the past few days, she began to stray into an unexplainable angst, having more faith in her vicious inner critic than blind faith. She started pacing the guesthouse and every decision, every bad choice, every deception, decidedly sealed her current fate. She'd learned how to live between the comfort of being alone and the ease and enjoyment of another's company. At some point she learned how not to need anyone. Yet the isolation was taking its toll.

She couldn't—not anymore—handle the not knowing, not having steady resources; not feeling confident what choice would lead her out of the present mess she'd boxed herself into. She didn't want to make yet another choice that would lead her right back where she was. She lost her home because of a bad choice. Phoebe understood it: she was starting to play it safe. What was she afraid of?

Then, she began to think of having placed her child up for adoption. Why, *why* was she thinking about this now? Was Joseph right? That she should look into finding her daughter? Was she up for something that required her to be entirely selfless? She stopped pacing and sat. She rocked back and forth, anxious, and feeling dreadfully insecure. She dashed for her papers and dug out Richardson's card. His daughter's card fell from the paperwork to the hardwood floor. She bent to pick it up. Phoebe called Venetia but received voicemail. "I need you to find something out for me. Call me as soon as you can."

For over thirty minutes, Phoebe sat in the corner of the small sofa, curled up, praying. She had never been this scared before. But she knew that she was scared. The telephone rang and she jumped to answer it. It couldn't possibly be Daniel or Richardson; neither had the number to the guesthouse landline. Unless—

"Hello!"

"You rang?" Venetia said. Her spirits were renewed since running into Joseph on the path earlier.

"I need a big favor."

"Okay, sure."

"Can you find out what hospital Brooke Richardson was born in, and her exact date of birth, and time?"

"I can make some inquiries. What's going on?"

"I gave a baby up for adoption when I was twenty-two."

"You have a child out there, Phoebe?"

"Yes."

"You never stop amazing me. And…What, you think it could be Brooke Richardson?"

"Well, I just felt something. I don't know if that's what really happens, that you feel some connection or something…I don't know. But can you find out?"

"Let me get back to you." Before she released the call, Venetia asked, "Are you all right? You sound…"

"I'm okay."

When she hung up from Venetia, Phoebe asked herself, "Should I be doing this?"

CHAPTER 17

"You're in a good mood, Dianne. Might I inquire as to why?"

With her legs crossed, Dianne indulged in a cup of black tea. For once she felt wonderfully rested. Less stressed.

"Torrick and I made love last night."

"I see. And how was it?"

"It was like we were when we were younger. When we first met and when we were more attracted to each other—when there was nothing to lose. Once, while I was carrying Daniela, we had sex—we didn't make love—in the shower of this upscale hotel. It was the most intense orgasm I had ever had."

"So what is the difference in making love and having sex...in your mind?"

Dianne sipped her tea. "The F-word, plain and simple. No kissing, hugging—no romanticizing the act. It's been a long time since Torrick and I were present during sex."

"Have you ever thought about the differences between Gregory and Torrick? These men have shaped you as a woman."

"Sexually, you mean?" The therapist nodded ever so slightly. "Well...Let's put it this way: Gregory was a clitoris man, and Torrick is more an intercourse partner."

"And the personal trainer?"

"What I got out of that was being totally uninhibited. I felt liberated. I needed that. And I did it I'm sure because I wanted to see what it felt like to be with someone different at this stage of my life…And I wanted to feel something new and with someone who didn't know my backstory. I get why people have affairs."

The therapist displayed no particular emotion. Her rust-red painted lips curved gently, but it was hard to read what was going through her mind.

"I love my husband, you know. What Torrick and I have—what we've had—has never been this rock-my-world love. I got pregnant; I was in my thirties. Torrick was successful, honorable. Marrying him was the logical choice to make." Her eyes roamed to the therapist. "I think authentic love is quiet and stable anyway. Not what I felt for Gregory; that was out of the realm of real. Not that I wish suffering for either of my daughters, but I would hope that they meet someone and fall dangerously in love and get their hearts broken."

With a curious brow, the therapist wondered, "Why?"

"So they could get it out of their system. And then meet someone like their father: trustworthy and caring."

"But, Dianne, bear in mind you did something similar and you still cling to some idea of Gregory. Remember, when Venice broke up, you suffered a profound sadness; you were depressed. Phoebe…"

"What does Phoebe have to do with this?"

"Venice, Phoebe, Gregory—the momentum of your history is haunting you."

"I don't know that I agree with that."

"No?"

"No."

"Your feelings have been underground for years. Are you familiar with klesha?"

"Klesha? What's klesha?"

"To simplify, conflicting emotions that cloud, or distort, the mind.

"Although you may not realize it, you have everything you want and *need.* There's no reason to hold on to resentment toward Phoebe."

"I don't actually consider myself feeling resentful. I ran into her and decided to start from that point. But when we were at Philipa's, and she started telling our story—her version of our story, which was wrong…"

"You're seeing this from your perspective. Can't you look at it as neither one of you being wrong or right: that your perception of events leading to the end of Venice was your version of it? Your reality; and based on how you filter through information. Phoebe has a different experience. Because you both are seeing things differently doesn't mean one is right and the other is wrong."

"How can that be?"

"You are experiencing this through hindsight bias."

The room was quiet for a little while.

"Is your marriage back on track, Dianne?"

"What do you mean?"

"A few weeks ago you weren't sure how you felt about remaining with Torrick. What has changed?"

"Daniela's party." Dianne stared into the air.

"What happened at the party that changed things for you?"

"We were happy again. Things were normal."

"What made things normal?"

"Torrick and me. I think we're in synch again. We're in rhythm."

"Okay," said the therapist. "And what about the med?"

"I'm…I try to take it as needed."

"Let's see what happens once you have waned off."

"I'd like that. I don't want to become dependent."

"Dianne?"

Her eyes met the therapist's.

"Remember, your past was once your future."

The workouts with his trainer put a spring in Joseph's step. He was starting to feel better about himself. The weight wasn't dropping off like he preferred it to, but he had to admit he was having a hard time letting go of some of his favorites, what the personal trainer called, "comfort foods." But he tried not to snack late in the evening, when his loneliness was most intense. He was making his way over to see Phoebe; the cold day on his skin felt rather good. When she called, Joseph felt flattered, but he wasn't sure why she wanted to see him. She said she'd discuss it when he got there.

He made a concerted effort not to come off too available. He thought if he said, "I'll come soon's I finish up around the house," that would indicate that he wasn't going to stop doing whatever he was doing merely because she called him.

By the time he reached the guesthouse, there were random snow-flakes floating in chilled, smoke-colored air. There had been no word about snow, but then the weather reports were never quite accurate these days. He stopped and said a prayer at the tree. Phoebe opened the door wearing a cropped sweater and a pair of closely fitted jeans that hung low off her waistline. Something she said when he was last at the guesthouse flashed through Joseph's mind: *I'm independent in my thinking. I don't have the same baggage other women my age typically have.* He wasn't sure why he thought of it at that precise moment.

When he entered, the guesthouse was quiet—no music, no tele-vision. And something spicy hung in the air.

"So, how you been, Phoebe?"

"Have a seat. I'm pouring a cup of cider. Would you like a cup?"

"Why not," he said.

When they were finally seated, relaxed, Phoebe folded her legs together. Leaning into the chair, she held her cider in both hands. "Have you reached out to Gloria?"

"Surely that's not why you called me over here."

"Just asking."

"We've communicated. By e-mail. She's actually interesting."

"Joseph…Come on, are you procrastinating?"

"Not really."

"But you find yourself a little curious, right?"

"Well, that's true."

"I won't bring it up again. Actually, I asked you over because I wanted to run something by you."

"Let's hear it."

"Remember when I told you that I'd given my baby up for adoption?"

"I recall, sure."

"Well, something's happened."

"Like?"

"I met this young woman two weeks ago. She made me think of my own daughter. When I met her there was…I told Venetia it was like a connection. But there was…she…something about her, and I haven't been able to shake it."

"You think this young woman might be your daughter?"

"It was strange—it's a long shot, I know. Running into a daughter I gave up for adoption? But I had Venetia look into her background. Because of pro bono work she does to help battered women and women transitioning out of prison, she's managed to acquire some notable friends."

"Oh, she no doubt has connections."

"Venetia's contacted someone. They're looking into this woman's background. We already know that she's adopted."

"How did that come about?"

"Venetia found out. I know that she's the same age as my daughter would be; I just don't know when she was born or where. It was a closed adoption, so Venetia's run into a brick wall."

"I think this is exactly what you should be doing. How can you give birth and not…? You underwent a profound change when you gave birth, Phoebe."

"You have to trust me when I tell you; I haven't given the adoption any thought until recently. Everyone senses something missing in their life, but I never connected the occasional void to not having known my daughter."

"I can understand that." *I love this woman.* "What happens if she is?"

"It's why I wanted your opinion: you're sensible. How should I approach her?"

"How was she with you when you two met?"

"We were informal and there was a natural relatability, if there's such a word. She even listens to Venice music on her iPod."

"Well," Joseph said, and took a drink of his cider. "That's very interesting."

"If I find out that this young woman is my daughter, how do I approach her?"

"How did you two meet again?"

"Her father…"

"Her adoptive father?"

"I interviewed for a position with his company."

"Oh, now that's tricky."

"Tell me about it."

"What's come of the job?"

"I don't know yet."

"Okay, look. If you don't get the job, it would be less complicated. But if you happen to get this gig, it's bound to be awkward."

"I could use an unbiased opinion."

"If you want to know if this young woman is your daughter, you have to take the chance and suffer any possible outcome, even if it's not in your favor. Can you do that?"

It took her a moment to reply, but when she did, Phoebe's

words were spoken with absolute sincerity: "Yes, I can do that."

Joseph thought, *I bet you can.*

When Torrick called and told Jacqueline that Henna would be going to L.A. with Dianne and Daniela, she saw this as an opportunity to spend quality time with Torrick. She had grown attached to the depth and richness he brought to her life. For three days he wouldn't have to sneak away to see her. She'd spent the past few days trying to determine whether she should tell him that she was pregnant. And while it would be difficult to tell him, she'd made the decision not to have the baby. It was the right thing to do, period. She rehearsed various scenarios in her head. But even before she began sleeping with Torrick, Jacqueline knew he wasn't the type of man who'd agree to terminate a pregnancy. Provided Jacqueline chose to have the child, there would be all kinds of repercussions. Torrick would face whatever he had to with Dianne, but he was pro-life to the bone.

"Jacqueline?" Claire stood inside the doorframe of Jacqueline's office, holding her tablet.

"Oh, yes?"

"How do you want to handle it?"

"Handle…?"

"The press conference?"

"Claire, a word. And close the door."

WTH did I do wrong?

After closing the door, Claire sat in front of Jacqueline's desk. She feigned being prepared to do whatever she was going to be instructed to do by balancing her tablet on her lap, hands in place. *She looks so serious. Did I screw up?*

Jacqueline slipped off her reading glasses and set them on a stack of paperwork piled in front of her, and rested her forearms on the desk.

"I thought we were moving toward being a paperless company. Look at this."

Claire shot a look at the paperwork the size of a ream. The day before, she'd gone through several stacks, sheet-by-sheet, and tossed everything remotely frivolous in Shred-it. The stack set in a neat pile on the desk required Jacqueline's approval, or Claire needed direction on how to proceed. Jacqueline was either sick or out of the office on business, so couldn't move forward.

"Is there anything I can help you with?"

"No. In fact you managed to make good notes so that I don't have to spend too much time on it. Actually, I want to ask something of you."

Hello! "Sure."

"You told me that you were interested in Strategy."

"That's right."

"If you promise to give me six months, I'll get you in Strategy."

Six months. That's it. Just six months. Claire, speak.

"Absolutely. Six months. Whatever you need."

"Thank you, Claire. That's all."

Taken aback, she said, "There's nothing else?"

"Oh, no. That's it. I'll go through the pile and sign off on anything that matters. And the press conference? Let's schedule it for tomorrow morning, say nine?"

Claire tapped her fingers against her tablet and stood in unison. "Nine. Well…"

"Is there a conflict?"

"Your meeting at the Monaco's is at eight forty-five."

"I need that press conference. It's a spot on MSNBC—I can't control the timeslot."

"Seven's early."

"That's all we have?"

"'Fraid so."

"Oy. Hold off for an hour. Get me in with Michael as soon as possible. And include Kerry, the branding coordinator."

"On it!"

When Claire left the office, Jacqueline called Torrick but received his voicemail. "I should be home by six-thirty. Seven at the latest. I can cook."

When Jacqueline pulled into the market parking lot, her cell rang. She reached for it and upon identifying the number, answered, "Hello, Sylvia. I've been meaning to call you. I still plan to terminate the pregnancy. Yes; I'm very sure. Schedule it for…? Well, I'll need my calendar." Jacqueline leaned against the headrest, listening. "I do understand. Of course. Can I call your office tomorrow? Thank you."

For well over twenty minutes, Jacqueline sat in her car; sadness rose to her chest but ceased at her throat. Before she knew it, tears rested at the edge of her quivering upper lip. Within a few minutes, she pulled herself together and went into the market. Blindly, she pulled items off shelves and grabbed produce and tossed it in the basket, not cognizant of what her hands came in contact with. They were out of the bread she liked, but Jacqueline chose a baguette that was too doughy although a passable substitute. Once she was in the car and driving home, it occurred to her she'd forgotten salad dressing and almond soy. *I'm too distracted.*

Torrick hadn't called her back, and when she got home, he wasn't there. She had given him a spare key for moments like this— when she was running late; that way he wouldn't have to wait. The condo was cold. Jacqueline dumped her tote bags on the kitchen counter and, blowing her hands, headed for the fireplace. It took a few minutes to get it going. She turned on music—an old Donny Hathaway CD she'd run across at a record store in London. Absentmindedly, she moved about the kitchen putting away items. Jacqueline picked up her cell phone to make sure she hadn't missed a call. *Where is he?*

She changed into more comfortable clothes. While the sauce was sautéing, she poured herself a few droplets of wine. Even though she'd made the decision to terminate the pregnancy, she'd chosen to slow down on her alcohol consumption. Spooning the sauce, her mind reflected back on Daniela's party. Dianne was happy. Torrick came across naturally devoted toward her. Was he doing that on a subconscious level; so as to not look at Jacqueline one too many times? Was he being himself?

What they'd chosen was immutable, and her relationship with Torrick had nowhere to go. He couldn't continue living his life between his devotion to his family and his desire to be with her. Jacqueline would never suggest he choose. It wasn't about choosing. And thus, she was knee-deep in a dilemma. She wanted to be with Torrick, but she wouldn't ask him, and nor did she want him, to leave his family. Where would their relationship lead? Where could it go? She needed to discuss this with Torrick. If this were, say, Daniel, they would naturally have taken their relationship to another level by now.

Her thoughts were interrupted by a call. *Oh, please don't let it be Simone.* When she reached for the cell, she took note of the number. "Michael?"

"Bad time?"

"No, never. What's going on?"

"I didn't get a chance to mention this to you earlier."

Jacqueline reached for her wineglass. "What's that?"

"Zachary Johansson is retiring."

"Retiring? He's, what, forty?"

"He's found a conscience. He wants to do 'good works' he said. He's going into environmental research. He wants to save the planet. Maybe even become a CNN Hero."

With laughter, Jacqueline said, "He's such an asset. The London office—what are they going to do? Have they found a replacement? Those are huge shoes to fill."

"They inquired about you."

"They? You mean London?"

"London seems interested in talking to you. I don't want to lose you here, especially so soon after Stefan's passing."

"What does this mean, Michael? I feel I'm being outsourced. You wouldn't have called me if you weren't going to suggest I take it."

"I wouldn't suggest you take it. I would prefer—I need you here."

"I left London because I wasn't going to advance beyond where I was. Now they want me to stop everything I'm doing here."

"It's a huge promotion."

"What's going on, Michael?"

"Listen, we can talk about this later. Zachary just gave notice. He won't leave before the New Year."

"What if I don't want to go back to London?"

"Nothing changes. Your name—it came up."

Jacqueline started biting the corner of her lip. She replaced the wineglass on the countertop with an unstable hand.

"Jacqueline?"

"Sure. Let's talk about this later."

"Enjoy your evening."

After this phone call?

Once he was backed into a parking space in front of Jacqueline's, Torrick ignored his ringing cell phone. He knew it was most likely Jacqueline wanting to know when he'd be arriving. When the SUV engine was turned off, Torrick took the key out of the ignition and rested in the seat, watching someone through a naked kitchen window at the end of the block. How ordinary, he thought. He had lived an ordinary life. The American Dream comprised of various things, but the basic concept of that Dream was to get an education, meet someone to share your life with, have kids to preserve a legacy, build a career to secure a life of comfort, and purchase a home. Torrick lived within those margins for quite some time. He had been faithful to his wife and worked diligently to secure a good and comfortable home. He never wanted for anything else; never cared about the distractions that were out there. But he was in the process of destroying all of that. And for what? Blithely, he started something he couldn't find his way out of. He loved Jacqueline; Torrick was definite about that. Yet a lot of what was happening between them was based on newness—something he hadn't had before, and it had been a while since he didn't turn over and fall asleep after sex. With Jacqueline he held, cuddled, spooned. Flashes of her came into his head throughout the day. He couldn't remember when last he was impatient to see Dianne when he got home. When she did come to mind during his day, it had more to do with *stuff*—their domestic life. It had been ages since they just *talked*.

"Dammit!" he hissed, hitting the steering wheel.

Inattentively, he waited for the elevator in the lobby of Jacqueline's building. Torrick looked at his handheld. He'd received a text from Daniela. He opened the text with a half-smile.

It read, "luv u."

CHAPTER 18

The sky was a pale blue, and the day was chilly, but a soft sun posed against the canopy, offering a splash of glitter on what was oftentimes a quite gloomy day. Phoebe looked up to the heavens. It was as though she anticipated the answers to her life's questions. She chose to walk with a brisk pace. Before her bungalow went into foreclosure, she walked the beach, sometimes for miles. Now her thighs felt loose and her lower abdomen began to protrude, slightly. While she'd lost a few pounds, her body was trying to tell her something. A woman walking toward her—straight-backed, swift, even while pushing a stroller—was talking openly on a cell. *What did we ever do before technology took over the human race?* For a brief moment, Phoebe felt a quiet sorrow rise to her chest. In some ways, she missed the days when things were less complicated, less stressful, less disconnected. Before everyone spent more time *looking down* instead of up. Despite the fact that the world was supposedly smaller because technology brought corners of the world closer, the masses were more isolated than ever.

When she reached the door of the café where she was going to sit and have a cup of tea, her cell rang. It was the Next Generation calling. She contemplated whether to answer, but she needed to work and she needed to be distracted by something. "Yes, it's Phoebe. Yes, I'm available. When? You'll shoot me an e-mail to confirm? Sounds good."

She entered the café and it was partially full—everyone was either on a laptop or using their mobile device. A barista whisked by but slowed to say, "There's a table over there. Can I get you something?"

"Green tea, thank you." She headed to the rear of the café. Al Green's "How Can You Mend a Broken Heart" began to play. Just days ago she'd heard "Strawberry Letter 23." Each song took Phoebe back to when music was relevant and the cultural landscape was less dense.

She spotted a young man seated at a table in front of her. He was viewing a video with his touchscreen cell. Handsome and stylish, he wore a designer scarf around his neck, his hair well-trimmed, and his fingernails clean. He was a little too young for Venetia, and she shouldn't jump into anything right now anyway. Her feelings were still raw. Every morning in the shower, Phoebe asked herself what she should do about Barry.

"This is Cornell," Phoebe overheard the young man say. *Is that Joseph's son?*

Her cell rang and Phoebe reached for it. "Hello. Yes, this is she." The barista placed her green tea and check on the table.

"When? Yes, I can arrange that. Can you send me an e-mail so… Oh, sure. Text me. Thank you." Phoebe breathed a sigh of relief. Her insecurity—or lack of faith—made her give into believing she wasn't going to hear from Kent Richardson.

"Hey, how's it going?" Cornell said to Phoebe, pulling out a few singles and left them on the table.

"Hello," Phoebe replied.

He turned to leave. Phoebe watched him with a curious eye. He reached for his buzzing cell with a rap song ringtone. "Zyn, what-up? True that," she overheard him say.

Luckily, the temp assignment Next Generation offered her

wouldn't interfere with the meeting she'd have with Kent Richardson's associate. Timing, they say, is everything. But she still hadn't heard from Daniel. Because she didn't know her all that well, Phoebe didn't want to call Jacqueline, whom she knew had a friendly relationship with Daniel. It would be too risky to make that move.

Damn, what would I wear?

Whenever Dianne came home, she oftentimes found herself not wanting to leave. She was in love with her hometown and it was never more apparent than when she stayed at her mother's house. Love circulated discernibly through every room. Dianne always felt safe here. When Venice broke up, she came home because she knew she would be protected. Although the temperature was a surprising sixty-five degrees, it was a stunning weekend. Disappointingly for Daniela, a light shower was predicted. Yet she was so thrilled about meeting Gwen and spending the weekend with her "friend," Dianne doubted whether her oldest would even notice. Henna's bottom lip poked out because she couldn't hang out with Gwen, too.

Dianne would find something her baby girl could do while Daniela and her boy hyphen friend went to the studio and the casual dinner Gwen arranged. Dianne and Torrick wouldn't agree to let Daniela go without Vanessa's daughter, Carmel, chaperoning her. Despite his having rap lyrics tattooed on his forearm, and the young man Daniela was fixated on at the moment was from a good family, Dianne didn't know enough about him; and then there was Gwen. If her reality show were even remotely an indication of her *real* life, Dianne didn't want Daniela to be influenced by all that Hollywood fakery and good-life nonsense. When she was a part of Venice, she herself had been exposed to insalubrious influences that naturally came with that lifestyle. It didn't take much to be seduced by the Hollywood mystique. At least superficially, Daniela didn't mind that her cousin Carmel would have to tag along with her. From all that Dianne could tell, nothing was going to rain on her daughter's parade.

Dianne and Vanessa decided taking Henna on a shopping spree would be a distraction. She wasn't having as much fun. Dianne felt sad when she said, "I could've stayed home with Daddy." Similarly, Dianne knew what it felt like to be on the outside looking in. They chose the Grove since it had great stores to shop in, and then there were more than enough eateries to select from, including Henna's favorite—the Cheesecake Factory. They walked leisurely through the exterior mall, Dianne and Vanessa arm-and-arm, while Henna was skipping along, her spirits starting to elevate, finally. She would stop at a window and peep inside, turn to Dianne, and with animation, ask, "Mama, can we go in here?" Solely to appease Henna, they did. Her eyes were attracted to plenty of things, yet Henna was more like her father. She wasn't impulsive, but deliberate in the way she approached just about everything.

When they came upon Barnes & Noble, Vanessa said, "Can we go in, Henna? I'd like a latte."

"Can I have a mocha Frappuccino, Mama?"

"We'll see."

They entered the bookstore and Vanessa said, "I miss L.A."

"Me, too," Dianne said, stepping on to the escalator.

"Why do we say that every single time we come home?" Vanessa joked.

"I was born here, right, Mama?" Henna's two shopping bags dangled from her wrists.

"Correct." Dianne stepped off the escalator.

With a cute grin on her face, Henna replied, "Cool!"

They laughed their way to the only available table.

"I'll order," Vanessa said. "What do you want, Henna?"

"A mocha Frappuccino. Can I, Mama?"

"Vanessa, get her a small."

Dianne was looking through messages on her cell and Vanessa was pouring raw sugar into her latte. Henna was in her own world. She was good at being with herself, but also liked being around others. She was so much like her father it was borderline unsettling to Dianne. She knew that secretly Henna was Torrick's favorite; she herself couldn't decide which of her daughters she *liked* more, but she loved them very, very much. However, the love she felt was unique with each girl.

"Mama, can I look at the books?"

"If you're taking your Frap, please, Henna, don't spill it."

Dianne and Vanessa observed her walk hurriedly to the books nearby. "God, she reminds me of Torrick," Vanessa said.

"I know." Dianne laughed.

"Listen, have you broken down…?"

"He knows about the personal trainer even though I haven't owned it."

"He's waiting for you to bring it up. That's who Torrick is. You know he's all about trust. You need to tell him the truth. If you don't, this will always be between you two; it will never go away."

"You should know. You left your first husband because he cheated. I'm not sure I could leave Torrick just because he cheated."

"You say that from someone who *has* cheated. Do you really think you'd be okay with him being with another woman? Not some one-time thing. I mean a relationship?"

"Torrick? Falling for someone else? I don't think so. He told me that he'd never been exposed to a black woman who was 'worldly'—he liked the idea of that. To Torrick, honey, I'm a catch!"

"You're looking at your husband from the perspective of someone who's known him a long time. People change; they evolve. Look at you! You went off and slept with a guy you scarcely knew. And didn't use protection, by the way. *I* would have expected differently from you. You can't make assumptions about your husband based on who you think he *still* is. Given the right opportunity, who knows?"

"If he wants to confront me, so be it."

Vanessa watched her sister closely. Dianne sipped her latte. She didn't know this side of her sister. "Have you learned anything in therapy?"

"Hey!" Dianne snapped. "I don't want to discuss this anymore." Dianne looked around for Henna and caught her talking with another young girl by the books, and then she heard her therapist's voice in her head: *Your past was once your future.*

Before she was fully awake, Torrick snuck out of Jacqueline's condo, and while driving toward home, he sensed that something had changed. He wasn't entirely cognizant of it. Yet between the time they each fell asleep and he woke up and stared at the ceiling, something—a detail that eluded him—was off. He moved about the empty house. He didn't sense the natural ebb and flow that infused throughout the house. It hit him that he'd taken his life's contentment for granted—Daniela's laughter from a distance; Henna jumping up and down in her room doing who knew what!; Dianne talking to someone on the phone. In the generous home, such simplicities shaped their lives. The silence made him aware that he and Jacqueline had reached an impasse, and that knowledge dominated his thinking. He liked the smell of something cooking or the sound of life in a house in which people *lived* there. He never felt that way at Jacqueline's: it was aesthetic, quiet and solemn, and not one object was ever out of place.

Since he purchased the house ten years ago, not once had he been in it alone for more than a few hours. Surely not days. He had been home for several hours, doing paperwork in his office, when Torrick stopped to answer a call. A VIP client, Kent Richardson, was arranging for security. After handling the provisions, which took ten minutes, he went back to his paperwork. A few minutes into it, Torrick found himself distracted. He rested into the back of the chair. With his arms folded over his chest, it became clear to him: perhaps had he gone straight to his office instead of coming home when he left Jacqueline's, in all likelihood Torrick wouldn't have become aware of such thoughts. Coming home, however, and feeling the emptiness, the quietude, it permitted him the luxury of gazing deeply at his marriage, at his life. Sitting in the stillness, he fully understood what he'd put in motion. A few weeks ago, Pastor Stevens asked him, "Do you end a marriage like yours because you ran into a few speed bumps?"

Torrick reflected more acutely on the pastor's words. He knew his marriage and its dynamics much more intimately than the pastor, and they hadn't run into a *few* speed bumps. Before he stopped to help Jacqueline two months ago, his marriage was strained and the link that naturally held a longstanding marriage together was compromised. He didn't go looking for another woman, but as the pastor so politely pointed out, because the opportunity presented itself didn't mean he was supposed to take the bait. He was to rely on faith and get his strength from the Lord; not give into fleeting temptation. Torrick and Dianne's relationship had been full and complete with all the ups and downs of any marriage—was he prepared to throw it all away? He had always been drawn to Jacqueline, but it was because of his marriage and the vows he took to remain faithful to his wife that he never so much as looked at Dianne's friend with lust in his heart. He respected her as a family friend—Daniela and Henna adored Jacqueline. He never, and nor had she, crossed lines. Mulling over everything—his marriage, his children, Jacqueline—Torrick had a better sense of what was at stake. With his mind clearer, he admitted to himself he always had a thing for Jacqueline. It was the *thing* that any number of men had for a beautiful woman—the *idea* of her.

He reached for his beer and took two long gulps. Still struggling with what exactly to do, Torrick went back to his paperwork. He was to hook up with Jacqueline later and he hoped by then his head was clearer. He would know fully in his gut what he needed to do. But no matter what choice he made, it would dramatically alter his, and Jacqueline's, fate.

Within a few minutes of finally concentrating on invoices that needed his approval, Jacqueline called.

"Where are you?"

Torrick, unconsciously, frowned. Her tone came across possessive. "Excuse me?"

On the other end of the line, Jacqueline felt put off, but repeated herself: "Where are you?"

"I'm at home. Why?"

Briefly, silence played through the wireless phones.

"So…what, are our plans cancelled?"

"Hey, you know what? I got caught up in paperwork." Torrick was only partially truthful. While he did get lost in work that was time-sensitive, he also had misgivings, which he'd only really begun to feel a few hours ago.

Jacqueline was no fool. Although she wasn't accustomed to having relationships with married men, she'd been around long enough to know the signs of a man getting restless. "Okay," she responded. "Call me if you want to do something."

Placing his phone on the table, Torrick felt a pang of guilt. He wasn't sure exactly where to place it, and on what. Dianne, Jacqueline—all of it? He had some owning to do—he got that. Still, he felt as though he was between a rock and a hard place. Either decision—to end things with Jacqueline or to dump his wife—would leave him feeling he made the wrong choice. He was torn between the woman he was *in* love with and the woman he *loved*—the mother of his children, and the woman he had built a life with for nearly two decades. Jacqueline was ambiguity, a bit of an enigma. Yet he knew the lights and shadows of his wife, and what buttons to push, and when. He was intimately familiar with every boundary; not even the possibility of her cheating on him was an outright surprise. Jacqueline, on the other hand, was a woman who had spent her entire adulthood deciding her fate independent of someone else. She was not used to seeking approval from a man. It was those attributes that made her even more attractive; Torrick had not yet ascertained how much of a risk he was willing to take. Suddenly, though, the decisive moment was starting to present itself.

What Torrick loathed most was how he'd placed himself in such a lose-lose position. Even if he slept with her that one night, when he rescued Jacqueline out of the rain and her stalled car; still, he'd be in a different place—psychologically.

"To hell with it," he fussed beneath his breath.

He stormed out of his office and went to the kitchen and grabbed the last bottle of Guinness. He tossed the top in the kitchen sink. He made his way to the family room and switched on the television. After locating the sporting event he'd wanted to watch, Torrick sat in front of the TV. The landline rang throughout the stillness of the house. His thoughts were dark and he wasn't in the mood to talk to anyone. He heard Henna's voice from the distance—"Hi, Daddy, it's me. I'm having a lot of fun. 'Byyyeee!"

It was one of those partly sunny days, and Jacqueline decided not to wait for Torrick. It was rare she had the opportunity to do something completely self-seeking and spontaneous. It was perhaps what she missed most about her post-college and pre-mortgage days: a time when she was a black urban professional—aka, buppy— and long before she received mail from AARP. That "thirties girl" would drive to the airport, park, walk inside, pick a location in which to travel—she didn't plan it. Sporadically, she found herself longing for the days of living abroad and being able to take the Eurostar to spend a weekend in Paris, or catch the TGV to Barcelona. But shy of forty, her needs changed. She herself didn't choose the change. Slyly, life itself made one conform to its natural order.

Jacqueline managed to find a parking spot near World Market.

For several blocks, she kept feeling this thing—her chest felt heavy. The market was crowded. Her eyes landed on a couple. The woman, Jacqueline guesstimated, was in her late thirties, and noticeable pregnant. Jacqueline's thoughts were interrupted by a merchant inquiring if she was interested in the prawns she stood in front of. She cleared her throat, speaking low but clear, "Yes, I'd like two, no, one pound." When she looked over her shoulder to seek out the couple, their backs to her, the man had his hand on the pregnant woman's backside. Jacqueline lost sight of them inside the cluster of heavy foot traffic. She intuited a discontent she couldn't recall ever feeling, not in this way.

She'd scheduled the termination of her pregnancy in a week, and felt no obligation to tell Torrick that she was pregnant. Jacqueline wasn't sure if it had to do with how he had been acting lately. Something was going on with him. He was changing his mind, and they were ending. Her body sensed it before her mind would allow the thought to develop. He wanted her, but there was more at stake than his feelings for her and Jacqueline wouldn't make it any more difficult for him.

When they started seeing each other, she understood other people had to be considered, and she made every effort not to be clingy, or to come across officious. But when she spoke with Torrick earlier in the day, he treated her like a woman who was getting on his nerves. As if she was suddenly acting too needy. She had been more than compromising. For starters, she was sleeping with the husband of a so-called friend. A friend she liked and cared about and—well, respected was debatable. The duplicity was in the worst way possible: she was having very intimate sex with her friend's husband. What's more, Jacqueline hadn't allowed a man to be the center of her life. As much as she had grown into a loving relationship with Torrick, she learned how not to put herself in a position in which she had no out. One thing had always, *always* been clear to her: Torrick wouldn't leave Dianne. Even if he entertained it, in the end he wouldn't go through with it. And frankly, if he left Dianne for her, he likewise had the potential to leave Jacqueline someday. Most importantly, if Dianne could loathe the very notion that Phoebe existed on the planet, where would that leave Jacqueline?

By the time she ran a few errands and unlocked her front door, Jacqueline was biting back tears. She was about to lose so much. There was the probability of losing her friendship with Dianne. Perchance, she and Torrick had reached a stalemate; where could they go from where they were without hurting people they cared deeply about? And then there was London. Her cell rang and she anticipated it to be Torrick. "Hello. Daniel? Who is she? Don't be daft. You've been off the grid, my friend. But I swear, you have the most impeccable timing."

When Joseph received an e-mail from Gloria inquiring if they could Skype, he was clueless. He'd held off responding so not to look the fool. Finally, he searched the word "Skype" on the internet, but was too self-conscious to even do it. This was all new to him: Skype, texting, and social networking. All this oversharing was like a universal high-school. This new technology, this always-accessible culture, was so amazing, but it demanded so much time. When did meeting people become so damn complicated? The twenty-first century had its perks, but the world was moving too fast. No sooner than he learned one thing, something else popped up. Joseph couldn't keep up. And now, people walked in malls and supermarkets with their dogs! When he was still working for the post office, dogs weren't allowed. Everything was so casual now—calling POTUS by his first name, like *Cher!*

He chuckled, recalling Phoebe asking him, "So what exactly do you miss about the so-called good old days, Joseph?" Joseph, with his wide grin, had said, "Larry King. I used to watch Larry King every single night. CNN—it's not the same without Larry King. I miss the gas station attendant asking me if I need my oil and water checked, and washing my windshield. I miss *holding* the *TV Guide* in my hands. That's what I miss."

Joseph was going to talk to his son about this Skype business. He knew all about this new-media stuff. He could tell him what he needed to do. Joseph was at the infancy stage of shifting in his thinking. If he wanted to Skype Gloria, or Skype *with* Gloria, he needed to adjust his mind-set.

He wasn't exactly sure when it crept in, but he was starting to get very interested in Phoebe's colleague. She sounded intelligent by her e-mails. With her sense of humor, their conversations flowed like water from a stream. Joseph had to admit, he'd found himself growing attracted to Gloria, and how he might feel about her in person was becoming less and less imperative. That could be a good thing, he decided. For someone's looks shouldn't take precedence over their character, their beliefs and values. In that regard, he liked the new way of connecting with people. Before he'd gone on one date with Gloria, he was getting to know who she was. Joseph, admittedly, liked it that way.

"Dad! Are you home?" Cornell called out from downstairs.

"I'm up here, Cornell," he yelled out.

When he came to his father's room, he held a protein drink in one hand, and his device in the other. "Hey!" he said. "I talked to Christine. She's getting two weeks off."

"Oh, now that's great."

"I'm going to take a shower…"

"Cornell?"

He stood in the doorframe. "Yeah, Dad?"

"What do I need to do to Skype?"

"Skype?" Cornell's head bobbed back.

"You do this kind of thing, right?"

Cornell laughed. "Oh, my God. Did this Phoebe put you up to this?"

"No, Gloria."

"Who the he—heck is *Gloria?*" Cornell's face went blank.

CHAPTER 19

In her youth, Phoebe juggled her life without effort. Before Venice became an overnight success story reaching the charts with hits like "Plan B" and "Destiny 4-Ever," she managed to sit with Dianne and Cordia in some of their stomping grounds like Pancake House in West Hollywood, and Copper Penny in Hollywood where they sat for hours having free refills of coffee. They'd sit at a table at the Red Onion nursing drinks until the last call. Young and still untainted by the complexities of life, they orchestrated their future by simply writing down the things they planned to accomplish in the next six months. A year before they set foot on a stage, they partied and club-hopped, topping the evening with Fatburger and Roscoe's Chicken and Waffles. They dreamed of "making it"—and they didn't know at what. They just *dreamed*. Until Phoebe said, "We look good. Cordia can sing. Let's start a group."

Phoebe still had, amongst her many possessions, all the lists they made which she'd framed, before their lives changed forever and they were—as the phrase was so loosely used these days— celebrities. That word—"celebrity"—had a different subtext when Venice was at its height of success. When they were popular, the ladies never considered themselves celebrities. Now, every musician, actor, athlete, politician, and on-air journalist was a brand— a marketed life. She certainly wouldn't want to be a celebrity these days, because reality TV had trivialized public persona. Besides managing to party until two and three in the morning, holding down a part-time job, attending Loyola Marymount and taking fifteen credits each semester she attended, *and* be in a girls' group, Phoebe slept very little in those days. She didn't *need* the sleep, and even now, she slept restlessly if she went to bed early. Those pre-Venice days taught her how to organize as well as compart-mentalize her life.

That stamina was gone now. In Lisbon, Paris, Sydney, Toronto, New York, San Francisco, Los Angeles? There was a transforma-tion bogging her down, or had she simply surrendered? Five, even three, years ago she wouldn't have sat in a hotel lobby feeling anxious, murmuring pseudo prayers to be hired. Up until not that long ago, just about everything came *to* her. And what didn't come directly to Phoebe, she went after and nine times out of ten, she attained that which she wanted to acquire. She would warn any woman under thirty-five not to depend too heavily on looks. When it faded—and it ultimately faded—it was impossible not to experience it both psychologically as well as physically. Even now, while sitting in the festive lobby of a grand downtown hotel, she could calculate when *age* began to alter her world. Sitting there, waiting, a profound sorrow rested inside her heart. Whatever happened today would be the beginning of the rest of her life. This opportunity she was hoping for wouldn't present itself again. By chance something else, yet it would not be *this*. And her age— the middle—would have some influence over whatever came to pass.

Phoebe pressed her eyes shut hoping her prayers were being carefully evaluated in spite of her agnosticism. Before Venice took the stage, Dianne reached for Cordia's and Phoebe's hands and she'd say a generous prayer. She was good at that. Dianne always went to church, even when they were on the road. She'd find what Phoebe defined as holy mysteries in farmhouse churches to gothic cathedrals—from the lushness of Charleston to the cobblestone streets of Rome. Quietly, serenely, Dianne would sit with her god. Phoebe wished she had the belief she had known Dianne to have, and she would truly pray.

"Ms. Pleas?"

Phoebe looked up to a young, quietly attractive blonde with loose curls resting on her shoulders. Her suit was a well-cut design. Phoebe knew the designer's signature style without having to look at the label. "Yes."

"Good morning!"

Phoebe came to her feet. "Good morning."

They walked toward the bank of elevators.

They arrived on the floor that Kent Richardson's people had reserved strictly for office use. Her escort instructed Phoebe to take a seat and someone would be with her momentarily. A stylish woman with a Bluetooth in her ear stopped and offered Phoebe water. She declined. The place was buzzing. Everyone was preoccupied. Several people huddled together talking. All those present were sharply dressed, and came across quick, efficient, *focused*. Phoebe leaned into the energy, feeling this desperate need to be a part of whatever was going on; it felt big and authentic. She made a mental note to send Michael a thank-you card.

"Phoebe?" She looked up to Brooke Richardson. "It's good to see you again."

"Hello!"

"My father has been delayed. Let's go chat."

They went into a connecting suite.

"Do we need to reschedule?"

"Kent Richardson is in the middle of a very complicated business transaction and it has taken longer than he anticipated. So he asked that I follow up with the candidates he's lined up. It's down to you and two other candidates in L.A."

They talked for no more than ten minutes. Brooke had developed keen emotional intelligence: she listened politely, posed well thought-out questions that weren't asked out of curiosity or politeness, but of genuine *interest*.

"So, relocating back to L.A. poses no problem?"

"Oh, no."

"In two days?"

Phoebe didn't hesitate. "Absolutely!"

"Good," said Brooke, standing.

Phoebe stood, too.

They walked silently to the elevator. Phoebe said, "There's no final decision? I mean, Kent Richardson doesn't have…"

"He trusts me to make the right decision."

When the elevator doors opened, Phoebe looked into Brooke's gentle cinnamon brown eyes—and she hadn't noticed it previously, but her eyes were the exact color of Gregory's bedroom eyes— and said, "Thank you very much, Brooke."

"I'll have your contract PDF'd to you by end of business. I look forward to working with you."

The elevator felt as if it was not moving, but it was going down. Phoebe saw the number to each floor flash. She shut her eyelids, and Phoebe said in a gentle whisper, "Thank you. Thank you, God."

"Are you mad at me?"

Jacqueline stood in her doorway holding a glass of almond soy. "It's hard to be mad at you, Torrick. Come on in."

"I got so caught up in the game…"

"There's no need to explain." Torrick felt a little chill in the air; he chose to overlook it. "I thought we could go to see a film. Then

I realized that would probably be risqué. Surely you wouldn't want to run into Pastor Stevens. We can always find something on Netflix."

Torrick sat on at the edge of the sofa. "Pastor Stevens, huh?"

She sat next to him. "Are you hungry?"

"I haven't eaten."

"I can order in Chinese."

With his fingertips, he rubbed his chin, contemplating. "Sure. That sounds good."

Jacqueline placed her glass of soy on the table. With her long legs, she straddled Torrick. "Want to make love first?"

"Mmmm, that's an idea."

He peeled off her leggings, and he was inside her without taking off a stitch of clothing. With every thrust Jacqueline bit back tears. When her heartbeat escalated, she let go completely, wrapping her legs around his waist tightly, squeezing, and mumbling words Torrick couldn't understand.

While he was in the shower, Jacqueline studied her nude body in the wardrobe mirror. She squeezed her breasts; they were so tender. There was no baby bump; not yet. Even she wouldn't have known she was pregnant if she hadn't been told by her physician that she was incontestably pregnant.

When Torrick came into the bedroom, he was caught short by Jacqueline admiring herself in the mirror. She was smoothing her tummy with the palms of her hands, which he found strange. She caught his reflection in the mirror and tried to be nonchalant by saying, "Does it look like I'm gaining weight?"

"You look stunning."

They met halfway in the middle of the full-sized bedroom and embraced. "Thanks for the new toothbrush," he said in her ear.

She untangled herself from their embrace. "I'm taking a shower. I left the menu on the table."

Torrick was sitting in the living room with the television on when Jacqueline joined him. She needed only two fingers to count the number of times he watched TV at her place, which included that early evening. While they most often made love, they also talked. Occasionally, they would sit at opposite ends of the sofa, she with her tablet and he with his laptop, and they worked while they sipped wine and every now and then, one or the other would get up and go grab something to snack on. They always caressed and laughed. They had passionate debates.

It was clear to Jacqueline now—that had changed. He was used to her and, as the B.B. King song put it so reverently, the thrill was gone.

"So what's on?" she asked, relaxing in the sofa.

"You smell nice," he said. He reached for the remote and put the sound on mute. "Nothing, really. There's what, a thousand channels on cable? You'd think there would be better programming to choose from."

"How about a game? Those are always on."

He chuckled, hoping to avoid the conversation about his not calling her to say he was going to stay home and catch a game instead of coming back to her place so they could spend some quality, uninterrupted time together. For once, he wouldn't have to check the time and leave to go home to his family. He'd asked himself on his way back to her place if Dianne and the girls had gone to L.A. three weeks ago, would he have chosen to stay home and watch a game or would he have chosen to spend the entire day with Jacqueline.

"Did you order?"

"Yep. It should be here soon."

Eventually, the food arrived and they sat on the sofa and ate from the cartons instead of plates, sharing their portions with chopsticks. Every so often Jacqueline's phone would ring, but she elected not to answer. However, on three separate occasions, Torrick answered his. All business calls that he handled expediently.

Jacqueline was stuffed. Her head rested in Torrick's lap. His eyes were closed as if he were trying to catch some shut-eye. Jacqueline's mind went from her conversation with Michael about London and then back to Torrick and his mentioning Daniel while they ate. How did he even know about Daniel? Not that there was anything to *know*. Could that have been why he was so distant of late? Oddly, in a conversation with Daniel a few hours ago, he'd asked her, "Who is he? Because you're in love."

She wasn't attached to the idea of having Torrick's baby. And withholding the information was probably iniquitous; frankly, though, it was her decision whether to terminate the pregnancy. She knew their relationship had reached its plateau. He was trying to find his way out of her life but didn't know how to do it. The longer he stayed, the more Jacqueline sensed it. It was if she could hear his mind. While she wanted to make it easy on him because in some ways it would make it easier on her, she chose to let him make the first move. She wouldn't beg or stop him, but he was going to have to be a man about it and end it—that would demonstrate a level of respect he had for her. For days now, she mentally prepared herself for his leaving her. But he wasn't sure how to do it; that became clear to Jacqueline. Despite that he'd cheated on Dianne, Torrick wasn't the type of man to sleep with a woman and then dump her. In fact, Jacqueline believed he'd convinced himself that he loved her enough to leave Dianne, when in fact, everything about who he was as a man resisted such an act. In Torrick's mind, even having an affair was sordid; the sneaking around, planning, keeping track of lies.

When Torrick's cell rang, Jacqueline reached for it and handed it to him.

"Torrick James," he answered. "Dianne?" He raised his torso, and Jacqueline's eyes popped open and she looked up to the expression outlining his face. "Slow down. What—what are you talking about? *What?* Dianne, take a breath. Let me speak to Vanessa!"

Jacqueline sat up, brushing her hair away from her face and tucking it behind her ears. By the very tone of Torrick's voice she knew something had happened. A nervous habit, she wet her dry lips.

"Where's she?" Torrick listened for a long while. "I'll get a flight out as soon as possible. I'll call Dianne back as soon as…What's that? You're breaking up, Vanessa." He covered the phone and whispered, "Turn on the television."

Jacqueline reached for the remote control and flicked on the television. "What am I looking for?" She was careful not to speak too loud.

"All right. I'll get back with you as soon as I can." He disconnected the call. "Turn to CNN."

Jacqueline flicked to the channel. Across the television screen were the words "breaking news." Jacqueline leaned forward, listening to a voiceover: "Gwendolyn Banks, the popular reality TV personality of the highly popular reality show, *Gwenology*, was in a car accident." The crawl on the screen mimicked the same information. A great deal of police presence surrounded an area that looked to be filled with foliage, and hilly. The correspondent was reporting, "It appears the SUV, registered in Gwen Banks' name, went off the cliff here along curvy Mulholland Drive, roughly a mile from Gwendolyn Banks' Hollywood Hills residence…"

"Dear God. Is she all right?" Jacqueline cried out.

Torrick rushed to his feet. "Daniela was in the car with her."

"What? Daniela! Gwen wasn't even supposed to be driving. Do we know if she was the driver?"

"Dianne and Vanessa were on their way to the hospital. They didn't have details. Only that Daniela was in the automobile when it went off the road."

"This makes no sense."

"I need a flight. Where's your laptop?"

"Use my iPad. It's in my office."

While Torrick was out of the room, Jacqueline turned up the volume. What she was hearing wasn't good. The Escalade swerved off Mulholland and flipped several times before plunging at the bottom of the hill. Although the aerial shot of the black vehicle was too far to see how badly damaged it was, it looked so ominous. The reporter, no babe in the woods, was good at keeping the flow of information going; still, there were discrepancies in her coverage. She mentioned that there were four, then three, and back to four passengers. Other than Gwen Banks, she could not give names or sexes of the other passengers. She alluded to Gwen being the driver, and backed away from that with, "There is no clear understanding of who was driving." She reported that two bodies had been thrown from the SUV while two—the fast-thinking reporter then said one but changed it again back to two—bodies were found at the scene inside the vehicle but not wearing seat belts.

"Wait, we have additional information…" the veteran reporter went on to say.

Gwen had been admitted to the hospital for observation. One other passenger, a male, was in surgery. Another "unidentified" female died while being transported to the hospital, and there was still no word on the fourth unidentified passenger, another female. *Who was the driver?* Was the initial report accurate: that Gwen was the driver? Was she under the influence and authorities were withholding that information?

"I can't get a damn flight!" Torrick rushed into the living room using a tone that threw Jacqueline for a loop. "What are they saying?"

Jacqueline's cell rang. She rushed to answer it with a breathless, "Hello!" She listened. "Yes, I just heard. What's going on? What happened?"

"I need a damn flight!" Torrick argued to the air. He rubbed his hands across his closely shaven head and circled the space he was standing in. He was becoming impatient, annoyed. Torrick was panicking.

Jacqueline said to the caller, "Yes, yes. Okay. Let me get back to you." Before she could put the phone down, it rang again. It was Michael. She wasn't sure she wanted to answer. "Yes, Michael?" she said. "Yes, I just heard." She listened to his instructions. "Sure. Michael, I need to take care of something. I'll call you back."

"I can't get a flight out. There are no seats—every airline is booked."

"Try standby."

"Standby!"

"I'm brainstorming."

"Kent Richardson! I do security for him when he's in town. He has a private jet. He was due in this afternoon but was delayed..... I don't have his number in my phone."

"Kent Richardson's a client of Michael's."

Spellbound, he couldn't turn away from what was happening on the large screen. Nevertheless, Torrick broke himself away and he began to surrender to God. He prayed. And he prayed even more. Why was Daniela with Gwen *in* a car? It was common knowledge to anyone who engaged in social media that she wasn't supposed to be behind the wheel of a car. Daniela was smarter than that. Jacqueline had arranged for her and her Friend to have a limo. Because he couldn't put two and two together, he filled in information to stay sane. Torrick tried to stay optimistic, which was his truest nature. Nevertheless, his mind kept coaxing him back to all kinds of bad thoughts.

"Okay, I tried Kent's cell, but no one's picking up. I didn't even get voicemail. But I do have his daughter's number. I know that she's been in town. She was handling some kind of deal...She's Gwen's attorney."

"What's the number?"

Jacqueline recited it, and Torrick pressed the digits.

"Brooke Richardson speaking."

"Hello, Brooke. Torrick James."

"Oh, yes, Torrick. How can I help you?"

"Can you tell me where Kent Richardson is right now?"

"Over the Atlantic, why?"

"I have something pressing...I was wondering when he'd get to town because I need to get to L.A. as soon as possible. My daughter..."

"His plans have changed. We cancelled security."

"Dammit!" Torrick said.

"Can I ask what this is about?"

Torrick explained the circumstances to Brooke Richardson in an anxious, tired voice. The urgent nature of his situation left her breathless. "Gwen's a client. I should fly back to L.A. as well. Are you available at this number?"

"Yes."

"Let me see what I can do."

"Whatever it costs, I'd be grateful."

"Give me ten."

"What?" Jacqueline said when he released the call.

"She's going to see if she can arrange something."

"Like?"

"I don't know. Maybe she can get me a flight. Her father golfs with the president so she no doubt has connections."

"Brilliant."

"Why hasn't Vanessa called me back?"

"They're probably trying to find out what's going on." She answered her ringing cell. "Jacqueline Daye. Yes? Who's this? I don't have a statement. I'm not Gwen Banks' agent. No, not her PR person either. Yes, I work for Media Capital. That's correct. I have no statement. Died? Yes, I heard that." Jacqueline glanced Torrick's way. He was staring down at his cell as if that would make it magically ring. He looked up to Jacqueline when he heard the word *died*. "I'm sorry; I have no statement at this time. Good-bye."

"What was that about? Who died?"

"It was a reporter. They were trying to confirm if one of the passengers in the car had been killed in the crash." With a shrug, Jacqueline said flippantly, "He was simply fishing for information. He didn't know if a person died or not." When her cell rang again, Jacqueline looked at the number but didn't recognize it; consequently, she rejected the call and let it go into voicemail.

"Dammit! I hate this waiting," he argued.

"Torrick…" When she reached out to him, he rebuffed her.

Jacqueline called Claire and assigned her the task of monitoring social media and instructed her to get ahead of the prevailing narrative but to tweet with care. She emphasized it was imperative to track black Twitter.

Torrick's cell rang and he answered immediately. "Yes, Brooke?" He listened for a few moments. "Yes, I can get there. No, it's no problem. I can make it." He listened further. "Yes. And thank you very much. Thank you," he said with intense fervor.

Jacqueline stood stock-still. She anticipated he would tell her what was what. Instead, Torrick reached for his leather jacket and slipped it on, then grabbed the keys to his automobile. Wordless, he checked his cell and turned to leave. Jacqueline trailed behind him. He opened the door, and Jacqueline felt that if she said nothing, he would have left without saying so much as a word to her. "Torrick, what's going on?"

"Brooke Richardson has a client, a soccer player, who's leaving for L.A. in ninety minutes. He's offered to let us fly into L.A. with him."

"Oh, that's wonderful."

For a split-second, he looked at her and then said, "I have to get to Boeing Field." When he turned to rush toward the elevator, Jacqueline's first impulse was to offer to drive him. Yet when she set foot out into the corridor, he was stepping into the elevator. He didn't need her. Finally, the last drop of hope came to pass. Jacqueline never quite knew how it would play out when it came to fruition.

She lost track of time flipping from one channel to the next, hoping to get new details, but the reporting was repetitive. Jacqueline mentally debated whether she should call Dianne, but that didn't feel right. After she called Michael and they spoke for a few minutes, he decided he would put publicity on it as soon as possible so that *if* Gwen had in fact been the driver, they could spin it in the best possible light. Worse, if she had been drinking and driving, they would have a difficult time keeping such details from the media and there was no good way to spin that. Should any passenger die as a result of the accident, Jacqueline and Michael both agreed, Gwen's public career was over.

She sat through the morning hours, channel-surfing and screening her incoming calls. Jacqueline attempted to stay on top of any new information. She dared not check social media because the narrative would be opinion-driven; however, Claire was a savvy social networker and could spin a persuasive tale even with less than 140 characters. At some point Jacqueline began to feel guilty. Had she not asked Gwen, as a favor to her, if she didn't mind letting Daniela hang out with her, sweet Daniela wouldn't have been in the car with Gwen, no matter who was driving. And Torrick wouldn't have treated her like a pariah instead of a woman he had been sleeping with for the past several months. A woman whose ear he whispered into dozens of times, especially when they made love: "I need you in my life."

With her face buried in her trembling hands, Jacqueline cried, "What have I done?"

Dianne and Vanessa pushed their way through a barrage of media. Vanessa kept shouting, "Get the hell out of the way!"

It was mayhem outside the entrance of the West Los Angeles hospital. It took them nearly fifteen minutes to get from the parking structure to the front entrance. They had no one to help them. In typical circumstances, this would have been exactly what Torrick's security firm would have been hired to do—shield Dianne and Vanessa.

When they entered the hospital, Dianne asked a passing hospital staffer, "Can you please tell me where I can find my daughter?"

"I'm sorry?"

"She was in a car accident."

"Check-in, straight down the hall, to your left."

Dianne started walking in a hurried pace, and Vanessa called out, "Thank you!"

When they reached reception, two uniformed officers were standing around along with two men looking ironically like Detectives Briscoe and Green from the glory days of *Law & Order*.

Vanessa said to a woman behind a busy desk, "Can you tell me where Daniela James has been admitted?"

"Family?" the woman asked.

"I'm her aunt; this is Dianne Lewis James, her mother."

"Fifth floor," she said. "See the attending nurse."

Upon arriving on the fifth floor, Dianne and Vanessa were wary of the reporters that managed to get there long before them. They weren't intrusive as was typically the case, but their presence was daunting.

"They must be here for Gwen," Vanessa said.

Dianne replied in a frustrated voice, "I just want to see Daniela."

When they reached the fifth-floor nurses' station, Vanessa's cell rang. "Hello." With her back to Dianne, she said, "Where are you? Oh, thank goodness. How long before you get to L.A.? Yes." Vanessa looked over her shoulder. "She's strong, Torrick. She'll be okay." Vanessa took notice of several uniforms nearby, and she was trying to make sense of all the police presence. "I'll tell her."

"When will I know?" Vanessa heard Dianne ask the woman behind the desk. "How long?"

"You'll have to wait for the attending physician." She reached for a ringing telephone.

Vanessa stopped a woman wearing hospital garb and said, "Where can we go? Away from all this…My sister's the mother of a young daughter who's—we've been told she's being prepped for surgery. She was in a car accident…"

"You're Dianne Lewis. Oh my God, Daniela's your daughter?"

Both Dianne and Vanessa looked on curiously. Dianne was struck that someone recognized her as Dianne Lewis. Vanessa answered for her sister, "Yes."

"Come with me."

Obediently, they followed the woman. Vanessa thought, *thank goodness you can rely on a sister*.

When they arrived in a small waiting area, at the other end of the floor and away from the swarm of police and media, Dianne asked, "Why are we waiting here?"

"I asked if we could go someplace less…intrusive. If she knows who you are…and when the media learn that Daniela is your daughter. Girl!" The hospital employee said, "I'm not sure of the status of your daughter. The last I heard, she was being prepped for surgery."

"What were her injuries? Didn't they have to wait for a parent's consent to?…"

"Ms. *Lewis*, your daughter was medevacked and admitted with life-threatening injuries. She's in excellent care…"

"Tell me," said Vanessa. "What about the other passengers?"

"Gwen Banks was released. She was taken into custody."

"Custody?" Dianne said, her voice troubled, her brow creased.

"I'll tell you this much: Ms. Banks was behind the wheel. Authorities practically bodyguarded her into the hospital; they wanted her to be tested for alcohol *before* she was treated for injuries. Her alcohol content was over the legal limit."

"What about the other passengers? Are they all right?" Dianne was desperate to know.

"One's staying overnight for observation. The other one was admitted to another hospital. I don't know the status of that patient." The woman touched Dianne's arm gently. "God bless," she said.

Dianne flopped in a hard chair and Vanessa mimicked her baby sister. Dianne, with her elbows to her knees, pressed her hands together in prayer-style. With her eyes tightly shut, she began to pray. She prayed and prayed and prayed until tears dripped uncontrollably down her face. Vanessa, who'd abandoned prayer many years ago, began to pray, too.

When Joseph learned that Phoebe had returned to California, he had a lingering bitter taste in his mouth. He was perturbed by the idea that he wouldn't be able to see her again; although there was the chance at Christmastime. Despite that she couldn't care less about him, Joseph looked forward to her company, and whenever he could get it. While he had been getting mighty friendly with Gloria over the past few weeks, he admitted it to himself: He wanted Phoebe more than he'd wanted any other woman since he'd first laid eyes on the woman that eventually became his wife and the mother of his two children. There had been no relationship in the real sense of the word, but Joseph did his fair share of fantasizing about Phoebe, and in his mind, they had something.

He was perhaps more disappointed that she hadn't come by or called him to say good-bye. He thought they had enough of a friendly relationship that when she left, she would have at least dropped by to let him know she was leaving. Candidly, their relationship was no more than two people having been in a right time and right place. There had been no love affair, or kisses or hugs— or sex. She was a woman he fantasized having in his life, even though, deep down, Joseph could never quite picture her in his wife's kitchen, or her fooling around in the tomato patch he planted a few years back. He couldn't actually see her waking up next to him. So what did that say? What did it all mean? Why was this woman placed in his life? How much of it was his doing and how much of it was a divine mystery?

Joseph pulled out his cell phone and was going to figure out this texting. Gloria said to text her with details about where they were going to meet. He couldn't bring himself to admit he'd never texted before. He made a series of bad judgments when it came to Phoebe; he didn't want to screw things up with Gloria. For so long, before he first met up with Phoebe, there were times when a quiet pathos reminded Joseph that he was deeply alone. He had his little interests and they served him. Once inside his own little bubble, he became comfortable, and relied on his own sense of order. Yet when he met Phoebe, his entire body reacted to the scent of her, the essence of the woman she had become long before he ever set eyes on her. He had forgotten what it felt like to like a woman, to be in her company and thoroughly enjoy her femininity. To lose track of time. Once that kicked in, Joseph wanted it all the time. He wanted to be with someone, and to know that he was needed and *wanted*.

"Let's see here." He fooled around with his cell for a while. He chuckled to himself when he thought about what Cornell had said a few days back: "Dad! Really, you need to invest in a new phone. At least get a smartphone. A flip-phone; it's like antiquated." He managed to find the texting in his menu. He pressed "create a message," but once he started using the keypad, it confused him because there were three letters to a button. How could he type the letters "S" or "O"? Where was Cornell when you needed him? It took him roughly forty minutes to finally get the entire text written out. When he pressed send, Joseph didn't just feel relieved; his self-confidence went up a notch or two.

Gloria responded almost immediately, but Joseph had to figure out how to open the darn message. When he managed to open it, Gloria replied with *c u there!*

EPILOGUE

I t was late when Torrick managed to reach the hospital. As someone who made a living providing high-level security, he knew how to dodge a crowd, along with various media outlets, in order to reach the floor where his daughter was currently fighting for her life. He was about to enter a side entrance when he was stopped by someone he didn't recognize. Torrick couldn't face a journalist right now.

"Marcus Pierce. We spoke on the phone. Your director of security reached out to me."

Relieved, they shook hands and acquainted themselves briefly. "It's-it's a lot of press presence. *A lot*," said Pierce. "Do you want me to call in some additional security?"

"No, no, that's okay."

They rushed through the hallway and to an elevator typically used for VIPs. When they made it to the floor, the police presence and the various media didn't necessarily surprise Torrick; still, he was unprepared. Surely by now these people had to know Gwen was no longer at the hospital and had been released and arrested. Why were they still here? After all, *she* was the story.

"Who else is admitted here?"

"What do you mean?"

"There's too much police activity, and media? What's this, gang related?"

When they slipped beyond the crowd hovering around, the security man said, "Not to my knowledge. Let me check it out." He stood to the side and made a call.

Torrick took note of the time on his watch. He sighed audibly. The private security man returned.

"No VIP, no gang-related gunshot wounds admitted."

Frustrated, Torrick said, "Let's go." When they turned a corner, Torrick's heart began to race. Something huge was going on. Was it about Daniela? When he spotted Vanessa, Torrick waved to her. With an energetic pace, she walked toward her brother-in-law. They embraced, and when he released her, his bloodshot eyes looked straight into her solemn face. "Where's Dianne?"

"She snuck off to the ladies."

"What's the word on Daniela?"

"She's out of surgery, but the doctors haven't come out yet."

With a frown, Torrick said, "This isn't good."

"We were told they would come out soon."

"I don't like this," Torrick said, his large hands shielding the pain in his face.

"There's a lot of hush-hush about what happened. One of the passengers—Daniela's Facebook Friend, he didn't make it."

"Marcus Pierce, hired security," the man said to Vanessa.

"Vanessa."

"Where was Carmel during all this? I thought she went with Daniela to Gwen's dinner party."

"She did."

"And?"

"I don't know all the details. She was taken to headquarters, downtown. They say for further questioning. I don't want her coming here. We haven't talked since she called to tell us that Daniela had been in an accident."

"Carmel was there for a reason. And what happened to the limo?"

"Torrick…"

"Torrick!" Dianne cried out, rushing into his arms. They held each other in a lingered, emotional embrace. Dianne began to sob while Torrick bit back tears. Finally, when Dianne pulled herself together, Torrick escorted her to a set of chairs and they sat. Her voice earnest, she said, "I'm sorry."

"Sorry for…?"

Dianne didn't say, *For everything.*

"What happened with Carmel?"

With a shrug, Dianne brushed away tears resting on her chiseled cheeks. "I don't know. No one's telling us anything. Not the police, not the doctors. We're just here and I feel so helpless."

Torrick took Dianne's hand. "We need to pray."

She nodded in agreement.

With their hands linked together, they prayed silently. They prayed from the heart, and with such sincerity. Tears caressed their chocolate skin, and mucus drained from Dianne's nose. They continued to pray until words failed them. The intensity of their faith was so compelling Vanessa and Marcus Pierce were in awe.

"Good evening," a man in scrubs said to Vanessa and Pierce.

Both Torrick and Dianne jumped to their feet, anxious.

"Good evening," Vanessa said.

"Are you my daughter's physician?" Torrick asked.

"You're Mr. James, Daniela's father?"

"Yes, and my wife." He barely looked to Dianne while she clung to his side.

"I'm Dr. Stein, your daughter's neurologist. She's suffered head trauma…"

"Dear God," Dianne cried out.

"Why has this taken so long?" Torrick asked.

"Is she all right?" Dianne was desperate to know.

"She's in a coma."

"And…" Torrick gave the neurosurgeon a hard look.

"We won't know if there's paralysis until…"

"Why?" Dianne cried out. "Why *her?*"

The neurologist explained in an empathetic yet professional voice the various medical outcomes, and was cautiously optimistic. "But," he stated further, "we're at wait and see. Mr. and Mrs. James, our chapel is on three."

"Oh, Torrick." She clung to him tightly.

"I love you," he whispered. "She's going to be okay."

While in his arms, feeling secure and safe, Dianne tried to believe it—Daniela *would* be okay. And out of nowhere her mind conjured up the early evening she and Phoebe had met for drinks at the Blue Bar. Dianne had asked Phoebe did she believe in karma. Dianne could barely breathe. Was this her karma?

It rained most of the morning. Joseph took a good walk along the path. He was about to head home when his tax attorney friend whizzed by him and spoke over his shoulder, "You shaved your head!"

Indeed he did shave his head. Impulsively, Joseph waltzed into his longtime barber and said to him, "Shave it clean."

"Watch it. Someone didn't curb their dog just up ahead!" Joseph called out.

The tax attorney wasn't the only person that took notice of his new look. The teller at his bank made a remark. And then there was his son, too. It boosted Joseph's esteem to a degree, and he was feeling self-assured, like when he was still working at the post office.

He made his way back to the house, reflecting on timing; the way it maneuvered through people's lives. While he was still cynical, he was beginning to relate to the new world he now stood in. Meeting Phoebe—did she have a hand in his new unfolding? Other than choosing to work with a personal trainer and to start paying more attention to how and what he ate, there was no other situation that came to mind. It had to be Phoebe. Maybe the reason she came into his life had more to do with his changing his life and not her being *in* his life. He didn't doubt that God used people for some purpose not perceptible on the secular level. For so long Joseph wandered around feeling out of touch, although he didn't see it that way at the time. He gave up in ways he hadn't known; meeting Phoebe, though, brought out something in him and not just his sexual attraction to her. He wanted to share his life and to have a purpose for living out his day. Not only going through the motions of life: getting up, having a cup of coffee while reading through the paper. He was middle-aged—this was supposed to be prime time.

Joseph found himself looking forward to his day, whereas previously, he'd crawl out of bed, do his usual, and perfunctorily move through the rhythm of his life. Yet by the day's end, Joseph became bored, which was how he found himself one day looking on porn sites. He needed something to get his attention. The porn was a diversion from his otherwise tedious life.

When he arrived home from his walk, Cornell's Jeep wasn't parked in its usual haphazard manner, which meant he was probably at work. Joseph took a shower and dressed. He still had a few hours to kill before he met up with Gloria. He had to admit he was rather edgy, like it was his first date when he was a teenager. Despite his anxiety, he was eager and filled with hope. He had come to like Gloria—her sense of humor, her intellect. How that would play out, Joseph had no clue. He just knew he wanted to meet her and see where it would lead.

This was all so new to him. He'd been married the better part of his adult life. He married young, and when his wife died, Joseph was left alone. The kids were old enough not to need him, but Joseph needed them. Except they were young, curious, *living*. Christine moved clear across the country to attend college, and immediately after graduating, found a job. His baby girl liked it back there, on the other side of the country. Before he moved back home, Cornell shared a place near the university; he had his own life—friends, school, kicking it, leading the life of someone his age. Before Joseph knew it, the years stacked up and before he could make sense of it all, he was old. He felt *old*. But Phoebe brought something out in him, and gradually he became aware of what was missing in his life. Being around her and knowing that she wasn't much younger than he was, he had led a life of convenience. He lost touch with his old friends from the post office. Joseph thought about it periodically: What happened? When did he let himself go?

"I should go," he reminded himself. There was the issue of parking, and Joseph didn't want to be late.

The drive took under thirty minutes. He decided it was better to park in a lot than on the street. Finally, the rain eased up and Joseph had to walk two blocks, which turned out to be nice. He didn't come downtown often. He steered clear primarily because it was too crowded, and there had been no reason to. When Cornell suggested a popular bistro near the waterfront, Joseph decided to recommend it to Gloria. Once he managed to make it to the bottom of the hill without feeling any discomfort in his joints, Joseph felt a resurging of spirit; even an ego he had long forgotten how to use. With every step, he felt a bit more confident, more comfortable in this new skin of his. Although it was subtle, Joseph sensed this was a new beginning, or was he simply in a good mood?

When he entered the bistro, the place was packed. He'd hoped for something quiet, out of the way, not the latest popular place to be seen. Even when he was younger, Joseph was never that big on crowds. People standing around in the front of the bistro were holding drinks of various kinds. They were younger, and buzzing with conversation about this and that. He wove between clusters of people, and overheard snippets of conversation. These were people who had demanding careers and stressful jobs and what they were discussing was related to one or the other. Did people talk about anything else besides their jobs and other people? He made his way to an area that was less crowded and began to seek out Gloria. He overheard two women, holding wineglasses in their hands, talking about that reality personality—Gwen Banks. Joseph had to chuckle to himself—even he'd gotten caught up in the blow-by-blow coverage related to that car crash. *What a dog-gone shame.* He prayed for Dianne's oldest to make a full recovery.

"Do you have a reservation?" A polite brunette interrupted his thoughts.

"Oh, yes. Morgan. For two."

"Wait here, Mr. Morgan."

Ever so slightly he turned, and a woman looked directly into his eyes. She was smartly dressed and attractive, perhaps in her early forties and well-maintained. Joseph wasn't sure, but he thought it could be Gloria. When they Skyped, her hair was pulled back and she was wearing glasses. The woman who stood in front of him wore her hair loose, and trimmed just above her shoulders, lacking the eyewear.

"Joseph?" The woman grinned.

Joseph took in a velvety-scented perfume. "Gloria?"

Prior to the recession, Phoebe was contented through the aughts. It felt as though it happened swiftly, her life savings diminishing to nearly nothing. Then precipitously, things she never had to worry about before were becoming paramount in her mind: health-care, and retirement. These were dangerously distracting thoughts and suddenly she was living through every impossibility. Since her early twenties, she'd led a good life. Venice was more than her rite of passage; being a part of the group sustained her financially. When money started coming in after the success of *Plan B*, Phoebe purchased her bungalow—three-bedroom, one-and-a-half bath, with the scent of the ocean. One couldn't feel the full effect of consequences until one reached a low point. The pain of losing everything was complicated to someone with faith. While Phoebe could have asked the man she'd spent the last two years with for help, because she'd been financially secure and independent through-out her adult life, she didn't know how to seek his assistance. And even Venetia offered to give her a loan. In her mind, the concept to seek someone's help was no more than an abstract principle. Venetia had told her, "You just need some time." Phoebe decided to trust time, and now she was pleased that she didn't have what-ever it took to depend on that man because she was spared the feelings of regret. For nearly thirty years, she had been successful on different levels. Success happened that way—in stages. When Venice broke up, she had cash to carry her for years, traveling throughout the world, until she discovered what she was supposed to do next. She had dropped out of college so as to devote her time to Venice, thus, she had no formal training to go out and start a career like—as Dianne once referred to it—"normal people."

Now, so many years having come to pass, she couldn't imagine her life any other way. She couldn't have known what she wanted over thirty years ago when she moved to Los Angeles to go to school but ended up being in a singing group that became an international success. At nineteen, she didn't know enough about herself—what she wanted, what she needed, and what mattered. Standing in this very moment, she knew one thing was indeed true: losing nearly everything, she discovered who she really was without a title, money. She learned she could live a simple life and not feel deprived, or be envious of those who had more tangibles. When all was lost but her breath and memories, she was never discontented, or unhappy. Phoebe didn't feel any less alive. She didn't feel any less loved; she wasn't small or insignificant.

In an hour, she would be picked up by a driver. She would be taken to an office building in Century City, and there she would meet with Kent Richardson. She was uncharacteristically tense. Potentially, this opportunity could be her last chance to salvage the pieces of her life. For a long time, after Venice, Phoebe saw her life take strange highs and painful lows. Her heart had been broken more times than she cared to admit to. She discovered that no experience was ever entirely good or bad.

Her cell rang and Phoebe answered. "Daniel? Well, I'm in L.A." Thoughtfully, she listened. "Can we arrange to meet in say…Oh, you're on your way to London? Well…so…You really liked it? Yes, I had a feeling the marketing analysis would need adjustments. Sure." She half-smiled, listening. "Sounds good. *Ciao!*" Earlier, she'd turned off the television, too emotionally fatigued to bear more inconsistent stories about Gwen Banks, and the status of Daniela's health. At cross-purposes, Phoebe wasn't certain how best to handle Dianne. On the one hand, she wanted desperately to reach out to her, and on the other, she was most likely the last person Dianne wanted to hear from. Venetia suggested she make the call on behalf of them both. Phoebe was still waiting to hear back from Venetia because she was tracking down additional details about Brooke Richardson's birth. Joseph was perhaps right when he'd told Phoebe that her life, on some level, lacked definition in not having known the child she'd given birth to. The choice, unknown to her until recently, transformed each and every choice. The sound of her cell nearby startled Phoebe out of her subdued state of mind.

"Hello," she answered.

"Just me," Venetia said. "I think we've got all the details, Phoebe."

Unconsciously, Phoebe sat at the edge of an ottoman. She paused; she allowed stillness to enter her heart.

"Brook Richardson was indeed born at Hollywood Pres, which is where I was also born. Her date of birth is the fifteenth of June in the year of nineteen eighty-two. Her birth was recorded at six-oh-one a.m. The date, hospital—it all fits. *This* woman could very well be your daughter…"

"Jacqueline Daye's office. Claire speaking."

"Claire, hi, it's Venetia Street."

"Well, of course. Hello, Venetia. How are you?"

"Good, thank you. Is Jacqueline available to speak with me?"

"She's off to London."

"Is she handling Gwen media-wise? I thought she might want me to do some Hollywood shuffling."

Claire chuckled. "Actually, I should forward you to Michael's office because…"

"When's Jacqueline due back in town?"

"She's…" Claire wasn't informed of exactly what was going on. She knew that Zachary Johansson's resignation had headquarters hustling to line up talented candidates before Johansson's departure; and Jacqueline flew to London to spend a week attending a number of crucial meetings to get up to speed. "I'm not sure, Venetia. Did you want me to forward you over to Michael's assistant...?"

"Thank you, Claire!"

"Absolutely!"

Several days ago, Jacqueline sat in quiet melancholy for nearly ten hours on a British Airlines flight. For the first time in her life, she experienced vague feelings of being lost. Her life, in just under forty-eight hours, morphed into something she could hardly believe was her own personal reality. The change was beyond the scope of words. Completely at a loss, she stared out at the bank of thick clouds high above the carpeted earth. Not three months ago, she was in the best place she'd ever been: Her working life and her personal life didn't clash. Years ago, she arrived at the conclusion that balance was no more than an illusion. She hadn't met someone special to ease the loneliness that sometimes accompanied single-hood; yet she had male friends and companions to fill in the sometimes empty spaces. Only from time to time did she ache for love, intimacy, and sex. Three months ago, Jacqueline *liked* her life and it took no more than a few calls to find someone to *be* with.

Her involvement with Torrick made her feel as alive and as curious and even more engaged, like when she was in her early thirties. Her relationship with Torrick had become an ignominious fate. The consequences were quite profound—she saw it so clearly while resting her eyes behind a pair of designer shades. When Stefan's cancer returned and his body rested into the earth, she felt vulnerable and insecure. Jacqueline would never, ever have started a relationship with Torrick under routine circumstances, and she truly believed the experience chose her; she didn't—she wouldn't have chosen it. While she understood her rationalization was no justification for her behavior, and it was without question cruel and selfish, it *was* the truth. She didn't recognize herself; looking back in hindsight. It was something she had only become aware of in recent days—that, in looking back, her relationship with Torrick silently evolved into an affair. While they remained coy about it, there had always been something elusive between them for years. Nothing happened out of nowhere. It quietly, gently, subtly breathed.

There came a time, in those dreadful long hours on the flight, where she began to mentally berate herself. How could she? *Why* did she? She'd allowed herself to get lost in the arms of a married man—the shame of it all. She couldn't introduce him to friends or show him off in public. With Media Capital's holiday party only a week away, she certainly couldn't walk into one of the most expensive restaurants in the city and with him on her arm. How degraded she began to feel. How *used*. Every single time she just happened to catch Torrick turning his silver wedding band around with his fingers, she knew. She *knew* it deeply; and how could she not know that she was no more than a distraction—a thrill lacking in his theoretically *solid* marriage?

Then there was that last night she saw Torrick. When he walked out of her condo, he barely looked at—no, he wouldn't look at her. Although she was saddened, Jacqueline likewise knew that Torrick was extremely distracted and his immediate concern was the welfare of Daniela. Hours went by and still no word from him put Jacqueline in an emotional tailspin. Surely he had a minute to call her and give her some news. He knew that she'd be frantic with worry, and news reports weren't particularly useful; only recycling the same details because they didn't have anything else to report. He could have texted her, which wouldn't require time or effort, and he wouldn't need to *talk* to her. When days went by, everything became clear to Jacqueline—she'd never hear from Torrick. He would make no endeavor to reach out to her. His silence made her feel disposable. Frankly, it was always there—the eventuality—hiding in plain sight.

Her last night at home, before she had to fly to London, Jacqueline passed the stage of tear-filled anxiety. When it all sunk in, with raw nerves, she called Dianne and left a message: "If you need me for anything…" Then she turned on the news. As someone whose career hinged on communication, she understood that a breaking news story was fluid, leaving producers scampering to fill in what the breaking news event itself lacked—a plethora of details. A news anchor Jacqueline knew casually was reporting that one of the passengers was the daughter of Dianne Lewis, a former member of the hit group of the early 1980s, Venice. Within hours of that detail being reported, it created a great deal of media buzz. On her first day in London, Jacqueline was crossing Regent Street when she heard "Plan B," Venice's signature hit, playing loudly in a passing Mercedes. The anchor reported further that Daniela was still in a coma; Gwen was out on $2 million bail; one other passenger had been released from the hospital, but Daniela's Facebook Friend had died of internal injuries. Although it had been erroneously reported that all four passengers weren't wearing seat belts, it was only Daniela and her Friend who were both thrown from the nose-dived vehicle because they hadn't buckled their seat belts. It was later reported that Daniela had been videotaping everyone in the car with her iPhone just prior to the crash. There was no way to determine if her videotaping contributed in any way to the accident.

Jacqueline sat in a sparsely occupied café in Notting Hill sipping tea. It was the exact place where Stefan, ten years ago, offered her a spot at his headquarters in the U.S. Her cell rang and Jacqueline, still operating with her old reflexes, expected the number to appear as Torrick's. "Daniel. Your voice, I'm glad to hear it. Excuse me! No, I'm in London. What's that? *You're* in London? Where?" Jacqueline instinctively looked around as if to spot him. "Tonight? Dinner? Daniel, you have no idea, my friend. Your timing's—it's so bloody perfect. How long will you be here?" She could feel her eyes form irrepressible tears, and for various reasons. "Yes, I know it. They have superb lamb. I'll be there. And, Daniel?" She spoke so softly Daniel could hardly hear her: "Thank you." No sooner than she released the call, her cell rang again. "Jacqueline Daye! Oh, Sylvia, hello. Yes, I know I missed my appointment. I know, I know! I had to fly to London on business." Jacqueline listened for quite some time and then interrupted her ob-gyn. "I need some more time. I understand that, I do. How much time do I have…? Certainly, of course."

Reaching for her cup of tea, Jacqueline, unconsciously, looked down at her tummy. She exhaled, and took a small sip. *Stefan, give me a sign.* Not long after she paid her check and strolled through the chilled holiday-decked streets, making her way past a row of terraced Victorians off Clarendon Cross, she eventually made her way to All Saints. Jacqueline walked inside and sat, reflecting on her life with all of her heart and soul.

Once it became clear to Jacqueline that she wouldn't hear from Torrick, she called her old beau, Gwen's father, and discovered the events that unfolded the night of the accident. Jacqueline didn't want the mediated version. She wanted an unabridged account of what happened the evening her life, and the lives of those she cared deeply for, would never be the same. Although most of the facts leading up to the accident hadn't been made public, primarily because the only two people who were able to give details were Carmel, Vanessa's twenty-one-year-old daughter, and Dianne's niece, and Daniela's driver. Conversely, Daniela's driver was outside the

Hollywood Hills residence and couldn't know what led everyone to leave Gwen's leased Hollywood Hills cottage and end up at the bottom of a cliff. According to Carmel, the evening was lively and Gwen was in good spirits. Photos were taken and Daniela sent out a tweet that she was having dinner with Gwen Banks. Carmel's account of dinner was that Gwen had, at minimum, five glasses of wine before and during dinner. Gwen was impetuous by nature. After dinner, she told her guests she had a taste for a slice of Marie Callender's Chocolate Satin. Out of the blue, she jumped up and said, "Let's go, chop-chop! My treat." Carmel couldn't recount exactly how Daniela and her Friend ended up in the Escalade. She reported to investigators that she stepped into Daniela's limo as Daniela, her Facebook Friend, one of Gwen's *Gwenology* crew and Gwen were getting into the SUV. Before Carmel could get one foot out of the limo, the SUV pulled out of the zigzag-like driveway and into the narrow street where homes on stilts hung like icicles along the curvy hills above Hollywood. Carmel jumped back into the limo and screamed at the driver, "Follow them. You can't lose them!"

Gwen was driving in the middle of the narrow, ill-lit street and made a wide turn into the main road, heading west. The limo, a good two-block distance behind, maintained surveillance on the SUV's taillights, and Carmel, her tone urgent, was insistent that the driver speed up and not lose them. Carmel recalled, once or twice, hearing the sound of tires screeching. She reached into her pocket for her cell to call Daniela to demand that Gwen stop the Escalade. She realized that because Gwen kept saying "chop-chop," Carmel became distracted and left her cell at the cottage. "Excuse me, but I need to use a phone." Her voice was anxious. The driver said something about using the limo phone. The very moment Carmel's hand reached for the phone, it struck her—she didn't know

Daniela's number by memory. She breathed heavily and covered her face. *Mom will never forgive me!*

Daniela's limo driver yelled out as if she were directing her exclamation to the windshield: "Watch out!" Instinctively, the driver slammed on the brakes. That's when Carmel heard the SUV skid and then it flipped over. The sound was haunting—the shiny black Escalade glided on its roof before tumbling over the guardrail. Sitting at the edge of the seat, Carmel's forehead and the tip of her nose pressed against the window. She was in utter shock, watching in slow motion, the nearly 7,000-pound vehicle plunge off the cliff and out of sight. She screamed, "Daniela!" Her heartbeat escalating, she said in a voice so soft and low she herself couldn't hear it, "Oh. My. God!"

The End

About the Author

Bonita Thompson is a freelance story analyst and reader. She has been educated at several universities, including The American University of Paris, in Paris, France. She has studied communications, international law, and media. Bonita has taught creative writing, and English as a second language. She volunteers for WriteGirl, a creative writing and mentoring program for teen-aged girls in Los Angeles.

IF YOU ENJOYED "THE NEW MIDDLE," BE SURE TO LOOK FOR

Vulnerable

BY BONITA THOMAS
COMING SOON FROM STREBOR BOOKS

Prologue

In a deep sleep Rawn kept hearing this faraway voice—*It's between you and me*—and the tone was eerily familiar. His eyes popped open. The syncopation of his day hinged almost entirely on how much sleep he had. If he could manage a good night's sleep, all the minutiae, which defined his day, would not be so exasperating. But like a sequence of mornings lately, he woke up having experienced another fatiguing night and he was bone-tired. Rawn adjusted his deep cognac-colored eyes to the essence of premature autumn sunlight. He wished like hell he could stay in bed and let the day that was about to unfold do whatever it was going to do without him contributing to the collective conscience. Annoyed, he tossed the bedding to the empty side of the queen-sized mattress. Finally, he was getting used to sleeping alone.

Absent-mindedly, he came to his feet. The room felt cool against his naked skin. Soft signs of early dawn trickled in from exposed roof windows which defined the neatly squared room. Rubbing sleep from his eyes, he became conscious of the fact that he was not sweating, nor had he been disturbed by a dream he could never quite remember. Immediately this struck Rawn cold; he had come to depend on trying to make sense of his dreams. Still not fully awake, he strolled to the bathroom.

He always let the shower run until the room was so steamy he could barely see a foot in front of him. Rawn observed his tired face in the bathroom mirror. Not long ago a young woman he knew only by sight approached him at his table. He was sitting at a neighborhood bookstore-café, and she said something about liking his "new look," followed by a wink. By chance was she referring to stubble that shadowed his cheeks and jaw line? Rubbing his face with his hands, he wondered was she throwing off an innocent flirtation or was she in effect hitting on him. Rawn could not recall exactly when he last noticed that a woman was flirting. He himself stopped flirting some time ago.

He was in and out of the shower in less than ten minutes. He was wrapping a towel around his lean waist when he heard the telephone ringing in the background, but he chose to ignore it. These days Rawn screened every single call; he made no exception. He was fed up with producers from every other television talk show calling him every other day. Even though the preoccupation with him had tamed to a degree over the past several months, he chose to buy a cellular because, despite it being unlisted, his landline was now public knowledge. In less than thirty minutes he was dressed in a casual Perry Ellis suit that hung tastefully on his tall and lean physique. He stood at the front door, his leather satchel slung across his chest. He bowed slightly as if he were saying a silent prayer. On his front porch he bent over and reached for *The New York Times*.

Fifteen minutes later, Rawn entered Café Neuf and it was typically crowded. The bakery-café was rich with the smell of strongly brewed coffee and scrumptious French baked pastry. He stood at the entrance and studied the room. Straightaway he caught the local dot-com millionaires, Rowena and Sean, at their regular table wearing their trademark all-black. The café became their temporary office while their rambling waterfront home was being renovated. Cellulars rang incessantly, and top-of-the-line laptops congested the birch and poplar wood table. Jean-Pierre, the owner of the well-liked Café Neuf, always accommodated his regulars and knew each one by name. Of course he was well-acquainted with Rawn because he was a frequent customer, not to mention he spoke French. Likewise, Jean-Pierre, like so many on Crescent Island, knew all the good, the bad, and the ugly details of Rawn's once private life. For months he was relentless Crescent Island gossip. What had happened last year forever changed the young man who dropped by Café Neuf most mornings for an espresso and rich buttery croissant. Jean-Pierre had a soft spot for Rawn. He gestured for the young man.

"Hey, good morning, Jean-Pierre," he greeted the Frenchman.

"I open terrace. Let you sit in back. It be not so stressful, *peut être?*" Jean-Pierre shrugged.

Rawn looked over his shoulder at the animated room. "I can wait until a table's free. It's cool, Jean-Pierre." He tried to pull off a nonchalant tone.

In his thick French accent, Jean-Pierre said, *"D'accord!* Take the table when it come, *oui-oui?"*

"Merci." Rawn knew how much Jean-Pierre preferred his native tongue.

He stood by a couple waiting for a table. It was impossible to not take notice that they were in the middle of a rather intense conversation. Politely, Rawn nodded to a young woman seated alone nearby, primarily because he felt her eyes trace his every move from the moment he entered Café Neuf. She slid a laptop inside a high-end brand-named backpack, and as she headed for the door, folded an issue of the *Weekly* under her armpit, offering Rawn a subtle nod when she passed. Rawn's eyes traveled to her excellently shaped legs, concealed by a pair of black opaque nylons.

Taking a deep breath, he flipped the newspaper to below-the-fold. More and more, he lost interest in what he read about in the newspaper or heard on the news. What was happening out in the world had no direct influence on him personally, not right now. It was rather apparent there was a moral crisis in America. Still, Rawn could not concentrate on teens with handguns, the political and intellectual climate, foreign crisis, the Middle East, the president and his conflicting approval ratings as a result of a scandal, and the *soi-disant* thriving economy. Although he was naturally curious and always engaged, the way the new worldview was rapidly transforming humanity—eco-friendly, technology, globalization—simply did not pique his interest.

When he turned to the sports page, Jean-Pierre approached him and said in a low voice, "A table, it come. Take it, *rapidement, mon ami.*"

Rawn looked to the couple a few feet away. They were caught up in a heated exchange and couldn't care less that a table had become available. Because seating was first-come, first-serve, customers generally dashed for a free table. The couple's conversation began to get increasingly passionate and Rawn caught "You have colossal nerve!" and "Go to hell!" through clenched teeth. The woman gave the man the finger and stormed out of Café Neuf. Rawn thanked Jean-Pierre and walked to the empty table. When he sat at the table-for-two, he could see beyond the French doors that the once tender blue sky had turned heavy, low, and gray.

"*Ça va?*" The familiar waitress greeted Rawn in good spirits. Her sultry mouth accentuated her strikingly attractive face.

He thought she might have quit, or he missed her whenever he

came into Café Neuf because Rawn had not seen the waitress in…
certainly before everything went down last year.

"*Ça va!*" he replied.

"What would you like this morning?"

Rawn was not up to meeting her warm, kind eyes; instead he
looked beyond her slender shoulder, concentrating on copper-
colored photographs of Paris *arrondissements*, which classily lined
the mauve-painted wall. "A café au lait and chocolate croissant."

"Would you prefer non-fat, low-fat, soy…?"

"Good old-fashioned milk," he spoke in a tone verging on sarcastic.

"*Oh*-kay! French or American roast?" She knew his preference.
Yet she was making every effort to engage him; throwing some
loving-kindness his way which did not accompany an ulterior motive.

He dropped his eyes to the newspaper and said, "French."

"The bowl or a cup?" The waitress shrugged subtly, her mind
playing with the idea that he was different now; aloof.

"Bowl." He purposely avoided eye contact. He stated, "*C'est tout.*"
Rawn preferred that she not hover.

With a tight smile, the waitress departed swiftly, and her very
gentle scent—jasmine or lavender, Rawn did not really know—
caressed the air. When he first laid eyes on her, he decided that a
man had to ease into the waitress. She was unapproachable, and not
because she was cold or standoffish. There was something about
her. The standard line—whatever a man generally used to get the
attention of a very attractive woman—would not work on this one.
She was classy, and more importantly, comfortable in her skin. She
was complicated—if not mysterious—because she was not average.

Minutes later she carefully placed his French roast café au lait
on the table, and Jean-Pierre's to-die-for chocolate croissant. "Here
you go," she said. "Anything else?" She pressed her plump lips

together as if doing so kept her thoughts buried deep inside her head.

"I'm good." Rawn sensed the waitress wanted to say something to him. He had learned the look, the demeanor. He assumed she was like most people who struggled to be appropriate. But what exactly was *appropriate?*

When the waitress left his table, she was so poised, so graceful. She stopped at the table next to Rawn's, and in a sincere voice inquired if the customers enjoyed their croque monsieur and whether they were ready for their check. Once, a little more than a year ago, Rawn ran into the waitress at PCC. Comfortably dressed in well-fitted jeans, her cropped lime-colored chenille sweater exposed a small butterfly tattoo a little left of her navel. Before approaching her, Rawn observed the waitress leisurely walking through the aisles of the market. A subtle detail made her eye-catching; a *je ne sais quoi*-ness. When he finally managed enough nerve to approach her, they held a casual conversation for a while, talking and laughing so effortlessly in a way that happened when two people naturally clicked—no pretense, no façade, no status-dropping nonsense like where-did-you-go-to-school and what-do-you-do? When he inquired about her to Jean-Pierre, the Frenchman simply stated that the waitress lived in Seattle, and her name was Imani.

Rawn was attracted to Imani the very first time he laid eyes on her. On at least one occasion, he sensed the attraction was mutual, and then out of the blue, she disappeared. A good year had come and gone since he last saw Imani, and it only struck him that particular morning. He had been suspended between the present and what used to be.

Standing, and taking one last sip of his café au lait, he considered, for one split-second, what his fate might have been had he been courageous enough to ask her out at least once.